A FIVE LETTER WORD FOR LOVE

A
NOVEL

# AMY JAMES

AVON
*An Imprint of* HarperCollins*Publishers*

A FIVE-LETTER WORD FOR LOVE. Copyright © 2024 by Green Couch Writing Inc. All rights reserved. Printed in the United States of America. No part of this book may be used or reproduced in any manner whatsoever without written permission except in the case of brief quotations embodied in critical articles and reviews. For information, address HarperCollins Publishers, 195 Broadway, New York, NY 10007.

HarperCollins books may be purchased for educational, business, or sales promotional use. For information, please email the Special Markets Department at SPsales@harpercollins.com.

FIRST EDITION

*Interior text design by Diahann Sturge-Campbell*

Library of Congress Cataloging-in-Publication Data has been applied for.

ISBN 978-0-06-339901-3

24 25 26 27 28  LBC  5 4 3 2 1

*For Rebecca, Julie, and Jen*

# CHAPTER 1

Just between you and me, I've always found crossword puzzles condescending.

And yes, I know. Crossword puzzles are inanimate objects. They can't be condescending or judgmental or smug.

But they totally are.

All those infuriating white boxes and pretentious clues, just laughing at you while you stare at them stupidly. Like, oh, you *don't* know who Deborah of *The Innocents* (1961) is? And you don't know a five-letter word for "simply be"? You poor, sad human. Do you even have a working brain?

I read somewhere that doing a crossword puzzle every day improves cognitive function and reduces brain shrinkage (which sounds like a bad thing any way you look at it) so about a year ago, I downloaded the *New York Times* crossword app and decided to try it out. I got up at seven a.m., sat myself down by a sunny window (also proven to be good for cognitive function), and was determined to make a go of it.

But . . . I couldn't do it. I literally could not get a single answer. I kept clicking to the next clue, then the next, just waiting for that "Aha!" moment when I'd finally get one.

Industrious animal in a classic fable. No idea.

*Steppenwolf* author. Nope.

Something that might be put on plastic bags. Immune system components. Unit in a duel.

No, nope, absolutely no sweet clue.

I called my father for advice, since I know he does the crossword every Sunday, and he said not to get frustrated and that it gets easier the more you do it.

Which ... *how*?

It's not like math. It's not like you learn what two plus two is and then the next day you can still remember that it's four. It's like learning that a brandy glass is called a snifter and then being asked the next day to fill in the last word of a Benjamin Franklin quote. Surely one does not inform the other?

But it must, somehow, because millions of people do these things every day. Millions of people are strolling along knowing a nine-letter word for "abruptly resign" and who the president of Finland is.

Honestly, it's no wonder I can't get a better job.

Anyway. I kept trying for about two weeks, waiting to get the hang of it (or for easier clues to show up) and for my morning routine to transform into a blissful, fulfilling experience that improved my cognition and stopped my brain from shrinking. But it never did. If anything, it felt like my brain was shrinking *more*, like it was contracting from stupidity or something.

I was just about to give up and revert to my old morning routine—scroll through cute animal videos on Instagram, realize I'm wasting my life on my phone, frantically look up job postings, change the font on my résumé for the fortieth time as though that might be the secret to getting an interview ("Helvetica? Let's call her!")—when I stumbled upon Wordle.

The instructions were simple enough for even my shrunken brain to grasp. You get six tries to guess a five-letter word. When you make a guess, the letters will turn gray, yellow, or green. Gray means that the letter isn't in the word at all. Yellow means the letter is in the word, but you have it in the wrong place. Green means that it's in the word and you have it in the right place.

It sounded doable, so I thought, what the hell, I'll just give it a try. Surely it can't be any harder than trying to figure out a seven-letter word for "Off-the-books business, perhaps."

So, I tried.

And I could *do* it.

It was easy enough that I didn't want to smash my phone against my skull but hard enough that I had to work at it a little. There were a few hiccups, like the first time I didn't get a word and IDIOT popped up on my screen (I genuinely thought the app was insulting me until I realized IDIOT was the five-letter answer), but after a while I got the hang of it. And it was thrilling! That little surge of satisfaction when I figured it out quickly, the adrenaline rush when I got it right on the last guess. I got a ten-day streak before KAYAK stumped me, then I made it twenty-nine days before I lost out to SQUAT. Then suddenly, somehow, I had a forty-nine-day streak, and when I made it to fifty—BLUFF—I genuinely jumped up and down.

And okay, look, I can see you rolling your eyes. Thinking to yourself, what kind of loser gets so much excitement out of a stupid app? Don't you have anything meaningful in your life? You're a twenty-seven-year-old woman, for goodness' sake, don't you have a career to build or beloved children to adore?

And to that I say, go do a crossword, you pretentious cow. I think you're the type of person who'll enjoy it.

No, I'm kidding.

You're entirely right.

The truth is, I don't have a lot going on for me right now. I don't have a career, just a low-paying job as a receptionist at an auto shop and a bachelor's degree in science that is entirely useless since I realized in my last year of university that I actually want a career in the arts. And I don't think I want any children, even if I had a boyfriend to make them with or a salary to afford IVF or adoption.

So . . . yeah. It isn't much, but I've got my Wordle. And I'm up to a three-hundred-day streak, now!

This morning, I put in DOUGH as my first guess (I was eating cookie dough for breakfast; don't judge). The H was yellow (right letter, wrong place), the rest of the letters were gray. Next, I tried PESKY (inspired by the housefly buzzing at my window), which gave me a yellow P and a green Y. Then my mom called to have a chat before she and my dad go off on vacation to New Zealand, so now I'm trying to finish the puzzle at work. Which might make me sound like an irresponsible employee, until I tell you a little more about my job.

First of all, before you ask, no, I don't have any particular interest in cars. I applied for this job for one reason and one reason only: it was near a cute house that had crazy low rent. See, in my last year of university, when I realized I wanted to work in a creative field like film or art, it was too late to go back and change my major. But I figured, hey, a bachelor's of science is still a *degree*. I could still apply for low-paying entry positions or internships in creative fields. Surely my passion and enthusiasm would make up for my lack of a BA.

(Spoiler alert: they didn't.)

The trouble was, for every job or internship I applied for, I was competing with equally passionate, enthusiastic people who had figured out what they wanted to do in the womb, like you're supposed to, and who not only had proper arts degrees but who had already done all these impressive, artsy things. Like when I applied for a job at an art gallery in Toronto that went to a girl who had won a National Geographic youth photography award. Or when I applied for an internship at a Vancouver film studio that went to a twenty-one-year-old who had directed an award-winning short film. And honestly, I don't blame them for not choosing me. I wouldn't have chosen me either. But it felt like I was trapped in a catch-22. I couldn't get a job without any experience, and I couldn't get any experience without getting a job.

To make some money in the meantime, I applied for a few entry-level jobs for people with a bachelor's in chemistry (my actual degree), but there I ran into the opposite problem. I had the degree and decent grades but absolutely zero passion or enthusiasm. I didn't want to be an agricultural chemist or a toxicologist or a water chemist (whatever that is), and I just couldn't fake it well enough to get past an interview.

So, after about a hundred rejections (and eighteen months of living with my parents in their tiny condo in Halifax), I made a new plan. I was going to go back to school and do a proper, creative degree. But I already had a twenty-six-thousand-dollar student loan from my bachelor's in chemistry, and no clue which arts degree I wanted to do. I wanted to choose the right thing this time, and every time I thought I knew for sure—Writing for Film and TV, yes!—I'd get prickles of doubt when I actually started the application. Was this what I was really passionate about, or did it just *sound* cool? What if I dug myself twenty-six thousand dollars deeper into my student debt hole and wound up with nothing to show for it?

I waffled and I stressed, and all the while my loan payments piled up and my living situation grew a little more strained. Not that I don't get along well with my parents or anything, but it was pretty tight quarters, and I just felt so pathetic every time I'd run into an old friend and they'd ask, "Where you living these days?"

So, when my mother's friend told me her sister was looking for someone to rent their house in Waldon, Prince Edward Island, for practically nothing, I jumped onto my computer to find jobs nearby. And there were exactly two: line cook at a local restaurant and receptionist at an auto shop called Martin Auto.

I applied for both. After a ten-minute phone interview with the auto shop owner, Fred Martin, during which he asked me zero questions and complained at length about his old receptionist leaving without any warning, I got the job.

(It's probably lucky for the people of Waldon that the restaurant never called.)

I work at the shop from nine to five, Monday through Friday. I could try to describe what the shop looks like for you, but that feels like a waste of both our time. Hop in your car and drive to the nearest auto shop. That. It looks exactly like that.

Martin Auto has two mechanics—Dave, who's old and car-obsessed, and John, who's young and car-obsessed—and only schedules about ten appointments a day. The owner, Fred, doesn't actually work in the shop anymore, so I've seen him maybe three times since I started. I answer the phone, check people in and process their payments, tidy up the break room, and empty the garbage cans. And . . . that's about it.

There are definitely good things about it. It pays just enough for me to chip away at my student loan, and it's not very busy, which gives me plenty of time to do Wordle and research arts degrees. And the town of Waldon is actually pretty lovely, with brightly colored buildings scattered around a small fishing harbor, red sandstone cliffs to the east, and a long stretch of farmland to the west. The air always smells like the sea, and in spring and fall, I wake up to the sound of lobster boats whirring in the harbor. If I was someone who wanted a small-town life, I might be perfectly happy here.

Hang on a minute.

*Happy.*

H, P, Y.

Of course! I smack my forehead with the heel of my hand and swipe open Wordle. I type in HAPPY and voilà. The letters turn green, one after another. My streak's up to three hundred and one days!

As I do a little celebration dance in my chair, the shop doorbell jingles and an elderly woman with curly white hair steps inside. She's wearing a heavy coat even though it's pretty warm out for May, and she looks vaguely familiar, although that isn't saying much. Waldon is such a small town that basically everyone looks vaguely familiar.

"Morning," I say cheerfully. "Do you have an appointment?" I glance down at the schedule and wonder if she's "Maud Williams, tire change, 9:30 a.m."

She looks a bit nervous. "No, there's something wrong with my car. It's making this awful sound."

"Oh no." I pull a sympathetic face. "Have you brought your car to us before? What's your name?"

"Ethel Cox."

I type her name into the awful, ancient program they use to keep track of customers and open her file. "You were here last month." I squint at the scanned receipt, struggling to make out a word of Dave's writing. "Your car was acting up then, too, wasn't it?" I squint harder. "For a—a squelching noise, it says?"

"A squeaking," Ethel corrects.

"And did they fix it?" I ask uncertainly. I can see that Dave charged her forty dollars last time, but I can't see exactly why.

"No, they couldn't find anything wrong! Then the squeaking stopped, just like that. I thought it must have fixed itself, but now there's a new sound." Ethel's brow creases. "Could someone look at it today? I've got bridge in Charlottetown at three."

She looks really stressed, poor thing. "It's a pretty light day," I tell her. "Let me go see if they can squeeze you in."

She brightens. "Oh, thank you."

I smile at her and then retreat into the garage to find Dave. He's got a car up on the lift that belongs to one of the local lawyers. It's an old Porsche that's apparently really rare or interesting or something. Dave and John both went nuts over it when she brought it in.

"Morning, Emily," Dave says. He's a tall white guy in his late fifties, with graying hair, broad shoulders, and large, calloused hands. He's divorced, with two adult children named Analyn and

Jenny. Or at least, that's what I've managed to glean from his Face-book page. He's not big on personal talk, Dave.

"Morning," I reply. "Do you have time for a fit-in today? There's a woman here whose car is making a weird sound."

"Not today," Dave says. "John might."

I turn away with an inward sigh. Great.

It's not that I don't like John, it's just—

Actually, no. That's exactly it. I don't like John.

His full name is John Smith (because his parents knew how boring he was going to grow up to be, I guess) and he's around my age. He's sort of good-looking, in a can't-be-bothered-shaving, too-cool-to-care-about-how-I-dress kind of way, and I'll admit, when I first met him, I kind of thought we might hit it off. I put extra time into my hair and makeup the first few weeks I worked here and tried to think of clever conversation to make.

But the thing is, John doesn't care about clever conversation. Or conversation in general, really. Like, there was this one time I walked into the break room and heard him speaking Spanish on the phone. So when he hung up, I said, all bright and interested, "I didn't know you spoke Spanish!"

And he said, "Yup," and started scrolling on his phone.

I waited for him to elaborate, but when it became clear that was never going to happen, I asked, "Did you learn as a kid or an adult?"

I was planning to tell him about this interesting study I'd read about how age impacts your ability to learn new languages.

Without looking up from his phone, he said, "My mom's Do-minican."

I already knew that because of the time John was away for a few days and Dave told me he was visiting his grandparents in the Dominican Republic, but I nodded like it was news to me. "That's cool. I wish I was bilingual. I'm trying to learn French, but it's super hard. I should've done French immersion in school."

To which he responded with a nod. No actual words, no "mm" of acknowledgment, just a slow nod, like what you do when someone is being really annoying and you're trying to get them to take the hint.

I should've just given up then, but at the time I thought he was cute enough to bother trying once more. So I asked, "What language do you think in?"

He stared at me. "What?"

"I just . . . wondered what language you thought in," I said. "Like, if you learn two languages in childhood, do you think in both of them, or just one? Or does it depend on the situation?"

He stared at me again—slightly incredulously, I might add— and then shrugged. "Dunno."

At which point I really did give up.

And look, I'm not saying it was a particularly genius conversation starter on my part, but at least I was *trying* to fill the silence. John has never once tried to initiate conversation with me, unless it's, like, to ask me what time a customer is coming in.

When he does talk—which is rare—all he talks about is cars. Even when he and Dave and I happen to be in the break room at the same time, all he talks about is the cars they're working on, or this race car he and his friend are fixing up to take to the local track. And he never even tries to include me in the conversation, like he just assumes I couldn't possibly be interested.

Which . . . okay, I guess I'm not. But it's still rude, and feels sort of sexist.

He's also a jerk to customers, which is why I wish I didn't have to ask him about this fit-in.

"What kind of noise?" he asks unhelpfully, when I tell him about Ethel's car.

"She didn't say," I answer politely. I'm always polite to John. When you only have two coworkers, you can't afford to be snarky to one of them. I don't think John has any idea I don't like him (or that he'd care if he did).

He sighs. "She out front?"

"Mm-hmm." Where else would she be?

I follow him back out to reception, where Ethel is sitting in one of the plastic waiting room chairs.

"This is John," I tell her, since John never introduces himself to people. "He might be able to squeeze you in, but he was wondering—"

"What kind of noise is it?" John interrupts. "Do you hear it all the time?"

"Oh, well, I don't know," Ethel says, looking flustered. "It started last week."

John frowns. "So do you hear it all the time? And is it a grinding or rattling or what?"

I have to stop myself from rolling my eyes. This is what I mean. It's not like he yells at customers or swears at them or anything, but he's so curt and impatient. Like he expects a seventy-five-year-old woman to walk in and say, "Why, good morning, young man. I'm afraid I've just heard a distinct ticking noise from the exhaust manifold, so I've popped in to see if the gasket needs to be replaced. I would do it myself, but silly me, I seem to have misplaced my torque wrench!"

Honestly.

"It's sort of a rattling," Ethel says. "You know, I had a Honda for years and it never gave me any problems, but then I got in an accident last year and I had to buy an old Toyota because the Honda dealership closed down—"

She launches into a story about her late husband, who didn't get along with the owner of the Toyota dealership, and how she can see why, because her new car isn't half as reliable as her old one. I can feel John growing irritated beside me. And okay, yes, this story is going on a bit long, but she's a nice old woman. There's no need for him to frown at her like that.

"I'll take a look," he says pessimistically, when she finally peters off. "Are your keys in the car?"

"No, I've got them here." Ethel rummages through her purse. "Will it take very long? I've got bridge at three."

"Depends what's wrong," John says, then heads off without offering any more information. I scowl at his back.

"Would you like me to call you a taxi so you can wait at home?" I ask Ethel.

"Oh, no, dear. I'll just wait here, if that's all right?" She eyes the tiny space. It's basically just my desk and four ugly plastic chairs. "I don't want to be a bother."

I smile at her, feeling a spark of warmth in the center of my chest. "It isn't a bother at all."

# CHAPTER 2

Since we're being honest with each other, I'll tell you another little secret: I don't really have any close friends. It's pretty embarrassing to admit it, but there you go.

I don't mean that I don't have *friends*. I do have friends. I have three friends from university I still chat to regularly, and a decent amount of high school and childhood acquaintances I occasionally touch base with. But none of them are *close* friends. You know the kind I mean. Those magical adult friendships you see in shows and movies, the ones who go to brunch together and share all their secrets and would help each other bury the body if they killed someone.

None of my university friends live within a thousand kilometers of me, so there's no chance of brunch dates, and if I killed someone, the police probably would've caught me by the time they showed up. Or the family of the person I killed would have murdered me for vengeance.

Okay, I've taken this to a bit of a dark place.

Sorry about that.

The thing is, if you think about the ways adults make close friends, it's usually through work or through their kids. Or maybe through some shared interest, like a book club or sport or something, but there just aren't a lot of opportunities for socialization in Waldon. So when I get customers like Ethel who have to hang around while they wait for a service, I really do enjoy it. Especially when they're older, which most people in Waldon are. Older people *love* to have a chat. Most people think it's boring to listen to them, but that's probably because they don't ask the right questions. You wouldn't believe what you can learn if you ask the right questions! Like Ethel, for example. She just told me she was born in 1948, and that she still remembers watching the moon landing with her husband and children in their first home. She made onion dip and they had Chicken à la King for dinner (no, I don't know what that is either).

I do some quick math and calculate that she was twenty-one when the moon landing happened. At twenty-one, she had a husband and children and a home. When I was twenty-one, I'd just broken up with my first serious boyfriend and spent a month drinking wine in bed and binging Netflix.

Yikes.

Ethel is there for nearly an hour, and I think she enjoys the time as much as I do. She looks disappointed when John returns, and downright devastated when he says, "You'll have to come back tomorrow. Suspension's worn out."

Ethel stares at him blankly. John never bothers explaining things to customers; he just assumes they know as much about cars as he does.

"Can you fix it?" she asks.

John nods without looking at her, absently wiping his greasy hands on an even greasier rag. "Not today. Come back tomorrow."

I almost roll my eyes. Honestly, can't he say it a bit more apologetically? Poor Ethel's brow crinkles right up and I just know she's worrying about missing her bridge club. I'm actually thinking of offering to drive her there myself when she sighs and says, "Oh, well. I suppose I'll have to go with Shirley or Dotty."

"Would you like to use our phone to call them?" I ask. "We've got a phone book."

Ethel laughs. "I don't need a phone book. Their numbers haven't changed in forty years!"

My smile is a bit hollow as I hand her the cordless phone. Even Ethel has close friends. If she murders someone at bridge club, Shirley and Dotty will help her bury the body and then drive her back home to share some Chicken à la King.

John disappears back into the garage and another customer comes in to drop their car off. By the time I'm finished with them, one of Ethel's friends has pulled in to pick her up. Ethel smiles and thanks me for keeping her company before she goes. I smile back, but once she's gone, I settle a bit heavily into my chair.

I desperately need a distraction from my gloomy thoughts, but the shop phone stays silent almost all day and the rest of the customers hurry in and out without any small talk. Around three, my phone dings with a text. I reach for it gratefully.

> [3:06] **Mom:** Off to New Zealand!
> Boarding plane now.

Safe flight! I text back.

They're traveling with another couple, Abe and Ann, and they'll be gone for six weeks. They've known Abe and Ann since before I was born, and now that they're all retired, they're going on trips to all sorts of incredible places, Costa Rica and Switzerland and South Africa.

At this rate, I won't have anyone to hang out with when I'm retired. I'll have to get a bunch of cats. (Which actually sounds quite nice, but you can't take a bunch of cats on vacation to Costa Rica, now can you?)

My phone dings again in my hand.

> [3:08] **Mom:** Your father is asking if you've heard anything from that film studio in Calgary?

My stomach twists unpleasantly.

> [3:08]: Nothing yet!

> [3:09]: Could be a while

This is a slight lie. I applied for an internship at this small independent film studio a few weeks ago, and about a week later, I got a rejection. But I'd already told my parents all about it, and how I thought it might be the perfect stepping stone into the industry because the posting specifically said, "People of all experience levels encouraged to apply!"

> [3:09] **Mom:** Hopefully you'll hear soon!

> [3:09] **Mom:** Going on airplane mode now. Love you!

> [3:09]: Love you too!

I put down my phone with a sigh. I should really stop telling my parents about all the jobs I apply for, but I don't want them to think I've given up trying. They've never once told me they're disappointed in how my life's turned out, but I think deep down, they sort of are.

Like, there was this one time when I accidentally overheard my mom talking to one of her friends in the kitchen, and her friend said something like, "What's Emily up to these days? Still doing fill-in jobs?" And when my mother confirmed I was still doing temp work, her friend clicked her tongue in sort of a regretful way and said, "She was always such a bright girl."

I don't remember exactly what my mom said in response—something like, "Oh, she's just sorting things out"—but I do remember her tone. Like she secretly sort of agreed. Like she didn't quite want to admit it, but deep down, she knew I was squandering my potential.

Which is why I keep telling her and Dad about all the jobs I'm applying for, even though they all end up in rejections. I *am* still sorting things out, and I *will* find my dream job. Someday, my mom's friend will ask her what I'm up to, and she'll be able to say, "Oh, Emily? She's doing such-and-such. Oh, yes, she absolutely loves it!"

This auto shop job, and Waldon, are only temporary. A stop on the road to my dream job. My dream *life*. A life where I'm happy and fulfilled and have close friends to share it with.

On impulse, I open the group text between me and my three university friends. The four of us really did have one of those magical friendships you see on TV. We met during frosh week and were basically inseparable for the next four years. Almost every photo I have from university is of the four of us. Squished together on the bleachers cheering on our university hockey team, posing on the library steps wearing matching sequin headbands (we were going through a Gossip Girl phase, all right? And I never said that we were cool). If I'd killed someone in university, they definitely would have helped me bury the body. If they weren't too hungover from partying the night before, I mean.

We've kept in touch since then, but our lives have gone totally different ways. Divya moved back to India for a while and now lives in Toronto with her fiancé, whom she met in law school. Fallon and her husband started their own company selling cold-pressed juices and they now have four locations across Canada. And Martha moved to Maine, where her husband is from, and is pregnant with her third child.

I scroll through our last texts—a debate on whether Martha should name her next child Harold (I voted no; I kept picturing this creepy old-man baby with wrinkles and a monocle)—and then start to type.

> [3:36]: Miss you girls! We should plan a reunion trip sometime soon!

I don't really have money for a trip right now, but if you book way in advance, you can sometimes get flights from Charlottetown to Toronto for less than a hundred dollars.

No one answers right away, which isn't unusual. I take my lunch break at my desk and scroll through information on a degree in classics. I think I can see myself doing that. I really like Roman history. Or at least, I really liked this podcast I listened

to last week about Julius Caesar. And I bet you could get a job in
an art gallery with a degree in classics. I picture myself striding
through a gallery, my hair drawn up in a bun, a long skirt swish-
ing at my ankles, my heels clicking on the marble floors, talking
to someone about . . . whatever art gallery workers talk to each
other about.

I'm Googling "What does an art gallery worker do" when my
phone dings.

> [3:38] **Fallon:** That would be so fun!

Divya texts a moment later. It's a GIF of a bunch of girls dancing. I quickly search flight prices on my phone.

> [3:39]: Maybe we could all meet
> in Toronto in September!

> [3:40] **Fallon:** I've got the new store
> opening in Calgary then

> [3:40] **Fallon:** Maybe next year!

> [3:41] **Divya:** I'll be way too
> pregnant in September lol

I blink at my phone. Divya's pregnant?

> [3:41] **Martha:** Omg!!!!!!!
> Congratulations!!!!!!!!!!!!

I type a little slowly.

> [3:41]: Omg! Congrats!

> [3:42] **Martha:** When's your due date?

> [3:42] **Divya:** September 30

September 30? That means she's like . . . five months pregnant, if my mental math is right. I wonder why she hasn't told us until now.

> [3:43] **Fallon:** Crazy

> [3:43] **Martha:** Have you found a good birth coach yet??

She and Divya talk about birth coaches for a while (I can't help picturing an angry hockey coach screaming at the obstetrician from the side of the hospital bed—"You call that an epidural? I'll show you an epidural!"), and when that peters off, I try again.

> [3:47]: All the more reason for a reunion trip! We can all come meet the baby!

There's a minute of silence.

> [3:48] **Divya:** Yeah, maybe!

> [3:48] **Fallon:** That would be fun

[3:49] **Martha:** Have you found a good preschool Divya?

The preschool talk goes on for a few minutes. I try to stick with the conversation, but I don't really have anything to add. As the conversation tails off, I half-heartedly suggest a group video chat sometime, which Divya and Martha agree to so enthusiastically that I know it will never happen. Fallon doesn't even answer. I'm pretty sure she dropped off the conversation the moment the preschool talk started. Fallon has complained to me more than once that all Martha ever wants to talk about is her children. Which is true, but at the same time, all Fallon ever wants to talk about is her business. Since I have nothing interesting to say about children or business, most of my conversations with them are pretty one-sided. And my conversations with Divya are usually pretty superficial. She can't talk about her work, since her law firm handles all these super-sensitive, confidential cases, and we don't have a ton of interests in common, so all we're left with is bland, soulless exchanges. *How are things? Great, you? Oh, not bad. Love your new haircut! Aw, thanks, girl!*

I put down my phone with a sigh. It's probably just as well. I can't really afford a trip right now, anyway.

The afternoon drags on. I practice a bit of French on a free language app (I have this secret dream of living in Paris someday—it'll be just like *Emily in Paris*, except I'll try not to be the worst), and I straighten up my desk and clean the windows. In desperation, I even wander back to the garage to see if Dave or John want me to make coffee (no).

Just before closing, John comes out to the front desk with a customer, arguing with him about . . . I don't know. Something to do with the guy's car. The customer, an older man, is a bit red in the face and John's voice is sharp with impatience.

"I don't know what you want me to tell you," he says.

"Well, thanks for nothing, then," snaps the red-faced man, and storms out.

"What was that about?" I ask.

"Huh?" John blinks at me like he hasn't noticed me sitting here. (He does that *all the time*. I'm one of *three* people who work here, is it really so hard to remember?) "Oh. Nothing."

Nothing? A customer storms out and he says it's nothing? Does he really not care, or does he think I'm too stupid to understand their argument?

All of a sudden I'm just furious, and I can't stop myself from snapping, "You should really be nicer to people."

He blinks at me again. "What?"

He doesn't sound offended, just mildly surprised, which if anything just irritates me more.

"You're rude to the customers," I say.

"Oh." He looks to the door and back again, like he's just putting together what happened. "That guy's a dick."

"He's still a *customer*," I say. "If you want to keep his business—"

"I don't," John says, then looks at me as if to say, *Are we done here?*

My hands clench in my lap. "Ethel isn't a dick, and you were rude to her too."

"Who?"

"Ethel! The woman with the worn-out suspension!" This is the only way John can remember customers, by what's wrong with their cars.

"Oh," he says, completely unconcerned. Then, "What time am I booked tomorrow? I've got a thing in the morning."

I want to scream in frustration. It's like trying to argue with a wall. A really flat, boring wall covered in stupid car posters.

"Nine thirty," I say through my teeth.

"'kay," he says, and wanders off.

Conversation over, I suppose.

I close up the front part of the shop at five and head home. John and Dave are still clanging around in the garage, but I've learned not to wait around for them to finish.

I drive home in a sour mood. My spirits are so low that not even the sight of my house can raise them. Maybe I'm being biased, but I'm pretty sure it's the prettiest house in all of PEI. If I showed you a picture, I bet you'd agree. It's set a little way back from the road, with two huge leafy trees in the front yard that partially conceal it from view, and a huge backyard that slopes down toward the harbor. The walls are white, and the window trim and metal roof are a matching shade of dark green. It has three bedrooms, two bathrooms, and an office, which makes it approximately one billion times larger than any house I could actually afford on my current salary. The owners are living in their condo in New Mexico for a while, and I'll tell you right now, if you're looking for me the day they tell me they want it back, you'll find me sobbing hysterically in the bathroom.

I pull into the driveway and get out to check my mailbox, hovering for a little while just in case my elderly neighbor spots me and wants to come out for a chat. After a few fruitless minutes, I give up and go inside.

I change into sweatpants and wander aimlessly around the house. I could make dinner, but I'm not really that hungry. I could go for a run, but all my limbs feel really heavy, like they're weighed down or something. I could have a glass of wine, but I'm starting to worry I'm becoming one of those people who drinks alone too much, and Canada's new alcohol guidelines (two drinks a *week*, what sadistic monster came up with that?) are stressing me out a bit. I pick up my phone to call my parents and then remember they're on a plane somewhere and will be out of touch for six weeks.

In the end, I curl up on the couch, put on *Anne of Green Gables*—the original one from 1985, which I've watched about fifty times since I moved to PEI—and cry a little bit when Matthew dies at the end.

Just because it's a sad movie, you know.

No other reason.

# C H A P T E R   3

O kay. New day. Here we go.

The sun is out, the trees are starting to bud, and as Anne of Green Gables would say, every day is fresh, with no mistakes in it.

(I think she actually said "with no mistakes in it *yet*," but I don't like that as much. It makes it sound like the mistakes are inevitable.)

I make myself a coffee and some crunchy toast with peanut butter and then sit down at my kitchen table and open up Wordle. Day three hundred and two, here we go.

I start with READY. Ready for a good day.

The R and E are yellow—the rest are gray. Hmm.

PRICE. As in, I can't afford the price of this organic peanut butter. (Plus it doesn't taste as good as the cheap stuff, and the weird layer of oil on top kind of grosses me out.)

Shoot. The R and the E are still in the wrong place, and the rest of the letters are gray.

Okay. Changing strategy here. I need to eliminate some other letters.

TOUGH. As in, I need to toughen up and stop feeling so sorry for myself.

The O is in the right place, the rest of the letters are gray. Still, that's a lot of options ruled out. And now I know three letters: O, R, and E.

O, R, E.

R, E, O.

O, E, R.

LOVER, I type. As in, it's been months since I've had one.

Aha! The L and V are gray, but the O, E, and R are green.

How about . . . MOVER. No, wait, I already know there's no V. MOWER? Like a lawn mower?

I type it in.

Crap. Crap, crap, crap. It's still wrong—and now I've only got one guess left.

_ O _ E R

Why are there so many words that could fit? POWER? POKER? No, those don't work. There's no P or W. COVER? HOVER? No, there's no V.

C'mon, brain. *Think.*

I close the app for a moment and try to let my brain wander. I check my email (nothing), my bank account (ha), the new dating app I'm trying out.

Oh! There's a message.

I open it with a bit of trepidation. The thing about PEI is, it's really idyllic and beautiful but the population is only, like, 150,000, and I'm pretty sure 80 percent of them are above sixty. So trying to use a dating app here is a bit risky. The last few guys who messaged me were in their fifties, which, like . . . maybe they were really lovely, and I'm sure some people don't mind a bit of an age gap, but my rule is, if you're closer to my parents' age than to my age, I'm going to have to politely pass.

But this guy, the one who sent the message, he looks quite young! I scroll through his profile. He's named Arjun, he's twenty-nine, he works as an engineer in Charlottetown . . . his favorite movie is *Die Hard* (that's such a common answer I wonder if the app shouldn't start making it the default for guys), favorite musician is Drake (another answer that should be the default) . . . his profile picture is a little blurry, but he's definitely cute, with short dark hair and a really friendly smile.

Best of all, his message isn't anything cringey or creepy, it's just normal. Hey, how's it going?

With a pleasant flutter of nerves, I message back. And by the time I get my second cup of coffee, he's answered!

We message back and forth a bit—the usual stuff, nice to meet you, how's your day going—and I make him laugh (or at least, type "lol") when I tell him how I think *Die Hard* should be the default movie choice for guys on the app. We banter back and forth about movies for a while (he tells me he waffled between *Die Hard* and *The Dark Knight* for his favorite movie, and I make an argument for why *A Knight's Tale* was actually Heath Ledger's most iconic work) and within half an hour, we've set up a date for tomorrow night in Charlottetown.

I get dressed for work, singing cheerfully to myself and thinking I should do a Heath Ledger movie marathon sometime. I can watch *A Knight's Tale, 10 Things I Hate About You,* maybe even *The Dark Knight,* although I'm not really into superhero movies—

Hang on a second.

*The Dark Knight.* Heath Ledger.

JOKER.

I grab my phone, swipe open Wordle, type the letters in—and that's it! JOKER! That's the Wordle answer!

I do a little spinny dance in my bedroom. Three hundred and two days! Only sixty-three days until I hit a year!

I stop dancing abruptly. Actually, sixty-three still sounds like quite a lot of days. What if tomorrow is some really weird word, like ERGOT or CRAIC? If I lose out after three hundred and two days...

Well. Nothing will happen, I suppose.

But I'll be *super* disappointed.

I grab my bag and head out to my car. My neighbor, Mrs. Finnamore, is watering her garden plants in rubber boots and a pink dressing gown.

"Morning, Mrs. Finnamore," I call.

"Morning, dear," she replies.

She's so sweet, Mrs. Finnamore. She's had me over for tea a few times since I moved here, and I try to keep an eye out for her in return. I think she forgets that she's eighty-eight sometimes, and I'll catch her trying to lift fifty-pound bags of gardening soil by herself or trying to clean out her gutters without anyone to hold the ladder steady.

"I'm going to the grocery store later," I tell her. "Need me to pick anything up for you?"

"No, thank you."

I wave again and climb into my car, humming to myself. I'm determined to be cheerful today. This is already a better day than yesterday, right? I've done Wordle, and I've got a date tomorrow! That's exciting.

Mostly exciting.

Okay, I'd say I'm feeling, like, 95 percent excitement, 5 percent dread. And I know *dread* probably sounds like a strong word, but trying to meet people using dating apps is kind of weird. It's like you're locking yourself into this weird social ritual called "The First Date." You arrive, you exchange pleasantries, you chat about this and that, you eat some food, maybe you laugh a little, but the whole time it's kind of like you're on a job interview. A strange, nighttime interview for a position where you'll do some of your work naked.

And, like, you and your date both *know* why you're there, but you don't talk about it directly, and at the end there's always this awkward moment when I want to blurt out, "All right, well, thanks for coming in. We'll check your references and be in touch."

And that's assuming the guy is nice, and not just trying to get you to come back to his place for sex. Which, can we talk about for a second? Because not only is it super annoying having to come up with excuses to get away from pushy guys (because if you try to tell them the truth, that you're just not interested, they either get sullen and defensive or straight-up nasty), but sometimes the idea of having a one-night stand actually does appeal to me. I'll see a guy on the app who's super hot but also clearly not long-term-commitment material, and I'll think, hey, maybe I should just go on a date, have a fun night, and be done. But that's the catch-22 about men. You don't want to have casual sex with the ones who are only on the app to get casual sex, but the nice ones will never push you for casual sex, which means it's up to you to suggest it, and I've just never been confident enough to do something like that.

I tried asking my friends for advice once, but none of them had ever used a dating app, so they couldn't really understand what I was talking about. Fallon met her husband, Ethan, doing her MBA (they were the two top students in the class; very Anne of Green Gables and Gilbert Blythe) and they got married straight after graduation. Divya's parents set her up with her husband, Ishaan, but they'd already known each other for a few years through their families, and they were going to the same law school. And Martha met her husband, Jason, when we were in university and was married and pregnant with her first child by the time we all graduated.

When I tried to talk to them about how tricky dating apps were, their replies were:

> **Divya:** omg, that sounds brutal

True, but not particularly helpful.

> **Fallon:** You don't need a guy!! Plus don't you want to get your career settled first?

Also true, also not helpful. I know I don't *need* a guy, but I would like one, and at this rate, if I wait until my career is "settled," I'll be about seventy-five.

> **Martha:** Is there a filter to show if they want kids?

Which is a valid question, I suppose, but probably the least helpful response of the three. I told Martha once that I don't think I want kids, but she shook her head and said, "Just wait," and then told me for the fiftieth time about how she thought she didn't want kids until she met Jason, and then the second he asked her to marry him she suddenly *knew* in the depths of her soul that she was ready to be a mother.

I'm not saying that it might not happen to me someday, but I always get a little annoyed when she says it. Just like Fallon's convinced that life is meaningless without a career, Martha is convinced that life is meaningless without kids.

I suppose my life is double-meaningless, since I have neither. It's meaningless-meaningless. Meaningless squared.

No, stop that, Emily.

I shake my head firmly, as though I can shake the negative thoughts away. I'm not going to let myself sink into a dark mood again. This is going to be a better day.

Dave's daughter Analyn is pulling out of the parking lot as I get to work. I wave at her eagerly and roll my car window down to talk to her. I've got a bit of a crush on Analyn. She's a little older than me, in her early thirties, I think, and from creeping Facebook I've learned that she then went to culinary school in France and now owns the highest-rated restaurant in Summerside. I have this secret daydream that she'll pop into the shop one day, and we'll get to chatting and become close friends. Which is extraordinarily unlikely, since she works about a million hours a week and probably already has hundreds of friends.

"Morning, Analyn!" I call brightly.

"Morning," she calls back, waving.

Then she pulls out onto the road and drives off. Which is totally fine. I need to get inside and get to work anyway.

I answer a few phone messages and clean off the layer of grime on the window that seems to have regrown overnight, then wipe down the bathroom taps, which are covered in Dave's and John's trademark black fingerprints. I don't know how they can stand it. I don't even work in the garage yet I still somehow go home with little smears of oil and grease on my clothes.

(Actually, who am I kidding? They probably don't even notice.)

John comes in a few minutes after nine from whatever nondescript "thing" he mentioned he had this morning and goes straight to the open garage without stopping at the front desk. The morning passes by unusually quickly, with plenty of phone calls and customers flitting in and out. None of them stay to chat, but there's a distinct sense of cheeriness in the air. It's the nicest day so far this spring. The sky is a really bright shade of blue and I can hear birds chirping outside the windows. It's like the whole world is conspiring to lift my spirits.

(And yes, obviously I realize the weather is not actually related to my life, but just—let me have this one, okay?)

At lunch, I sit down in the break room and pull out my hand-written "Dream Job List." It's a list I started a little while ago of all the things I want my dream job to have. So far, it's this:

1. Located in a big city (i.e., New York, Paris, London)

This one's a biggie. Don't get me wrong, I think small towns are lovely, but I want to be somewhere *vibrant*. Somewhere I can meet incredible people and go to art galleries and theater shows. Somewhere I can be a part of something important, somewhere I can really make something of myself.

2. In a creative field

This one is also a biggie. I'm not sure why I decided to major in science, except that it felt like what I was supposed to do. All of my high school teachers always said the same things: I was such a smart girl; I had such a bright future. Smart girls with bright futures didn't waste their potential on something as fickle and self-indulgent as the arts.

I don't know exactly which creative field I want to work in yet, but I'm casting a wide net, keeping an eye out for internships in film, photography, art history . . . anything rooted in creativity. If I keep an open mind, I just know the perfect job will present itself someday.

### 3. In person

I added this one after the COVID pandemic. I was doing a few temp jobs in Halifax at the time, and all of them got switched to virtual only. I was obviously really lucky that switching to virtual was an option, rather than just getting fired, but the experience taught me I am just not cut out to work from home every day. It's nice once in a while, for sure, but I like seeing people every day. And I like having an excuse to get dressed up nicely (and not just from the waist up).

Those three are all I have so far, the only absolute *musts*, but today I take out my pen and add a fourth.

### 4. Six-figure salary

I know it sounds shallow, but it's something that's been pricking at me ever since I looked up those flights to Toronto. I want to be able to enjoy little luxuries—girls' trips or spa days—every now and then without completely stressing over every dollar. And when I say six figures, I'm not saying I want to earn $999,999 or anything. I would be perfectly content with $100,000. (Perfectly content? Who am I kidding, I would be *thrilled*.) And I don't expect to earn that right away. But if I'm going to go back and do another degree, I want to be working toward a career that will give me more financial security in the long run.

I nod at my list, pleased, just as John steps into the lunch room. In a rare moment of interest, he leans over the table.

"What's that?" He squints and reads the title aloud. "Dream job list."

I scowl. It sounds stupid when he says it with that tone.

"Yes," I say with dignity, while simultaneously shifting my hand to hide the "six-figure salary" bit.

"This isn't your dream job?" he asks, pulling open the fridge.

He doesn't say it sarcastically, which somehow makes it more insulting. "You think it's my dream job to be a receptionist in an auto shop?"

He unwraps a sandwich and shrugs. "I dunno. It's a good job, isn't it? Pays benefits and stuff?"

Well, now I feel like an elitist jerk. "Yes, it is a good job," I say tersely. "But that's not the same as a *dream* job."

He takes a bite of his sandwich and says, through a mouthful, "What d'you mean, a dream job?"

I'm flabbergasted. Partially because this is the longest conversation John and I have ever had, by about a hundred words, and partially because how can he not know what a *dream job* is?

"It's something you're *meant* to do," I say. "Your passion. Your purpose in life. Something you love so much it doesn't even feel like a job!"

John snorts. "I don't think that's a real thing. All jobs feel like jobs."

I roll my eyes. "No, they don't. You think—" I grasp for a good example, an example he'll actually understand. "You think professional race car drivers see their work as a *job*?"

John stares at me blankly. "Yes. Even if you like what you're doing, it's still going to feel like a job sometimes."

"Is this *your* dream job, then?" I demand. "Or just something you settled for?"

He shrugs. "I like working here. And being happy with your day-to-day life isn't settling."

"Well—good for you," I say stiffly. "Some of us are still looking, so if you don't mind, I'm going to get back to my list now."

He takes another bite of his sandwich and wanders off. I scowl at his back and then add another item to my list.

5. No irritating, one-dimensional coworkers who don't understand anything about <u>dreams</u>

# CHAPTER 4

The sun is setting as I arrive in Summerside the next night for my date with Arjun. I'm a teensy bit stressed because I'm running late—the shop owner, Fred, showed up just as I was leaving and decided, after nearly twelve months of showing no interest, that he'd check in to see how I was doing—and also because my car wouldn't start right when I left home. I had to try four or five times before it worked. I wonder if it's a worn-out suspension, like in Ethel's car. After I pull into the restaurant parking lot, I step out and kneel to look underneath it, but since I don't know what I'm looking for (or even exactly what the suspension is), it's hard to say if something's wrong.

I brush the dirt off my knees and stand. Before I go inside, I quickly pull out my phone and open Wordle. That's the other reason I'm stressed. I still haven't figured out today's word. After two entirely wrong words (MONTH and PILED), I tried FRACK. The F and R are yellow (right letters, wrong place), and the A is green, but the rest is wrong. I eliminated a lot of letters with my three wrong words, but I'm still completely stumped, and I only have three guesses left.

What word has an F, R, and A in it?

FARMS?

No, I already know there's no M.

FARTS?

I snort out loud, then shake my head at myself. Grow up, Emily.

The *New York Times* isn't going to make FARTS a Wordle answer. Plus, the A is in the wrong spot.

I stare at the screen for a few more seconds before I remember I'm running late. I swipe open my camera and switch it to selfie mode to quickly check my reflection—yep, same as always: hazel eyes, long brown hair, tons of freckles—then pocket my phone and hurry into the restaurant, where I find Arjun waiting by the door. He's just as cute as his photo and nicely dressed in a button-up shirt and dark pants. We do that awkwardly cheerful, "Excuse me, are you—?" "Oh, yes, of course, so nice to meet you," and then we approach the hostess for a table. We don't have to wait at all, thank goodness, and we're taken to a table near the window.

"Your server will be with you in a moment," the hostess says.

As Arjun and I settle into our seats, I look around the restaurant, which is surprisingly full for a weeknight.

"Busy place," I say, shaking my napkin onto my lap.

"Super busy," Arjun says.

We smile at each other for a brief, slightly awkward beat.

"Er—so," I say brightly. "What do you do for work?"

"Engineering," he says.

"Oh, right." I smack my forehead with my palm. "That was on your profile."

"And you're a receptionist somewhere, right?"

I nod. "At an auto shop, yeah."

He nods. "That's cool."

I pull a face. "Not really."

"No, it is," he says. "I mean, the world needs receptionists, right?"

He doesn't say it in a mean way, really, but I'm not quite sure what to say in response. I smile and nod, then another silence falls. Almost in unison, we look to the window, as if we'll be able to mine some conversation from the quiet Summerside street. Usually, I'm pretty good at coming up with things to talk about on first dates, but my brain feels sluggish today. Plus, a large part of it is still trying to think of the Wordle answer.

R, F, A.

F, R, A.

FRAYS. That's a word, isn't it? Like . . . this sweater *frays* if you put it in the dryer. I know it's not the right word, because the F and R don't go at the start, but I could still use it to rule out the Y and S. I glance surreptitiously at my phone, but it would be beyond rude to pick it up right now.

"Weather's great today," I say instead.

"Definitely," he replies.

I try to think of something clever to add, but my mind is totally blank. "Feels like summer is right around the corner," I say finally.

Arjun nods politely but doesn't answer. I don't really blame him.

We're saved by the waitress, who appears with a notepad and a smile. "Something to drink?"

"Just water, thanks," I say.

"You don't want a drink?" Arjun asks.

I shake my head. "I wish. I have to drive back to Waldon."

"Ah." Arjun nods in understanding, but I see the flash of disappointment in his eyes. This is not a surprise. I've been on enough first dates to realize that a lot of guys think that no alcohol equals no fun (aka no sex), which is irritating but also a pretty useful litmus test. This one guy I went out with last month kept pushing me so much to order a drink that I wound up faking an emergency call to get out of there.

Arjun orders a beer for himself and the waitress smiles and disappears.

I take a steadying breath and lean forward with a determined smile. I'm not going to sit here like a lump just because I'm having a bit of an off day. "So," I say cheerfully, "do you like your job?"

"Oh, yeah. How about you?"

I hesitate. "It's okay. I'm still trying to find my dream job."

"Dream job." Arjun chuckles. "Like being famous or something?"

"Er—no. I mean, not that I would be against it!" I laugh. "But I just want to find something I'm more passionate about, you know?"

"Yeah, I get it," Arjun says. "I thought about doing chemical engineering for a while, but then I was like, nope, way too boring."

I smile. "You know, I have to admit, I've never actually understood all the different types of engineering." (Or even exactly what an engineer *does*, but I won't mention that right now.) "Like, I've heard of chemical engineering, but I don't actually know what it means."

"Oh, right." Arjun nods. "So, chemical engineering is like treatment plants and things, super boring, but civil engineering—"

"That's what you do?"

"Yeah, it's way more interesting. Like, right now I'm a project engineer for this huge company Traho—you've probably seen their buildings in Charlottetown, plus they're really huge out west—"

He keeps talking about his company for a while. So long, in fact, that my attention starts to flicker. I swear I'm trying to be polite and pay attention, but my mind keeps wandering back to Wordle.

F, R, A.

R, A, F.

RAFFS. No, that's not a word.

RAFTS? That's a word, but the A isn't in the right place.

REAFS. Like, coral reafs?

No, I'm pretty sure it's spelled "reefs."

"You know what I mean?" Arjun says.

Crap.

Do I know what he means about *what*?

I open my mouth to give him some vague nonanswer, but the waitress saves me just in time, arriving to take our orders. I pick something randomly from the menu and force myself to focus properly after she's gone. I ask Arjun where he went to school and listen attentively as he tells me a few stories about university, but after a half hour or so, I can already tell that he and I are just not meant to be. He's friendly enough, and he doesn't say anything *wrong*, exactly, but we don't have the same sense of humor, and he doesn't ask me any questions about myself, not even when I intentionally let the silence stretch out to see if he'll speak first. I end up pitching question after question at him like I'm a late-night TV host or something. He seems to enjoy it (everyone loves talking about themselves, I learned that about fifty first dates ago), and while he talks, I tuck into my meal, a lobster roll and fries.

When he steps away to go to the bathroom, I immediately take out my phone.

FRAYS, I type.

Hmm. The S is yellow, so that's something, but I can't think of a single word that has an A, R, S, and F in it. (Besides FARTS, which I really need to get out of my brain.) My mind is totally stuck on words that start with FR, even though I already know that's wrong.

"Everything okay?" Arjun asks as he returns to the table.

"Oh, yeah." I force a chuckle and show him my screen. "I've been doing this Wordle app thing, but I can't figure out today's word."

"Bummer." Arjun drains the last sip of his beer and then pulls out his own phone. "I'll Google it for you."

"No!" I cry, as he starts typing. A woman at the table next to us jumps half a foot.

Whoops. That was too loud.

"I mean—no, thank you," I say, flushing. "I just—I don't want to ruin my streak. It doesn't count if you cheat."

"How long's your streak?"

I sit up a little straighter. "Three hundred and two days."

"You've done it every day for, like, almost a year?"

"Yep! It's become sort of a routine. Every morning, I get up and do Wordle with a cup of coffee." I lean forward eagerly, planning to tell him about the hardest words I've run up against—then I notice his expression. It's the same polite, glazed look I expect I have on my own face when I'm forced to listen to John and Dave talk about cars. I chuckle feebly and sit back in my chair. "It's not that interesting, really."

"No, it's cool," he says politely. Another silence falls between us. He fiddles with his empty glass. I watch a woman park her car across the street. I'm trying to think of more questions to ask him, but honestly, I've completely run out.

Our waitress reappears and takes our empty plates. "Did you two want to see the dessert menu?"

Arjun and I glance at each other, and for the first time all night, I think we're on exactly the same page.

"Just the bill, please," I answer for both of us.

# CHAPTER 5

Five minutes and one awkward end-of-date hug later, I'm sitting alone in my car, glaring at my cell phone.

A, R, F, S.

F, R, A, S.

R, F, S, A.

What the *hell* is this word?

Exhaling in frustration, I put my phone away and pull out onto the back road that leads from Summerside to Waldon. I drive a couple of kilometers over the speed limit, keeping a wary eye out for wildlife on the side of the road. The important thing is not to panic. It's 10:45 p.m. now. By 11:15 p.m., I'll be back at home, and I can make a cup of chamomile tea and write down every possible combination of the remaining letters until I figure out this stupid—

*BANG.*

I yelp as my car shudders beneath me. I maneuver frantically off the road, pulling onto the slim gravel shoulder not a second before the whole car just goes *dead*, no lights, no engine noise, nothing. I frantically twist the key to turn it on again, but absolutely nothing happens.

I put the handbrake on and take the key out of the ignition, and then I just sit there in the sudden silence, my heart thumping loudly in my ears.

What just *happened*?

I put the key in the ignition again, only to take it out immediately. What if I try to turn the car on and something bad happens, like the engine explodes? Is that a thing that engines can do? God, why haven't I listened to some of the boring crap Dave and John have said about cars?

I rake my hand through my hair and then twist in my seat, taking in my surroundings. I'm completely alone. There isn't a single other car in sight. There are deep, dark woods on either side of the road, and as I stare into the bit nearest me, I swear I see a dark figure moving between the trees. My mind floods with images of bears and coyotes and serial killers.

Okay, no.

This won't do.

"You're okay," I tell myself firmly. "No need to panic."

I grab my phone and look up "car towing service PEI" and thank the heavens, two twenty-four-hour towing businesses pop up. They're both in Charlottetown, about an hour away, but the first website clearly says "Serving all of PEI since 1982." I don't know exactly where I am right now, but I know it falls within "all of PEI."

I take a deep, steadying breath and click call.

Then I hang up again.

I'm just going to quickly look up how much a car tow costs, first.

"Car towing cost PEI Canada," I type into the search bar.

Um . . . hang on.

This can't be right.

Up to two hundred and fifty dollars? For a *tow*?

I keep scrolling through the search results, waiting for one of them to say something different, but for the first time in the history of the internet, no one is disagreeing.

This tow could cost me up to two hundred and fifty dollars.

I open my bank account, which I know for a fact only has nine hundred dollars in it. My rent is due next week, and my student loan payment is due the week after that, and then my cell phone bill . . .

I can't afford this. I can't afford to pay for a tow. And I can't even call my parents to ask to borrow money because they're off in some beautiful, remote town in New Zealand without any cell service. And I can't call anyone else, because I don't have anyone else to call.

A hot, thick lump suddenly forms at the base of my throat, and my eyes start prickling ominously. I shake my head angrily. I am not going to cry about this. I'm *not*. I'll just have to suck it up and pay for the tow with my credit card, and then pay one of my other bills late. Or I'll beg Fred for an advance on my next paycheck. Maybe I'll offer to do some extra overtime, or to clean up that big nasty stain behind the fridge that's been there since I started.

A bright light flares in my rearview mirror. I flinch in alarm—coyotes and serial killers are still lurking at the edges of my mind—then relax a little when I see it's just a car.

I mean, it could be a car *filled* with serial killers. Or a car filled with coyotes, although that would be weirder.

The car is coming closer. Time to make a decision. Get out and flag them down and risk ending up as the subject of one of those awful murder documentaries (I have a vision of our waitress from the restaurant giving a tearful interview to the camera, saying something like, "If she'd only ordered dessert, maybe she'd still be alive . . .") or sit still and let them drive past.

I'm leaning toward letting them go by when I realize it's too late. They're slowing down and pulling up on the shoulder behind me. It's a low-riding car with a long hood, the exact kind of car I imagine a murderer or a drug dealer would drive.

Oh god. My heart starts thumping anxiously. This feels like the start of a very scary movie.

Okay. Focus, Emily.

I've taken a few self-defense courses, and the instructor said the most important thing is to take charge of the situation. If it's a murderer, I need to get the element of surprise, not sit here trapped in my broken car. I grab my purse—there's nothing valuable in it, but I can hurl it at their face and make a break for the woods—and push the car door open determinedly.

The other car's door swings open—a man's legs appear—I clutch my cell phone tightly in my hand, ready to dial 911 at a moment's notice—

"Emily?"

All of the air rushes out of my lungs.

It's *John*.

Oh, man. I have never been so happy to see John in my *life*. (Although I suppose that's not saying much, since I'm not usually happy to see him at all.)

"Hey," I say shakily. "What are you doing here?"

"Driving home." His footsteps crunch on the gravel. "Is something wrong with your car?"

I nod. "It just went *bang* and stopped working." I'm embarrassed to hear how thin and frightened my voice sounds. I clear my throat. "I was going to call a tow truck."

He frowns. "Keys?"

I hand them to him and he gets into the driver's seat of my car. I take a wary step back. "Are you sure it isn't going to explode?"

He stares at me, like he's trying to figure out if I'm joking. "It isn't going to explode."

He turns the key, but nothing happens. I follow him uncertainly as he goes to the front of the car and pops the hood. He stares at the engine for a few minutes and pokes and prods at random things. I watch in silence, shivering slightly in the cool air. It's weird seeing John outside of work. He looks kind of . . . different. He isn't wearing his work coveralls, for one thing, and his hands aren't covered in grease. In jeans and a dark T-shirt, he looks . . . well, he looks kind of handsome, actually. For an emotionless block of wood, I mean.

"When was the last time your battery was replaced?" he asks.

Uh-oh. Is that a thing I'm supposed to do?

"Um . . . I think the people that owned it before me probably changed it," I say.

"When did you buy it from them?"

"Er . . . nine or ten years ago." I won't mention that it was already twenty years old back then. I clear my throat. "How often are you supposed to change it?"

John raises an eyebrow. "More than once a decade. Didn't the engine light come on?"

My cheeks darken. "There was a light on. But I thought it was just like . . . a warning."

"It is a warning," John says. "It's a warning that something's gone wrong with your engine."

"Oh, you know what I mean," I say crossly. "I thought I had more time to deal with it."

"How long has it been on?"

"Er—a few weeks," I say. (Twelve weeks, if I'm being exact.) "Can you fix it?"

"Yeah. Just get it towed to the shop."

My shoulders sag. "You can't fix it here?"

"Nope." John wipes his hands on the hem of his T-shirt. "My buddy has a truck, you want me to call him?"

"Like a tow truck, you mean?"

John nods.

"Well . . . I don't know. I can just call a towing company." And then miss my student loan payment and eat Kraft Dinner every day for the next month.

John frowns. "Those places charge too much. Liam won't charge you anything. He races with me out at the track. Owes me, like, twenty-four hundred in spare parts."

"Oh." I shift awkwardly on my feet. I want to say no, but what choice do I really have? He's offering me a perfect solution, even if I do feel really weird about accepting it. "Well . . . yeah, all right. I mean, if you're sure that he won't mind."

"Lemme call him," John says.

He heads back to his own car to get his phone. I glance at my own phone while he talks. It's 11:07 p.m. John's poor friend is probably asleep, and who knows where he lives? If he has to drive a long way to get here, he'll probably be really annoyed.

And I'll miss the Wordle deadline. Midnight will come and go and my streak will be over.

That's less important than inconveniencing John's friend, obviously.

(But my *streak*.)

"Hey, man," John says, wandering back to me with his phone to his ear. "Do you still have that flatbed, the one Randy and I used that time? Ah, sweet. Any chance you can come pick a car up?" He listens for a moment, then laughs at something the guy says. "No, did I tell you what happened with the radiator?"

The guy on the other end of the phone says something else, and John goes silent for a while. Surreptitiously, I swipe open my phone and go to Wordle. It's not too late. I can do this. I already know there's an F, R, A, and S, and I know that A is the third letter. I only need one more letter. I'll just go through every unused letter in my head and see what words I can make.

Q, R, A, F, S.

QRAFS. SQAFR.

Nope. Nonsense.

W, R, A, F, S.

SRAWF. FRAWS.

Is FRAWS a word? It sort of sounds like it could be. Something from old-timey English, maybe, like a word in a Tennyson poem. I mean, the only Tennyson poem I know is that one that Anne of Green Gables recites at the start of the movie, and I only remember a few lines of it, but the word *fraws* definitely could've been in there. It still won't help me much, because I know the word doesn't start with FR, but I can't think of anything else to try.

With my heart in my mouth, I type it in and click enter.

Crap. Not in word list.

"Emily?"

I glance up. John is off the phone, staring at me.

"Sorry," I say hastily.

"It's fine. Liam's coming."

I feel a rush of relief. "Thank you. That's really nice of him. I hope he doesn't have to come too far?"

"He's just up the road. You want to wait in my car? It's kind of cold out."

"Yeah, thanks," I say, a little awkwardly. We get inside John's car, which, upon closer inspection, is some kind of vintage . . . something. It's nice on the inside, though, and much cleaner than my car's ever been. John gets into the driver's seat, and for a moment we sit in silence.

"It was nice of you to stop," I offer. "I was glad it was you and not, like, a serial killer."

"Like the start of a bad horror movie," John says.

"Yes, exactly!" I laugh a little, then the awkwardness descends on us again. My eyes shift to my phone. 11:16 p.m. Forty-four minutes until midnight.

I clear my throat. "Were you in Summerside for something?" I ask. Then I pause, realizing I don't know where John lives. "Or do you live there?"

"My parents live there."

"Oh." Another silence falls. Seriously, could he help me out a little here? This is like part two of my awkward date with Arjun. "Do they . . . like living in Summerside?"

John nods. "They retired there."

"Where did they live before?"

"Montreal."

"Ooh." I sit up a bit straighter. "Do they speak French?"

"My dad does. He was born in Toronto, but he mostly grew up in Quebec. And his mom's family's from France."

France! I look at John with new interest. "Have you ever been there?"

"A few times."

"And?" I press. "What's it like?"

"It's cool."

I try not to roll my eyes. *It's cool.* France should put that on tourism posters.

"Wait, does that mean you speak French too?" I ask. "French *and* Spanish?"

He nods.

"Wow." Now I'm really curious what language he thinks in. I don't dare ask again, though. I don't want to get another incredulous look. "That must be really helpful."

He raises an eyebrow. "In Waldon?"

"Er—well, no, maybe not. I meant like, for traveling and stuff . . ." I trail off into silence, and John doesn't say anything in response. Honestly, I don't know why I keep trying with him.

Oh, screw it. If he doesn't want to talk to me, I might as well keep working on Wordle. I pull my phone out a little pointedly (not that John will notice) and open the app. I've got two guesses left. I can do this.

A, R, F, S.

F, R, A, S.

What about . . . AFARS. Is that a word?

I type it in slowly and click enter. And—oh, crap, it *is* a word. But it's wrong. The first A is gray, the F is yellow, the A and the R are green, and the S is yellow.

I stare at the screen helplessly. I only have one guess left, and I can't think of a single word to try. My brain is totally, utterly blocked.

"Crap," I mutter.

John glances at me. He doesn't ask me what's wrong—classic John—but his expression looks vaguely curious.

"Are you good with words?" I ask him in desperation.

He shrugs. "I dunno." He glances at my phone. "Is that Wordle?"

I'm surprised he's even heard of it. I nod miserably and tilt my phone toward him. "I'm about to lose my streak."

He leans a little closer to look at my phone screen, and despite my frustration with him, a tiny part of my brain can't help registering that he smells really nice. Sort of like firewood burning on a crisp fall night.

"You've almost got it, though," he says. "You already know it ends in A, R, F."

I frown at my phone. Do I know that?

Oh, crap. He's right. From my earlier guesses, I know that the F isn't the first or second letter, which means it has to be at the end.

_ _ A R F.

One of those two blank letters is an S.

"QSARF," I try. "WSARF. YSARF. Those aren't words."

John's mouth turns up slightly. "No," he agrees.

"SUARF. That sounds like a word. Like . . . a combination of SUAVE and BARF. That outfit is totally SUARF!"

John looks at me, and something about his flat expression makes me snort.

"Okay, never mind," I say. "Not SUARF." I move through the remaining letters. "ASARF. SSARF. FSARF."

John snorts. "You're not very good at this."

My head snaps up indignantly. "I am too! I have a three-hundred-and-two-day streak, I'll have you know. I'm just totally blanking. It's been a long day," I add. "My car's broken, and I just had the most mediocre first date in the history of time, and I'm broke and destined to die alone—"

"What if the S is the first letter?" John interrupts. "Did you try that?"

"We already ruled out SUARF, and U's the only vowel left. Unless you think SBARF is a word—"

Hang on.

I swear I hear my brain go *click*, like something's slotted into place. Because you know what rhymes with SBARF?

"SCARF," I say aloud.

John nods. "There you go."

I start to type it in, then I put my phone down, uneasiness curling in my gut. "What if it's wrong?"

John's only response is a shrug, which would usually make me want to throttle him but which right now I feel is probably a fair response. If it's wrong, it's wrong. And it's not like I can think of any other words to try.

I bite my lip and nod. "Okay. Let's do it."

S, C, A, R, F.

I hold my breath, click enter—

I let out a squeal of excitement and dance around a bit in my car seat. John's eyebrows lift, but not in a mean way. He actually looks kind of amused.

Beaming, I show him my phone screen. "It's right!" I do another little jig in my seat. "Three hundred and three days!"

"Nice," he says.

I let out a loud sigh of relief and slump back in my seat, grinning contentedly. "Man, that was so close."

"Mm."

Normally, a nonresponse like that would make me want to smack him, but right now I just beam at him appreciatively. "Thanks for your help," I say. "I don't know why I couldn't get that."

"No worries," he says. "I had trouble with it too. There's Liam," he adds, as bright lights flash in the rearview mirror. A truck is approaching, flashing its four-ways as it turns onto the gravel strip behind us. John opens his car door, but my brain is still stuck on what he said.

*I had trouble with it too.*

"You . . . do Wordle?" I say.

John glances back as he gets out of the car, flashing me a smile that appears on his face out of nowhere, like a splintery burst of lightning.

"Yeah," he says. "All the time."

# CHAPTER 6

John does Wordle.

*John* does Wordle.

John does *Wordle.*

Nope. No matter how many ways I think it, it still sounds strange. I can't reconcile this new information with reality.

Don't get me wrong, it's not that I don't think John is smart, it's just . . . well, look at him! He and Liam have been staring at Liam's tow truck with their arms crossed for, like, ten minutes now, talking about its towing capacity like it's the most interesting topic in the entire world. John actually kneels down on the ground to inspect—I don't know, that metal thing that connects the truck bit to the towing bit—and stands up again with his hands dirty and an impressed look on his face. You're telling me that same man goes home and curls up with a cup of tea to do his daily Wordle?

No. I just can't believe it.

I hover awkwardly to one side as the two of them load my car onto Liam's truck, then John says, "Thanks, man" to Liam and heads back toward his own car. I start to follow him, but he frowns at me like I'm being odd and says, "Liam will take you."

Then he gets in his own car and drives away without another word.

Seriously, you're telling me *that* guy does Wordle?

I walk back to Liam's truck, acutely uncomfortable, but it turns out he's actually a really nice guy. Unlike John, Liam's capable of talking about more than cars, and he tells me about his wife and kids as we drive. He drops me off at my house and says he'll take my car to the shop. I thank him profusely, but he waves me off.

"Don't worry about it. I love an excuse to drive this thing."

I glance dubiously at the truck, a thousand tons of ugly, rattly, metal, but Liam really sounds like he means it. No wonder he and John get along.

I thank him again and head inside, fighting a yawn. I don't have the energy to do anything but change into sweats and crawl into bed. I stare up at the ceiling with a faint buzzing in my head, like the ringing you get in your ears after you've been to a loud concert. It's been a very long, very weird day. My date was disappointing, my car is broken and will cost god knows how much to fix, and I scraped through my three hundred and third Wordle day by the skin of my teeth. Really, nothing has improved from this morning. If anything, things are even worse.

And yet . . .

"Scarf," I whisper into the darkness, then squish down into my pillow with a small smile on my face.


I DON'T HAVE time to do Wordle the next morning. My parents call from New Zealand at 4:30 a.m. (my dad makes a lot of jokes about calling from the future, since it's already tomorrow there, which I would appreciate a lot more if it wasn't *4:30 in the morning*), then Mrs. Finnamore waves me down for a chat while I'm waiting for the local taxi to pick me up to take me to work.

When I get to the shop, I'm immediately accosted by a man who has been waiting in his car for the shop to open. He's jittery and strange, talking rapidly about a receipt he needs to "prove how bad his accident was" and lifting his hands over his head to show me how limited his range of motion is. It doesn't look limited at all to me, though I'm not about to say that to him. I get him a copy of his receipt and then turn pointedly to my computer, but he lingers for several minutes, leaning all over the desk and reading the receipt out loud to me.

"Four-inch scratch on driver's-side door—see?" He pushes the receipt toward me. "*Driver's-side door*, that's where the impact was, that's what threw my shoulder out of alignment."

John walks in halfway through the guy's lengthy monologue about how he's going to sue the person who hit him, the police officer who refused to arrest them on the spot, and the doctor who told him there was nothing wrong with his shoulder on his MRI scan. For once, I'm deeply grateful for John's rudeness, because he cuts right across the guy's speech to ask me when his first appointment is and then leans against the desk with his back to the guy, totally blocking me from his view. The guy scowls at his back for a minute but then finally leaves the shop.

I let out a sigh of relief. "That guy was weird."

John makes a vague "mm" of agreement, his typical nonanswer. But then he surprises me by adding, "Some people spend their whole lives looking for something to blame their problems on."

I blink. "Yeah, exactly."

He pushes himself off the desk. "Liam get you home all right?"

"Er—yeah, thanks," I say. "He's a really nice guy."

John nods in his signature slow, absent way and then wanders off to the garage. I swear he has some sort of word limit for conversations, or something.

Still, his comment about that customer sticks with me the rest of the morning. I can't help but wonder if I'm one of those people, trying to blame all my problems and inadequacies on the world. I don't think I'm quite as bad as that guy—I would never try to claim that a four-inch scratch on my car caused "catastrophic damage" to my body—but maybe I have been feeling a bit too sorry for myself these past few years. I think back on all the job rejections I've collected, and I'm embarrassed to admit that beneath the disappointment and self-loathing I always felt when I got them, there was also a vein of defiance. Like, how can they not see that I'm worth hiring? How can they not see that I'm special?

But it isn't the world's job to tell me that I'm special. It's my job to work hard enough to make it true.

Gripped with a sudden surge of determination, I sit up straighter in my chair and take out my phone. Over the rest of the morning, I make out a new, stricter budget for myself so I can pay off my student loan a bit faster (goodbye name-brand Mini Wheats, hello generic "wheatie squares") and cross about twenty jobs off my "Potential Careers List." I need to get this thing down and start taking decisive action in my life.

Gallerist—gone. Just because I like wandering around art galleries doesn't mean that I'd actually like working in one. Plus, I think I'd feel really bad trying to pretend it's okay to charge fifty thousand dollars for a piece of canvas with two blobs of paint on it.

Photographer—gone. I like the *idea* of being a photographer, but if I'm honest, thinking about all those complicated buttons and settings on fancy cameras makes my head hurt.

Web designer—gone. I don't want to sit at a computer all day.

Makeup artist.

*Makeup artist*? Was I high when I put this on the list? I can't even do my own makeup, for goodness' sake. Gone.

At noon, I head into the break room, where John is sitting at the lunch table eating a sandwich and staring at his phone.

I clear my throat. "Hey."

He glances up briefly and then looks back down at his phone. "Hey."

I feel a teensy spark of curiosity. Could he be doing Wordle right now? I surreptitiously peek over his shoulder as I walk to the fridge to grab my yogurt.

Nope. He's just scrolling through Kijiji, shopping for some sort of car part.

"I'll fix your car later," he says. "I took a look at it this morning, it's your alternator that's shot."

"Oh, no rush," I say automatically.

He frowns. "Don't you need it to get to work?"

"Er—well, yeah. But I can take taxis, if you're too busy with other stuff today."

"I'm not. It won't take long."

"Oh. Well . . . okay. I'll pay you, obviously," I add.

He shrugs. "Don't worry about it."

"No, I will. Just let me know how much I owe you."

He takes another bite of his sandwich. "It's no big deal. It's going to take, like, ten minutes, and there's an alternator in the back from Dave's old Corolla."

I know I should argue more, but then I think of my bank balance and decide to bite my tongue.

"Thanks," I say awkwardly.

"No worries."

A silence falls. I don't know why, but I feel sort of disappointed. Which is stupid because what did I expect? The slightly interesting fact that John does Wordle doesn't change the millions of *un*interesting things about him. Just because we have this one tiny thing in common doesn't mean we could ever be friends.

I sit down with a sigh and pull the lid off my yogurt. Out of the corner of my eye, I see John glance up from his phone.

"Did you do Wordle today?" he asks.

My spoon of yogurt freezes halfway to my mouth.

Did he just initiate a conversation?

I force myself to act casual, swallowing my bite of yogurt and reaching for a napkin with deliberate ease. This sort of feels like when someone's standoffish cat suddenly hops onto your lap. If you pay them any attention, they're going to give you a withering look and leap away.

"Not yet," I say. "I was going to do it now."

"Cool," he says. "I'll do it too."

I take out my phone and open Wordle. "Don't tell me any hints," I say quickly. "That's cheating."

He nods, chewing a bite of sandwich. He swipes Wordle open on his phone and then frowns at it, a pensive little crease appearing between his brows. Which is . . . kind of cute. Objectively speaking, I mean.

I shake my head and turn my attention to my phone. I start with a banker word, OUIJA. When I was first doing Wordle, I read online about good words to start with, and I use this one occasionally. It's nice because it knocks out a bunch of vowels right from the start.

Like today—the O, U, *and* A are right. They're all in the wrong place, but that's still better than nothing.

O, U, A.

A, O, U.

I bite my lip, running through all the unused letters.

ABOUT!

I type it in eagerly, sneaking a little glance at John as I do. He's still chewing thoughtfully. There's a smudge of black grease on his cheek.

Hmm. ABOUT is wrong, but the B is yellow. I bite my lip.

B, O, U, A.

B, A, O, U.

Something lights up in the back of my brain. There's a word that I know . . . it's hovering at the edges of my mind . . . it's got something to do with—with crocodiles, I think, and swamps . . .

BAYOU.

It hits me in a sudden flash of inspiration. I type it in, and voilà! Three hundred and four days! I do a little dance in my chair.

"You got it?" John asks.

I grin. "Got it."

"That's, what—three hundred and four days?"

I blink at him, strangely touched that he remembered. "Yep."

"That's cool," he says. He doesn't put any inflection into the words, but it still feels kind of nice to hear.

"Do you have a streak going?" I ask.

"Nah, I can't remember to do it every day. Is there a G in it?" he adds, turning his phone toward me. I peer at his screen curiously. He started with MOTOR—classic John—then tried DONUT.

"No G," I say. "Why don't you put something like PLAID to get rid of a bunch of the other letters?"

"I've got it on hard mode," he says. "Have to use the O and the U in the next guess."

I stare at him again, my brain glitching like it did last night. Not only does John do Wordle, he does it on *hard mode*?

Nope. Does not compute.

I watch as he starts typing and then snort in surprise. "OPIUM?"

"It's a word."

"I know that," I say. "It's just a bit random."

He raises an eyebrow. "How do you choose words, then?"

"Just . . . randomly," I say. "Oh, shut up," I add tartly, as his mouth curves up in amusement. "You've still only got O and U. Want a hint?"

"No. Just tell me if there's a double letter."

"That would be a hint," I point out. "And no."

"Okay." He frowns again, then types ABOUT.

"I used that one too!" I say brightly. "It's still pretty hard to guess—" I start, but he's already typing in BAYOU.

"Cool," he says, as the letters turn green.

Damn. How did he figure it out so quickly?

"How'd you get that so fast?" I ask.

He shrugs. "There's a guy at the track from Louisiana. His team's called Bayou Racing." He swallows the last bite of his sandwich and stands. "Later."

He heads out of the room without another word, leaving me staring at the empty doorway, feeling off-balance and oddly giddy.

Weird, I think, as I take another bite of my yogurt. That was very, very weird.

# C H A P T E R  7

The sun emerges from the clouds just after lunch, and the rest of the day is bright and warm. All the day's clients are nice, and I spend a few fun hours researching degrees in paleontology, which is one of the careers that survived my "Potential Careers List" pruning earlier. I can totally see myself working at some beautiful, remote site, digging up dinosaur bones and brushing them off with those tiny little brushes. (It's always seemed to me like it would go faster if they used larger brushes, but maybe they get paid by the hour or something.) I think it would be so cool to hold something in your hand that's *millions* of years old. And who knows, maybe I could discover a brand-new type of dinosaur, and they'd name it after me! The Emilyosaurus.

Actually, no. That's stupid.

They shouldn't name it that.

Just past five, Dave comes out to the front desk and hands me my car keys.

"John had to head out to some family thing," he says. "He said it's all fixed. Have a good night."

"Oh—you too," I say, though he's already out the door. I gather my things with a strange feeling in my stomach, almost like disappointment. Which is silly, because talking to John is always so awkward. Still, it would have been nice to thank him.

Maybe I'll make him a thank-you card. That's a polite thing to do. Plus, I love making people cards.

Spirits lifted, I head out back to find my car. I let out a breath of relief when it starts normally. For a moment I think it looks sort of different inside, then I realize it's because the engine light on the dash has finally gone off.

The next time it comes on, I swear I'm going to get it fixed right away.

I sing to myself on the drive home, wrapping up an enthusiastic and off-key rendition of Kelly Clarkson's old song "Miss Independent" as I pull into my driveway. I'm in such a good mood I decide to pop in to visit Mrs. Finnamore. I ring her doorbell twice, since she sometimes doesn't hear it the first time. I wonder if her hearing aids need to be looked at.

A minute later, the door swings open, revealing a very thin, very rude middle-aged woman.

(And before you say anything, I know what you're thinking. How can I know that she's rude just from looking at her? But can't you just tell sometimes that people are going to be rude, just by the look on their face when you lock eyes with them?)

She frowns at me. "Can I help you?"

"I just came by to say hi to Mrs. Finnamore. I live next door." I point to my house.

"Is that Emily?" Mrs. Finnamore asks, appearing behind her.

"Hi, Mrs. Finnamore," I say.

"This is the girl I was telling you about," Mrs. Finnamore says to the rude woman. "Emily, this is my daughter, Debra."

The woman—Debra—purses her lips. "You're the one that helps with her groceries?"

Her tone is accusatory. I glance at Mrs. Finnamore uncertainly. "Er—sometimes, yes."

I've actually only done it once or twice. I'm not sure why I'm lying, except that I have a sneaky feeling I know why Mrs. Finnamore told her daughter about me. A few weeks ago, Mrs. Finnamore told me that her family wants to put her in a home. They all live out west, and they think she's too old to live by herself.

"Emily's very helpful," Mrs. Finnamore says.

Debra makes an impatient noise. "You need help with more than groceries, Mom," she says. "She hasn't taken her meds properly for weeks," she adds to me in an undertone. Which—excuse me? Why is she talking to me like her mother isn't there?

My hackles are rising, but I force myself to smile politely. "I think she's doing pretty well."

Debra lets out a disbelieving breath. "Yes, well, she can't be depending on strangers all the time."

"What?" Mrs. Finnamore says.

"I said *you can't be depending on strangers,*" Debra says loudly.

"I don't mind helping," I say.

Debra gives me a condescending look. "Are you a certified home care nurse?"

Okay, I really don't like this woman. "No," I say. "But I don't mind helping with groceries and laundry and things."

"See?" Mrs. Finnamore says. "Pay the girl to do more, Debra, if it'll stop your endless fussing."

Wait, what? I try to backtrack hastily. "Oh, no, I didn't mean—"

"I'm not going to hire some random stranger," Debra snaps. "If we're going to get you home care, it's going to be a proper nurse."

"I don't want a nurse, I want Emily," Mrs. Finnamore says. "And it's foolish to pay a trained nurse to get groceries."

Debra rolls her eyes. "I'm going to be the one paying for it, Mom. It's not about the *money*."

Okay, things are getting way out of hand here. "Look," I say quickly. "You've got the wrong idea—"

"How much do you charge?" Debra interrupts.

I stare at her, totally thrown off-balance. Five minutes ago, I was singing Kelly Clarkson in my car. Now I've been dragged into a very uncomfortable, private family dispute.

And yet . . . why *shouldn't* I do it? I don't mind helping Mrs. Finnamore, and if it would get her daughter off her back about going to a home, isn't that a good thing? Plus, I can tell just from looking at Debra that she's got lots of money. Look at those perfectly pressed clothes, look at those shiny Chanel earrings.

"For groceries and laundry?" I ask, to buy myself some time to think.

"*And* make her take her blister pack meds properly, and keep the house from turning into a pigsty," Debra says.

I bite my lip, thinking quickly. How much do I think a private caregiver charges? Forty dollars a week? Fifty?

"Sonny McNeil's girl charges two-fifty a week," Mrs. Finnamore says. "And she doesn't even do the laundry."

My mouth drops open. Two hundred and fifty dollars? A *week*?

Luckily, Debra is frowning at her mother when she says it, which gives me time to rearrange my face into a look of calm composure.

"Two-fifty seems about right," I say, nodding like someone who totally knew that information beforehand.

Debra heaves an aggrieved sigh. "I'll have to think about it," she says.

"Of course," I say. Then, because I'm feeling a bit evil, I add, "Just let me know soon, before my schedule fills up."

It has the effect I intended. I can practically hear Debra's unpleasant brain whirring. To her, her mother is a problem, and this is a quick solution.

"I'll let you know," she says stiffly.

I smile at her. "Very good. Have a nice night."

I catch Mrs. Finnamore's eye as I turn to leave, and I could swear I see a mischievous glimmer in her eyes. I have to fight to keep from laughing. How did such a cool lady wind up with such a nasty daughter?

I head home and make myself some pasta, and I'm not ten minutes into an episode of *Schitt's Creek* when the doorbell rings. Fifteen minutes later, I sit back on my couch with a grin on my face and a crisp check for a thousand dollars in my hand. In cramped, slanted handwriting, Debra's written on the memo line: *For private caregiving services, May 23–June 23.*

I prop the check up on my coffee table and beam at it.

I guess I'm a private caregiver now.

# CHAPTER 8

As awful as Debra is, I'm determined to do an amazing job at caregiving, for Mrs. Finnamore's sake. The next morning, I pop over to her house before work to sort out a list of things I'll do for her.

"You don't have to do anything," she says, pouring tea into my cup. "Just keep the money, buy a little treat for yourself."

"I can't do *that*," I say, aghast. "Your daughter gave me a check for a thousand dollars."

"Debra's got more money than brains," Mrs. Finnamore says. "She'd pay ten times that to get out of caring for me herself."

I shift in my chair. "I'm sure she's just worried about you."

Mrs. Finnamore makes a dismissive noise. "Biscuit?"

"Er—sure." I take a chocolate biscuit from the box she offers me. "Really, though, I can't just take her money. I wouldn't feel right about it. And there must be something you need help with," I add. "Some chore that you don't like to do, or something you don't have time for . . ."

I trail off, glancing around her kitchen. I don't know how Debra could worry about this place turning into a "pigsty." It's the cleanest, neatest home I've ever been in. It is a bit cluttered, I suppose, with hundreds of porcelain figurines arranged artfully on little tables and shelves, but it's so clean I could eat off the floors.

"I manage just fine," Mrs. Finnamore says. There's a distinctly stubborn edge to her voice.

My shoulders sag. "Then I can't take your daughter's money. No, I mean it. It wouldn't be right. She paid me to be a caregiver."

Mrs. Finnamore watches me for a long moment. So long, in fact, that I sneak a glance at her wall clock to make sure I'm not going to be late for work. I don't rush her, though. I've found that some older people need a little time to gather their thoughts. I think that's why a lot of young people get so impatient with them. But I don't mind waiting. I take a few sips of my tea and take another chocolate biscuit.

"I suppose you could get the groceries," Mrs. Finnamore says finally. "They keep that store far too cold."

I nod. "I can do that." I hesitate, then add, "What about setting out your medicines? Debra seemed pretty worried about them."

Mrs. Finnamore lets out a harsh breath through her nose. "Debra's worried about everything. But if it'll stop her fussing, I suppose."

I nod. "Anything else? Laundry, maybe?"

She eyes me. "Do you know how to do laundry properly?"

"Er . . . yes." She looks so doubtful that I glance down at my clothes, suddenly worried I have a huge stain or something.

"I've got a new machine," she says. "It's very complicated to use."

"I'm sure I can sort it out. I mean, if it would be helpful."

She hesitates and then nods. "Fine."

"What about meals? And dishes?"

I realize right away I've pushed too far. Mrs. Finnamore's mouth tightens at the edges. "For goodness' sake, I'm not an *invalid*. I'm perfectly capable of making my own meals. And I've seen what you young girls think meals are, all that microwaveable nonsense and pasta from a box. No, thank you."

I hide a smile. "Fair enough." I look around her pristine house again. I wonder how much time it takes her to keep everything clean like this, and how often she gets out of the house. "We should go out once a week, too," I add determinedly, "to do something fun in town."

She looks skeptical. "Like what?"

"I don't know. There's a museum on Main Street I've been meaning to go to since I moved here."

Mrs. Finnamore raises an eyebrow. "What on earth could they make a museum about in Waldon?"

"Oh, c'mon," I say encouragingly. "It'll be fun. A girls' outing on Debra's dime. It's supposed to be rainy tomorrow, we could go then. Rainy days are the best for museums."

She looks at me—a bit pityingly, I might add—and then grudgingly relents. "If you really want to. I think my old friend Jim works there."

"There you go," I say brightly, then rise to my feet. "I should get to work. Thanks for the tea."

I sing along with the radio as I drive to the shop. I can't believe I'm going to make two hundred and fifty dollars a week just to help out a cool old lady. Think of all the interesting stories I'll hear! I make a mental note to ask Mrs. Finnamore if she remembers where she was during the moon landing. In fact, maybe today I'll do a little research about the fifties and sixties, when Mrs. Finnamore would have been around my age, and make a list of interesting questions to ask her. I want to make sure she has a good time on our outing, and like I said on my date with Arjun, there's nothing people like more than talking about themselves. Whether they're thirty years old or ninety years old, the rule still holds true.

When I arrive at the shop, John is at the front desk talking on the cordless phone. He's frowning heavily, like he's annoyed with whatever he's hearing. He wanders off as soon as I come in without so much as a nod of acknowledgment—thanks, John—and I sneak a glance at the number on the phone dock. He's talking to the shop owner, Fred.

Huh.

I've never seen Fred and John interact, but I have occasionally wondered if they don't get along. I've heard John complain about the state of some of the garage equipment, and when Fred popped into the shop the other day he made a few weirdly defensive comments when he was checking the books, like, "See? Plenty of business. If it's not broke, don't fix it, Emily. That's what I always say."

I hesitate for a few moments, then surreptitiously rise to my feet and drift toward the hallway. Just to stretch my legs, you know.

Coincidentally, it allows me to hear a few snippets of John's conversation.

"I really think—no, but—" An impatient sigh. "No, I realize that, I'm just saying—"

Man, I haven't heard John sound this angry since that time a customer asked him to paint their Volkswagen Beetle bright pink. (I believe his exact words were "You want to pay me to make your stupid car look even stupider?")

"Fine. No, fine," John snaps.

Shoot—his voice is getting louder. He's coming back.

I hustle back to my desk. By the time John reappears, I'm frowning thoughtfully at an old receipt.

"Oh, thanks," I say casually, as he returns the phone to the dock. He kind of grunts in acknowledgment and then disappears into the garage. I put down the receipt—which I've just noticed is from 2009, how the heck did this get here?—and prop my chin on my hand, frowning thoughtfully.

It never occurred to me to wonder if Fred runs this shop properly, because honestly, I've never really cared. But now that I think about it, there are a lot of things around here that need updating. The booking system is ancient, for one thing, and I know for a fact the security cameras in the back are broken, since Dave warned me not to park there when I first started working here. And I'm no mechanic (obviously), but I've heard Dave and John cursing out some machine called a tire balancer about a billion times. I wonder why Fred hasn't bought them a new one.

Oh, well. I'm not going to get involved. Fred has always been nice to me, but he seems like someone who could fly into a temper pretty quickly, and I don't want to get on his bad side. Plus, it's not like I'm going to work here forever. In fact, with the new money coming in from helping Mrs. Finnamore, I might be able to get out of here even sooner. If I don't change my lifestyle at all, I can use the caregiving money to pay down my student loan. This time next year, I could be debt-free and ready to dive into a new, exciting career!

This encouraging thought carries me through the morning, and I pass most of the time looking up things that happened in Canada in the fifties and sixties. I even track down a list of the top ten most popular songs in Canada in 1962, which is when Mrs. Finnamore was my exact age. Maybe I'll make a playlist of them for the drive to the museum.

A few times during the morning, I find my thumb hovering over the *New York Times* app, but every time, I decide against opening it. It just makes more sense to do Wordle at lunchtime, when I can focus more. And if John happens to be doing it then too, well, so be it.

I head back to the break room just after noon. John is sitting at the table, unwrapping a ham-and-cheese sub.

"How's it going?" I ask, opening the fridge door.

He shrugs.

That's his answer to the question "How's it going?" A *shrug*.

I turn away and roll my eyes. Okay, maybe we're never going to be BFFs, but I've still decided I'm going to make him my Wordle work buddy, whether he likes it or not. I've got to keep my streak going, and it can't hurt to have someone to bounce ideas off of.

I put a pot of coffee on, spoon some granola and yogurt into a bowl, and sit down across from him. "Wordle time."

He raises an eyebrow at my tone (which, okay, was kind of bossy) but takes out his phone.

"What's your first word going to be?" I ask.

He shrugs again. "You?"

"HELPS," I say. "As in, my neighbor's daughter just hired me to—er, *helps* her out around the house."

"That sentence doesn't make sense."

"Yes, I know," I say tartly. "But 'help' is only four letters. What's your first word?"

"COURT."

"As in . . . ?"

"As in nothing." He types it into his phone. I look away before he clicks enter. I don't want to accidentally cheat. "So are you, like, trained to do home care or something?" he asks.

"What? Oh—no. I'm not doing actual nursing stuff." I spent a good hour last night making sure that I didn't need any specific training to be a caregiver in Canada, but it seems like as long as I stick to strictly nonmedical things, I'm okay. "I'm just going to help my neighbor out with groceries and chores and things. She's eighty-eight," I add.

He grimaces. "Brutal."

"No, it's fun!" I insist. "I love older people. They have such interesting stories."

He looks at me like I'm crazy. "Okay."

"Don't you ever ask your grandparents to tell you stories from when they grew up?"

"No."

I frown. "Well, you're missing out. Too many people think of their grandparents as just, like, generic old people who only exist to send them money at Christmas. They don't think of them as real people with feelings and hopes and dreams." John is still looking at me like I'm nuts, but I ignore him. "I bet your grandparents could tell you really interesting stories if you just asked them the right questions," I chide him. "Like, wouldn't your mother's parents have been alive during the April Revolution? Or were they living in Canada then?"

John frowns. "How'd you know my mom's Dominican?"

With effort, I refrain from rolling my eyes. "You told me."

"Did I?"

This time, I actually do roll my eyes. "Do you remember any conversations you have that aren't about cars?"

He blinks at me, looking faintly surprised. "Yes. Just because I don't remember every single thing I've ever told you—"

"Every single thing?" I repeat. "You've told me, like, *three* things about yourself."

He stares at me, and for once I think I've actually startled him out of his usual apathetic stupor. My cheeks grow a little hot under his gaze.

"Forget it," I say. "Let's just finish Wordle."

I turn back to my phone determinedly. HELPS gave me a yellow E and a green S. Time to rule out some other letters.

CRAZY, I type. As in, I must be CRAZY trying to have conversations with John.

It's a better choice—the C is green and the A is yellow.

C, E, A, S.

C, A, E, S.

Hmm.

CAVES, I type in.

Shoot. Every letter is green but the V, which is wrong.

CANES, I try.

Crap. Wrong again.

I skim through the remaining letters.

Oh! CARES! It must be CARES. I confidently type it in and click enter.

Crap, *crap*. How can that not be right?

Oh. Wait a second.

CAKES. It could be CAKES.

Or . . . CAGES.

. . . and isn't CATES also a word?

Oh, god. This is my worst nightmare. Any one of those could

be right, but I've only got one guess left. My streak might end right now, just because of pure bad *luck*.

I swear under my breath.

"What?" John says.

"I've got one guess left, and there are three words that it could be."

"Show me."

I turn my phone toward him. "CAGES, CAKES or CATES."

"Or CADES," he adds.

"Is that a word?"

"I think so. A cade is, like, a barrel."

I drop my head into my hands and rake my fingers through my hair. "I'm screwed."

John studies me for a moment and then looks down at his own phone. "Do you want some help?"

I shake my head miserably. "My streak won't count if I cheat."

"Well, then, you've just got to guess."

I bite my lip. He's right. There's no other way.

"CATES and CADES are too weird," I say. "I'm not going to use them."

"CAKES or CAGES, then."

"Yeah." I roll both words over my tongue, trying to see if I get a gut feeling for one of them, but all I feel is slightly anxious.

"Do you have a good feeling about either of them?" I ask John.

"What do you mean, a good feeling?"

"Like, does either one of them *feel* right?"

He stares at me like I'm nuts for a moment, then shrugs. "I'm putting a roll cage in that Miata later."

I nod tersely. That'll have to do. "CAGES it is."

I take a breath—type the letters—

"I can't look," I say, squeezing my eyes shut. I stab my thumb in the direction of the enter button. A moment of silence, then—

"Nice," John says.

I crack one eye open. "Seriously?"

"You got it," he says.

A childish squeal of excitement slips from my lips. I bounce around in my chair a little and then stop when I see John watching me.

"What?" I say, a little sharper than I mean to.

He watches me a moment more. "You're kind of weird."

He doesn't say it like an insult. In fact, it almost sounds like a compliment.

I lift my chin up. "Yep. And you're good luck," I add generously. "That's twice now you've saved my streak. If I have to guess again tomorrow, I'm going to have to hunt you down at home."

"Or you could just text, like a normal person."

I brighten. "Ooh, yes. Give me your number."

He dictates it to me, and I save it as "John Smith (Auto Shop)." I shoot him a quick text so that he has my number and then rise to my feet. "I should get back to the desk."

"Later," he says.

It's not until that evening, when I'm driving home, that it occurs to me that I've accidentally asked John for his number. I squirm uncertainly in my seat. I hope he didn't think I was like . . . *asking* asking. Like, in a romantic way.

Then I laugh out loud. What am I, crazy? Of course he doesn't think that. There's nothing romantic between John and me. He made that abundantly clear when I first started working here, and every single day since. And I'm definitely not interested in him. This is a Wordle friendship, plain and simple.

No, not even a friendship. A Wordle *alliance*.

That's all there will ever be between John and me.

# CHAPTER 9

I wake the next morning to the sound of rain thundering down on the roof. I stretch my arms and legs out wide and then shift a little deeper under the covers. Honestly, is there a sound in the world that's more comforting than rain on a metal roof? Go ahead, try to name one.

See? You've got nothing.

I turn on my bedside kettle (which I have for days exactly like this) and snuggle up under the blankets to sip tea and do Wordle. When I'm done (easy-peasy, WRECK in four guesses), I grab the book I've been reading and dive into the pages.

I'm so engrossed in the story, I almost forget about my museum date with Mrs. Finnamore. I leap out of bed the second I remember and rush to get showered and dressed. I decide on a knee-length skirt that I've always thought looks sort of old-fashioned, a short-sleeved blouse, and a pair of tiny brass earrings that are shaped like hammers. Weird, yes, but I think it's pretty fitting since we're going to the local barrel-making museum.

(Yes, I said barrel-making. We're in small-town PEI, what did you expect, an exhibit of Terracotta warriors?)

Mrs. Finnamore's in a bit of a sour mood, and she fusses a little about going, but I dig my heels in and shoo her to my car.

"It'll be good to get out of the house," I say firmly.

The rain splatters the windshield as we drive into central Waldon (aka the one long street with all the shops and the post office) and find a parking spot near the museum. To my surprise, there's a line to get inside. I think all the tourists must be desperate to find something indoors to do. I see a lot of grumpy-looking parents wrangling restless kids.

The museum is built inside of this huge, historic-looking house on the waterfront. It sort of looks like an old schoolhouse, with a big veranda out front and a gable roof with a dormer window framing the center of the house. It's really quite gorgeous, even in the pouring rain.

"Look at this building!" I say.

"It's falling apart," Mrs. Finnamore says, unimpressed. "Look at those planters."

I follow her gaze to the big stone planters that flank the museum entrance. I suppose she's right—they do look a little neglected. I'm not an expert gardener like Mrs. Finnamore, but even I know that those are all weeds.

"Well, still," I say, tilting my head back to admire the house again.

"Oh, for goodness' sake," Mrs. Finnamore says, grabbing the handle of my umbrella to tilt it forward.

She keeps grumbling as we wait, but when we get to the front of the line, she waves me away when I offer to get the tickets. She pays ten dollars for our admission and two dollars for the coat check. I hang up our dripping coats and umbrella and then rejoin her at the entrance to the exhibits.

"Doesn't it smell good in here?" I ask, breathing deeply through my nose. "Like sawdust and history."

"History?" Mrs. Finnamore repeats. "I'm older than this factory."

I pretend I don't hear her. We walk slowly around the museum, which is quiet and echoey and dimly lit, peering at the old barrel-making equipment and watching a worker demonstrate how they used to make barrels. It's a shame that it's no longer a viable career option, because it looks quite peaceful. For a moment I envision myself as a barrel-maker. I can see the website now—EMILY EVANS: HANDCRAFTED BARRELS FOR ALL YOUR BAR-RELING NEEDS.

Amazing.

"Oh, there's Jim," Mrs. Finnamore says, gesturing toward an elderly gentleman sitting in the corner. He has a vest on that says Security, which is . . . kind of hilarious. What are people going to steal? The barrels must weigh a hundred pounds each, and most of the old equipment wouldn't even fit through the doorway. Also, Jim looks like he's about ninety. I can't really see him chasing down barrel thieves.

"His daughter just got out of the hospital. I should go see how he's doing," Mrs. Finnamore says, and then walks off to talk to him.

"I'll be here," I say cheerfully, trying to ignore the fact that I've just been ditched by an eighty-eight-year-old.

I watch the barrel-maker for a while, then my phone dings in my pocket. I pull it out, absently wondering if my parents have caved and bought New Zealand cell phone plans.

Instead, I find a text from John Smith (Auto Shop).

[12:21] **John:** get Wordle today?

I blink at it in surprise. I know I gave John my number, but I never thought he would actually use it. I guess he must be having trouble with Wordle.

[12:22] Yep! How bout you?

[12:22] **John:** yep

Huh. Maybe not.

I'm about to put my phone away when it dings again.

[12:22] **John:** what word did you start with?

I stare at it for another incredulous moment. Is John actually *continuing* the conversation?

[12:23]: WATER.

[12:23] **John:** as in . . . ?

A surprised noise slips from my lips. I sort of want to grab the tourist next to me, show her my phone, and say, "Are you seeing this?"

Unless . . . maybe John is actually super talkative, but only in texts? I had a friend like that in high school. She was super shy in person but crazy chatty in texts.

[12:24] As in, the WATER for my tea was boiling!

[12:24] **John:** tea is nasty

(Okay, maybe not *crazy* chatty.)

[12:24]: Tea is the best

[12:24]: After coffee

[12:24]: And milkshakes

[12:24]: And wine

[12:25] **John:** lol

Well, would you look at that? I got an "lol" from John. This is probably what it feels like to get a high five from the pope.

I consider typing something like, "What are you up to this weekend?," but I feel like that would be pushing my luck. For the second time, I'm just about to put my phone away when it dings.

[12:26] **John:** what are you up to this weekend?

Okay.
This is seriously bananas.

[12:27]: Have you been hacked??

[12:28] **John:** what?

[12:28]: You've never asked me this many questions before

[12:28] **John:** ?

[12:28] **John:** sure I have

[12:29]: You definitely haven't

[12:29]: And I'm at a barrel museum

[12:30] **John:** . . . why?

*Four* questions! This is definitely a record.

[12:31]: For fun!

[12:31]: Duh.

[12:32]: I took Mrs. Finnamore, the lady I'm helping out at home

[12:32]: She didn't really want to come, though

[12:33] **John:** smart lady

[12:33]: Pffft

[12:33]: You wish you were at a barrel museum right now

[12:34] **John:** I really don't

[12:34] **John:** but have fun, I guess

[12:35]: I will, thanks!

[12:35]: Enjoy your sad, barrel-less weekend

[12:35] **John:** haha

[12:35] **John:** thanks

Well, would you look at that? An "lol" *and* a "haha." Somebody alert the media.

I chuckle at myself, then lurch sideways as someone's toddler rams into my legs. I smile at the kid's mother, who apologizes wearily.

"No problem," I say.

I watch the kid run off to barrel (ha!) into someone else, then smile a little to myself. Maybe John and I are more than Wordle allies. Maybe we're Wordle acquaintances. Heck, maybe we're even approaching Wordle friends!

I wander around the museum, peering at exhibits and just taking in the general atmosphere. It's been so long since I've been to a museum, I forgot how much I love them. They're so quiet and peaceful, and it's so fun to learn something new—even something as objectively dry as barrel-making. It would be cool to work here, watching people mill about, soaking up little bits of knowledge. I wonder if they ever need anyone to help out.

Just as I think it, my eyes land on a poster pinned to a nearby wall.

## VOLUNTEERS WANTED

Like *fate*.

I glance over to make sure Mrs. Finnamore isn't looking for me (she isn't; apparently Jim is much better company than I am) and then head back to the main desk where we bought our tickets. I wait for a young family to finish their purchase and then step up to talk to the middle-aged woman working the desk. Five minutes later, I'm chatting with the museum manager in a back room. Five minutes after that, I have my first shift! From noon to five tomorrow, and every Saturday and Sunday after that. The museum manager, Shelley, says I'll start at the ticket desk, but once I feel comfortable, I can move on to guided tours.

Well, okay, actually she said that all I had to do was sell tickets and keep an eye out for kids trying to push barrels over, but when I suggested doing guided tours in the future, she looked at me funny and said, "I guess."

Whatever. I'm going to take it. I've been looking for something to fill up my weekends a bit, and this is going to be perfect. Plus, museums are kind of creative places, aren't they? Plenty of "scope for the imagination," as Anne of Green Gables would say.

Grinning cheerfully, I make my way back to Mrs. Finnamore, who is still talking with Jim.

"Ah, Emily," she says briskly. "I was just telling Jim how you're going to be helping me out around the house. She's going to get my groceries," she tells Jim. "And she's going to do the laundry, once I've taught her how to use the machine properly."

"Is that right?" Jim asks. He's very tall and thin, with a few strands of white hair combed over his crown. He's got a kindly look about him, and even though his hands are swollen and curled around his cane, he seems pretty hale for his age.

"She could do the same for you," Mrs. Finnamore says.

Hang on, what?

"Well, now, I don't know," Jim says, while I hastily raise my hands up in protest. "I'm doing all right."

"You're too old to be standing in those grocery lines," Mrs. Finnamore scolds. (Which, please! She's one to talk.)

"How much does it cost?" Jim asks, looking at me.

I open my mouth to tell him apologetically that my arrangement with Mrs. Finnamore is really more of a one-off, but Mrs. Finnamore answers before I can.

"It's two-fifty for the week, but that's with her sorting out all those pills the fool doctor thinks I should take. For groceries and laundry I'm sure it's no more than a hundred."

"Oh—not that much," I say hastily. Honestly, I am going to kill Mrs. Finnamore. "Plus, I don't really have time—"

"I'll give her your phone number once I get home," Mrs. Finnamore says, speaking over me. "You'll be home later tonight?"

Jim nods.

"Very good. Emily will call you then. Tell your daughter I'm thinking of her."

I smile weakly at Jim and then hurry after Mrs. Finnamore, who is heading for the exit. "You can't be telling other people I'll work for them!" I tell her as we get into the car. The rain is still pouring down, bouncing two inches off the windshield.

"Oh, it's only Jim," Mrs. Finnamore says, waving me away. "He really shouldn't be living alone. He hasn't done well since his wife died last year. Bowel cancer, you know. And none of his children

live here anymore . . . plus his daughter's in and out of the hospital
with her lungs . . ."

Well, crap. I can hardly refuse to help poor Jim out now, can I?

"I mean . . . I guess it might be fine, for a little while. No one else,
though," I add firmly. "I don't have time."

"Oh, what do you girls do today? Spend all your time tapping
away on your phones. Plus, my friend Doris could really use help
with her pills. You know she's on twice as many as I am, and hers
are the kind you have to take every day—"

"Mrs. Finnamore," I groan.

"What? It's a little extra cash, and it won't take you five minutes.
She just lives up the street from us, you know, you could pop in to
her place on those little runs of yours—"

I sigh inwardly and resolve myself to helping out this Doris
woman too.

Honestly, before you know it, I'm going to be the unofficial
caregiver for the entire town of Waldon.

# CHAPTER 10

True to her word, Mrs. Finnamore makes me call her friend Doris as soon as we get home from the museum, and I spend Sunday morning visiting both her and Jim to set up a weekly caregiving plan. Between the two of them and Mrs. Finnamore, this new job is going to take up about eight hours a week, which is time I really should spend sorting out my life. But it also means 1,450 extra dollars a *month*, which means I can pay off my student loan and move on to my dream life even sooner, so I figure it's more than worth it.

Jim is easy. He needs his laundry and his groceries done, and he desperately needs someone to tidy up his house a bit. He's a really sweet man—ninety-six years old and still living at home! He's a bit quiet at first, but I draw him out by asking lots of questions about the people in the photos at his house. He tells me the most heart-wrenching story about his youngest daughter, who died of leukemia when she was a teenager, and I learn that he worked at the local post office for nearly fifty years. I just know he has all sorts of stories to tell, and I can't wait to hear them.

Doris is a bit of a different story. She's stooped with arthritis and so thin that I can see all the knobby bones of her spine, but her spirits clearly haven't been impacted by her age. She greets me by saying, "You're the girl Betty's hired, are you?" And then, "I thought she said you were pretty."

Without pausing to let me answer (not that I'm sure what I

would've said to that) she proceeds to dictate exactly what she wants from me. "None of this caregiving nonsense, I'm perfectly capable of doing everything except my groceries. That fool doctor took my license away after I had one teensy little accident."

She tells me several times that she thinks I'm overcharging her and tries to demand I use her ancient car when I get her groceries because she doesn't trust my "flimsy modern car." Five minutes in, I decide to be amused instead of offended, but I'm still glad I won't have to see her more than once a week.

I go for a quick run when I'm done (I feel like I need to run off the whole interaction, to be honest), then I shower and get ready for my first shift at the museum. I put on cropped pants and a button-up blouse that I think looks sort of vintage, and pull my hair into a bun on the top of my head. I scrutinize myself in the mirror, trying to sort out if I look museum-y enough. Maybe the next time I'm at the pharmacy, I'll buy a cheap pair of those fashion glasses, the ones that don't have any prescription lenses in them.

I snap a picture of myself in my mirror and send it to the group chat with Fallon, Martha, and Divya.

[11:02]: Image sent.

[11:02]: Starting work at a museum today! Do I look the part?

As I put on some mascara, my phone dings with an answer.

[11:06] **Fallon:** So cute!

[11:06] **Fallon:** Did you finally get out of that gas station job??

[11:07]: Auto shop lol

[11:07]: And no, I'm still there

[11:07]: The museum is just a volunteer thing

[11:08] **Fallon:** Ooh I see haha

[11:08] **Fallon:** Still no luck on the job front?

[11:08]: Nothing yet, but getting closer!

(That's a tiny lie, but I'm hoping karma will overlook it.)

[11:08] **Fallon:** Yay!

[11:08] **Fallon:** You're way too smart to be a secretary forever lmao

She sends a string of emojis afterward, the one with the girl wearing a graduation cap. I bite my lip.

[11:09]: Lol

[11:09]: What are you up to this weekend?

I wait a few minutes, but she doesn't answer. I turn back to the mirror and apply another layer of mascara, feeling a bit squicky inside. Talking to Fallon does that to me sometimes. Out of our group, she was the one I was closest to in university. She had this way about her, this sort of sparkly, infectious energy, and whenever we used to talk about the future she would grin at me and tell me we were destined for great things. I know she's disappointed in me for winding up where I am. Sometimes it seems like she's my alter ego, like a successful version of me. I'm really happy for her, don't get me wrong, but sometimes it makes it sort of painful to talk to her.

I sigh and give my head a little shake. Jealously is a bad color on anyone, and I'm not going to become one of those people who resents anyone who's better than them. I need to use Fallon as a source of inspiration, not resentment. I'm going to find a job that I love as much as she loves hers, and I'm going to live in a big, exciting city and achieve all the great things she always said that I would. And in the meantime . . . in the meantime, I'm going to have a little silly fun at the local barrel-making museum.

I nod determinedly at my reflection and head out to my car. I arrive at the museum thirty minutes before my shift, just in case I need to do any training before I start, but the manager, Shelley, just sits me at the front desk and shows me where the cashbox is.

"Do you take credit cards?" I ask.

"The machine's broken," she says, scowling like the machine is personally conspiring against her. "I'll be in the back if you need anything."

She heads off before I can think of any more questions. I'm a bit nervous to be left on my own already, but at the same time,

I'm glad I don't have to work beside her all day. She seems a tad unpleasant.

I straighten out the pamphlets on the desk, clean a coffee stain off the cashbox, and then count all the money in it so I can make sure the balance is correct at the end of my shift. Then I sit up straight and wait, eagerly, for someone to show up.

But fifteen minutes pass by and the place is as empty as it was when I arrived. I think yesterday might have been an anomaly. The sun is out today, and although plenty of people walk by, no one even glances at the museum.

Tucking the cashbox in a drawer, I get up and take a quick spin of the place. I know it's just a small, kind of random museum, but it really is incredible. I feel like I've been transported back a hundred years. The floors are made of thin hardwood planks that creak underfoot, and the glass in the windows is warped with age. And whoever designed the exhibits clearly knew what they were doing. As you move through the rooms, they take you through the history of barrel-making, ending in the largest room in the back, where the barrel-maker was doing demonstrations yesterday. He isn't here today, though. Maybe he only comes on Saturdays.

My footsteps echo as I loop the rooms once, then again. I reread all the little placards that explain all the different tools and peer out the windows to the enormous yard in the back. It's really beautiful, with a few big shady trees and a pier overlooking the water. It's a shame they don't use it as part of the museum. They could put in a barrel-themed playground for kids. Maybe in the summer they could even put a barbecue out there and sell burgers and hot dogs.

"Hello?" calls a voice.

I jump and hurry back to my desk, where two middle-aged women are waiting.

"Hi!" I say brightly. "Did you want to buy tickets to the museum?"

"Oh, no," one of the women says. "Do you have a bathroom?"

I hesitate—something tells me Shelley wouldn't approve of this—then nod. There's nothing worse than being stuck somewhere and having to pee, and something tells me these two women are tourists. "Of course," I say. "It's right through there."

"Thanks," says the woman, and heads off.

Her friend peers past me into the museum. "What's this place about?"

"Barrel-making," I say. "The town of Waldon was once the second-largest manufacturer of barrels in the country." I know this because I read it on one of the museum placards. "Ten thousand barrels a year, all of them made by hand."

The woman nods politely. "Well, maybe I'll take a walk through while I wait for her," she says. "How much is it?"

"Five dollars."

"Do you take credit cards?"

I pull an apologetic face. "Machine's broken."

The woman frowns. "I don't know if I have any Canadian money." She digs in her purse. "These funny little coins you use," she muses. "What are these ones called?"

"Toonies," I say, hiding a smile. She's American, surely. "Where are you from?"

"New Jersey," she says. (I knew it!) "My sister and I are here for a week." She hands me three toonies.

"Your change," I say, opening the cashbox. "One loonie."

"Ha! A loonie. How strange." She heads off into the museum. I can tell she's not that interested in barrels, really, but she seems like the type of person who enjoys poking around places. I smile as I watch her wander around. It really is peaceful in here.

The other woman, her sister, emerges from the bathroom. "Where'd Anne go?" she asks me.

"She went through the museum," I say. "Do you want to buy a ticket too?"

"For five dollars?" the woman says incredulously, reading the sign. "Yeah, right. Tell Anne I'll be outside when she's done."

I stifle a snort. How rude.

I smile extra politely at her, because rude people never seem to know what to do in the face of excessive kindness. "Absolutely," I say cheerfully. "You have a great day, now. Enjoy the town!"

She looks vaguely confused and annoyed, just like I hoped she would. I giggle to myself as she leaves. Five minutes later, her sister—the nice one in the family, I'd say—reappears and thanks me.

"Enjoy the rest of your visit," I tell her. "Good luck with your awful sister," I add under my breath after she's gone.

No one else comes in afterward, and I start to get a little bored. I do Wordle (QUIET, in four guesses) and make a list of all the ideas I have to boost interest in the museum—barrel-themed playground, hot dog stand, guided tours—then I rummage through the desk drawers until I find the broken credit card machine. It's one of those small handheld ones with a separate piece for people to tap their credit cards. Someone has shoved it back into its box, which thankfully still has a manual inside. It takes me a good forty-five minutes, but by the end, we've got a fully functioning credit card machine again.

I wander back to Shelley's office, where I find her scrolling through Facebook on an old desktop computer.

"I fixed the credit card machine," I tell her.

She glances up briefly. "I'm sure it'll just break again. That thing's a piece of junk."

Okay, that wasn't quite the praise I was looking for, but whatever.

"It's pretty quiet here today," I say.

"You can leave if you want to," she says without looking away from Facebook. "I'll watch the desk."

I frown. "No, I don't mind staying. But I was thinking—wouldn't it be fun to call the local schools and see if they want to bring their kids here for field trips?"

Shelley snorts. "Pretty boring field trip, looking at a bunch of barrels."

Okay, what is *with* this woman? Honestly, why work in a barrel-themed museum if you don't like barrels?

"Er—have you worked here long?" I ask. Maybe she's gotten jaded over the years. Maybe she used to be a hardcore barrel-enthusiast, but the rough world of barrel museum curating wore her down.

"My aunt ran it before me," Shelley says, with the tiniest eye roll. "I could've sold this building for, like, half a million, but the town historical society conned her into letting them take over the lease right before she died."

Yikes. "A tad unpleasant" may have been a serious underestimation of Shelley.

"I think it's cool," I say stubbornly. "I love museums."

Shelley gives me a slightly incredulous look and then goes right back to scrolling on Facebook.

I escape back to my desk and sit down again, feeling a bit perturbed. Fortunately, I don't have much time to sulk before a young couple peers uncertainly into the door.

"Come in!" I say eagerly, beckoning them inside.

They're in their midtwenties, I'd say, and they tell me they're visiting from Japan. When I ask what brought them to PEI, the girl says, "Anne of Green Gables."

"Ooh, I *love* Anne of Green Gables!" I say earnestly. How cool that someone traveled here from so far away because of a lovely old children's book.

The two of them clearly know how to appreciate a museum properly, and after paying for tickets, they spend nearly an hour walking around. They're in the back room when I hear them speaking in English to someone with a deep, male voice. I twist around, confused. Did someone else sneak into the museum while I was talking to Shelley?

I wander back there and find the barrel-maker from yesterday back at his post, carving off thin ribbons of wood from a log with a two-handled blade. He's probably about fifty years old, with tanned white skin, muscly shoulders, and an impressively bushy beard. If he had old-fashioned clothes on, he could be in a photo titled "Ye Olde Barrel Maker."

The Japanese couple and I watch quietly as he works. He's got a really natural way about him, explaining what he's doing in a deep, calm voice. It's strangely soothing to watch him, and it's clear he cares deeply about his craft. I feel a pang of longing in the center of my chest. I want to find something I care about that much.

After about fifteen minutes, he comes to a natural stopping point in his work and says it's time for a coffee break, then tells us all to enjoy the rest of the museum.

I hurry after him, eager to introduce myself.

"That was great," I say, following him into the tiny break room near Shelley's office.

"Er—thanks," he says, looking surprised to see me behind him. "Are you visiting Waldon?"

"No, I'm volunteering here. This is my first day." I stick out a hand. "Emily Evans."

He shakes my hand. "Trey Fisher."

"Nice to meet you. I wasn't sure if you were here every day. I'm so glad that couple got to see you!"

"I usually come down a few times a day," Trey says, grabbing the empty coffeepot. "My shop's just up the street."

"What do you sell?"

He gives me a funny look. "Barrels."

"Oh!" I laugh at my own stupidity. "Duh. I didn't realize people still made barrels by hand."

"What did you think whiskey was made in?" Trey asks. "Or wine?"

I grin sheepishly. "I guess I've never really thought about it. Or I guess I thought they'd have, like . . . barrel-making machines, or something."

"They do, but they don't make them as good as a cooper does."

"Ah." I nod sagely. "And a cooper is . . ."

Trey laughs. "Are you sure you should be working at this museum? A cooper is someone who makes barrels and casks."

"Oh, sure. I definitely knew that," I say. "Just like I *definitely* know the difference between a barrel and a cask."

"All barrels are casks, but not all casks are barrels," Trey says.

"Thanks," I say dryly. "It's totally clear to me now."

He laughs, a deep, warm rumble. I'm not going to lie to you, I'm kind of rethinking my "no dating guys in their fifties" rule before I spot the wedding band on his left hand.

"Coffee?" he asks, pouring water into the machine.

I smile. "Sure!"

"I'll stick around for another half hour or so, but if more people show up after I leave, feel free to text me. Did Shelley give you my cell?"

"Er—no." I take out my phone and type as he tells me his number. I sit down on the edge of the break room table as he scoops coffee into the filter. "Do you like working here?"

"Working?" Trey laughs. "This place makes, like, fifty bucks on a good day. I'm a volunteer, same as you."

"Oh. Well—do you like it?"

"Sure. It's a nice break from the shop. And it's fun to pretend that people actually care about barrel-making a couple times a day."

I laugh. I definitely like this guy. "How does the museum stay open if it doesn't make any money?"

"Grants from the historical society, mostly."

"It's a shame there aren't school tours," I say. "Or how cool would it be to have a barrel-themed playground in the back?"

Trey chuckles. "A barrel-themed playground. That's a good idea. Shelley would never go for it, though."

I glance at the door, conscious that Shelley's office is just down the hall. "Why not?"

Trey's expression sours a little. "Her aunt Josephine ran this museum for years. She was a cooper herself, actually. One of the only female coopers in Canada, back then. She died a few years ago. Shelley would've just sold this place, but Jo signed it over it to the historical society."

"Er—Shelley mentioned that, yeah," I say. "Why does she still work here, if she doesn't like it?"

"No clue." Trey shrugs. "She probably gets a decent salary from the society to manage it."

To scroll through Facebook, more like. "So there's no way of improving things here?"

"Not unless it costs zero dollars," Trey says. He pours me a cup of coffee from the half-full pot.

I take a sip, frowning thoughtfully. "I bet there's still a way."

"Well, if you come up with anything, let me know if I can help."

"Really?"

Trey nods. "I wouldn't mind seeing a few more people come through this place. Kids these days should learn more hands-on skills."

An idea strikes me. "Would you be willing to teach kids' classes?"

Trey frowns thoughtfully. "I guess. As long as they're old enough to use the tools safely."

"So like . . . six?"

Trey snorts. "You don't have children, do you?"

"Er—no."

"Twelve and up," he says. "And we'd need parent consent forms."

I grin. "Let me look into it."

I hold out my coffee cup for him to clink. He looks amused but does it anyway. I walk back to my desk with a little more pep in my step. It's not a career or anything, but I bet I can make a difference here.

I sit down at the front desk, take a deep swig of coffee, and open a blank note on my phone. I've got a lot of work to do.

# CHAPTER 11

B arrel into summer,'" John reads over my shoulder.

I jump half a foot off my chair. I didn't even hear him come into the break room.

While my heart rate returns to normal, I hold up my notepad. "Clever, right?"

"Clever for what?"

"For the event I'm going to throw at the barrel museum!"

He stares at me incredulously. I swear, that's what my conversations with John usually are. I say something, he stares at me.

"I volunteer at the barrel museum now," I explain.

"You're kidding."

"No, I'm not. It's really fun! Or—well, I've only done one shift so far, but it was really fun. The cooper there—that's someone who makes barrels—"

"I know."

"—he's going to help me put together a barbecue event, to help stir up a bit of interest in the museum. And I've got to call the local schools to see if they want to bring their kids for field trips." I glance down at my to-do list to make sure that's on there.

"Schools?" he says. "I would've thought nursing homes were more your thing."

I open my mouth to make a sharp retort, then close it again. Huh.

"I know you're making fun of me, but that's actually a brilliant idea," I say. "I wonder if nursing homes do field trips. I should call and find out." I scribble it onto my list.

John sits down opposite me and takes out his lunch. "Did you already do Wordle?"

Something in his tone makes me look up. John rarely uses any inflection in his voice, so it's hard to read anything into it, but does he sound sort of . . . hopeful?

No. Can't be. He's probably just inhaled a bunch of car fumes or something.

"Not yet," I answer. "Just give me a sec, I've got to finish this first."

I look down at my lengthy list. I never realized how much planning you have to do to throw an event. I've got to figure out food, decorations, advertising . . . plus, I've got to convince Shelley to actually let me do it. That's number one on the list.

"Do you know anything about making websites?" I ask. "I'm thinking I should set one up for the museum, to help advertise the event."

"You know the average age of this town is, like, seventy-five, right? Put a flyer on the community center bulletin board and call it a day."

Hmm. That's actually not a bad idea.

"And at the grocery store," John adds.

Damn. Another good idea.

"Thanks," I say. "I'll add 'design super-cool flyer' to my list."

"It's a flyer for a barrel museum," he says. "You might want to lower your expectations a bit."

I laugh automatically, then do a double take. John made a *joke*.

Oh, we are definitely becoming Wordle friends.

I hide a smile and put my list away. "Okay. Wordle time."

"First word?"

"MONEY. As in, I still have to figure out where to get the money to pay for this event."

"Won't the museum pay for it?"

I sigh. "Trey says Shelley—that's the museum manager—won't pay for anything extra."

I type MONEY into Wordle, but only the Y is yellow. Shoot.

"Could you buy the supplies yourself?" John asks. "If you charge people, like, two or three bucks for a hot dog, you'd probably break even."

"But what if I shell out a bunch of my own money and no one shows up?"

He shrugs. "I'm sure people will go. What else is there to do here?"

I frown at him. "Why do you live here, if you hate it so much?"

John looks vaguely surprised. "I don't hate it."

"You talk about Waldon like it's super boring and filled with old people."

"It *is* super boring and filled with old people."

"So move somewhere else."

He shrugs. "I like it here."

I hesitate. "Why?"

"I dunno. The rent is cheap. It's quiet. It's by the water. What else do you want?"

"I want to live somewhere exciting, like New York or Paris."

He raises a doubtful eyebrow. "Really?"

My frown deepens. "Yeah. So?"

"I don't know. Volunteering at the barrel factory—"

"Museum. Barrel *museum*."

"—and working with a bunch of old people . . . you just seem like more of a small-town girl. I can't really picture you living in a big city."

I look down at my phone. I don't know why it hurts my feelings so much, but it does. The rational part of me knows that there's nothing wrong with being a small-town girl. But that's not *me*. That's not what I want.

"Thanks," I say shortly.

John frowns. "I didn't mean—"

"Let's just do Wordle," I interrupt.

"You're mad."

"I'm fine."

He raises an eyebrow. "You're clearly mad."

I exhale impatiently. "No, I'm not. I'm just—thinking about my next word."

"Fine." He turns back to his phone. "What word are you going to use?"

"I don't know." I stare at my unused letters, struggling to focus. "YACHT."

"As in?"

"As in nothing," I say (okay, snap). "I'm just trying to rule out more letters."

He's silent for a moment, and I'm already regretting my temper. He probably didn't mean to insult me. He probably thinks being a small-town girl is a good thing.

"What word are you using?" I ask stiffly.

He turns his phone toward me.

His word is SORRY.

Damn it.

That's quite cute.

The corners of my lips twist up. "It's fine," I say, more honestly this time. "It's just . . . I don't know. I don't want to be a small-town girl. I know there's nothing wrong with it," I add hastily, "and I don't mean anything against people who like small towns . . . It's just not who I want to be."

"So why not go somewhere else?"

"I can't afford it. I've got this stupid student loan I'm trying to pay off . . . plus I don't want to move somewhere until I know for sure what I want to do there."

"Your 'dream job,'" he says. It still sounds slightly sarcastic when he says it. I swallow a stab of irritation.

"Yup," I say shortly. "But I'm stuck here for now, so I'm just trying to make the best of it and find fun things to do." I gesture to my Barrel Into Summer to-do list.

"And you think planning a barbecue at a barrel factory is fun," he says.

"Barrel *museum*. And yes."

He stares at me for a while and then turns back to his phone. I bite down another wave of irritation and force myself to focus on my next word. The Y in YACHT was yellow, the T was green. John's SORRY also accidentally helped me, because now I know there's an R and S somewhere in the word. But what word has a Y, R, S, and T in it?

S, Y, R, T.

Y, R, S, T.

YURST.

Is that some sort of sausage, like a bratwurst? A bratyurst?

I type it in and click enter. Nope. Not in word list.

"One of my racing buddies plays guitar," John says. "He plays at the track sometimes, and some of the bars in Charlottetown pay him to do gigs."

I frown, wondering where he's going with this.

"Want me to ask him to play at your . . . barrel thing?" he asks.

I sit up a little straighter. "You mean it?"

"Sure."

"Wouldn't I have to pay him, though?"

He shrugs. "I did his alignment last year for half price. He owes me one."

I break into a wide smile. "That would be awesome!"

"I can call him later. Just text me the date and time and stuff."

I nod, grinning, and reach for my to-do list. Live music wasn't on there (I hadn't even though of that), but now I add it, just so I can check it off.

Live music—check!

"You think this thing has a double letter in it?" John asks, holding up his phone.

I open my mouth to say no, then I pause.

A double letter. A double *T*.

T, R, Y, S, T.

TRYST.

I type it in, click enter, and one by one, the letters turn green. Three hundred and eight days!

I beam at John. "I think it does."


AFTER WORK, I head to the store to buy groceries for Mrs. Finnamore, Jim, and Doris. While I'm waiting in line, I take out my phone and text Fallon.

> [5:42]: Hey girl! I need to pick your brain on something. Any advice on how to plan events? I'm organizing this summer barbecue thing at a local museum and I want to make sure it goes well. You have to plan a lot of events for your stores, yeah?

I'm not expecting her to text back right away, so I'm surprised when three dots appear almost instantly.

> [5:43] **Fallon:** Omg that's too funny, I was just about to text you!

> [5:43] **Fallon:** I'm going to send you a post to share on all your social

> [5:43] **Fallon:** New promo launching on the website next week

I shift uncomfortably on my feet. Fallon asks me to do stuff like this every now and then. And obviously I want to support her, but it always feels kind of weird. I basically never post anything on any of my social media accounts, which means that 90 percent of what's on there is just ads for Fallon's business. I'm pretty sure Instagram thinks I'm a bot.

But I guess I shouldn't complain. If I ever have a business, I'll probably be asking her to do the same thing.

> [5:44]: Of course! Just send me what you need me to post.

[5:44] **Fallon:** Ahhh you rock girl

[5:44] **Fallon:** Sending now!

Sure enough, seconds later a notification pops up for my Facebook and Instagram. (And yes, I know, no one under the age of sixty actually uses Facebook anymore. I only have it so I can see all the pictures from my parents' trips.) I obediently repost what Fallon's sent me.

[5:46]: Done!

[5:47] **Fallon:** Amazing . . . thank youuu

The line ahead of me inches forward. The teenager working the checkout line must be new. I swear it's taking her five minutes to scan each item.

[5:50]: So, any advice on planning events? I'm mostly wondering how much food I should buy. I don't want to run out, but I think I'd rather that than buy too much . . .

[5:52] **Fallon:** Hmm dunno girl

[5:52] **Fallon:** We use event planners

[5:52] **Fallon:** Good luck though!

I frown, slightly annoyed, and start to pocket my phone without answering. Then I shake my head at myself. It's not Fallon's fault she's successful enough to afford event planners.

[5:53]: Thanks! Good luck with the website promo!

Fallon sends back a fingers-crossed emoji and a string of money-bag emojis.

The line moves forward again—another worker has come to help out the new girl—and I unload my cart onto the conveyor belt, sorting Mrs. Finnamore's, Doris's, and Jim's things into three separate piles. They've all given me cash to pay with (Doris kindly explained that she didn't trust me with her credit card), and after I check out, I carefully count their change into individual Ziploc bags.

"Are you sure you got everything?" Doris asks a quarter hour later, as I carry the last bag into her kitchen.

"I'm sure," I say.

"Hmm," she says skeptically. "Don't scare the cat."

Her cat, whom she hasn't named ("Names are for people, girl, not animals"), is asleep on the top of the fridge. I don't know how I could possibly scare it, since I'm pretty sure it's possessed by the devil. I love cats, but this one seems to exist solely to hiss, bite, and scratch. I think that's why it gets along so well with Doris.

She and the cat both supervise as I unpack all the groceries. I nod absently while Doris tells me her opinion on the day's weather ("Far too hot"), the evening news ("Why would I care about all that foreign nonsense?"), and her nephew's recent haircut ("Stupid"). Honestly, I don't think there's anything in the world that Doris doesn't have an opinion on.

Which, now that I think of it, actually might be useful to me.

"Hey, Doris," I venture. "If you were in a nursing home, would you want to go on field trips to museums?"

"If I were in a nursing home, I'd want to be shot."

Okay. I probably should have seen that coming.

I bid Doris good night ("What exactly do you think will be good about it? Don't you know I'm eighty-six?") and head to Mrs. Finnamore's.

"I don't think anyone is that interested in barrels, dear," she says, when I ask her the same question I asked Doris. "Plus, that old building is far too drafty."

"Okay, but if you *had* to go," I press. "What would you want it to be like?"

"I don't know," she says uninterestedly. Then, perhaps seeing the disappointed look on my face, she heaves a sigh and adds, "You should put in more seating, if you're going to drag folks there from their nursing homes. Those wooden floors are terribly hard."

"More seating." I nod. "Thanks!"

When I ask Jim, he has even more helpful ideas. In fact, it sort of seems like he's been waiting for someone to ask him about it.

"That place is too dark," he says. "You can hardly read anything on those tiny exhibit signs. Not that anyone really bothers reading them. People spend most of their time watching Trey."

*More lights, more Trey*, I mentally add to my list.

"So if you went on a tour there, would you just want to watch Trey?"

"Oh, I don't know," Jim says. "Might be nice to sit around and chat a bit, maybe have a pot of tea."

I nod thoughtfully. We could set up tables outside, maybe serve tea and snacks . . . I wonder if I could even find some mugs shaped like barrels. That seems like something that should exist, like for pirate-themed birthday parties.

Hang on a minute.

*Birthday parties.*

What a genius idea! What kid wouldn't want to have their birthday at a barrel museum? Once I add the super cool barrel-themed playground, I mean.

I thank Jim enthusiastically and head home. After dinner, I hunt down the contact information of the local schools and nursing homes. There are only two schools—an elementary school, and a combined junior high/high school—and one nursing home just outside of town. There are more nursing homes in Summerside and Charlottetown, but I think I'll wait to approach them. I don't want their residents to drive an hour to get here until I'm confident I can give them an awesome day.

Around nine, I curl up in bed with a glass of wine and scroll absently through Instagram. Fallon's shared my post about her website promo on her story (along with about a hundred others) with the caption "We've got fans all over Canada!!!" Further along in her story is a photo of her and her husband outside their Toronto location. They both look really tan, like they've been on a trip down south, and their staff are gathered around them holding up bottles of juice. They all look really happy, and not just in a fake Instagram sort of way. They've got their arms wrapped around each other and some of them look like they've been caught mid-laugh.

I click onward to Martha's story. She's posted about fifty pictures of her and her kids visiting a zoo. They all look really happy too (even if I privately think their matching T-shirts are a little cheesy).

I put down my phone with a sigh. I was having a fun day plotting out all the ways I could improve the museum, but now it all feels sort of stupid. I probably shouldn't be wasting my time on all this stuff. It's not like it's going to get me any closer to my dream job.

I sink down into the covers and take an unhappy sip of wine. I should spend my night looking for more jobs I can apply to, but that suddenly seems pointless too. Like I'm just flailing about, applying for anything under the sun, desperately trying to find something that will stick.

I'm scrolling through Netflix to find a sitcom to distract me from my sorrows when my phone dings with a text from an unknown number.

[9:07] **Unknown:** Hey, Emily – this is John's friend George. He told me you're planning some outdoor event up in Waldon and might want me to play?

I sit up a little straighter. I totally forgot about that. I'm surprised John's already reached out to him.

[9:08]: Hey George! Yes, I'd love that, if you're available?

[9:08]: I can't pay anything, though, so totally understand if you can't do it.

[9:09] **Unknown:** Sounds great!

[9:09] **Unknown:** Don't worry about payment, I owe John like two grand lol

[9:10]: Awesome!! I'm still waiting on a few details

(Like, if Shelley will even let me do this thing.)

[9:10]: But I'll get back to you ASAP to confirm

[9:11] **Unknown:** Sounds good. Thx!

I smile at the screen for a moment, then open a text to John Smith (Auto Shop).

[9:12]: Hey, your friend George just texted me! Thanks for reaching out to him.

[9:13] **John:** no worries

[9:13] **John:** he's weirdly excited about it

[9:13] **John:** I guess he's been trying to break into the barrel museum scene

I laugh.

[9:14]: Well, it is very competitive

[9:14]: I've already had a call from Beyoncé, begging me to let her perform

[9:15] **John:** lol

I chew on my lip, wondering if I should say something else. It still feels weird talking to John like a (sort-of) friend, but it's not like I'm overwhelmed with options right now. I might as well ask his opinion. It can't be any meaner than Doris's.

[9:19]: Do you think this whole event idea is kind of stupid?

[9:19] **John:** no

[9:19] **John:** why?

[9:20]: I don't know

[9:20]: It's just like, a silly barrel museum, right?

[9:20]: I don't think I should be spending so much time on it

There's a brief pause. I wonder if I've overshared.

[9:21] **John:** you think too much

[9:21] **John:** are you having fun doing it or not?

My brow furrows thoughtfully.

[9:22]: Yeah

[9:22]: I am

[9:23] **John:** well, there you go

Then he sends a little emoji of a guy shrugging. The corner of my mouth twists up.

[9:23]: Thanks 😊

[9:23]: Headed to bed now. Night!

[9:23]: Or as Wordle would say

[9:23]: NIGHT

[9:24] **John:** lol

[9:24] **John:** night

I take another sip of wine, put my laptop away, and reach for my to-do list again, smiling to myself just a little.

# CHAPTER 12

At work the next morning, I wait until I have a break between customers (not hard, considering we only have four people on the books), and then determinedly pick up the phone. I dial the number of the local high school and wait for it to ring. The second it does, I hang up.

Crap.

It feels *way* too weird to do this over the phone. Sort of spammy, like a telemarketer, and also kind of creepy. What am I going to say, "Hey, you don't know me, but do you want to bring your kids to the place where I volunteer for a guided tour?"

See? Creepy.

What I *want* to do is go to the schools in person so I can A) prove that I'm a normal person and B) bring them some of the brochures I swiped from the museum. I think I'll be more persuasive in person too. I can talk about Trey's demonstrations, and maybe even mention the Barrel Into Summer event.

But the thing about schools is, they're open during the day, just like the auto shop. I could pop out really quickly at lunch, but I have a feeling school teachers won't appreciate being bothered during lunchtime. I seem to remember it being the most chaotic time in high school, a hundred hormonal teenagers swarming around trying to get all their socialization done in one sixty-minute period.

I glance at the clock. It's 10:50 a.m. There are only two customers booked this afternoon, because Dave is off today. I bite my lip. Maybe . . . maybe I could say I'm sick and take the rest of the day off.

And yes, I know it's wrong to skip work when you're not actually sick. I actually sort of hate people who do that, to be honest. I worked in a restaurant during the summers when I was in university, and there was this one girl who used to call in sick *all the time*, like she didn't realize (or care) that it meant the rest of us would have to work twice as hard to pick up her slack.

But I've never taken a sick day since I started working at the shop. Would it really be so wrong to take one teensy little day?

I push my chair back and walk to the garage before I can lose my nerve. I have to yell John's name three times before he hears me over the sound of the machinery.

"What?" he says, when he finally spots me.

I affect a grimace. "I'm headed home. I've got a brutal headache."

Instantly I feel awful, because he puts his tools down and comes toward me, looking—well, not *concerned*, exactly, but maybe slightly less indifferent than normal. "Do you have the flu or something?"

"Er—no. Just . . . y'know, a little headachy and dizzy. Probably just stress or something."

"You need me to give you a lift home? You shouldn't drive if you're dizzy."

Crap. He's right.

"I'm not dizzy right *now*," I backtrack. "I was earlier, but now it's gone."

"It could come back, though."

"No, no," I say hastily. "I'm sure it won't. This happens sometimes . . . I get these sort of . . . spells . . ." I trail off feebly. The concerned look on his face has vanished, replaced by a slightly dubious one.

I'm really not pulling this lie off, am I?

"Okay, look," I say sheepishly. "I'm not really sick. I just need to leave for, like, an hour or two, so I can run these museum brochures to the schools and see if they want to come for a field trip. I know it's stupid, but I want to go today, because school will be over in, like, a month, so it's my only opportunity. I can forward all the phone calls to my cell, and when the customers check out—"

"No worries." John cuts me off. "Just go."

"What?"

"Just go," he repeats. "I can check people out."

I hesitate. "Are you sure?"

"Yep."

Still, I waver. "But what if Fred comes in?"

"Fred's in Florida. But if he flies home to check that you're working the front desk, I'll be sure to tell him you went home sick."

I swallow a laugh. "Oh. Well . . . okay, then. I promise I won't be long."

"I really don't care."

I scrutinize his face. He definitely means it.

Feeling a little less guilty, I jog out to my car and head off to the local high school, which is only ten minutes away. Even though it houses both junior high and high school, it's not very big. As I step inside the main entranceway, I feel like I've been transported back fifteen years. It's wild that so much time can pass but high schools always seem to look the same. This place even smells like my old high school, as if all schools in the universe are bound by law to use the same lemon-scented floor cleaner.

I find my way to the principal's office and knock lightly on the door. It swings open a moment later, revealing a tall bald man whom I instantly like. His name is Mr. Peterson, and he lets me into his office and listens as I ramble eagerly about the museum. He even makes me a cup of tea from a little kettle on his desk. He says he thinks field trips to the museum sound like a good idea for some of their younger kids, though maybe not their high schoolers. I'm secretly relieved when he says it. I don't want any high school kids rolling their eyes and pretending to be too cool for my museum.

He says he can't promise me anything—this close to the end of the year, their schedules are pretty booked—but that he'll be in touch. And I know it sounds like a line you say to get rid of someone, but I swear he really means it.

I leave the school in high spirits and head to the nursing home. It's about the same size as the high school, but the atmosphere couldn't be more different. The school had that squeaky-shoe silence, whereas this place is filled with the warm rumble of voices.

I hover in the entryway for a moment, feeling a bit nervous. I've never actually been to a nursing home before, and I'm scared it'll be this super depressing place filled with sad people waiting to die. But actually, once I step inside, it seems really lively! There's a young woman guiding a group of people in wheelchairs through a seated exercise routine, a nurse helping an elderly woman do a puzzle, and a man playing piano in the corner. I make a mental note of everything I see, to tell Jim about later. He mentioned to me that he's not sure how much longer he can stay in his house. I think it's too full of memories of his wife. Maybe a place like this would be good for him. Less lonely.

It takes me a little while to track down the person in charge, a short, heavy woman with frizzy hair. She's pretty preoccupied during our chat—her phone rings about every five seconds, and three people come in to ask her questions while we talk—but she listens to everything I have to say and takes the brochures. Like Mr. Peterson, she says she'll think about it and be in touch. I'm not *quite* sure she means it, but I figure at least I've made a start. I can always check back in next month and see if she's thought about it. This isn't like school. The residents will be here all year.

My last stop is the elementary school. For all my good intentions earlier, I accidentally arrive just as the lunch bell rings. Hundreds of kids spill out of the doors, all of whom seem to be hollering at the tops of their lungs.

Honestly, I don't know how teachers do it. I'm exhausted just *watching* them trying to establish order. I hurry inside, dodging and weaving around tiny kids, and find my way to the principal's office. As I feared, she's eating lunch when I knock on her door, and she doesn't look super keen on being interrupted.

I shorten my speech to sixty seconds, hand over the brochures, thank her for her time, and make a break for it.

I arrive back at the shop at half past twelve, sweaty and slightly flustered.

"Oh, man," I say, collapsing into a chair at the break room table.

John looks up from his phone. "I thought you were taking the day off."

"I said I was taking an hour or two," I correct. Then I let my head flop into my hands. "That was exhausting."

"You didn't have to rush back. I told you I could manage here."

"Oh, I know, I'm just worn out from the elementary school," I say. "How on earth do people have kids?"

John unwraps the foil from his sandwich. "You don't like kids?"

"I like kids just fine, when I can play with them for five minutes and then hand them off to someone else. But actually having kids myself..." I shake my head. "I know people say it's a full-time job, but I think that's total crap. When you have a full-time job, you go home at the end of the day and relax. Having a kid seems more like two full-time jobs, and your boss never lets you go on break and sleeps in your house every night." I let out a weary breath. "I really don't think I ever want kids."

"Same," John says. "Some parts seem cool, but I think I'm good with nieces and nephews."

"My friend Martha says I'll wake up one day and change my mind."

John takes a bite of his sandwich. "Kinda rude."

"It is, right? Like I'm not mature enough to know what I want, or something." I go to the fridge and grab my usual lunch, a cup of yogurt and little baggie of granola. "She also says I'll regret it when I'm older, because there'll be no one to take care of me."

John makes a doubtful face. "Is that a good motivation to have kids? So that you can force them to take care of you when you're old?"

I laugh. "That's exactly what I said! She was not impressed."

"Does she live here?"

"No, we went to university together. She lives in Maine now."

I hesitate, then add, "I actually don't really know many people around here."

"That sucks," John says.

"Yeah. It does." I'm quiet for a moment, then I brighten. "Maybe I'll meet someone through the museum tours!"

John snorts through a mouthful of sandwich. "What, like a high school kid?"

"*No.*" I roll my eyes. "Like a cool, artsy teacher. You know I actually thought about being a teacher once."

"You just told me you can't stand kids."

"I said I didn't *want* kids and that they seem incredibly exhausting," I retort. "But yes, that was part of the reason I didn't do it."

"You should meet my sister," John says. "She's not a teacher, but she likes to think she's cool and artsy."

I try to picture a girl version of John and come up with the image of a very intimidating woman with a leather jacket and hundreds of tattoos. I'm not sure I'm cool enough to hang out with that kind of girl. Plus, I know he's not really offering. He's just making polite conversation. (Which I'm not complaining about, mind you. This is a huge step up from last week.)

"That would be cool," I say. I glance at the clock. "Do you have time for Wordle, or do you have to get back?"

Before he can answer, the front desk bell rings. Our first afternoon customer must be here.

I pull a face and rise to my feet. "I guess Wordle will have to wait."

I take my lunch with me and head back to my desk, where a pretty, dark-haired girl in her late teens is tapping her foot impatiently, waiting to drop off her parents' car for a tire change.

"Is there somewhere to wait?" she asks, looking around the shop as if she expects me to fold back a red curtain and reveal a pedi-spa.

"Just those chairs there," I say, pointing.

She looks vaguely offended and takes a seat with a small, almost inaudible huff. Two seconds later, she pops a pair of earbuds in and blares her music so loud I can hear the tinny sound of it from my desk.

I spend the next twenty-five minutes finishing my lunch and checking phone messages, and then I've got nothing to do but sit there and be annoyed by the girl's music.

I glance at her surreptitiously. She is definitely not from Waldon. I bet her parents have a cottage here or something. She's dressed pretty casually in jean shorts and a sweater, but I can spot the tiny signs of wealth, like the Tiffany bracelet peeking out from her sleeve and the Louis Vuitton purse thrown over her shoulder.

She looks up and catches me staring. Whoops. I give her a polite, apologetic smile. She responds by sweeping her gaze from my head to my toes, then pretending to smother a smirk.

My face burns red hot.

What a jerk.

I run my hands self-consciously over my hair and clothes. I did Jim's laundry last night instead of my own, so I'm wearing one of my oldest sweatshirts over some plain black leggings. I didn't think it looked that bad when I glanced in the mirror this morning, but it's clear what that girl is thinking when she looks at me. John's blunt words from yesterday echo in my ears.

*Small-town girl.*

I force myself to sit up straighter and lift my chin up stubbornly.

Fine, maybe I am a bit small-town right now. That doesn't mean I'm going to be forever. I have a brief vision of myself sitting behind a vast desk, decked out in Balmain and Prada with floor-to-ceiling windows behind me overlooking Fifth Avenue. I raise my bejeweled hand and wave in the next candidate interviewing for my lowly assistant position. And what do you know, it's Little Miss Jean Shorts! Her eyes widen as she recognizes me—she plasters on a fake smile and opens her mouth to talk—but nope, too late. I'm giving her the same cutting head-to-toe gaze she once gave me and ordering her out of my office.

I stifle a snort. Okay, that was an immature daydream.

I do feel a little better now, though.

I leaf through the barrel museum brochures for the fifteenth time and then do some research on barrel-making online. If Mr. Peterson calls me about bringing his kids in for a field trip, I want to make sure I've got lots of really fun things to tell them about barrels.

The trouble is, there's really not much to say about barrels, unless you want to talk about wine or whiskey, which I don't think is super appropriate for junior high school kids.

I chew on my lip, trying to think of what I would've wanted to do on a field trip in junior high. Honestly, I probably wouldn't have wanted to hear stories about barrels. Especially not in the last weeks of school before summer. The only thing I would've cared about was being out of class and having fun with my friends.

Ooh! Maybe I can let them do some sort of activity in the backyard. Some sort of . . . barrel-rolling race, maybe. Barrel rolling is a thing, right?

I do a quick Google search, and yes, yes it is. But honestly, it sounds a little dangerous for kids. The article I'm reading keeps going on about the importance of wearing steel-toe boots.

Oh, well. I'll think of something else.

I drum my fingers on the desk. Think, brain, *think*.

My gaze drifts to the snooty girl again. There's no way she'd be caught dead in a barrel museum.

Hmm. That's a thought.

I waver for a few minutes, then think to myself, *Screw it.*

"Excuse me? Miss?" I wave my hand until the girl finally notices me.

Reluctantly, she removes one of her earbuds. "Is the car ready?"

"Er—no. I wanted to ask your opinion on something." She scowls suspiciously, but I press on. "Do you like museums?"

She blinks her mascaraed eyelashes at me. "What?"

"Museums," I repeat. "Like, if you went to a museum in a small town, what sort of things would interest you?"

She's looking at me like I've absolutely lost my mind. "Are you, like, fundraising or something?" she says suspiciously. "Because I already donate a *ton* to charity."

Somehow, I keep from rolling my eyes. Yeah, I bet she donates to charity. "No, I'm just trying to help out the local barrel-making museum."

"*Barrel*-making?" she repeats derisively.

"Yes, barrel-making," I say. Then I heave an exaggerated sigh. "Never mind. I'm sorry I bothered you. I just thought I'd ask you, since you're so young and obviously really stylish . . ." I wave my hand to encompass her outfit. "I thought you might be able to help me figure out what junior high kids might be interested in. I'm *way* too old to understand," I add for good measure.

My god, that was too easy. The girl looks instantly mollified. She sits up a little straighter and takes her other earbud out.

"Well, I don't go to museums because, like, most of history is super offensive—"

"Of course," I say, straight-faced.

"But I get invited to a bunch of art exhibits, y'know, for my Insta? I have, like, thirty thousand followers."

I tilt my head and put on a confused expression. "What's Insta?"

She stares at me. "Instagram."

"Oh, *Instagram*." I nod wisely. "My niece told me about that. I could never figure it out. Phones these days have too many buttons!"

Okay, I'm enjoying myself way too much right now. And Jean Shorts Girl doesn't even look snooty anymore, just deeply pitying of me, the ancient barrel museum worker who doesn't know what Instagram is.

She flicks her glossy hair over her shoulder and leans forward conspiratorially, like she's going to share the secrets of the universe. "Right, well, what you need to do is get an influencer to come to your museum and take a bunch of pics there and make them look super artsy. I'd offer to help, but I'm, like, way too swamped right now. Plus my feed is aqua-themed, so, like, barrels wouldn't fit."

"Feed?" I ask innocently. "Like animal feed?"

Don't laugh, Emily. Don't laugh.

"That means the pictures on Instagram," she says slowly. She turns her phone toward me and scrolls through her aqua feed. "See how good the colors look?"

"Wow," I say obediently.

"Anyway, that's what you have to do. Hire a bunch of influencers and get them to hype up your barrel . . . thing."

"Thanks," I say, injecting just the right amount of profound gratitude into the word. "That's so helpful."

She smiles beatifically and puts her earbuds back in. I drum my fingers on the desk again, turning an idea over in my head. Jean Shorts Girl actually was helpful. Not her idea about influencers, I mean, that's bananas. But I think I might now have an idea on how to make the museum just a tiny bit cooler for kids.

I pick up my phone and open a new text to Trey.

[1:42]: Hey, Trey! Are you working this Saturday?

[1:42]: I've got an idea for the museum.
Would need your carpentry expertise. 😊

He doesn't answer straightaway. I answer a few phone calls, then Jean Shorts Girl approaches the desk and asks for a Post-it note to write her Instagram handle on for me.

"You'll really love it," she says. "I do, like, style tips for people and stuff."

She glances subtly at my outfit again as she says it. How sweet.

I take the Post-it with a grateful smile and make a show of looking it up, muttering, "Instagram . . . dot . . . com. Oh shoot, spelled it wrong. Instagram . . . d-o-t . . . c-o-m. Ah, there we go." Then I try not to burst into laughter at the look on her face.

I scroll through her feed for a while, which looks like every other influencer's feed I've ever seen. You might think I'd be the kind of person who would find this kind of stuff appealing, since

I'm always going on about my dream job, but I don't actually have any appetite for social media. I don't care about amassing followers or getting likes. That kind of success has always felt a bit hollow to me. I don't even care about money, really, beyond the fact that I don't want to have to stress about it. I don't want wealth and status, I want happiness and purpose. I want to wake up every morning and be excited to go to work. I want to fall asleep every night thinking, *Yes. This is what I was put on this earth to do.*

I give Jean Shorts Girl a few compliments on her photos, which she's obviously waiting for, and by the time her car is ready, she's entirely warmed to me. John comes out with her keys and is scribbling on her receipt as she says to me, "You should give me your email, 'cause, like, I was thinking of doing a bunch of makeover profiles, and it would be so cute to do them about people from here. I'm staying at my parents' cottage for a few weeks"—Ha! I knew it!—"and I could, like, go shopping with you and fix your clothes and stuff."

John gives me a sideways glance, but I'm not going to drop my act just because he's here.

"That would be so cool," I gush. "I've always wanted a makeover, because—well, you know." I wave a hand over myself and pull a face.

"Don't be so hard on yourself," she says. "You're, like, really pretty for your age."

"Aw, thanks." I hand over her receipt and scribble my email address for her on the bottom. She'll forget about me the minute she walks out of this shop, so I'm not particularly worried about giving it to her. "Have a great day!"

"You too." She smiles pityingly at me, gives John an appreciative once-over (I guess *he's* not too old), and then flounces out.

John frowns at me after she's gone. "What was that about?"

I snort. "I was just playing around. She was sort of rude when she came in, so."

"So you retaliated by acting really nice to her?"

I chuckle. "Yep. The ultimate revenge—making her accidentally like me."

John blinks. "That's so weird."

"Mm-hmm." I glance at the clock. "Your next appointment isn't here yet. You want me to call them, see if they're running late?"

As I say it, my phone dings with a text. I glance at it quickly.

[2:06] **Trey:** Happy to help. Tore my hand open yesterday though, so might not be able to do much until stitches are out.

*Stitches*? Poor Trey.

Also . . . crap.

"What is it?" John asks.

"Oh . . . it's just Trey, the cooper at the museum. I was hoping he'd help me with this weird exhibit idea I have for the museum, but he's got stitches in his hand." I sigh. "I don't suppose you're good at carpentry stuff?"

John shrugs. "I'm all right. When do you need help?"

I blink. "Seriously?"

"As long as it's nothing too crazy."

I hesitate. I'll need to approve this with Shelley, but I can do that on my shift on Saturday. "Could you come by the museum this Sunday?"

"Sure."

I beam at him. "Thanks. Now hang on, I'll call Mrs. Manthorne."

I dial the number we have on file and reach a very sweet, very flustered-sounding woman who is at a hair salon and has obviously completely forgotten about her appointment. I reschedule her and then hang up the phone with an apologetic grimace. John hates when people cancel. Or at least, I think he does. He gets a bit frownier whenever it happens.

"She's not coming," I say. "Want me to call the next person and see if they can come early?"

He shrugs. "I guess." Then, after a tiny beat, "Unless you wanted to do Wordle now."

I brighten. "Ooh, yes, please."

He leans against the desk and takes out his phone. "First word?"

I think for a second. "SAVER. As in, you're a total lifesaver for helping with the museum stuff. You?"

John's mouth twists thoughtfully. "PIZZA."

"As in . . . ?"

"As in, you can pay me in pizza."

I chuckle. "I can do that."

We fall silent, both of us studying our phones. The S in SAVER is green, and the E is yellow. I think of Jean Shorts Girl and wonder if INSTA is a word.

Nope. Not in word list.

How about . . . SMOKE. As in, when John's sitting this close to me, I can smell that same smoky smell I noticed that time we were in his car. I've never noticed it at work before. I wonder if it's his shampoo. Or maybe it's some random car fluid that just happens to smell like firewood smoke, like how antifreeze apparently tastes like sugar. (I know that because when I was a kid my mom warned me never to drink it, and for a while I thought that anything that tasted sugary was secretly deadly.)

Either way, it smells really nice, like a bonfire on a crisp autumn night. I take a deep breath in through my nose and then surreptitiously move my gaze over his frame. He's got his coveralls undone to the waist, revealing a black T-shirt that fits snugly on his shoulders. He's actually really good-looking, John. His hair is dark and slightly wavy and his arms are all strong and veiny, and if you ignore all the grease stains, he's got really nice hands. I bet they're really strong from all his work in the shop.

I'm admiring them absently when he glances up and catches me staring.

Whoops.

Hastily, I turn my attention back to Wordle. The S, O, and E of SMOKE are green.

S _ O _ E.

SCOPE. As in, it would be so embarrassing if John thought I was scoping him out just now. We're finally becoming friend-ish, I don't want to ruin it by ogling him when I already know he's not interested. Plus, I'm not interested in him. I just happened to notice that he smells really nice and his arms are really strong, that's all. And if I'm feeling a little flushed all of a sudden, that's just because it's warm in here today.

Obviously.

SLOPE, I type into Wordle. As in, I need to be careful here, because this is a very slippery slope.

One by one, the letters turn green, as if Wordle is agreeing with me.

"You got it?" John asks, leaning closer to glance over my shoulder. And damn it, that smoky smell really is enticing.

"Got it."

"That's, what—three hundred and nine days?"

I smile a bit unsteadily. "Yep."

"Nice." John hops off the desk and holds out his fist for me to bump, which could not be a more obvious "just-friends" gesture and yet still somehow makes my heart beat a little faster. He shoots me a lightning-flash grin before he heads back to the garage, leaving me shaky and electrified.

The moment he's gone, I thump my head down against my keyboard.

Uh-oh.

# CHAPTER 13

O kay. The important thing, I've decided, is not to make mountains from molehills. Yes, I find John objectively attractive. So what? This isn't news. I thought he was hot when I first met him, until I found out about his personality (or lack thereof). And yes, I've come to realize he has a *bit* more personality than I originally gave him credit for, but he's still Boring John. He still cares about cars more than people. He still answers half the things I say with an incredulous stare.

Honestly, I think this is more a reflection of how starved I am for a proper crush. Like, if you're lost in the desert for a month, even a dirty old can of soda is going to look just as good as a strawberry daiquiri, right?

Okay, that was mean.

John's not a dirty old can of soda.

But he also isn't the kind of guy I want to date. I like really driven, outgoing guys. Like my high school boyfriend, who was class president and the captain of the soccer team. Or my university boyfriend, who was pre-law, or even my post-uni fling with that slightly eccentric (but very engaging) medical student. I like guys who want big things from life and who push me to want more from my own. What's John going to push me to do? Work at the auto shop forever? Die with grease stains on my clothes?

. . . okay, that was also mean. There's nothing wrong with working at an auto shop forever.

But it isn't *me*.

Anyway. I slept on it last night, and I've decided the thing to do is just ignore my inconvenient physical attraction to John and focus on something else, like my Barrel Into Summer event.

On Wednesday, I design a flyer and use the auto shop's printer to print off a prototype. John helps me change out the color cartridge, and I don't pay any attention to how warm his arm is when it brushes against mine.

On Thursday, I make a list of all the places I can put the flyers up, and John and I practically die of laughter when the Wordle answer turns out to be FLYER. I definitely don't notice how nice his laugh is or that he gets dimples on his cheeks when he laughs really hard.

On Friday, I walk into the break room to find him and Dave watching a YouTube video of some big crash in Formula 2, and when I comment that I thought it was called Formula 1, not 2, John subjects me to a twenty-minute lecture on all the different racing leagues on the planet. I don't want to interrupt him, since it's the longest he's ever talked to me, which feels kind of nice, but it's all incredibly confusing and more than a little boring. So really, you can hardly blame me for spacing out and getting lost in the honey-brown shade of his eyes.

Needless to say, by Saturday, I'm very glad to have some time away from the shop. I get up early and have a cup of coffee on the back porch, soaking up the warmth of the fragile May sun. At nine a.m., I head out to the breakfast date I've set up with Jim.

It isn't part of my caregiving service, really, I just felt like he needed a little company this weekend. His wife's birthday is next week—she would've turned ninety-four—and I can tell he's really torn up about it.

I drive to the bakery downtown and buy a box of freshly baked cinnamon rolls and then head to his house. It's an old-fashioned farmhouse that sits on the top of a hill, with a wide porch overlooking his neighbor's farmland. We sit outside and have tea and cinnamon rolls and watch the neighbor's horses graze. There's a white one who I've decided is named Ghost, and a brown one I've named Epona.

I ask Jim to tell me about his late wife, and the memories roll out of him slowly. It's less of a story of their lives together than a collection of unrelated snapshots. She always put a half-cup of sugar in her tea. She stepped on a snake once in the garden and hollered so loudly that the neighbors came running over. She didn't like to drive. She cooked chicken and boiled potatoes on Sundays.

Listening to him talk, I can't really glean much about their relationship, or even what kind of person she was, but I know that doesn't matter. He's reliving those tiny moments with her as he tells me about them, and after an hour or two of talking, the lines of his shoulders seem a little looser.

"You're a good girl," he says, as I return from taking our teacups back into the kitchen. "Spending your Saturday with an old fella like me."

"I'm happy to," I say honestly. "I wish I could stay longer, but I've got my shift at the museum. I'm going to ask Shelley if I can throw that event I was telling you about."

Jim lets out a breath. "Shelley," he says, with a dismissive shake of his head. "I don't have much to do with her. You know she tried to stop me working there after Josephine died? She said the place didn't need security."

"You're kidding," I say indignantly. What sort of person tries to fire a ninety-six-year-old volunteer? "What did you do?"

Jim shrugs. "I kept showing up anyway."

I giggle. "That's amazing."

"If you want to throw your party, just do it. Don't pay that woman any mind."

I smile. "Thanks, Jim. See you tomorrow?"

"I'll be here."

I wave goodbye to Ghost and Epona and head to the museum, practicing my argument for Shelley as I drive. I'm going to put all the food on my credit card, so it isn't going to cost her anything, and Trey and I will handle everything the day of the event. I'm not sure why she would say no—and yet I have a sneaking feeling that she's going to.

The morning volunteer, a nice older woman named Brenda, is struggling to use the credit card machine when I arrive. I help her sort it out and resolve to make a cheat sheet for her for the future. She agrees to watch the desk an extra five minutes while I go talk to Shelley. My palms are a bit prickly with nerves. I rub them on my jeans and then knock on her office door.

"What?" she calls.

I open the door. Soup is dripping from her spoon onto her desk as she scrolls through Facebook on her computer, and there's a crumpled fast food container on the floor. I swallow down a spike of annoyance. Her office could actually be really cute, if she made any attempt to keep it clean. There's a big window overlooking the backyard and a bookshelf on either side of the desk, giving the place a cozy, reading nook kind of vibe.

"Hi, Shelley," I say politely. "Do you have a minute?"

She glances up. "What's up?"

I take a breath and launch in. "I was thinking it would be fun to host an event here next weekend, to celebrate the start of summer and maybe draw in a little extra business."

"We don't have money for that," Shelley says, half-turning back to her computer.

"No, I know," I say hastily. "But I've got it all planned out so it wouldn't cost a thing. There's a local musician who can play for free, and Trey's got a barbecue we can use, so we can sell hot dogs and hamburgers and lemonade—"

"I don't have time to plan something like that."

"You wouldn't have to do anything," I say. "I can plan it all. You could just—show up and enjoy!"

Shelley lets out an impatient breath and glances back at her computer, like I'm keeping her from some important work. "When did you want to do this?"

"I was thinking next Saturday. The weather is supposed to be really nice, and it'll be a week before the kids get out of school, so I was thinking we could call it the Barrel Into Summer event." I force a cheery smile. "Kind of a cute name, right?"

Shelley scowls. "A week isn't enough time to plan something like that."

She's turning away again. Her tone is final.

"I think it's a good idea," says a voice from the door. I glance back to see Trey leaning against the doorframe with his arms crossed.

Shelley's lips press together. Her eyes move between Trey and me, as though she's weighing whether or not it's worth arguing with us.

"Oh, fine," she says ungraciously. "But you two have got to sort it out yourselves. I've got too much on my plate already."

Too much on her *plate*? What, is she trying to scroll through the entirety of Facebook or something?

But, whatever. She said yes. That's all that matters.

"Awesome," I say. "Thanks."

I turn to leave and then hesitate at the door. I consider telling her my other idea, the one that Jean Shorts Girl gave me, but then I think, screw it. I'm going to take Jim's advice and just do it without her. She probably won't even notice.

Out in the hall, I hold my hand up to Trey for a high five. "Success!"

He chuckles. "Success. You need me to do anything for it?"

"Could you help me set some stuff up outside? Or wait—your hand—" I peer at his hand, which I've just noticed is bandaged.

"Eh, I can still lift stuff."

I frown. "Are you sure? Didn't you say you got stitches?"

"It's fine." He peels back the bandage—which, yuck, I didn't ask him to do—and shows me the long line of black stitches underneath. "It's not that bad."

It looks pretty bad to me, but I can tell there's no use arguing with him. "I'll do all the carrying," I say instead. "I just need you to tell me which stuff I can take outside. And I want to tell you about this exhibit I want to make. If you think it's a good idea, I mean."

I take him to the back of the museum, where there's a big stretch of empty wall. Because of the way the building is designed, this part of the wall goes all the way up to the second floor.

Trey looks amused as I explain my idea. "Do you think it's possible?" I ask.

He studies the wall. "Should be. I'll need another pair of hands if you want it done by next weekend, though."

"My friend John said he could help out tomorrow. He works with me at the auto shop."

Trey nods. "See if he can come by around noon."

He heads off to his demonstration station and I walk back to the front desk, doing a little celebration dance as I go. I relieve the other volunteer, Brenda, then settle into the chair and take out my phone to text John.

[12:19]: Any chance you can still come by the museum tomorrow to help Trey?

He sends back a thumbs-up.

[12:19] **John:** what time?

[12:20]: Would noon work?

A pause.

[12:21] **John:** WORKS

I stare at it for a moment, confused. Did he accidentally put caps lock on or something?

Then I laugh.

[12:21]: Ha!

[12:21]: If that's really today's answer, I'm going to be pissed.

[12:22] **John:** lol

[12:22] **John:** I haven't done it yet

[12:23]: DITTO.

I put my phone down for a minute to help a lovely middle-aged couple who come in to buy tickets. They're visiting from Australia and they seem genuinely interested in the museum. I chat with them for a few minutes and they tell me that they own a vineyard! Hence the interest in barrels, I suppose.

"Make sure you tell Trey that," I tell them. "He's our cooper."

They head off eagerly into the museum. I pick my phone back up and see I've missed a few texts.

[12:24] **John:** lol

[12:24] **John:** first word?

[12:37]: EVENT

[12:37]: As in, Shelley just agreed to let me do the Barrel Into Summer event!

[12:38] **John:** nice

[12:38] **John:** let me know if I can help

[12:39]: Thanks!

[12:39]: I'll probably take you up on that.

[12:40]: What's your first word?

[12:41] **John:** umm

[12:41] **John:** ORDER

[12:41]: As in??

[12:42] **John:** as in nothing

[12:42] **John:** you know you don't have to pick every word based on something happening in your life, right?

I laugh aloud.

[12:43]: I know you don't HAVE to, but it's more fun that way

[12:43]: Plus, I'm convinced the Wordle answers are connected to my life

[12:43] **John:** . . .

[12:44] **John:** what?

[12:45]: Like on Thursday, when it was FLYER!

[12:45]: And remember yesterday, when the answer was SPILL?

[12:45]: I spilled coffee all over the desk an HOUR later

[12:45]: Coincidence???

[12:45] **John:** yes

[12:46] **John:** that is a coincidence

[12:47]: Nope

[12:47]: Wordle was trying to warn me about the future

[12:48] **John:** what if today's answer is DEATH?

[12:49]: Speak well of me at my funeral.

[12:50] **John:** lol

[12:51] **John:** . . . you don't really think Wordle answers are connected to your life, do you?

[12:51]: You'll never know for sure until you read my autobiography

The museum door swings open again and a slightly flustered woman comes in with a young boy.

"Hi, there," I say.

"Hi," she says. "Do you have a bathroom we could use?"

"Er—of course." I point. "Right through there."

"Thanks."

Darn it. I swear, more people come in here to use the restroom than to see the barrels. What is wrong with people?

Then I have an idea. I grab the Barrel Into Summer flyer from my purse and quickly make ten copies on the museum's ancient copy machine. I get back to the desk just as the woman and her child are stepping out of the restroom.

"Thank you," she says.

"Of course." I smile. "Are you visiting Waldon on vacation or—?"

"Oh no, I'm from here. We were just at the park up the street."

The park up the street? I wonder if there's a bulletin board there.

"Well, if you're around next weekend, we're having an event here," I say brightly, handing her a flyer. "There's going to be music and a barbecue, and er—fun stuff for kids."

I can't be more specific than that, mostly because I haven't planned any stuff for kids. What would kids enjoy that costs zero dollars?

"Like a scavenger hunt?" asks the boy.

I beam at him. "*Exactly* like a scavenger hunt. How did you know?"

The kid grins at me proudly and his mother thanks me again. As the door swings closed behind them, I add "Plan scavenger hunt" to the to-do list on my phone. What a perfect idea! I can make a treasure map and hide clues around the museum. I'll have to get prizes, but maybe I can find something cheap at the dollar store. I wonder if they have barrel-themed toys.

(Probably not.)

My phone dings on the desk.

> [12:57] **John:** is there a double letter?

> [12:58]: Hang on, just starting now

I open Wordle and type in EVENT, which gets me nothing. Shoot. I look around the room, drumming my fingers on the desk. From inside the museum, I can hear the clanking of Trey's tools.

CLANK.

The C is green; the rest is gray. Hmm.

TOUGH. This puzzle is tough.

Ooh, that's more helpful. The U and H are both green.

C_U_H

I scan the unused letters. CQ, CW, CR...

CR!
CRUSH!

[1:04]: Got it

[1:04]: No double letter

[1:04] **John:** nice

[1:04] **John:** and is it connected to your life? lol

I glance away from my phone and catch sight of my reflection in the window opposite the desk. My cheeks are slightly flushed and I'm smiling foolishly.

I look down at Wordle, those five green letters staring back at me mockingly.

*CRUSH.*

[1:06]: Nope.

[1:06]: I guess I was wrong.

# C H A P T E R  1 4

I don't need all those," Mrs. Finnamore says.

It's 10:45 a.m. the next day, and I'm sitting in her kitchen with a half-empty cup of tea in front of me. I should have left for my museum shift about ten minutes ago, since I need to pick Jim up on the way, but Mrs. Finnamore is really digging her heels in about taking her medications today. When I came by to set them out at 8 a.m. (the time she's actually supposed to take them), she told me she would take them after breakfast. When I stopped by an hour later, she said her heartburn was acting up. Now, it's that she doesn't need them.

"I mean . . . it's up to you," I say uncertainly, "but you know Debra wants you to take them."

"Debra is not in charge of me."

"I know. But the doctor wants you to take them too." I actually looked all her medicines up online, and some of them seem really important.

Mrs. Finnamore makes a dismissive sound. "Doctors these days don't know what they're doing. Bill didn't take a single pill his entire life and he was fit as a fiddle."

Bill was Mrs. Finnamore's husband. I hesitate. "Didn't he die from diabetes, though?"

She looks at me sharply. "That was *genetic*."

I sigh and put her med pack down. I have a feeling this isn't happening today. "Okay, well . . . I really need to get going."

Mrs. Finnamore fiddles with the handle of her teacup. "Those doctors didn't do anything for Bill," she says, as though I haven't spoken. "They just wanted him to take insulin. Twenty years, they kept pushing those shots on him. And then when he finally gave in, it wasn't six months later that he died."

I bite my lip. I'm not a doctor, but I'm pretty sure Mrs. Finnamore is misunderstanding the situation. I think *not* starting the insulin for twenty years might've been the problem. But I'm not about to say that to her. I bet it helps having someone to blame.

"Do you miss him a lot?" I ask.

"Oh, you know," she says vaguely.

"Not really." I give her a small smile. "The longest relationship I've ever been in was only two years. Weren't you and Mr. Finnamore together for, like, forty?"

Mrs. Finnamore fiddles with her teacup for another moment and then lets out a heavy breath. "You young girls are smart not to get married too quickly."

I hesitate, then say tentatively, "Were you . . . not happy with Mr. Finnamore?"

"Oh, we were very happy," Mrs. Finnamore says colorlessly. "But youth is a precious thing." She looks at me. "You should be very careful not to waste it."

An unpleasant shiver runs over my skin. I'm definitely going to have to dig into this Bill situation way more sometime. But right now, I really have to go.

"I'll stop by later," I promise her. "We'll have tea."

She nods and says she'd like that, but I can tell her mind is still far away. There's a heavy feeling in my chest as I drive to Jim's. I was mostly joking when I told John I think the Wordle answers are connected to my life, but I can't fight the sense that Mrs. Finnamore's warning really *is* related to me. Youth is a precious thing, she said. And mine is slipping away by the second.

Jim is waiting for me outside of his house, dressed in his museum security vest.

"Hello, dear," he says, getting into the passenger seat.

I force myself to put on a sunny smile. "Sorry I'm late. Ready to fight off barrel thieves?"

Jim chuckles. "Ready."

I roll down the windows to let in the warm, sweet-smelling breeze, and connect my phone to the car speakers. A bright, lively song starts up.

"What station is this?" Jim asks.

I smile. "It's not the radio. I made a playlist of songs from the fifties for you."

Jim listens for a moment. "Is that the Diamonds?"

I nod.

He chuckles. "I haven't heard this song in years."

"I could make a playlist on your computer for you, if you wanted."

"Oh, you know I don't fuss much with that thing." He's quiet for another few minutes, tapping his fingers gently to the music. I have to admit, the fifties music is really growing on me. It's so folksy and cheerful. It's not doing much to lift my mood right now, though. Mrs. Finnamore's words are still sitting like a weight on my chest.

"Is everything all right?" Jim asks, as we pull onto the road into town.

"Oh—yes, sorry. I'm just thinking." I pause for a second, then ask, "Do you ever have any regrets about your life?"

"Of course not," he answers, without even a second of hesitation. "Why? Is something wrong?"

"No. Not exactly." I flick my blinker on at the stop sign. "I guess I'm just worried I'm wasting my youth."

"You don't like living here?"

"It's not that I don't like it," I say, feeling a stab of loyalty as I turn onto Main Street. "I'm just not sure I'm happy enough, I guess."

"You'll never be happy if you think too much," Jim says.

I chuckle. "So your advice is to think less?"

"Exactly. It's a nice day, isn't it?" He gestures to the cloudless sky. "We've got good music, good company. What else do you need?"

"I'm not sure it's that simple."

Jim waves a dismissive hand. "Life is only as complicated as you make it."

I twist my mouth doubtfully. "But didn't you ever hope your life would turn out to be . . . I don't know, bigger than it was?"

"What do you mean, bigger?"

"I don't know. More important, I guess. Not that your life wasn't important," I add hastily. "I just mean—I don't know, was it your dream to work at the post office all those years? Or was there something else you wanted to do more?"

Jim considers this as I pull into the museum parking lot. "There were thousands of things I wanted to do, I'm sure," he says. "But you can't do everything you want to do in life."

He says it like it's simple, but if anything, I feel even more stressed than before. Because he's right. You can't do everything you want to in life. Which means I have to be even *more* certain about what I decide to do. I don't want to wind up like Mrs. Finnamore, mourning her lost youth and talking about her husband in that flat, lifeless way.

I sigh and follow Jim into the museum, where I settle in at the front desk and Jim heads off to the back. I take out a stack of bright yellow Barrel Into Summer flyers, which I printed at the library last night. I've already put up about fifty around town, at places like the community center and grocery store and pharmacy and bakery. I tape a few to the wall behind the front desk, then, for good measure, I tape one across from the toilet in the bathroom. I'm determined that everyone who comes in here to pee is going to leave knowing about this event.

I'm deciding whether or not I should put flyers near some of the exhibits when my phone buzzes in my bag.

[11:24] **John:** heading your way

[11:24] **John:** you want a coffee?

I bite the inside of my lip. Yesterday, I'll admit, this text might've given me a fizzy little burst of excitement, but now I'm not so sure. This is probably how Mrs. Finnamore got into trouble. She probably thought Bill was a bit of a looker, and then he asked her out and she thought, sure, no harm in having one date with a good-looking chap, even if he's clearly not husband material. But then, boom! Eighty years pass by and her life is nearly over and she's wishing she could go back and get a do-over.

On the other hand, Jim would tell me to stop overthinking and just focus on being happy in the moment. Plus, the situation with

John is totally different, since I already know he isn't interested, which means I don't have to worry about getting trapped in a second-rate marriage. This is just a silly little one-sided attraction. There's absolutely no harm in enjoying it for what it is.

Yes. That makes sense. I'm going to go with that.

I turn back to my phone.

[11:25]: Would love one. ☺

Five hours later, John still hasn't left the museum.

He and I did Wordle together over coffee (PLEAT, on the fifth guess), then I took him to the back room to introduce him to Trey. They've been back there ever since, hammering and drilling and having enthusiastic arguments about—I don't know, how to hammer and drill things properly, I guess. It sounds like they're having fun, so I mostly leave them to it, popping back every once in a while to make sure they haven't lost sight of my (slightly whimsical) artistic vision.

Shelley is eventually drawn out of her office to complain about the noise, but she stops short when she sees that it's Trey's doing. I think she might be a little intimidated by him, actually. She limits her complaints to a sour frown and then retreats back into her office without even asking what they're up to.

About ten minutes after she leaves for the day, a pretty, heavyset woman with short brown hair pokes her head in the front door. She's carrying two pizza boxes in one hand.

"Shelley gone yet?" she asks me.

"Er—yes," I say uncertainly. "Were you hoping to speak with her? Or did you want to buy a ticket to the museum?"

She grins. "I'm hoping you'll let me in for free. I'm Rose. Trey's wife."

"Oh!" I smile and offer my hand. "I'm Emily."

"Figured I'd bring you all some dinner," Rose says. "But not Shelley," she adds conspiratorially.

I stifle a giggle. "The boys are out back."

I lock the front door and turn the Open sign to Closed, then we head to the back room, where Jim is watching Trey and John work. They're only halfway done with the exhibit, but I can already tell it's going to look amazing.

Rose balances the pizza boxes on a nearby barrel and we all gather around to eat. I'm a bit worried it will be awkward, but Rose is one of those rare people who can make everyone feel instantly at ease. She chastises Trey for working with his injured hand and gets a laugh out of Jim by calling his son a "total looker." (Apparently Jim's son was her teacher in high school.) When I tell her about the Barrel Into Summer event, she offers to take flyers around her neighborhood to drum up interest.

"It's about time someone did something with this place," she says. "It's such a beautiful building. And totally wasted under Shelley's management."

"Rose and Shelley went to high school together," Trey adds.

"And we used to work together at the grocery store," Rose says. "She used to bounce around from job to job, putting in a million complaints about her coworkers and managers and trying to get put off on stress leave . . . When Josephine died, everyone hoped the historical society wouldn't hire her, but I guess they wanted to keep things in the family, for Jo's sake. But Jo would be rolling in her grave to see her running this place. They never got along when she was alive." She shakes her head. "Maybe you can take over her job someday."

I point at myself. "Me?"

"Why not?" Rose says. "You'd do a way better job than Shelley. And tourism is really skyrocketing these days. Mark my words, this place will outstrip Summerside in a few years."

I smile a little guiltily and say nothing, because it would be way too rude to say how I really feel. I love this place, but being the manager of a tiny museum in small-town PEI is pretty much the opposite of my dream job. And even if it was my dream job, there's no way Shelley will ever give it up. She gets paid to sit in her office scrolling through Facebook while volunteers do the actual work. Why on earth would she ever leave?

Rose changes the subject to ask how Jim's daughter is doing since getting out of the hospital, and then she tells a story about a customer at the grocery store who tried to smuggle a thirty-pound bag of dog food out under his T-shirt, which leaves us all laughing over our last bites of pizza. A little after six, we all head out to our cars.

"Want me to drive you home, Jim?" Rose asks. "We live just up the road from him," she adds to me.

Jim agrees, and the three of them head off in Rose's car. John has parked a little farther up the street, near me. We walk along the sidewalk together in silence. The air is cool and sweet-smelling, and the trees that line the road rustle gently in the breeze. I glance sideways at John, who's walking with his hands shoved in his pockets. I wonder if he thinks it's strange to be hanging out with me like this outside of work.

"Thanks for all your help today," I say as we reach my car.

"No worries." He pulls his car keys from his pocket. "It was fun."

"I told you, barrel museums are super cool."

John chuckles. "'Super cool' might be a stretch."

"Extraordinarily cool, then."

"Passably cool," he counters.

I grin. "I'll take it."

A little silence falls between us, but for once, it doesn't feel awkward. If anything, it feels sort of charged. Like the end of a date, almost.

I bite my lip. I'm tempted to say something flirty to keep the conversation going, but that would be stupid. This isn't a date, and I don't have a crush on John.

"Well, night," I say hastily.

"Night," he says. Then, as I open my car door, "Don't start Wordle tomorrow without me."

My heart does a stupid flip-flop inside my chest. "Or what?"

"Or nothing," he says. "Just don't do it."

He shoots me a grin after he says it, and I'd be lying if I said it doesn't do seriously twisty things to my insides.

"We'll see," I retort. Then I get into my car and let my head drop onto my steering wheel as he walks away.

I hope tomorrow's Wordle answer is MORON.

# CHAPTER 15

I have to say, I've picked a *very* inconvenient week to suddenly become attracted to John. After more than a year of basically ignoring me at work, all of a sudden he's at the front desk, like, every five minutes. By five o'clock on Monday, we've spent an hour adjusting the shop schedule so he can fit in some appointments for his race car friends, a half hour figuring out how to order a tire balancer (I guess he finally convinced Fred to buy a new one), and then another hour at lunchtime doing Wordle (CHOIR, on the fourth guess) and talking about the Barrel Into Summer event. And that's not even counting all the times he's popped to the front desk to write out a receipt or double-check an appointment time.

What would be really helpful to dispel this teensy little attraction is some classic John behavior, like staring at me blankly when I make a joke or saying something snippy to a customer.

On Thursday morning, it seems like my wish might be granted. A middle-aged woman with very bright orange hair and slightly eccentric clothes has come in for a tire change, and while John is writing out her receipt, she asks him the same question no fewer than five times. Even I'm getting a little annoyed with her.

"So you're sure the tires are on *firmly*?" she says. "They aren't going to fly off?"

I glance at John, waiting for the explosion.

"Nope," he says.

"Because I read online that tires can fly off while you're driving if they're not put on firmly."

"They're on firmly," John says.

She frowns suspiciously. "You've tested them properly? Not just by hand, but with a proper tire machine?"

"Yes, ma'am," he says. "We use the Tire Flex 3000 to check that all tires are on firmly. But," he adds, as she snatches a breath to speak again, "I also used the Tirenator 4000 on your car, just to be extra sure."

"Hmm." The woman looks mollified. "Well, as long as you checked it on both."

"Of course," John says.

I run her credit card, give her a copy of the receipt, and bid her a good day, to which she responds with a pessimistic "We'll see."

When she's gone, John gives me a sly grin, a sharp glimmer in his eyes.

"What?" I ask warily. "You did double-check her tires, didn't you?"

"I did," he says. "But I didn't use the Tire Flex 3000 or the Tirenator 4000. Mostly because neither of those actually exist."

I let out a startled snort. "John!" I say, half-reproachfully. "That's terrible."

"What? You told me to be more polite to people."

"I didn't tell you to *lie* to them."

"And how was that any different than you and that rich girl the other day, exactly?"

"I—well—"

He raises an eyebrow. "Well, what?"

The corner of my mouth twists up. "I suppose it's better than your usual approach to customer service."

He grins. "Thanks. Now you have to try my way."

"What, be rude to people for no reason?"

"Not for no reason," he says. "But the next time someone's a jerk, you're not allowed to smile and be polite to them." He sticks out his hand. "Deal?"

"I suppose," I say grudgingly, shaking his hand. His grip is warm and strong, and there are callouses on his fingers. I let go very quickly and clear my throat. "I should get back to work."

"Right." He pushes himself off the counter. "Are you doing your old-people job tonight? 'Cause Trey and I were thinking we'd finish up the exhibit."

"I do my *caregiving* job every night," I say. "But I can come by afterward."

"Sounds good," he says, then heads off to the garage. I turn back to my desk, biting down on a tiny grin. Then I shake my head at myself.

"Get a grip, Emily," I say firmly.

The rest of the day passes by pretty uneventfully, except for this one time when I pop back to the garage to bring the phone to Dave and accidentally witness John using the hem of his T-shirt to wipe his face, revealing a very impressive set of abs. After work, I pop over to Mrs. Finnamore's to see if she needs anything, and also to dig into the situation with her late husband a little more. I think that's what I need right now: a cold, cautionary tale on the dangers of settling for the wrong man.

"I was at Jim's house last weekend," I tell her, while she makes us a pot of tea. "His wife's birthday would have been this week."

"Poor Jim," Mrs. Finnamore says. "That must be hard."

I nod, and then ask casually, as though it's just occurred to me, "When was your husband's birthday?"

"March," Mrs. Finnamore says, rummaging through her cupboards. "When you go to the store next, can you get some more of those wafer biscuits? The ones with the vanilla filling. The chocolate ones are too rich."

"Er—sure," I say distractedly.

"I like the lemon ones too. They're not too tart. Most lemon biscuits are much too tart."

"Vanilla or lemon," I repeat. "Got it." Then I clear my throat and try again. "Do you get a little down when his birthday comes around?"

"When whose birthday comes around?" she asks, pouring us both a cup of tea.

"Your husband's."

"Oh, I don't know," she says vaguely.

I hesitate, then decide to dive in. "It's just that the other day, when you were talking about him, it seemed like—I don't know, like maybe you two weren't always perfectly happy all the time?"

She gives me a sharp look. "I'm sure I don't know what you mean. Bill was a very good provider. He was a senior manager at the fish plant, you know."

"That's really impressive," I say hastily. "I didn't mean to pry. I was just . . . looking for advice, I guess."

"Advice?"

"Yeah. Just, like . . . how to know which guys to date. Not that I have anyone specific in mind," I add. "I'm just worried about settling down with the wrong person, you know?"

Mrs. Finnamore looks more interested now. I swear, if there's one thing people love more than talking about themselves, it's giving advice.

"Well, you won't find any good men on those silly apps you young girls use," she says briskly. "You should get your mother to suggest someone for you. That way you can be sure he's got a good character."

"Er—right," I say politely.

I'm pretty sure if I asked my mother to set me up with someone, she'd think I'd lost my mind. Plus, my mother spends all her time these days on bus tours for over-sixties. Where exactly is she supposed to be meeting men my age?

I take a sip of tea. "When you say a good character," I say, "you mean someone who's like . . . respectful?"

"Kind, respectful, that sort of thing," she says, with an absent wave of her hand. I settle back in my chair, feeling a bit disappointed. That wasn't exactly the groundbreaking advice I was hoping for.

But then she fidgets with the handle of her teacup and adds, "You should find someone who's helpful. Most men aren't, you know. It isn't in their nature."

"Helpful," I repeat.

"Mm."

I hesitate for a second, then ask, "Was Bill helpful?"

"Oh, he always did things when I asked him to," she says, in that airy tone I'm starting to realize is her way of deflecting. "But I suppose it would have been nice," she adds, "if I hadn't had to ask."

My brow furrows thoughtfully. I think I know what she means. My university boyfriend was like that. He was always happy to do things for me if I asked him to, but he never did anything spontaneously. Like, we had one class together in our fourth year, and he always used to go to the coffee shop near his house before class. He never once brought me coffee, even though he knew it was my favorite coffee place. I'm sure he would have, if I had asked him to, but that wasn't really the point. When someone does something for you, without you having to ask, it's just really nice, isn't it? It shows that they're thinking about you, even when you aren't around.

"That's good advice," I tell Mrs. Finnamore. "Thanks."

"No problem, dear."

"I've got to run," I say, rising. "I've got about a million things to do before the weekend. You're going to come, right?"

"If you want me to," Mrs. Finnamore says.

She doesn't sound particularly enthusiastic, but I'll take it.

I head straight to my car without going into my house. I'm absolutely starving, but I don't have time to make anything. The Barrel Into Summer event is the day after tomorrow, and I still haven't picked up paper plates and cups or figured out prizes for the scavenger hunt.

My phone dings in my pocket.

[5:57] **John:** what do you think?

I tilt my head, confused, but a second later, an image comes through. It's a box full of medals, the kind you get for high school sports.

[5:57] **John:** they're my sister's old volleyball medals

[5:57] **John:** fortunately our school was too cheap to buy specific medals for different sports, so they just have a generic pattern on them

[5:57] **John:** I thought you could use them for the scavenger hunt

[5:58]: That would be perfect!!

[5:58]: Thanks 😊

[5:59] **John:** no problem

[5:59] **John:** heading to the museum soon, just going to grab pizza

[5:59] **John:** want me to see if they sell paper cups/plates?

Yes!!! I type frantically. That would be so—
My fingers still on the word.
Helpful.
That would be so helpful.

I bite hard into my lip. Dammit. Talking to Mrs. Finnamore was supposed to warn me off of John, not make him seem more appealing.

With a resigned sort of sigh, I delete my half-written text and start again.

[6:01]: Yes, please!

[6:01]: That would be great. 😊

# C H A P T E R  1 6

All right, then. This is it.

Saturday. Event day.

Or, as I've taken to calling it—

B-day.

(And yes, I know that usually stands for birthday, but today it stands for barrel day, okay?)

I've been at the museum with Trey, Rose, and John since seven a.m., and to say I'm being extra would be the understatement of this still very young century.

"Do we have enough ice?" I ask. "Do the balloons look okay?"

None of them answer me, which is probably because I've asked both questions fifteen times already. I don't mind being ignored. I'm pretty sure I'm only talking to try to expel some of my nerves.

By ten a.m., we're ready to go. And I don't want to sound braggy, but this place looks really good. Like really, *really* good.

I shelled out a hundred of my own dollars to buy decorations from the dollar store, and I've gone with a red and gold theme. The museum entrance is framed with red and gold balloons, the trees in the backyard are artfully draped in red and gold streamers, and all the barrels in the backyard are adorned with red and yellow construction paper chains (I couldn't find gold construction paper, so yellow is the best I could do). I wanted to put a paper chain on the barbecue, too, but Trey pointed out it probably wasn't a good idea to put flammable material over an open grill.

The best bit, though, is the new exhibit, which John and Trey finished last night. It's basically a huge stack of barrels fitted into the wall, but they're placed so that someone can pose underneath them, pretending to carry them all. From the other side of the room, you can take the perfect picture of your child or friend pretending to have superhero strength. John and Trey even fitted the barrels into the wall so some of them look like they're about to tumble off the top of the stack.

And look, I'm not saying it's a work of genius or anything, but it's cute and funny and I think tourists will really like it. I think even Jean Shorts Girl might approve.

While Rose and Trey fire up the barbecue and John helps his friend George set up the speakers for his guitar, I head to the front desk alone to officially open the doors. I haven't looked outside for the last thirty minutes because I was too scared I'd see an empty parking lot, but when I swing open the door . . .

There's a line.

A *line*!

I mean, okay, it's not like a queue for Taylor Swift tickets or anything, but there are at least five families and a big group of older tourists. A few of them are clutching Barrel Into Summer flyers, and someone's kid is throwing a temper tantrum about the wait.

I beam at all of them. "Welcome!"

For the next two hours, I only leave my post to help people take pictures of themselves at the new wall exhibit. It's absolutely adorable watching everyone come up with funny poses with the barrels. My favorite is a young girl who does a handstand underneath, so it looks like she's balancing all the barrels on her toes. The atmosphere is bright and happy, the barbecue smells absolutely delicious, and Trey's station is a huge hit with all the kids. The scavenger hunt is going really well (even if one kid did accidentally tip over a barrel looking for a clue), and Rose came up with a fun activity for them in the backyard, a kind of ring-toss game where kids try to throw rings into barrels.

Around lunchtime, the museum's other regular volunteer, Brenda, arrives to take my place at the front desk. She looks shocked at how busy the place is, and I can't wipe the proud grin from my face as I head toward the backyard.

Things are in full swing back here. John's friend George is playing folksy songs on his guitar and Rose is dishing out burgers and hot dogs as fast as she can cook them. I wave at her over the heads of a group of American tourists and wander toward the back of the yard, where John is manning the drinks station.

Halfway there, I spot Shelley chatting with a group of older women. My feet reluctantly slow. I suppose it would be rude of me not to go say hi to her.

I force a smile as I approach. "Hey, Shelley," I greet her, and smile at the three women gathered around her. "Are you all having fun?"

"Absolutely," says one of the women brightly. She has curly white hair and an old-fashioned pantsuit with an official-looking pin on her lapel. "We're all members of the town's historical society," she says, holding a hand out to me. "And you are—?"

"This is one of our new volunteers," Shelley says.

"Emily," I say, shaking the woman's hand.

"How lovely," she says. "Did you help plan all of this?"

"She and Trey both pitched in," Shelley says, before I can answer. My mouth nearly drops open with shock. *Pitched in*? We planned the whole thing!

"How nice," says the white-haired woman. "I hope it hasn't cost too much?"

"Oh, no, I've budgeted it all out," Shelley says. "We'll make a tidy little profit."

"You can put the money toward another event," the woman suggests. "Maybe something for Canada Day!"

"That's exactly what I was thinking," Shelley says.

The women smile and head off toward the barbecue. I return their polite smiles with difficulty. My cheeks are burning, and my chest feels kind of tight.

Shelley gives me a bland smile. "Some kid spilled their soda in the back hall. Be a dear and clean it up, will you?"

My cheeks burn hotter. I open my mouth to mutter "Sure," then I stop myself. John's voice suddenly echoes in my head.

*The next time someone's a jerk, you're not allowed to smile and be polite to them.*

Shelley's definitely being a jerk, but even so, I'm not sure I have the guts to say anything.

Oh, screw it. It can't hurt to try.

I snatch a nervous breath and blurt out, a bit shakily, "That was a bit rude."

Shelley raises an eyebrow. "Excuse me?"

I lick my lips. "You didn't budget this event," I say. "I did. And Trey and I didn't 'pitch in.' We did everything."

Shelley gives a condescending little chuckle. "This isn't about taking *credit*, Emily. And there's a lot more to managing this place than you might realize. Now, why don't you go take a little break? I'll take care of the spill."

I open my mouth to retort, but it's no use—she's already walking away. For a second, I think about storming after her, but if I'm honest, my legs are feeling a bit shaky. I don't usually talk to people like that, ever. It made zero difference, obviously, but it was still kind of exhilarating. My heart is thumping a bit faster with adrenaline.

I cross the lawn and approach John, who's grabbing a can of soda from the cooler.

"Guess what I just did?" I say, taking a soda for myself.

"Bored someone to death talking about barrels."

"Ha, ha. No, I just stood up to Shelley. She was being a huge jerk, and I totally called her out on it."

"Nice." John holds his can of soda out for me to clink. "Well done."

"I'm not sure it made a difference, though."

He shrugs. "Probably not. Still cool, though."

"Yeah." I grin. "It was. How are things going here?"

Before he can answer, someone calls his name behind me. I turn to see a middle-aged couple approaching us. The man is quite tall, with very tanned white skin and wiry dark hair, and the woman has short dark-brown hair, light-brown skin, and a smile that looks kind of familiar.

"Oh, hey," John says, stepping forward to greet them. The woman kisses him on the cheek. "You guys been here long?"

"A little while," the woman says, smiling. She looks at me with interest.

"This is Emily," John says. "Emily, these are my parents."

I blink, startled. John invited his *parents*?

I reach out hastily to shake their hands. "Nice to meet you, Mr. and Mrs. Smith."

"Call me Carla," his mother says, leaning in to kiss my cheek. His father does the same and introduces himself as Laurent. He has a faint French accent, and his eyes are the exact same shade of brown as John's.

"Are you having fun?" I ask.

"Absolutely," Carla says. "This place is beautiful."

"Really impressive," his father adds, looking around. "Are you from Waldon?" he asks me.

"Halifax, originally," I say. "John told me you're from Quebec?"

"Not exactly," Laurent says, and launches into a story about the Toronto suburb where he grew up, and the business he started there that eventually took him to Montreal, and how that led him to the Dominican Republic, where he met his wife. I listen politely, marveling at how different he is from his son. He's exuberant and slightly loud and really chatty—so chatty, in fact, that Carla and John both tell him to stop talking after about ten minutes.

"You're going to put her to sleep," Carla chastises him.

"Oh, nonsense. Emily was interested, weren't you?" Laurent says.

"Yes, sir," I say.

Carla puts a hand on my arm. "Don't humor him," she advises me. "You'll end up stuck here all day listening to him go on and on."

I grin at her. She's standing so close I can smell her perfume, a bright, floral scent. Laurent smells great, too, a very subtle peppermint scent. It must be a family thing.

"John said you both retired to Summerside?" I ask.

Carla nods. "I still do a bit of work there, just to help out the hospital. They're so desperate for doctors. I'm an endocrinologist," she adds.

"Oh, wow," I say. Then I hesitate. "Er—and what is that, exactly?"

She chuckles. "It's a doctor who specializes in hormone problems. Adrenal disease, thyroid disease, that sort of thing."

"Wow," I say again. "Very cool."

"Well, it can be. Health care is in such a state right now." She shakes her head and gives a tiny sigh. "John tells us you've started some caregiving work recently?"

He did? I glance sideways at him, but he just looks back at me blandly and takes a sip of his drink.

"Yes, ma'am," I say. "Not, like, important nursing stuff or anything. I just do chores and keep people company, really."

"There's nothing unimportant about that," Carla says. "The hospitals on this island are full of people waiting for long-term-care beds, all because they've got no one to help them out a little at home."

I wince. "That's awful."

Carla nods. "No one in this country ever seems to think about the future. They think they're going to be healthy and independent forever, and then they're absolutely astounded when they get old! As though they didn't realize it would ever happen to them."

I nod earnestly. Doris is definitely like that, and Mrs. Finnamore too. Even Jim tells me all the time that he was shocked when his wife died, because he thought they had years left together. Which is heartbreaking, obviously, but also . . . his wife was ninety-three when she died. Jim talks about her like she should have had twenty or thirty years left, which even I know isn't medically realistic.

"If you ask me, we keep people alive far too long these days," Carla adds. "I hope I die in my sleep the day I turn seventy-five."

"That's cheerful," Laurent says dryly.

"You'll be lucky to reach seventy," Carla retorts, "with all your red meat and cigars."

"Speaking of which," Laurent says, "I've got my eye on one of those burgers. Very nice to meet you, Emily."

"You too," I say. They both smile at me and then head off to the barbecue, leaving John and me alone. "I can't believe you invited your parents," I say.

I say it to tease him, but he just shrugs. "They like stuff like this."

"Well, it was really nice of them. They're both so impressive too! A doctor and a businessman." I almost add something else, then think better of it and quickly shut my mouth.

John looks at me for a moment. "Maybe I was dropped on my head as a child."

"Um—what?"

He raises an eyebrow. "You were wondering how an endocrinologist and a successful businessman wound up with a son who's a mechanic. Weren't you?"

My face turns bright red. "Oh—no—"

"So maybe I *was* smart when I was born, but then I was dropped on my head as a kid, and that's how I wound up like this. I'll have to ask my parents sometime." His voice is dry, but there's an edge to it.

And he's right. That *is* what I was wondering.

"I don't think you're stupid," I say, mortified.

"Mm." He takes a sip of soda. "You sort of do, though."

"I don't! I swear I don't."

He just looks at me, and I feel a sharp twisting in my chest.

He's totally caught me out.

"I don't think you're stupid," I say. "I really, really don't." I hesitate, then add, "It just sometimes seems like . . . I don't know."

"What?"

"Well . . . like you might've settled a bit, I guess."

He snorts. "I know it's hard for you to believe, but I like working at the shop. And I like living in Waldon. My parents are both successful, but they'd tell you themselves, it hasn't always made them happy. They'd rather me and my sister do something we like rather than work ourselves to death."

"No, I get that. I just feel like—I don't know—"

"Like I should be chasing after some big, important 'dream job'?"

"Well . . . yes," I say helplessly. "I mean, it doesn't have to be big or important—"

"Because that would be beyond me," he says dryly.

"No! I just mean, you should do something you love."

"Okay, well, I *love* working on cars. Just because you're not interested in something doesn't mean it's totally useless."

"I know!"

"I don't think barrel museums and old people are very interesting, but you don't hear me questioning your life choices, now do you?"

"No." I rake a hand through my hair. "I'm such a jerk, John. Seriously. I'm really sorry."

He studies my face for a moment and then chuckles, all of the tension instantly vanishing from his frame. "Don't worry about it. I'm just giving you a hard time."

"Well, I deserve it. You've been so helpful all week, and this is how I repay you."

He laughs again. "It's fine. Tell you what: go buy me a hamburger and we'll call it even."

"A two-dollar hamburger is going to make up for me being a total asshole?"

"Good point. Two hamburgers, then."

I crack a small smile. "I really am sorry."

"I know. Now go get us some food, before I decide it should be three hamburgers."

I give him a grateful smile and head to the barbecue, mentally kicking myself all the way. I can't believe I was such a jerk.

Rose looks up as she hands a hot dog to Trey. "You want something, Emily?"

"Two hamburgers, please, and a hot dog."

"I can do the hamburgers, but Trey's just stolen the last hot dog," she says. Trey grins at me apologetically through a mouthful of hot dog.

"We ran out? Seriously?"

"Yep." Rose smiles. "And we're on the last pack of burgers. I think we can officially call this thing a hit."

I exhale in relief. (Just between you and me, I didn't *technically* have enough money to pay off my credit card if we didn't break even on all the food I bought.) "Thank goodness. I'll have three burgers, then, if you've got them."

"On it," Rose says.

"All the kids really love your new exhibit," Trey comments.

"Our new exhibit," I correct. "You and John did all the work."

"Yeah, well. It's nice to see people enjoying this place." He grins and takes another bite of hot dog, and for a minute or two we watch all the people milling around the yard. Everyone really does look like they're having a great time.

When I glance back at Trey, he's looking at me with a thoughtful expression.

"What?" I ask, a little self-consciously.

"You're good at this."

"Planning events for barrel museums?" I laugh. "Shame it's not an Olympic sport."

"I mean it," Trey says. "You should be manager of this place, not Shelley."

"Hear, hear," Rose adds.

Embarrassed, I wave them away. "You know that'll never happen."

"Yeah, maybe not," Trey says. "But I bet there are museums in Charlottetown that would love to have you work for them. Although I guess you probably wouldn't want to commute that far from Waldon." He swallows the last bite of his hot dog. "I should get back to it. No rest for the wicked."

A moment later, Rose hands me three burgers wrapped in paper. I smile and thank her. Back at the drinks station, John has been accosted by about thirty kids who have all just finished the scavenger hunt and are clamoring for a drink, so I hand over his burgers with an apologetic smile and take over the station while he eats. I hand out soda and juice until John shoos me away again, ordering me to go eat my own burger.

I head inside to get out of the sun and duck into the break room to eat. Afterward, I take a spin through the museum. I should really head back to the front desk to check on Brenda, but I don't want to go just yet. Trey's words are ringing in my ears, and there's an idea percolating at the edges of my mind.

*I bet there are museums in Charlottetown that would love to have you.*

He's probably right. There are probably museums there looking for workers.

But there are probably museums in other places looking for workers too. Places like New York and London and Paris. Places where museums span several blocks and tourists line up for hours to get in.

I turn slowly on the spot, taking in the scene around me. Laughter and music filtering in from the backyard. Tourists lining up to take pictures of an exhibit I helped make. Families making memories at an event I helped create.

*Dream job,* whispers a voice in the back of my mind.

Dream job.

# CHAPTER 17

APPLY is not a good word to use in Wordle. It doesn't rule out enough vowels, and it totally wastes a letter with the double P. It would be stupid for me to use it as my first word this close to the end of my yearlong streak.

On Sunday morning, I use it anyway.

APPLY.

As in, I'm going to apply for a degree in museum studies today.

I researched it all night, after I got home from the museum. Apparently there are people called exhibition coordinators whose entire job is to create museum exhibitions, just like I did at the barrel museum. When I think of spending my life building places for people to learn, places that can give people that warm, quiet feeling that museums have always given me . . . it feels perfect. It feels right.

I was planning to apply to ten or fifteen places in the United States and Canada, but then I saw how much it costs to apply to university. A hundred and fifty dollars just to *apply*? Who can afford to apply to more than one?

It's taken several hours to narrow it down, but I've decided to apply for an MA in museum studies at NYU. The application deadline is two days from now, which I think is a sign. I found this just in time.

I pour myself the world's biggest cup of coffee and then knock out my entire application in one sitting. The hardest part is the personal essay. I want to gush about the feelings museums give me, the long circuitous journey I've been on to realize this is my dream job, and all my goals and aspirations for the future, but when I put it all down on paper, it just seems sort of cheesy and off-putting. I delete it all and try again. I lay out my interest in the degree in a plain, simple way and briefly describe my experience at the barrel museum and the success of our new exhibit. For my writing sample, I write a short essay on the value of rural museums.

I load in all the documents they ask for and then I reach the references page. Three letters are required. I bite my lip for a long minute, then type three names.

Trey Fisher, Cooper, Waldon Museum of Barrel-Making.

He was the one who gave me this idea, and I'm sure he'll be willing to do it.

Fred Martin, Owner/Manager, Martin Auto.

I'm less sure that he'll be willing to be a reference, but I think he needs to be on the list, since he's my current boss.

Jim Williams, Security Officer, Waldon Museum of Barrel-Making.

I'm a bit nervous to put Jim as a reference, but I don't really have anyone else. Shelley would never agree to write me a reference (let alone a good one), Mrs. Finnamore doesn't know how to use her computer, and Doris would probably write fifteen pages about how I don't know how to use coupons properly. Jim knows how to use his computer reasonably well—his granddaughter taught him when she visited from Ontario—but submitting a reference letter through NYU's online system might still be beyond him. And

I'm not sure I can offer to help him. That seems ethically sketchy, like I'd be standing over his shoulder making sure he wrote good things.

Oh, well. This is a long shot anyway.

I pay my application fee—goodbye, eighty US dollars—and then reach the final page. I pace the kitchen for about ten minutes before I work up the nerve to click submit.

An impersonal page thanks me for my application, and that's it. I did it.

I let out a shaky breath and start closing out all the tabs I've opened since I started this application—hundreds of Google searches, my old university portal where I got all my transcripts, my online bank account, Jean Shorts Girl's Instagram (don't judge, I needed a five-minute break)—beyond ready to stop staring at this damn computer screen. I'm about to close the final one when something snags my eye. It's a search result buried halfway down the page.

Internships | The Metropolitan Museum of Art.

I click it so fast I get dizzy.

Five minutes later, I've got another huge cup of coffee in hand (never mind that it's nearly eight p.m.) and I'm starting my application for a yearlong internship at the Met.

This, I know, is a real long shot. Almost entirely outside the realms of possibility. These internships are made for eager undergrads just starting their first degrees, not auto shop receptionists whose greatest accomplishments are Wordle-related. But it can't hurt to try, can it? And the application is free.

When I finally step away from my computer two hours later, my vision has gone spotty from staring at the screen so long. I pick up my phone (yes, I know it's a screen) to finish Wordle and catch up on the texts I've missed.

First, Wordle. APPLY got me a yellow A.

TIRED. As in, I am so freaking tired.

Oh, nice! The R, E, and D are all yellow.

A, R, E, D.

R, E, A, D.

READS. As in . . . if Emily READS anything else on her computer, her eyes will fall out.

Shoot. Nope. The S is wrong, the rest are all yellow.

DREAD. As in, I'm dreading waking up for work tomorrow.

D, R, E, and A are all green.

D, R, E, A.

DREAM.

The answer is DREAM.

As I watch the letters turn green, a little shiver runs up my spine.

This has got to be a sign.

I admire my streak count for a moment and then flip to my texts.

> **[1:00] Rose Fisher:** Everyone at the grocery store is talking about how good yesterday was!

> **[1:01] Rose Fisher:** Would you like to come for dinner at our place this Friday?

[3:17] **Fallon:** Hey girl!! Amaaaazing new discount code on the website if you want to use (or promote)!

[3:17] **Fallon:** Sending a link to your insta!

I shoot off a quick response to Rose, make a mental note to look at Fallon's thing later, and then open up a text to John. Things got so crazy at the end of the event yesterday with cleanup and thanking everyone for coming and trying not to be furious when Shelley vanished without helping, John and I never really got another chance to talk before he left to have dinner with his parents. I know he accepted my apology, but I still feel really bad about what happened.

[9:42]: Hey! Hope you've had a good Sunday.

[9:43]: Thanks for all your help yesterday!!

[9:43]: And sorry, again, for being such a douchebag ☹

My phone dings as I'm pulling on my pajamas.

[9:49] **John:** lol

[9:49] **John:** no worries

[9:49] **John:** what'd you get up to today?

I start to type about NYU and the Met internship, then I stop. It feels a bit squicky to talk about dream job stuff after what happened yesterday.

[9:51]: Not much!

[9:51]: Just recovering from yesterday, really

[9:52] **John:** and plotting to overthrow Shelley, I hope

[9:52]: Haha

[9:53]: Yeah, I'm designing a new exhibit

[9:53]: Well, not so much an exhibit as a way to balance a barrel on Shelley's office door so it'll fall on her head when she walks in

I add a row of evil smiley faces.

[9:54] **John:** lol

[9:54] **John:** I'll help with that one

I pause, then type again.

[9:56]: See you tomorrow for Wordle?

[9:57] **John:** GREAT.

[9:57] **John:** 😊

The smiley face sends a warm little fizz through my chest. My lips stretch into a smile.

[9:58]: Great. 😊

# CHAPTER 18

D on't judge me, okay, but I may have done a stupid thing.

Last night, after I texted with John, I was feeling all giddy and squiggly, so I decided it was a perfectly good time to have my two acceptable weekly drinks. And since I didn't see anywhere on the new alcohol guidelines about how quickly you're supposed to drink them, I saw absolutely no harm in downing two full glasses of wine like they were tequila shots.

Whoops.

After they kicked in (and after I spent about thirty minutes dancing around the house to ABBA's greatest hits), it suddenly seemed like a *really* good idea to make John a thank-you card for fixing my car and helping out with the event.

And yes, I know what you're thinking. What am I, twelve years old? And *yes*, I do vaguely remember making a birthday card for a boy I had a crush on when I was twelve. But I didn't do this because I have a crush on John, okay? I just think it's polite to make people thank-you cards. I made one for my dentist last year, and you're not going to accuse me of having a crush on her, are you?

(Actually, it would be way more likely that I'd have a crush on her than on John. She's seriously gorgeous, and she owns like five dental practices around the island, so she's clearly a very driven person.)

Anyway. Stupid decision or not, I've made John a homemade

thank-you card. It's in my bag right now, and I have to admit, I'm pretty proud of it.

I take my bag with me to the break room at lunch on Monday, and while John's heating up a bowl of pasta in the microwave, I take the card out all casual-like.

"Oh, I almost forgot," I say (okay, lie). "I made you this, for fixing my car. And for helping out so much with the museum."

He wipes his hands on his coveralls—it makes zero difference, they're still covered in grease—and takes the card from me. On the front, I've drawn a Wordle game, exactly how it looks on the app. The words are MOTOR, BRAKE, AXLES, THANK, YOUTH, and JOHNS, but I've done it so that all the letters are gray or yellow, except for green letters that spell out "THANK YOU JOHN."

It's pretty cool, if I do say so myself.

John's eyebrows knit together for a moment, then he grins, like he thinks it's pretty cool too.

"This is awesome," he says, flashing that lightning-strike smile at me. My cheeks grow hot under his gaze, and I have to bite my lip to keep from smiling like an idiot.

And okay, fine. I'll admit it.

I have the *tiniest* crush on John.

(At least try to pretend you're shocked, will you?)

But still, it's not a big deal. What's wrong with having a fun, silly crush? It's harmless. It's obvious he's not into me that way, so there's no pressure, and I can just sit back and enjoy my secret crush in peace.

He grins at the card for another second, then the microwave beeps and he turns away to get his pasta. I run my eyes surreptitiously over his frame. Now that I've admitted I've got a little crush on him, I'd say I'm allowed to admire how broad his shoulders are.

I clear my throat as he turns around and reach for my phone. "What word are you starting with today?"

John sits down across from me with his pasta. "Dunno."

"I'm going to do BROKE. As in, even though I made my money back from the food yesterday, I'm still totally broke."

John laughs, and for a moment we're both quiet, tapping at our phones. I use BROKE as my first word, and all but the O are right. I type in the obvious answer—BRAKE—with a pang of disappointment. It's kind of a letdown these days when I get it too quickly.

"Got it," I say.

"Already? Nice."

"Mm. Let me know if you need a hint."

He doesn't answer, so I get up and put on the kettle to make tea. I lean against the counter and drum my fingers absently on the linoleum.

"BRAKE," John says. "Got it." Then he laughs. "Hey, like your card."

He's right. I did use BRAKE on his card. I chuckle. "I guess I'm clairvoyant. But only for Wordle. It's a very specific type of clairvoyance." I frown. "Clairvoyance? Is that a word? Clairvoyancy? Clairvoyitude?"

John laughs again. "Clairvoyitude."

The kettle is boiling; I flick it off and search the cupboards for a tea bag.

"What are your plans for the week?" he asks.

"Nothing much. Hanging out with Jim, letting Doris yell at me . . . oh, and I might do a Heath Ledger movie marathon."

"Like with friends?"

"No, just by myself. I love solo movie marathons," I add, a touch defensively.

"That's cool." John clears his throat. "Is that tonight? 'Cause there's this firelight festival thing in Charlottetown, if you wanted to go."

I go perfectly still.

Did he just—?

No.

Can't be.

. . . but what else could he possibly mean?

I lick my lips and attempt an offhand voice. "You mean, like . . . together?"

John clears his throat again. "Yeah. If you wanted to."

I turn around, my heart beating somewhere around my throat. "Like . . . a date?"

He snorts. "Yeah, like a date."

"But—you don't like me," I blurt out.

"I wouldn't ask you out if I didn't like you. But if you don't want to go—"

"No, I want to go!" I say hastily. "I mean, if *you* want to."

John looks amused. "Okay. We'll have to leave around seven, if that works."

"Seven's fine," I say faintly. I feel like I'm having an out-of-body experience, like I'm floating on the ceiling watching two strangers arrange a date.

"Why did you think I didn't like you?" he asks.

I flush. "I don't know. You just . . . didn't seem that interested, I guess. You never really talked to me."

"We've been talking for weeks."

I roll my eyes. "Yeah, *now*. But when I first started here, you basically ignored me every time I tried to talk to you."

John shrugs. "I'm not super chatty. Plus, I thought you were kind of a snob."

My head jerks backward. "What?"

"You just seemed like you didn't want to work here or be in Waldon at all," he says. "And you did think I was stupid," he adds with a wry grin, "no matter what you might say now."

I fall silent, my cheeks burning furiously. Did I really come off like that? I wrack my brains, trying to think of things I said to John when I first started working here. I guess I may have mentioned once or twice that this receptionist job was only temporary. And I may have made a few jokes about how small Waldon was. The really pathetic part is, I think I did some of it to try to impress him.

Oh, god.

"I'm a *snob*," I say miserably.

John snorts. "Not really. You just sort of seemed like that at first."

"No, I am!" I insist. "I think I'm better than the people who live here."

"You probably are better than some of them," John says. "There are some really shitty people here." He laughs again at the look on my face. "I didn't mean to make you feel bad. I just thought you were kind of stuck-up at first. Now I know you're not. I mean, can you honestly say you liked me when we first met?"

I hesitate. "Er . . ."

He chuckles. "See?"

The corners of my mouth twist up. "Do you always insult people when you ask them out?"

"Do you always expect people who ask you out to think you're perfect in every single way?" John counters.

An embarrassed laugh bubbles out of me. "Yes. You should think that I'm flawless. Obviously."

"Obviously," John agrees. Then he stands, says, "Later," and wanders off, like we've been having a totally normal, everyday conversation. I fight a sudden urge to chuck my cup of tea at the back of his head. I may be a snob, but he is seriously such a weirdo.

(A weirdo who likes me.)

(A weirdo I have a *date* with.)

I forgo my tea-throwing plans and do a little spin instead.

I have a date with *John*.

# CHAPTER 19

I don't want to sound like a bad person, but I swear Doris pretends to have hearing trouble sometimes. Like right now, she's telling me a long story about her childhood, and any other time I would be happy to hear it (well, maybe not *happy*, since so many of her stories are just thinly veiled complaints about every person she's ever met, but I wouldn't *mind* listening), but right now I'm desperate to get home and get ready for my date.

(My date with *John*.)

Every time she pauses for breath, I tell her loudly that I have to go, but she just barrels on like she hasn't heard me. If she really can't hear me, then I guess I'm a horrible person for thinking it, but if she's pretending . . . well, it's kind of genius, isn't it?

Finally, I give up and just back out the door. "I'm really sorry!" I holler. "I'll hear the rest tomorrow!"

I swear I hear her snicker as the door swings shut.

Back at home, I spend a half hour restraightening my hair, which has gone all limp and tangly at work, and put on some dark eyeshadow that I think makes me look sort of cool and flirty but probably actually just looks like normal eyeshadow.

Normally for a date I'd put together a pretty outfit—for my date with Arjun, for example, I wore an A-line dress and strappy sandals—but knowing John, he'll show up in jeans and a T-shirt and I'll look way overdressed by comparison. I pull on a pair of dark jeans that an ex once said made my butt look good and a black T-shirt and slim-fit bomber jacket. I'm toeing on my sneakers when bright lights swing through my living room. A few moments later, there's a knock on my door. I shove my phone, credit card, and money in my pocket, smooth down my hair one last time, and open the door.

John is dressed in a T-shirt and jeans (I knew it!), but he somehow looks nicer than normal, like he's done his hair differently or something.

"Hey," I say, my voice a little high-pitched from nerves. "Er—how's it going?"

He looks amused. "Good. You?"

I shrug casually. "I'm cool."

(I'm *cool*? Good lord.)

John snorts. "You're cool?"

"Oh, shut up," I say, shooing him off the doorstep. "I say stupid stuff when I'm nervous."

"You're nervous, are you?"

He looks way too pleased. I glare at him. "Not about *you*. Just about the state of the world. Climate change. Rising oil prices. The inevitable heat death of the universe."

He laughs. "Of course. Your house is really nice," he adds, as we walk to his car.

"Isn't it?" I say, walking backward to admire it. "It'll look even better in a few weeks, when all the flowers are out."

"Do you own it?"

I grimace. "I wish. Who can actually afford a house these days? The market is awful."

I explain how I wound up in the house as we drive to the highway. He says "mm" a few times and nods once, but when I stop talking, silence falls. I glance around the car, looking for something to say.

"Isn't PEI pretty?" I ask finally.

"Mm."

I point out the window. "Ooh, look at the cows."

John glances over but says nothing.

"John," I say sternly. "You're being too quiet."

He laughs. "I don't have anything to say. And I'm not chatty. You know that."

"Yeah, but this is a *date*," I say, swiveling in my seat to face him. "Conversation is supposed to *flow*. We're supposed to talk for hours and hours without noticing the time pass by."

"That sounds awful."

"John!"

He grins. "What? Wouldn't it be nicer to just chill and enjoy the drive? You can hook your phone up to the speakers if you want to listen to music."

I scowl at the side of his head. Ridiculous.

That said, it would be kind of nice to listen to music. Plus, I have the perfect "relaxing drive" playlist on my phone.

"I'll put music on," I say, "but only if you tell me three facts about yourself."

This is a trick I've used on several first dates. I've told you before, people love talking about themselves.

"Pass," John says.

I throw my hands up. "You can't *pass*. Honestly, do you want me to enjoy this date or not?"

John looks at me. "Are you not having fun?"

My lips twist, fighting a smile. Because, yes, maybe it is sort of fun bantering with him.

"Three facts," I say stubbornly.

"Three facts, and then ten minutes of silence," John counters.

"Why did you even ask me out if you don't like to hear me talking?" I say indignantly.

John snorts. "I don't mind you talking—"

"How romantic."

"—but there's no point in talking just for the sake of talking. If you have something to say, I want to hear it. But you don't have to talk just to fill the silence."

"You and I are very different people," I say dryly, which makes him laugh again. "But fine, deal. Three facts for ten minutes of silence. I'll go first. Let's see. I've never broken a bone . . . I had my appendix taken out in high school . . . and I think beer's disgusting."

"I like beer."

I roll my eyes. "Of course you do. That doesn't count as one of your facts."

"Fine."

"And nothing boring!" I add quickly. He gives me an exasperated look, and I grin.

"Three facts . . ." He drums his fingers on the steering wheel. "Okay. One: I bought this car in Calgary and drove it back here last summer. Two: I'm going to Toronto later this summer for my buddy Kareem's wedding. And three . . ." He thinks for a minute and then shakes his head. "I've got nothing."

"You can't have nothing," I scold. "Surely you can think of *one* other fact about yourself. I could name five facts about you myself!"

John snorts. "Can you?"

I sit a little straighter. "Sure can. Watch this." I count on my fingers. "You drink your coffee black. You don't wear a watch. You speak Spanish and French." I hesitate. This is a little hard, now that I think of it. "Ah! Got it. You like old cars, and you're a little rude to customers."

"Vintage cars," John corrects. "And I'm wearing a watch right now."

I roll my eyes. "I mean *most* of the time."

"You mean at work."

"That's most of the time! It counts. I win."

"Was this a competition?"

"Duh. I bet you couldn't name five things about me."

I'm expecting him to brush me off, but instead he looks at me, his brow crinkled in thought. The silence stretches out a moment, long enough for me to get a bit nervous about what he might say. "You're too nice to customers," he says finally. "And you feel like you have to talk a lot to entertain people."

"Hey!" I say.

"You like talking to old people way too much," he continues. "And you're a little idealistic."

I plant my face into my palm, torn between amusement and aggravation. "You were supposed to say facts about me, not insults."

He raises an eyebrow. "Were any of those untrue?"

I consider them. "I'm not a little idealistic," I say finally. "I'm *extremely* idealistic."

He laughs. "You're right. My bad."

I laugh with him. "I can't help it," I admit. "I don't mean it to be snobby, though. It's just, like . . . I don't know. Don't you ever want your life to be more exciting and like—important?"

"Important how?"

"I don't know. Like when you die, don't you want people to remember you for something?"

"I'll be dead. I'm sure I won't care."

I snort. "You don't get it."

"Nope." He gestures out the front windshield. "Some drunk moron could swerve into our lane and kill us both right now. We wouldn't be any less dead if we were world-famous billionaires."

"Okay, but don't you think we'd be happier right *now* if we were world-famous billionaires? Or even better, if we'd done something important that people would remember us for?"

"I suppose I might be happier if we were rich enough to be driving a McLaren. But otherwise, no."

I study his face. I think he really means that. "Well, I want my life to be meaningful," I say stubbornly.

"And I don't think what makes your life meaningful is what happens after you're dead."

I open my mouth to argue, then close it again.

Huh.

He has a point.

"Hey, you only said four things about me," I realize aloud. "You need to say one more. Maybe one that's slightly less emotionally devastating this time."

He frowns at me thoughtfully for a moment, then nods. "You have a nice ass."

A laugh splutters out of me, embarrassed and pleased. "Good lord," I say, blushing, and lean forward to turn up the music. "Let's do our quiet time now, please."

# CHAPTER 20

The edges of the sky are tinted purple as we pull into Charlotte-town. It's only early in the tourist season, but the streets are still pretty busy. We find a parking spot a few blocks away from the festival and walk over in silence. An hour ago, I might have called it an awkward silence, but after practicing in the car on the way here, I've decided to rename it an amiable silence. And I have to admit, it's pretty nice. Every few minutes, an annoying voice in the back of my head whispers, *Say something!* but I've decided to ignore it. It's nicer just to walk side by side, breathing in the cool, salty air and admiring the fairy lights strung over Charlottetown's main street.

The festival itself takes place on a wide waterfront street lined with shops. They've closed it off to traffic, so people are just wandering around, peering at the menus for the food trucks or looking at the craft booths set up along the street.

"Want to get some food first?" John asks. "And a beer?"

I open my mouth to remind him I don't like beer when I realize he's messing with me. "Ha, ha," I say dryly. "Food first, please."

We do a loop of the street to read the different menus, then I save us a spot at a picnic table while John goes off to order for us. I sit cross-legged on the bench and rest my chin on my hands. Now that the sun is going down, the twinkly lights above the street look even prettier, and someone has started playing guitar outside one of the shops. I take a deep breath and let it out again happily.

I wonder if I would enjoy this moment more if I was famous or a millionaire. My clothes would be nicer, that's for sure, and I'd have a personal makeup artist to do fancy eyeshadow for me. But the lights wouldn't be any twinklier, and the smoke wafting from the food truck grills wouldn't smell any more delicious.

Still, I don't think it's wrong to want a job that I love. My NYU and internship applications flash in my mind, but I push the thought away. It's such a long shot, honestly, I don't even want to bother getting my hopes up. Plus . . . my eyes drift to John, who's approaching with two cans of soda in one hand and a carefully balanced pile of cardboard take-out containers in the other.

Maybe it wouldn't be so bad to stay in Waldon a little while.

"What're you looking at?" John asks, as he sits down opposite me.

I clear my throat. "Just those shops there." I point. "I wonder if I'd like owning a shop. Thanks," I add, taking my food from him.

"What would you sell?"

"Good question. Clothes, maybe. Or jewelry." Though even as I say it, it sounds kind of dull. I like clothes and jewelry well enough, but I don't think I'd actually want to make them. "Ooh, or maybe I could own a bakery!"

"Can you bake?"

"Well . . . no. I mean, a little, but nothing fancy. But I could go to culinary school. That would be fun, wouldn't it? Like going to school, but your homework is cookies."

John laughs. "I don't think that's what culinary school is like. My sister's friend did it, and she said it was a lot of, like, food costing and learning back-of-house stuff. Plus a lot of butchery."

I grimace. "Okay, that sounds less fun." I take a bite of my food, a spicy curry dish. "Oh man, this is good," I say. Then, through a mouthful, "Is your sister older than you, or younger?"

"Two years older. You have any siblings?"

I shake my head. "Only child. But my cousins lived next door to us when I was growing up, so I didn't turn into one of those weird only children who don't know how to share."

John snorts into his soda. "Is that a thing?"

"It's called Only Child Syndrome," I tell him. "It's this theory by some ancient psychologist that says that all only children are destined to be spoiled, selfish brats. I wrote a paper about it in high school."

"That's so random," he says.

"Yes, well. Welcome to my brain."

John laughs. We eat in (amiable) silence, then throw our trash away and wander around the booths. Most of it is a bit too crafty for my taste, but I do buy a box of homemade chocolates.

"For my movie marathon," I explain to John. "What are your plans for the rest of the week?" I add, as we move on to wait in line for one of the most popular booths, which seems to sell some kind of jewelry.

"Just working on the race car."

"Oh, right. You do . . . racing stuff?"

John laughs. "Yes. Just at the local track. Me and my buddies have an old Nissan we run."

"So you race against other people?"

"Mm. I mostly take care of the car stuff. My buddy Tim does most of the driving. You should come out to a track day sometime."

I raise a teasing eyebrow. "Are you sure you want to commit to a second date before this one's even over? Things could go south from here, you know. I might tell you I'm in a cult or something."

"Are you?"

"No. But you might've agreed to go out with me again before you knew that, see? First dates," I add wisely, "are like interviews. You wouldn't hire someone halfway through an interview. HR wouldn't allow it."

John stares at me, a mix of amusement and incredulity on his face. "You're so weird."

I open my mouth to retort, but we've reached the front of the line. The owner of the booth, a pretty woman with light brown skin and tightly curled hair, smiles at us.

"Hi, there," she says.

I smile back. "Hi."

"What do you think of this stuff?" John asks, pointing at the table.

I lean closer to inspect the jewelry laid out on the table. It's actually really cool, sort of gothic and dainty at the same time, like a delicate silver ring with a tiny skull carved into it, or a miniature medieval-looking sword hanging from a very fine silver chain.

"It's awesome," I say. "I like that one." I point to the tiny sword. "It looks like something out of *Zelda*."

"Oh, good," John says, with a strange smile on his face. Then he gestures to the booth owner. "This is my sister, Kiara, by the way."

All the blood rushes to my face. I smack John hard on the arm. "Oh my god." I cover my face with one hand. "What if I said I didn't like it?"

"I would've laughed."

"You're such an ass, John," his sister says, laughing.

"He really is," I agree. "Nice to meet you," I add, holding out my hand. "I'm Emily."

"Oh, I know," she says. "John's told me all about you."

I raise a doubtful eyebrow. "He has?"

She snorts. "Okay, not really. Just that you two were coming tonight. He doesn't ever tell me anything interesting."

I grin. That makes more sense. "Did you make all this your-self?" I ask, gesturing to the table.

"Yep. I sell stuff on Etsy and in a few shops around town."

"That's awesome."

Kiara shrugs. "Eh, it's just a way to pass the time. I'm stuck on the island until my dumb husband finishes vet school."

"Vet school," I echo. "That's so cool."

"Maybe that should be your dream job," John says.

I wrinkle my nose at him. "I don't think I could ever put dogs down. I'd wind up crying as much as their owners every time."

"Same," Kiara says. "Unless they were tiny yappy dogs."

"Hey!" I protest. "My parents have a tiny yappy dog, and the little maniac's kind of grown on me. He's, like, an overly violent, overgrown rat. But in a cute way."

Kiara cackles. "Ooh, I like her," she says to John.

"Oh, good, because your approval is super important to me," he says.

"Shoo," Kiara says, waving him away. "Unless you're going to buy something, go bother someone else."

"I'll buy something," I say. It's not a great idea, given my current bank balance, but I really like Kiara's stuff. Plus, it would seem rude not to buy something.

"Don't give her money just to be polite," John says. "She's only pretending to be a hippie jewelry maker. She's actually a drug rep."

"Yeah, a Canadian drug rep for boring diabetes drugs," Kiara says. "I'm not swimming in cash like the Viagra reps in the States."

I laugh. "No, I want to. I really like the tiny sword necklace."

"Yeah?" Kiara holds it up. "I made it after watching that old *Sword in the Stone* cartoon."

"Ooh, I remember that movie!"

"Which one was that?" John asks. "The one with the depressed unicorn?"

Kiara and I roll our eyes in unison. "That was *The Last Unicorn*," I say.

"Obviously," Kiara adds.

I grin at her and then reach in my pocket for my wallet, but John waves me away. "I've got it."

"Oh—no, really—" I protest.

"Please, let him pay," Kiara cuts in. "I was going to give it to you for free, but this way I get some of John's money."

"How much is it?" I ask uncertainly.

"Depends. John, how much cash have you got?"

"I can see the price tag," he says, handing her a twenty.

"But can you not read?" Kiara asks. "Because it says twenty-five."

"Family discount," John retorts, but he gives her a five-dollar bill anyway.

Kiara turns away to wrap the necklace up in a tiny cloth bag and then hands it to me with a smile. "Nice meeting you, Emily. You seem really nice, although you've obviously got weird taste in men."

"Nice to meet you too."

I kind of want to add something like, "See you around," or blurt out "Can we please be friends?" but instead I manage to smile like a normal person and follow John to the next booth.

"Your sister's so cool," I say wistfully, looking over my shoulder at her. "I wish I could make jewelry like that."

John laughs. "You wish you could do a lot of things."

"I know. There are just too many options! How does anyone find their calling in life when there's literally a million different careers? And what if you *do* find your calling, but by the time you realize it, you're too old to do it?" I sigh. "It's overwhelming."

"Maybe you should think less about it," John says. "Or stop looking so hard."

"Maybe. Like how people say you'll only meet your soulmate after you've totally given up looking."

John makes a face. "Who says that?"

"The people in my cult."

It makes him laugh, like I was hoping it would. I laugh with him, then stifle a yawn.

"You want to head home?" John asks.

"Is that okay?" I ask. "I swear I'm having fun, I just usually go to bed at ten like a loser."

"I don't think that makes you a loser. Let's go."

We head up the street, waving at Kiara as we pass by, and walk back to the parking lot. Another silence has fallen between us, but this one feels slightly charged, almost electric. We're getting into end-of-date territory, now.

My feet slow as we approach the car. I'm not sure why, but I want to do this now, not after he's driven me home. "This was fun,"

I say. After the low rumble of the crowd at the festival, my voice sounds loud in the quiet side streets.

"It was," John agrees.

After another few steps, I stop walking altogether. John stops walking, too, and turns to face me. We're standing in the middle of a parking lot, and there's a woman loading boxes into a van nearby, but I don't care. This night was nothing like I expected. It was— quieter. And more relaxing. And really, really fun.

My heart is pulsing in my ears, and the tips of my fingertips feel prickly. "You still want me to come watch you race sometime?" I ask.

John nods. "Definitely."

I lick my lips. "Maybe you could come over for a movie marathon before that. We could watch *The Last Unicorn* and *The Sword in the Stone.*"

"Sounds horrible," John says. "I'm in."

I take a half-step closer to him. "Cool."

"Cool," he agrees.

The corners of his lips turn up, and then he steps closer and puts his hands on my waist. I can smell his bonfire-smoke cologne, along with a faint scent of gasoline that reminds me of being in the shop. I slide my arms over his shoulders and look up at him, waiting.

There's a single, delicious moment of tension, then he leans down and brushes his mouth over mine. His lips are dry and warm, his stubble rough and prickly. He kisses like he talks, slow and lazy, and I press myself against him, feeling a sort of arching deep inside me.

He pulls back first, but I wrap my arms around his neck and

kiss him again, chasing the light, giddy feeling that's spreading through my chest.

We stay that way until the woman loading boxes drops one with a loud curse. We break apart, breathless and grinning, and head to his car. It's a thirty-five minute drive back to Waldon, but neither of us says a word. I feel no need to break the silence. This silence is perfect—this silence is *sparkly*. I sink comfortably into the car seat and lean my head against the window, smiling as I watch the dark road slip by.

# CHAPTER 21

A late-spring storm descends on the island the next morning, buffeting my bedroom window with erratic splatters of rain. I was hoping to get an early-morning run in, but that's okay. Nothing can dampen my spirits today.

I roll out of bed, shower, and plait my wet hair into a French braid, then I make a pot of coffee and flop down happily into my couch. Every so often, I remember last night and a little fizzy burst of energy shoots through me.

I kissed *John*.

As I sip my first cup of coffee, I take out my phone and open Wordle. John isn't working at the shop today—he's taking a vacation day to go to a dentist appointment in Charlottetown—so there's no point waiting until lunch to do it.

LIKES, I type in. As in, John *likes* me.

Shoot. All gray.

SHOCK. As in, I'm still shocked at how great our date was.

Damn it. Nothing again.

Okay, maybe it's time to stop using romantic words.

I go back to my usual boring, sensible method and within a few minutes, I've figured out the right word. TRAIN, for three hundred and twenty-three days!

I sink back into the couch, grinning at my phone. I should text John and see if he's done Wordle yet. Or would that seem too eager? We just went out last night. Maybe I should wait for him to text first.

I spend about fifteen minutes waffling on it, then another fifteen trying to craft the perfect casual text. Then I catch sight of the time and realize I'm wasting my whole morning on this. I shake my head at myself and put my phone down determinedly.

Yes, my date with John was great, but I'm not going to be one of those people who makes their whole life about a relationship. Like Martha, back in university. The first two years of school, all she ever talked about was how much she wanted to be a self-help guru. She used to drive us all bonkers, actually, always looking down on us for eating sugar ("That's literally more addictive than meth") or getting annoyed when we wouldn't read all the books she recommended. They all had titles like *Winner, Winner: Five Foolproof Life Hacks to Become an Instant Success Story* or *The Happiness Game: Ten Secrets from the World's Happiest People*. I actually tried to read that one, but I didn't make it past secret number one: "Put down your morning coffee." Honestly, if that's the secret to happiness, I think I'd rather die miserable.

Anyway, then Martha met her husband, Jason, and we literally never heard about any of it again. All she ever talked about was Jason. Fallon actually made a drinking game out of it. If Martha said Jason's name more than twenty times in a day, we all had to take a shot.

We eventually had to stop, because we were getting wasted, like, every night.

So, yeah. I definitely don't want to be like that. Which means I can't stop trying to sort my life out just because of one tiny little (amazing) date with John.

I finish another cup of coffee (I'm officially losing at *The Happiness Game*) and spend the rest of the morning making a homemade card for Divya to congratulate her on her pregnancy, and another for Martha, whose third child should be born in a few weeks. I even call the bank to get a new debit card, since the tap function on mine stopped working a few months ago. And if I daydream a little about John while the bank has me on hold, well, that's nobody's business but mine.

At nine, I head into the shop. There are about fifteen phone messages waiting for me—I guess the whole town woke up and realized that it's almost summer and they should really get their snow tires taken off—and the first three customers of the day are kind of impatient, but today, I don't care at all. Time flies by in bright, happy bursts, and when I'm not reminiscing about all the best bits of my date with John, I'm planning out the next event for the museum, which I'm going to do on Canada Day. I want to make this one even bigger than the last one. Our final tally of guests for the Barrel Into Summer event was eighty-eight. On Canada Day, I'm determined to break a hundred.

At lunchtime, I pop down to the grocery store. Jim and Mrs. Finnamore both need a few things, and I buy myself a bunch of discount candy and chocolate.

In the checkout line, my phone dings with a text.

[12:14] **John:** how's it going?

My heart does a somersault in my chest.

[12:15]: Good!

[12:15]: Just buying my body weight's worth of candy at the grocery store

[12:15]: Snacks for my movie marathon tonight 😊

[12:17] **John:** Heath Ledger movies, right?

[12:17]: Nope, changed my mind

[12:17]: Nostalgic movies

[12:17]: Although I'll probably watch A Knight's Tale

[12:17]: That's Heath Ledger AND nostalgia

[12:17]: (And yes, I know I'm weird.)

[12:18] **John:** lol

[12:18] **John:** sounds fun

I glance up to make sure I'm not holding up the line, then shift my weight from foot to foot. Should I invite him to join me? Or would that be too weird? Normally I would space dates out more. Although that's because I usually find it kind of tiring being with someone that much. Like I feel that I have to be extra peppy and entertaining or something.

I don't feel that way with John. Things with him are somehow . . . different.

[12:20]: You're welcome to join if you want

[12:20]: Though I will make you watch The Last Unicorn.

I don't even have time to get properly nervous before John's answer pops up.

[12:20] **John:** sure

[12:20] **John:** sounds good

I grin down at the words.
Easy, I realize. That's how things are different.
Things with John just feel *easy*.

EASY OR NOT, having John inside my house is definitely kind of weird. Not weird in a *bad* way, but it's just a little bizarre, like seeing a penguin in the desert. I hang back a few steps and watch him wander the living room, his skin bathed in red from the sunset.

He's super interested in the house and asks me a bunch of questions I don't know the answers to, like when it was built and if it has a drilled well or a dug well.

"How on earth would I know that?" I say.

"You could've asked before you moved in."

"They're charging me two hundred dollars a month. The only question I asked was 'When can I move in?'"

"Two hundred a *month*?" He whistles. "That's insane. This place is incredible."

"I know, right?" I beam around the living room. "I guess they just wanted someone to look after the place while they were gone."

"Is that a wood-burning stove?"

"Yep." I don't add that I've never used it before, because I'm not actually sure I know how to start a fire.

"When d'you think the owners will want it back?"

I grimace. "I don't know. My parents say they really love it in New Mexico, so I think I've got a while longer."

I give him a tour of the rest of the house, beaming every time he points out the cool things I'm secretly hoping he'll notice, like the clawfoot tub in the master bathroom and the huge mahogany desk in the office. I even take him out to the garage, a standalone building set a ways back from the house that I think I've only set foot in once. The garage door hasn't worked since I moved in, so I've never parked my car inside it, and anyway, it's half-full of boxes of the owner's stuff and a bunch of broken lawn furniture.

"Holy shit," John says, staring at the large, cobwebby space like it's the Shangri-La. "This is insane. You could fit a huge workbench in here. And is that another room back there?"

I rise up on my tiptoes. It does look like there's a door hidden behind that pile of boxes. "Maybe."

It takes ten minutes for us to shift enough boxes to see, and another five for John to jimmy the door open. A shower of dust and dead bugs rains down when he finally gets it open, but he doesn't seem to notice.

"There's a whole other space back here," he calls.

I'll have to take his word for it. No way I'm walking through that dead bug shower.

John walks backward on the way back to the main house,

admiring the harbor view. "This place is seriously awesome. You couldn't find something like this in a big city," he adds.

"If you could, it would probably cost about a million dollars."

He snorts. "More like ten or twenty. Cities are insanely overpriced. My buddy in Toronto bought the tiniest two-bedroom apartment for one and a half million."

"Is that the one whose wedding you're going to this summer?" I ask, as we step into the kitchen.

"Mm." He peers at the radiator. "Does this place have a wood furnace, or oil?"

"No idea." I ignore his slightly affronted look and swing open the fridge. "Want a drink?"

After John takes a trip to the basement to confirm that it's an oil furnace, we stretch out on the couch with sodas and popcorn and I pull up our first nostalgic movie of the night—*A Knight's Tale*. I'm kind of expecting John to be one of those guys who's too cool for any movie that isn't a dark action film or violent thriller, but once again, he surprises me. He pays attention the whole time, even if he does have a habit of forgetting which characters are which. "Who's that guy?" is his constant refrain. In anyone else, it might be annoying, but with John it just makes me laugh.

"That's Heath Ledger," I say, for the fourth time. "He's the main guy."

"Ah." John nods. "He looks different now."

He definitely doesn't, but I just roll my eyes and hold my hand out for the popcorn bowl. He hands it to me without taking his eyes off the screen, frowning at Heath Ledger like he still secretly suspects it's a different character. I hide a smile.

My eyes linger on him a few moments more, watching the lights of the TV move over his skin. It's still a bit weird seeing him out of his work clothes. In a T-shirt and jeans, you can really notice things like the swell of his biceps and strong lines of his neck.

He notices me watching him, and something shifts in the air as our eyes meet. There's a pleasant warmth stirring inside me, but I just smile and turn back to the movie. It's more fun this way, letting the tension build naturally.

The last guy I slept with was someone I met online and had a few dates with over the winter. He was nice enough, don't get me wrong, but it all felt so dreadfully formulaic. Plus, I think he must've read somewhere that girls really get turned on by kissing. I like a good make-out session as much as the next girl, but this was, like, *forty-five minutes* of kissing. I kept trying to move things along, but he kept pulling my hands away and murmuring cringey things like, "There's no rush" and "We've got all night." I wanted to say, yeah, dude, I know we've got all night, so let's move along to the fun stuff, please.

I probably shouldn't be so harsh. I could tell he had good intentions, but I was so bored by the first ten minutes that he wound up doing the opposite of what I'm sure he intended.

I can already tell it won't be like that with John. Over the next hour, we slowly drift closer together. I shift on the couch to lean against his shoulder. He puts his hand on my leg. I trace my fingertips over his arm. His thumb moves over my knee.

By the end of the movie, we both totally know where this is going, but I like that he asks me anyway.

"Do you want me to head out?"

I look up at him with a grin. "What's a five-letter word for 'hell no'?"

Laughing, he pulls me closer and captures my lips in his. I throw a leg over his knees, straddling him on the couch. Our kisses are bright and breathless, his hands warm as they slide down my back. They move lower, strong fingers digging into my flesh, and then he pulls me against him, a rhythmic, dizzying friction. He scrapes his lips over the shell of my ear, and a breath of startled laughter slips from my lips. He laughs too; I think he knows just how I'm feeling. For a year we worked side by side, barely polite acquaintances. Now his warm, bare skin is sliding against mine, and my breathing is ragged in his ear, and it's all the more intimate after being strangers for so long.

His mouth moves down my neck, over my collarbone; a noise slips from my throat as it moves lower still, his tongue moving over raised flesh. My bra is on the floor—I vaguely remember discarding it—and the rest of our clothes follow shortly after. We break apart so I can hunt down a condom, and I laugh again as I sprint naked through the house, giggling harder as I duck under the windows.

"You're so weird," John says, laughing with me as I hop back on the couch.

"Yeah, yeah," I say with a grin. A moment later, he pulls me back into his lap, and my laughter gives way to soft, shallow panting. His hands are on my hips again, recapturing that steady rhythm, but now there's nothing between us. Everything gets hot and blurry, my world narrowing down to John's skin, his fingers, his lips. He's very quiet—not surprising—but I can feel his breathing changing as our movements become quicker. Then my head is on his shoulder, and I'm crying out and clutching him, and his groan is a rumble I feel inside my bones.

I come back to myself in stages, finally shifting my weight to collapse beside him on the couch. We're not touching anymore, but we're both breathless and grinning.

"That was fun," he says, and I laugh, because what a very John way to put it.

"Very fun," I agree. "Want to stay over tonight? Have some more fun later?"

He grins and echoes my words from earlier. "What's a five-letter word for 'hell yes'?"

# CHAPTER 22

Have you ever had one of those nights where you sleep really, really well? Like, you wake up and all of the aches and pains you didn't even really notice were bothering you are totally gone, and all your limbs feel loose and liquidy and warm?

Well, that's how I feel waking up the next morning. Like all of my insides have turned into warm, shimmery goo.

I stretch my arms out and roll over in bed to face John. He's sleeping on his side, with one hand resting loosely near his pillow. My gaze moves over his fingers, remembering the strength in them, remembering the way they felt moving over my skin. The night comes back to me in flashes—the slide of his mouth over my neck, the feel of the hard planes of his chest, the sound of our laughter. It was easy and intimate and *wonderful*, and I can't remember if I've ever felt so relaxed waking up next to someone before.

"Morning," he says, stirring.

"Morning."

He scrubs a hand over his face, blinking blearily. "Have you just been lying there staring at me?"

"Yep."

"That's super creepy."

I grin. "Yep."

He laughs and pulls me toward him, one strong arm wrapping around my waist. I slide my leg between his and run my hands up his chest, and it's some time before we make it out of bed.

Later, we sit down on the couch to tackle the day's Wordle, balancing our breakfast plates on our knees.

"What word are you starting with?" I ask.

"TOAST," he says, taking a bite of it as he speaks.

I laugh. "I'll do BACON."

I type it in, and—

No.

No way.

It's *right*!

I've never gotten it on the first guess before, not once!

I try to hide my reaction so I don't ruin the answer for John, but he notices anyway.

"Was that right? BACON?"

I grin and show him my phone. "Yep."

"Awesome," he says, then he puts his phone away without typing the answer in. I smile at him fondly. What a weirdo.

He heads to the shop early to align the tuning on his race car's differential (okay, fine, I wasn't actually listening when he said what he was going to do) and I get ready for work in a fizzy, sparkly state, like a glass of champagne in human form.

I'm a teensy bit nervous about how things will be at work—what if it's super awkward now that we've slept together? What if Fred somehow finds out and fires us for being unprofessional?—but to my relief, not much changes. John and Dave work on cars, I check people in and out. Only now, when John comes out to the front desk to write out receipts, he grins at me in this warm, easy way that makes me want to spin around in my chair.

Dave heads home around five, and shortly after, I close up the front part of the shop and head back to the garage to say goodbye to John, who's still working. The garage is so packed full of cars right now, I can't even see where he's at.

"I'm heading out," I call, in the direction of the clanging.

His head pops up from behind a dark blue car in the corner. "Oh yeah?"

"I've got a hot date with a ninety-six-year-old," I say. "Try to not be too jealous."

He laughs. "I'll try."

I hesitate. "I'd come kiss you goodbye, but there are about five million cars in the way."

"It's good, right?" he says, looking around at them. "I told all the local racers they could bring their cars here for stuff instead of going into the city. Fred is pissed."

"Why would he be pissed? Isn't this a lot more business?"

John rolls his eyes. "He's worried I'm bringing in a 'bad crowd.' I think everything he knows about racing comes from watching ten minutes of one of the *Fast and the Furious* movies on a plane."

I step carefully over some huge car part on the floor and start to pick my way toward him. "You like this sort of stuff more, yeah? Race car . . . stuff?"

He laughs. "Yeah. I'd like to do some dyno tuning and bolt-ons and stuff like that, but you know." He shrugs. "Fred."

"Which car is yours?"

"This one." He thumps the side of the dark blue car he's working on, then reaches out to help me balance as I shimmy around a hulking piece of machinery.

"It's . . . nice," I say uncertainly, peering at it. He raises an amused eyebrow. "Well, the color is nice," I amend. "Is it fast?"

He chuckles. "Not right now. The whole engine's shot. Over-heated at the last race."

"Bummer."

"Eh, it happens. I'm kind of looking forward to fixing it."

"Er . . . why? No, I'm serious," I add, laughing, as he gives me a dry look. "I want to understand."

He shrugs. "I don't know, it's just fun. Like, you found it really satisfying watching all those annoying kids having fun with your exhibit at the museum, right?" I nod. "Well, it's the same thing. This engine is totally shot, but I'm going to figure out why, fix it, and get it up and running again."

I lean forward to look under the hood. I suppose it is kind of interesting, thinking about how all those pieces work together. "How are you going to sort out what's wrong?"

I listen as he describes something called a compression test, pointing to different bits of the engine, and walking me through what each of them does. It's strange, because I've heard him talk about cars a million times before, but for the first time, I can hear the quiet passion in his words. He really does love this work—and it seems like he's really good at it.

"How'd you learn all of this?" I ask.

He chuckles. "Some of it at school, but most of it from just messing around. When Kiara and I were in high school, our dad bought us an old 2003 Jag to drive to school. He doesn't know much about cars," he adds ruefully. "I think he just thought it looked flashy. Anyway, Mom was pissed. She always said we were never going to get a car, because she didn't want us to become pretentious brats."

I laugh. "Your mom's awesome."

"Yeah. She's also an evil genius, because when she saw Dad roll up with one of the world's most unreliable cars, she said that we could keep it, so long as Kiara and I took care of any issues by ourselves. She made us learn how to change the oil and the tires and everything, and then just waited patiently for it to break down—which it did, like, a week after we got it." He grins. "It took me a year to get it running again. I basically had to rebuild the whole engine."

"And you were hooked," I say.

"Something like that."

"Do you still have the car?"

John snorts. "Hell, no. I sold it the day after I got it running again. Kiara and I split the money. I bought a cheaper, less shitty car, and she got a tattoo."

"Man." I shake my head. "She's so cool."

"She definitely isn't."

"Well, *I* think she is. I'd hang out with her in a heartbeat," I add wistfully.

He raises an eyebrow. "So, why don't you?"

"What?"

"I can give you her number. Just text her and see if she wants to grab coffee or whatever."

I shift uncertainly. "You think she'd want to?"

"I don't know, probably." He shrugs. "Can't hurt to ask, can it?"

"I guess not." I take my phone out. "Hit me."

I type her number in as John dictates it and then open a new text. "'Hey, Kiara—'"

"You're doing it now?" John asks, amused.

"Before I lose my nerve," I say. "Now hush. 'Hey, Kiara,'" I read aloud as I type, "'this is Emily—we met the other night.'"

"She knows who you are."

"'I hope it's okay John gave me your number—'"

"Why would she care?"

"'—but I wanted to text and see if you maybe wanted to grab coffee sometime this week, or whenever works. No pressure if you're busy! And sorry if this is super random!'"

"Good lord."

"It's polite!" I argue, as I click send.

"It's deranged. You know you don't have to apologize for politely asking someone to coffee, right?"

"I know I don't *have* to. But she probably has tons of cool friends to hang out with. Plus, I don't want her to feel, like, obligated to hang out with me just because you and I are—" I clear my throat hastily. "You know, just because we went out once."

He snorts. "She won't feel like that. And she doesn't have that many friends. Why do you assume everyone's life is so much cooler than yours?"

"Because it probably is."

"Your life is cool. Not your barrel obsession, I mean. That's still super lame. But Trey and Rose are pretty cool, and I can see why you like that Jim guy."

"He's great, isn't he?"

"Mm." John nods. "You shouldn't stress so much about stuff."

My lips twist into a reluctant smile. "Maybe you're right."

"Oh, I'm definitely right."

"Yeah, yeah." We grin at each other for a few seconds, then I rise on my toes to kiss him goodbye. It's nothing more than a quick brush of my lips against his, but the warm scrape of stubble does shivery things to my insides. His hands settle on my lower back and his thumbs slide under the hem of my shirt, and before long we're full-on making out against the front door of his car. He pulls me hard against him, and I slide my hands under his shirt, digging my fingers into the warm, strong muscles of his back.

I never really saw the appeal of having sex in public places—do people not realize how many germs there are everywhere?—but a thought is stirring in the back of my mind. I break apart from John and reach behind me for the door handle. "Ever done it in your race car?" I ask with a grin.

Then I pull open the door and go still.

Um . . .

Huh.

There's only one seat in this car. The rest of it is literally just a hollowed-out piece of metal. And the driver's seat is insanely tiny. Seriously, how does John even fit in there?

"I don't think anyone's ever done it in a race car," he says, looking amused. "At least not without removing the roll cage."

I peer at the thick black bars that crisscross through the whole car, halving the already limited space. "Any chance that can be done in, like, five minutes?"

"Nope."

"Hmm." I look around a little helplessly. "Maybe . . . on the hood?"

"You do know this whole place has security cameras," John says.

"I . . . did not. Does anyone actually look at them?"

"Fred can. I don't know if he actually *does*, but . . ."

I grimace. Yeah, I seriously do not want Fred having access to a sex tape of me.

"Maybe this isn't the best idea," I admit.

"Maybe you should come by my place later," John says. "After your hot date, I mean."

I laugh and lean up to give him another kiss. "That sounds good."

# CHAPTER 23

John's apartment is on the top floor of a large brick building off Main Street. I find a parking spot not far from the barrel museum and walk along the sidewalk with my hands shoved in my pockets and my head tilted back to admire the pink-and-gold sky. The air smells delicious, like sea salt and freshly cut grass. My chest feels light and airy, like there's more space in it or something. Only half of it is because of John. The other half is because of the text Kiara sent me earlier, saying she'd love to have coffee and asking if tomorrow morning would be too soon. Apparently she's gotten addicted to this hazelnut cappuccino the local bakery makes and has been going there every morning for weeks. Maybe, if we hit it off, morning coffee will be our thing (even if I do plan on buying the ninety-nine-cent black coffee rather than a five-dollar cappuccino).

The building John lives in is a tiny bit run-down, but his apartment is actually really nice. The floors are hardwood and the ceilings have a cool, sort of old-fashioned molding pattern, and there's one exposed-brick wall that gives the whole place an artsy vibe. There are a few big squashy couches in the living room and mismatched rugs strewn around haphazardly and a small balcony in the back overlooking the harbor.

I wander around while John opens a bottle of wine, peering into the bathroom (surprisingly neat), the closet (unsurprisingly messy), and finally the bedroom, which has big windows, a king-size bed, and—

Hang on.

Is that a *fish tank*?

"What?" John calls from the kitchen. He must have heard my excited gasp.

"You have *fish*!" I holler back.

A moment later, he appears in the doorway. "I have fish," he agrees.

"They're so cute!" I peer at them through the glass. One of them is tiny and golden, one is orange and pointy, and the third one is a gorgeous shimmery color and half-hidden between two rocks. "What are their names?"

"They don't have names."

I gape at him. "You haven't *named* them?"

"No. That one's a *Rasbora*—"

"A raspberry?"

"And that's a swordtail—"

"That tail looks nothing like a sword."

"And the one back there's a *Geophagus*."

"Those are all terrible names."

"They're not names, they're species."

I roll my eyes. "Well can I give them better names?"

"Nope."

"C'mon," I wheedle. "I'll come up with really good ones."

He shakes his head. "Not going to happen."

"Why not?"

"Do you like it when people name their cars?"

I pull a face. "God, no."

"Well, that's how I feel about people naming fish. You don't name your car, I don't name my fish."

I sigh and relent. "Sorry, boys," I tell the fish. "If one of you starts drowning, I'll have no way of telling John which one of you it is."

"Fish don't drown. And you can use their species names."

"Raspberry sherbet, sword in the stone . . . geophysicist?"

John laughs. "You can call them Fish 1, Fish 2, and Fish 3. That's the best I can do."

I grin. "I'll take it."

We spread out on his couch to sip on wine and pick at half a leftover pizza he found in his fridge. We make noises about watching something on Netflix, but in the end we just wind up chatting a while. He tells me about all the local racers who have brought their cars to the shop, and all the different race car services (or, as he and the racers call them, "performance car services") he wants to convince Fred to offer at the shop, and I tell him about the flowers Mrs. Finnamore is going to help me plant this summer around my house.

As we talk, I'm struck by the same feeling I had the other night. Being with John is just so easy. I don't feel like I have to be cute or funny or sexy or interesting. I *can* be, if I want to, but I don't *have* to be—and that makes all the difference.

"Did you have a good time with Jim?" he asks, as he gets up to get rid of the empty pizza box.

"Yeah. He showed me all these old photos of him and his wife from their wedding day in 1949. I took some pictures of them."

I hold my phone out to show him the black-and-white photos. "Aren't they cool?"

John takes the phone from my hand. "Damn—look at that old Porsche. Is that a 356?" He zooms in on the blurry picture. "I think it is."

"I can ask him."

"That's awesome. See, now I understand why you like old people."

I snort. "Yeah, exactly. It's all for the cars."

He laughs and heads off to the bathroom. I scroll through the pictures again. Jim and his wife were an insanely good-looking couple—she looked a little like Julie Andrews, and he had this really wide, dashing smile—and you can just tell from their photos that they were really in love. In practically every one, they're beaming at each other like they can't believe their own luck.

"Hey, you're staying here tonight, yeah?" John calls. "I can try to hunt you down a toothbrush."

I smile. "Yeah," I call back. "Thanks."

I look down at the pictures again. I've never really thought much about getting married—I still don't feel that fussed about it, to be honest—but I hope that someday I have a stack of photos like this, where anyone who looks at them can tell I was really happy.

And if I happen to be imagining John standing next to me in the photos . . . well, let's just keep that between you and me.

THE NEXT COUPLE of weeks fly by alarmingly quickly. I've somehow gone from having no friends in Waldon to being slightly overwhelmed with them. My early-morning coffee date with Kiara is amazing—she's just as cool as I thought, and really funny and smart—and our morning coffee dates really do become part of my daily routine. It means an extra ten dollars out of my budget every week (even though Kiara keeps rolling her eyes and saying, "Just let me pay, for Christ's sake!"), but it's more than worth it. Trey and I are also spending loads of time together to plan the Canada Day event, and he and Rose have John and me over for dinner twice. John's parents even take us out for a long lunch one day in Summerside. And that's not even mentioning all the time I spend with Jim and Mrs. Finnamore.

I spend nearly every night with John, either at my house or at his apartment. It still amazes me how easy it is to be with him. It's so easy that it almost feels anticlimactic, if that makes sense. I kind of thought that when I met "the one," it would be some grand, dramatic romance. But that's probably the product of watching too many movies. And anyway, isn't this better than drama? Someone you can be totally relaxed around, but can still make you feel all sparkly inside?

On Friday, during a boring hour at work, I decide to text Martha, Divya, and Fallon and see what they think. It's been weeks since I heard from them, and they've all found "the one," haven't they?

I open our group chat.

[10:01] Hey guys!! Hope you're all doing great. Random question for all of you – how did you know your husbands were the one?

I don't expect them to text back right away, so I put away my phone and go back to researching community grants. Trey and I have been talking about building a barrel-themed playground in the backyard, but I had no idea how expensive playground equipment is. I'm sure Shelley would lose her mind if I went to the historical society for money behind her back, so I'm trying to find a grant Trey and I could apply for on our own.

My phone doesn't ding until lunch, but I swipe the notification away without looking at it. John and I are about to start Wordle. I need to be *focused*. My streak is getting tantalizingly close to a year.

"Starting word?" John asks.

"GRANT," I say.

Hmm. Not a bad start. The G is green, and the T is green. The rest of the letters are gray.

BUILD, I try.

Crap. Nothing.

C'mon, brain. *Think*. What's a five-letter word that starts with G and ends with T?

I'm totally blanking. Okay, let's try to eliminate some other letters.

I look at all the letters I haven't used and come up with POWER. The O is yellow, the rest are gray.

G . . . O . . . T.

GOAT. No, that's only four letters.

GLOAT. No, there's no L.

GWOAT. Nope, that's not a word.

"Crap," I mutter.

"What've you got so far?" John asks.

"G, O, and T."

He looks down at his screen and raises an eyebrow. I can't tell if he's got it or not. Damn his inscrutable face!

"Do you have it?" I ask.

"I do now." He types a word. "I had the two letters you don't have."

I chew on my lip.

G, O, T.

"Is there a double letter?" I ask.

"Nope."

My phone dings with a text again, then twice more. I swipe the notifications away impatiently. "Is it a weird word? Something I wouldn't have heard of?"

"Nope."

I carefully run through all the letters I haven't used, trying to guess the second letter, at least. GQ, GW, GY, GS . . .

None of them make any sense.

Argh.

My phone dings again.

"Is that your parents?" John asks. "Are they back from New Zealand?"

"Nah, not for a couple more weeks," I say. I swipe to my texts. "It's just a group chat with my old university friends." I swipe back to Wordle, but a moment later, the bell at the front desk chimes. I look toward it with a sigh. "I should get that."

John nods. "Let me know if you want more hints."

I help the customer out front, who needs a copy of their receipt for their insurance company. By the time I'm done, John's gone back to work as well. I pour myself a cup of coffee and take it to my desk. I stare at Wordle for a little while before I shake my head. I'm totally blocked. Best to come back to it later.

I swipe open the group chat with Fallon, Divya, and Martha to see all the texts I missed.

[12:32] **Fallon:** Oooh, Emily, have you finally found a man?

I roll my eyes. Thanks, Fallon.

[12:32] **Fallon:** Jk girl

[12:32] **Fallon:** Sooo exciting

[12:33] **Fallon:** There's no such thing as the one, though, that's made-up Disney bullshit

[12:41] **Martha:** You're such a cynic, Fallon!

[12:41] **Martha:** Don't listen to her, Em. Soulmates are 100% real. I would know!

I grimace at my phone. Yuck. I think I preferred Fallon's insult.

[12:43] **Divya:** lollll

Okay, that's the least helpful of the three. And that's not saying much, because none of them actually answered my question. I'm frowning at my phone, wondering if it's even worth answering, when it dings again.

> [1:17] **Martha:** Just make sure he has the same family values as you do. That's all that really matters.

The same family values . . . like, if he wants kids or not? He already told me he doesn't think he does, same as me. But it feels like there should be a few more criteria than that for deciding if someone's "the one." The weird clerk at the Waldon liquor store who always stares at my breasts probably doesn't want kids either. Doesn't mean I'm going to wind up with *him*.

Fallon sends an eye-roll emoji.

> [1:18] **Fallon:** That's not ALL that matters

> [1:18] **Fallon:** You need someone who has the same interests as you

> [1:18] **Fallon:** Like me and Ethan

> [1:18] **Fallon:** We both love business and fitness

I drum my fingers on the desk. John and I definitely don't have all the same interests. We have Wordle, yes, but other than that, we're pretty much polar opposites. He likes motorcycle races (spare me), and camping (kill me), and cars (yawn). But I don't think that's necessarily a bad thing. Plus, my tastes are pretty eclectic. I doubt I'm ever going to find a twenty-seven-year-old guy who likes doing puzzles, learning French, and watching *Anne of Green Gables*.

[1:22] Hmm, interesting. Thanks!

(And yes, that's a lie. I'm just being polite, okay?)

[1:22] Divya, what do you think?

Fifteen minutes pass by. I take payments from two customers and answer a few phone calls. I don't know if Divya will answer later, or if she's just ghosting us.

Hang on a second.

*Ghosting.*

GHOST.

I snatch up my phone again and type the word into Wordle. And it's right! GHOST!

I'm doing a victory spin in my chair when John walks in. "What's the celebration for?"

"GHOST," I say triumphantly.

"Nice," he says. "Hey, I'm heading out early, but are we still good for the race tomorrow?"

I stop spinning. I kind of forgot I'd agreed to go to John's car race this weekend. I see now why Fallon said common interests are important. I can't think of any worse way to spend a weekend than standing around some loud, grimy racetrack.

But I promised him I would. And anyway, it's not like he wants to do all the stuff I want to do. (Even though my stuff is awesome, like my *Legend of Zelda* drinking game.)

"Of course," I say. "What time will you pick me up?"

"Practice starts at nine, and I've still got some work to do on the car, so I'll have to leave here at like . . . four?"

*Four?*

In the *morning?*

"Or you could drive up with Kiara. I think she and Jake are leaving here around eight."

I hesitate, trying not to look too eager. "I don't want to miss anything in the morning."

John shrugs. "It's just practice."

Thank god. "Well—okay, then. I mean, if Kiara and Jake don't mind."

"I'm sure it's fine. I'll text them now."

"Thanks. Drive safe tomorrow," I say.

He waves a hand in acknowledgment and heads out the door.

My brain is a bit frazzled from reading about community grants, so I wile away the rest of the day straightening up the office and planning my schedule for the next week. Trey wants to get lunch sometime to do a bit more planning for our Canada Day event, and Jim and Mrs. Finnamore both need their laundry done.

I leave the shop around five and head home. Something is nagging at me as I drive, and for a while I can't figure out what.

I throw my keys on the coffee table and sit down on the couch, swiping open my texts to send Trey a few links about potential community grants. The nagging feeling gets stronger as I reply to a text Kiara sent me offering to ask her craft booth friends to set up booths at our Canada Day event.

[5:37]: That would be amazing!

[5:37]: That's such a good idea! 😊

I would only be exaggerating slightly if I said I have a bigger crush on Kiara than I do on John. She's so witty and clever, and she's thoughtful too. Like when I mentioned to her that I wanted to have cupcakes for the Canada Day event, and two hours later she sent me a text connecting me with her friend Cara, who runs a bakery in Charlottetown.

Something clicks in my brain as I realize what's bothering me. Divya never answered my text in the group chat. My text— "Divya, what do you think?"—is the last one in the thread.

I open the group chat and scroll back through it slowly, going farther and farther. The nagging feeling grows stronger the longer I scroll.

For the last year, the only one who's ever started conversations in this group is me.

I toss my phone aside and go to the kitchen to make some food, but I'm so distracted I'm barely aware of what I'm doing.

I remember how close Martha, Divya, Fallon, and I used to be. We'd go out on weekends and get hangover brunch together afterward, we'd have movie nights at our apartment and commiserate with each other about bad exams, bad breakups, bad days. Sure, we annoyed each other sometimes, but we also had a ton of fun together. We really were best friends. I'm not misremembering it.

But I suppose it's only natural it couldn't last. University was a long time ago now, and we've all gone our different ways and grown into different people. And if I'm being totally honest with myself . . . even if they lived here in Waldon right now, I'm still not sure we'd still be close friends. We're too different now. And it isn't a bad thing, it's just . . . a thing. It's just the way it is. I think I was just trying to hold onto it because I was lonely, or because I felt like I still needed them. Even if what I needed was something they were never going to give me.

I sit down at my kitchen table and take a bite of my dinner. And yuck, okay, I should have paid more attention while I was cooking. I've definitely put sugar on this haddock instead of salt.

Oh, well. I take another bite of sugared fish. This was an important revelation.

My phone dings with a text, and for a split second I wonder if it'll be Divya, saying something that will prove my whole theory wrong. But it isn't. It's Kiara.

> [6:07] **Kiara:** Awesome! We can chat more about it tomorrow—I hear you're riding with us?

> [6:07] If that's okay? 😊

> [6:08] **Kiara:** Duh. Pick you up at eight?

I smile.

> [6:08] Sounds great.

# CHAPTER 24

Motors growl in the distance, and the air is thick with the smell of gasoline and burning rubber. I rise up onto my toes to see the race cars approaching, winding around the last corner of the track.

They roar by, one by one, and I grin a little wider when John's car goes by. He's not actually driving it—his friend Tim does most of the driving—but he's up in the control tower with a radio, giving Tim updates on his lap times and waiting to leap into action whenever there's a pit stop or when the car breaks down (which it's done, like, three times already).

"Are they winning yet?" Kiara asks. She's lying on a blanket on the grass beside me, with her sunglasses on and her hands thrown up over her face to block the sun.

"Nope," I say, sitting back down beside her. "Still second."

It's the third race of the day, and I'm getting better at being able to tell what position John's car is in. It sounds like it would be obvious—if he's the second car that whizzes by, they're in second place, right?

Wrong.

All the cars are in different classes—John and Tim's car is in GT3, which means . . . I don't know, something about the speed—so he's not actually racing everyone that's out on track. And after a few laps, the cars in the slower classes have been passed so much that it's hard to tell who's doing well.

I take a slice of watermelon from the container Kiara brought and turn my face up into the sun. This whole day has been way more fun than I thought it would be. The racetrack has wide green fields and trees all around it, and there's this one slope of grass that overlooks most of the track, so all the spectators (and by that I mean me, Kiara; her husband, Jake; and like twenty other people) sit on blankets or lawn chairs on the grass.

The atmosphere is kind of fun too. It's a community of Johns, people who love talking about cars and looking at cars and thinking about cars, but everyone's really friendly and all the drivers visit each other's trailers to chat between races. And whenever something goes wrong with one of the cars (which happens, like, every ten minutes), people drop by to help out or loan out a tool or replacement part.

When Kiara and Jake and I arrived, we sat in John's trailer for a while, watching people come and go. And I swear I'm not being biased, but it seems like whenever something goes wrong, people want John's opinion. It's kind of cool, seeing how knowledgeable he is—even if I don't understand half of what he's saying.

It's also kind of cool to see him and his friends racing. It's just a small track, but they still drive crazy fast, and it's sort of thrilling when John or Tim pass another car (sorry, "overtake" another car—no one here calls it passing) or win a race. Meanwhile, Kiara and I nibble on snacks she brought from home, and Jake tells us stories about vet school, and it's all just really lovely and fun.

Kiara and Jake make a really good couple. She's super cool, and he's sort of nerdy, so they kind of balance each other out. They bicker a lot—we got a bit lost on the drive down and I thought

Kiara was going to murder him—but you can tell it's just their way of communicating with each other.

"How long have you two been married?" I ask.

"Too long," Kiara says.

"Seven years," Jake answers.

"Wow." I take a bite of watermelon. "When did you know Kiara was the one?" I ask Jake. I say it in a teasing way, like I'm not seriously asking, but Kiara isn't fooled.

"Ooh, thinking John might be the one, are we?" she teases.

"No," I lie. "We've only been dating, like, a few weeks."

She shrugs. "You don't need much longer than that to figure out if someone's right for you. It's a total gut thing. If you don't feel it right away, you never will. Like with you. I knew right away that we could be friends. And with Jake, I knew right away that he was a boring nerd who I should avoid at all costs."

"Joke's on you, you married me," Jake says.

"Only for the money."

"I haven't made any money yet."

"Yeah, but you will," Kiara says. "The minute you graduate, I'm putting you to work."

I fall silent for a moment, thinking. "So it's really just a gut thing, you think?"

"Yep. Look, are you and John happy together? Don't think about it, just answer yes or no."

I bite my lip. "Yes."

She shrugs. "So that's that."

My brow wrinkles. "It isn't that simple, though. I think I could be happy with a lot of people, for a little while. I could date you for a few weeks and be perfectly happy."

She puts her hands to her heart. "Aw."

"But that doesn't mean you can be happy with someone *forever*. Tons of people get married, and they're happy for years, but then it doesn't last. Er—no offense," I add hastily. "I just don't know how you can ever know for sure that you'll be happy with someone forever."

Kiara takes a bite of watermelon. She's still lying down, so the juices run down her cheeks into her hair. She sits up and wipes it off with the back of her hand. "Look, you want to know what I think the real secret is to being happy with someone in the long term?"

"*The* secret?" Jake says. "This ought to be good."

I smother a smile. "Tell us."

Kiara pushes her sunglasses up. "Your happiness cannot depend on them. So many people think it's their partner's job to make them happy, and that's just total bullshit. Jake makes me happy, but it's not his *job*. It's my job to make me happy. Just like it's his job to make himself happy. Our individual happiest lives will either be compatible or they won't. Take John." She gestures toward the racetrack, where John's car is thundering around the last corner. "His happiest life is living in Waldon and doing shit like this and working in the shop. Is your own happiest life compatible with that, or not?"

I hesitate. That was part of why I didn't want to have a crush on John in the first place, because I felt like he wasn't the type of guy who would fit into my dream life. But things are different now. Aren't they? I know John so much better. And things between us are really, really good.

Still, do I really think I can build a life in Waldon that will make me truly happy? Because if I can't, then Kiara's right—it doesn't matter if John might be the one. I won't be happy in my own right, and even if I can push it aside for a while, resentment will start to bleed in. I'll start to blame him for my unhappiness, even though, like Kiara says, my happiness is not his job. It's my job to build a life that makes me happy. So can I do that in Waldon, or not?

"I think so," I say.

Kiara raises an eyebrow. "Better make sure," she says. For the first time, I hear a hint of older-sister-protectiveness creeping into her tone. "John may be a bit of an idiot, but he's one of the good ones. And he really likes you."

I watch the cars slow down and file into the pit lane. The race is over; I'm not sure if John's car won. I stand up and walk a few steps away from Kiara and Jake, watching John approach the car as Tim gets out and pulls his helmet off. They chat for a few minutes, laughing about something. John spots me watching and gives me a thumbs-up, and I feel a strange twisting in my gut.

I glance back at Kiara, and I think about all our coffee dates, and how I already feel like she's one of the best friends I've ever had. Then I think about Jim, who called me his guardian angel last week when I went with him to the cemetery to visit his wife's grave. I think about the guided tour I gave last week to a bunch of kids from Mr. Peterson's school, and how much fun they all had with the new exhibit, and how Trey and I are working on setting up summer classes for kids.

I do think I could make a life for myself here. I really do. But there's a prickly thread of uneasiness underneath my contentment, something I can't quite pinpoint or name.

John walks toward me, looking happy and handsome. "Having fun?"

I draw up a smile. "Definitely."

"Cooler than a barrel museum."

I make an indignant noise. "As if."

He leans down and casually brushes his lips over mine. I lean into the kiss, trying to wash away the strange, prickly feeling inside me.

"I've got to check a few things and then I'm going to run to the food truck to grab us some tacos," he says. "You want anything else?"

I shake my head. "Nope. Thanks."

But as I watch him walk away, his innocuous question swims around in my brain. I've got a great boyfriend who totally gets me, a volunteer job I've fallen in love with, and a group of friends who feel a little more like family with every passing day.

*Do* I want anything else?

# CHAPTER 25

Over the next few days, summer hits the island with a vengeance. Every morning is dazzlingly bright and warm, every songbird has come out singing, and Kiara and I swap our hot coffee for iced coffee and start planning picnics on the beach. I'm going to invite Rose along, since I just know that she and Kiara will hit it off (and because I have a secret plan to merge all my tiny friend families into one).

The Canada Day event is right around the corner, and John has been putting in nearly as much time on it as I have. We're still spending almost every night together, and the prickly feeling I felt at the racetrack has almost completely gone away. I don't even know what it was about. John is the perfect boyfriend. Like, the other day, he actually cleaned out a drawer at his apartment for my stuff, without acting like it was a big deal at all. And then when I mentioned to him that I was thinking I'd stay around Waldon a while longer, he gave me this casual shrug and said, "That'd be cool"—but then I caught him grinning to himself as he made us coffee. It makes my heart fizzy just remembering it.

Honestly, I'm probably just not used to things being so easy. I remember my university boyfriend throwing a fit when I put a thing of floss in the bathroom cabinet at his house. He said it felt like I was trying to move in with him.

(With a thing of *floss*.)

(Which I wouldn't have had to put there, by the way, if he ever bought floss for himself.)

So, yeah. That prickly feeling obviously has nothing to do with John himself. And it's basically gone now, anyway.

On Wednesday, the week before the Canada Day event, I spend most of my day at the shop running through my event checklist for the millionth time and trying to figure out if I've missed anything. Craft booths, check. Food and drinks, check. Entertainment, check. Give Shelley just enough to do that she feels important but not so much that she starts whining about it, check.

At five o'clock, I say goodbye to John and Dave, who show no sign of finishing anytime soon, and head out into the parking lot. On the way to my car, my phone rings. It's Mrs. Finnamore's daughter, Debra.

My stomach tenses unpleasantly.

"Hello?" I say warily.

"Emily? It's Debra."

Uh-oh. She sounds pissed.

"Hi, Debra. How are you?"

"I've been better," she says, her voice dripping with nasty sarcasm. "I suppose you've heard what's happened?"

My stomach tightens. "No."

She lets out a harsh, disbelieving breath. "My mother has been taken to the hospital," she says. Every word feels pointed, an accusation rather than a statement.

My hand flies to my mouth. "What happened? Is she all right?"

"She's broken her hip," Debra says tersely. "And the doctor said her blood pressure was sky-high. *Clearly* she hasn't been taking her medicines properly."

"But—she has been!" I stammer. "I swear—"

"I have to go," Debra says coldly. "I'll expect reimbursement for the remainder of the month." She makes that harsh noise again. "This is exactly why I wanted her to have *proper* help."

I open my mouth to say, I don't know, something—but she's already gone. I stand frozen with my mouth open, my phone screen blank in my numb hand.

Mrs. Finnamore broke her *hip*?

I have to get to the hospital, right now.

I leap in my car and drive there in a blind panic. My mind is running through every visit I've had with her over the past week. Did I leave something on the floor that she could have tripped over? Did I actually see her *swallow* her medications after I handed them to her? I'm struck by a vision of her taking the pills from me and then stuffing them in her pocket when I'm not looking. Oh god. I should have watched her take them, I should have made her open her mouth after she swallowed them.

The local hospital is small, only two stories, but I still get lost three times on the way to the emergency room. The waiting room is completely full, a hundred curious eyes boring into me as I walk up to the doors and press the buzzer. After a few minutes, I press it again. A moment later, a young woman in scrubs opens the doors. She looks irritated.

"Take a number and the triage nurse will call you when they get to you," she says, pointing to a big sign that says the same thing in huge letters.

"Oh, no," I say hastily, before she can close the door. "I'm just looking for someone who was brought in earlier. Betty Finnamore?"

The girl calls over her shoulder to someone I can't see. "Do we have a Finnamore down here?"

"Exam 2," someone hollers.

"Exam 2," the girl repeats to me, pulling open the door just enough to let me in. I don't really blame her. I can feel everyone in the waiting room staring, as though they'll be able to guess how long they'll have to wait by glimpsing through the doors.

Based on the chaos going on back here, I expect they'll be waiting a long time. In my short walk to Exam 2, I see a woman with a huge bloody gash on her forehead, a toddler screaming bloody murder as a nurse tries to give him a needle, and a terrifying middle-aged man hollering furiously at a doctor.

I rush into Exam 2 and hastily close the door behind me, but the scene inside is no less frightening.

Mrs. Finnamore is laid out on a stretcher with an IV bag dripping fluid into her arm. She's dressed in a flimsy hospital gown, and her hair is sticking up on one side, and she just looks so . . .

*Old.*

I mean, I know that she's old. She's eighty-eight. But at home, with her hair done up and her day clothes on, puttering around her house, it's easy to forget how old she really is. Lying there on the stretcher, she looks so incredibly frail. If I saw a picture of her as she is right now, I would say, yeah, that's someone who shouldn't be living alone.

God, what have I *done*?

I approach her timidly. "Mrs. Finnamore?"

No response.

I try again, a little louder. "Mrs. Finnamore?"

Still nothing. I reach out nervously and touch her shoulder. She stirs, her eyes opening slowly. Her gaze is cloudy. She stares at me, but I don't think she really sees me.

"Mrs. Finnamore, what *happened*?"

She doesn't answer. Her eyes close again, and within seconds, she's asleep.

I step back from the stretcher, feeling cold and slightly nauseated. I look around the room, taking in the scary IV; the awful, astringent smell; the frantic beeping of an alarm sounding from somewhere outside the room . . . all of it coalesces into one single, awful thought.

Debra was right.

Mrs. Finnamore needed a nurse, not a naïve, unskilled receptionist whose only qualification was "liking old people."

The door swings open and a tall man in blue scrubs comes in. His badge says Ethan Edwards, RN.

"How's she doing?" I ask anxiously.

"Ah, she's still pretty loopy from the pain medication," he says. "Her blood pressure's better, though. Are you a relative?"

I shake my head. "No, I'm . . . her neighbor." I almost say *caregiver*, but I'm too scared he'll judge me for doing the job so poorly. "Is it okay for me to be in here?" I ask.

"Yeah, but she'll be heading out soon."

"Heading out?"

"The closest orthopedic surgeon is in Charlottetown. The ambulance should be coming to get her any second."

"Why does she need to see an ortho—a surgeon?"

"She needs surgery to fix her hip."

"Can't you just—put a cast on?"

"Not for a hip fracture, no."

I look at Mrs. Finnamore again. What if she doesn't survive the surgery? What if she *dies*, because of me?

"Are you all right?" the nurse asks, peering at me.

"Oh . . . yeah. Sorry."

"No worries." He leaves the room, only to return again seconds later. "The ambulance just pulled up," he says. "We'll get her ready to go now."

I step back out of his way, and soon the room is crowded with two nurses and two paramedics. I back up against the wall, trying not to get in anyone's way. Before long, they've strapped Mrs. Finnamore onto a wheelable stretcher and are maneuvering her out of the room. She barely stirs as they move her, beyond groaning once in pain.

"You following us there?" a paramedic asks me suddenly.

I blink at him in alarm. *Should* I go with her?

I hesitate, then shake my head jerkily. She needs nurses and doctors, not me.

The paramedic nods and they wheel Mrs. Finnamore away. I take a half-step after them, the word *wait* on the tip of my tongue. But it's too late; she's out the door.

I wander back through the hospital and out into the parking lot in a daze, a hundred horrible thoughts running through my mind. I take out my phone and open my contacts, scrolling until I find the name I'm looking for.

John picks up on the third ring. "Hey." Then, when I don't answer, "Emily?"

My eyes fill with tears at the sound of his voice. "Hey," I choke out.

His tone sobers. "Is everything okay?"

I shake my head, sending a flood of hot tears spilling onto my cheeks. "No."

# CHAPTER 26

"That Debra bitch is nuts," Kiara says.

I crack a thin smile over my cup of tea. "Yeah. Maybe."

"Maybe?" Kiara rolls her eyes. "Her mother fell in the *shower*. Unless you were showering with the woman—which would have been way more concerning than you being neglectful, by the way—there's no way you could've stopped it from happening."

"Yeah, but if she'd had proper home care, the kind that help with bathing and things—"

"You said she didn't want that," Kiara interrupts.

Across the table, her mom, Carla, nods in agreement. "You haven't told me anything to make me think this woman has dementia, or anything else that would impact her capacity." She gets up and walks to the kitchen, returning with a packet of biscuits, which she offers to me and Kiara.

I take a biscuit with a sigh. It's been two days since Mrs. Finnamore broke her hip, and John's parents invited me over for dinner to cheer me up. He and his dad are outside on the deck, throwing a ball for the dogs.

"I see this sort of thing all the time at the hospital," Carla says, watching me. "Adult children don't want their elderly parents living at home anymore, so they try to demand we hold them in the hospital until they can get to a nursing home." She takes a sip of tea. "They think it's a terrible decision for their parent to stay home, and sometimes, they're right. But what they don't seem to realize is, people have the right to make bad decisions. We can't force people to accept home care or go into a nursing home against their will, not unless they've clearly been proven to lack the capacity to make medical decisions. And that usually happens from something like advanced dementia. Being stubborn and set in your ways doesn't count."

"I know," I say heavily. "I just feel so bad. And Debra's never going to let me help her mother out anymore."

Carla snorts. "You may be surprised. If her mother won't accept home care, the only option is for Debra herself to care for her. Somehow, I don't see that happening. Not from everything you've told me about her."

I sigh again. "Maybe."

"Don't stress about it too much," Kiara says. Then, through a mouthful of biscuit, "I can't wait for this weekend. I've made the cutest barrel-themed necklaces to sell. And Cara's still baking stuff for you, right?"

"She is, yeah!" I say, grateful to change the subject. "She said she's making a bunch of Canada Day–themed stuff. Cupcakes and cookies and things."

"She's really good," Kiara says. "She made the best cake for my birthday last year."

"What cake?" John says, stepping in from the deck. His father is still outside; I can hear him trying to coax their German shepherd to come inside.

"That cookies-and-cream cake Cara made last year," Kiara says.

"Oh, yeah." John nods. "That was sick."

He sits down beside me, throwing an arm over the back of my chair. I lean into him a little. He's been really great these past two days. He called the Charlottetown hospital to ask for news on Mrs. Finnamore when I was too nervous to do it myself, and at work he's been popping out from the garage every hour or two just to check on me. Kiara and Rose have also been amazing, texting me all the time to see how I'm doing. Even Doris has been helpful, in her own way. When I told her what had happened, she snorted and said, "Boo-hoo. I've broken both my hips, and no one threw me any pity parties."

John's father, Laurent, comes in, and the conversation turns to the trip that he and Carla are planning for this winter. As we listen to them talk, John shifts his chair a few inches closer to mine. Carla refills my empty teacup, and Laurent says, "You would love that, Emily," when they're talking about a hiking trail in Scotland. The tight knot that's been living in my chest since Mrs. Finnamore's fall loosens up a little, and I lean a bit more into John's arms.

"John says you're looking into museum jobs in Charlottetown," Carla says later, as I help her take the dishes to the kitchen.

"Oh, yeah," I say brightly. It's part of my "staying in Waldon" plan. If I'm going to be truly happy here, I need to find a job I'm more passionate about. "I really love volunteering at the museum in Waldon, but it doesn't actually pay anything. And there are some really cool museums in the city."

Like the Anne of Green Gables museum, for example. I had a total fit when I found that one, even if they don't technically have any job openings right now. I sent them an email anyway, just to inquire, but I haven't heard anything back.

Carla puts a hand on my shoulder. "I hope you find something good. I know a lot of young people want to get off the island these days, but"—her eyes twinkle mischievously—"I think John would like it if you stuck around."

I smile at her a bit shyly. I still get a tiny bit nervous around her and Laurent. I really want them to like me. Just because it's nice to be well-liked, you know. Not because I secretly think they might be my in-laws someday.

"I'd like it too," I say honestly.

THE NEXT DAY is Saturday, only two days before Canada Day. My shift at the museum doesn't technically start until noon, but I head in around ten because there's still so much I need to do, not least of which is inflating about a million red and white balloons. I get lightheaded just thinking about it.

There's a small line at the door when I arrive at the museum.

"Excuse me," I say, stepping around people. "I'm not cutting," I add hastily, seeing some dirty looks come my way. "I work here."

"Is the front desk opening up any time soon?" demands a woman balancing a toddler on her hip.

I frown. "It should be open . . ." I trail off as I reach the front of the line. There's no one at the desk. Weird. I thought Brenda was supposed to be here this morning.

"I can get you all sorted," I say to the people in line. "It's five dollars a person, three for children under ten."

For five or ten minutes I answer questions and hand out tickets, until the final visitor disappears into the museum. I peek outside to make sure no one else is about to come in and then head to the break room. There's no one there, but Shelley's voice is emanating from her office. Taking a steadying breath, like I always do before I talk to Shelley, I head over there.

Her office door is open. She has her phone pressed to her ear and is laughing loudly at something. I don't know why, but her laugh is almost more unpleasant than her usual scowl. I can't hear what the other person is saying, but I just have a feeling it's something mean-spirited.

She frowns when she sees me in her doorway. I turn to leave, but she waves a hand for me to stay.

"I've got to run," she says to the person on the phone. "Talk to you later."

I force a smile. "How's it going?"

"Great," she says.

And, ugh, even the way she says that is annoying. Sort of condescending, like, "*Obviously* I'm great, my life is so much better than yours."

(Okay, I may have developed a serious grudge against Shelley.)

"Did Brenda call in sick?" I ask. "There's no one at the desk."

"Oh, no," she says. "That's why I wanted to talk to you. I've spoken with the board of the historical society, and they think it's time we have some consistent staffing. Especially now that things are picking up so much."

I frown. Consistent staffing, what does that mean?

"We've hired two paid staff to work the front desk for the rest of the summer," Shelley goes on. "Really bright college girls looking for summer jobs."

"Oh." I try to think of something to say. "That's great," I manage finally.

And it *is* great, actually. This place should have consistent, paid staff. And it's the perfect job for college students, since the museum is busiest in the summer.

I just . . . wish I could have been considered. Not that I mind volunteering, but it would've been nice to start getting paid a little for my work.

"So, anyway, we won't really need volunteers anymore," Shelley says.

My heart does an awful thud-thud in my chest.

"Oh, I don't mind staying on!" I say quickly. "I like working here. Maybe I can just . . . focus on the events and the school tours."

That wouldn't be so bad, really. It's my favorite part of the job.

"Oh, the girls can handle that," Shelley says. "Thanks, though."

I stare at her for several painful heartbeats. Does she mean—

Is she *firing* me?

"I can help with other stuff," I say in a thin voice. "Whatever would be useful."

"Oh, no," Shelley says. "It's fine. Thanks, though." She repeats that stupid, condescending phrase again. "And you're still welcome to come to our event on Canada Day," she adds. "It's going to be really wonderful."

My mouth drops open. I'm still *welcome*? She says it like it's *her* event. Like I should feel lucky she's even giving me an invitation.

Suddenly I want to burst into tears. This is *my* event. I did so much work!

I open my mouth to try to argue, but before I can speak, a pretty girl in her early twenties edges past me into the room. She has two coffee cups in her hands.

"Should I, like, go sell people tickets?" she asks, as she hands one of the coffees to Shelley.

"Thanks, hon," Shelley says. "Sit down a minute, first, we need to talk about the Canada Day party."

*Hon*? Who is this girl, her daughter?

The girl in question looks at me inquisitively. "Do you work here too?"

"She used to volunteer here," Shelley answers, before I can speak. "She helped plan the Canada Day event."

Helped? *Helped*? I planned the whole thing! Me and Trey and Kiara, I mean.

"Cool," says the girl.

"Are you two—related?" I ask. Somehow, I keep my voice from shaking with anger.

"Oh, yeah," the girl says pleasantly. "Shelley's my mom. Mom slash boss, now." She cracks a white-toothed grin.

I fix Shelley with a frank, incredulous stare, but not a lick of shame crosses the woman's face.

"Close the door when you leave, will you?" she says. "We've got a lot of work to do!" she adds to her daughter, in a bright, jovial tone that makes me want to smack her.

My fists clench at my sides. I can't just let her fire me. I have to stand up for myself.

"I don't think this is fair," I blurt out.

Shelley raises an eyebrow. "Come now, Emily," she says. "You're being a bit rude."

There's an edge to her words. A bit rude. That's just what I said to her at the Barrel Into Summer event.

That's why she's doing this. She's probably been planning it ever since then. She just needed me to plan the whole Canada Day event for her first.

"You can't just—"

"The door, please," she interrupts. "Thanks."

Her daughter is looking between us uncertainly. Shelley's smile is smug.

With shaking hands, I turn on my heel and storm out, leaving the door wide open behind me. She can close it her damn self.

My fury carries me all the way to the parking lot and into my car, and then it gives way in a big painful *whoosh*. I stare blankly at my steering wheel for a moment, processing what's just happened.

Then I burst into tears.

# CHAPTER 27

At eleven a.m. on Canada Day, I wake up to the smell of freshly brewed coffee. I squint around in the darkness, disoriented for a moment before I remember I stayed at John's apartment last night. Then I remember what day it is and let out a long, heavy breath.

I drag myself out of bed, pull on one of John's hoodies, and head into the kitchen. John is sitting on the couch in the living room, drinking coffee and watching a motorcycle race on TV.

"Ooh, is this Formula 1?" I ask.

He stares at me, affronted, then sees my face and realizes I'm teasing. "So funny," he says.

"I thought so." I get my own cup of coffee and join him on the couch. "How'd you sleep?"

"Good. You?"

"Good. A bit disappointed to see the sun. I was hoping karma would punish Shelley with a freak July first blizzard."

"Are you sure you still want to go?"

"No," I say. "But we should, to support Kiara."

Kiara was adamant she was going to pull out of the event and tell all her craft booth friends to do the same, but I convinced her not to. I want the event to succeed, even if Shelley's going to take all the credit.

(Okay, maybe 90 percent of me wants the event to succeed. The other 10 percent wants it to be a total flaming disaster that ends in

Shelley getting fired and the historical society begging me to take her place.)

"Wordle first?" John says.

"Wordle first. I'm going to start with BITCH. As in, Shelley is the world's biggest—"

"I don't think Wordle uses curse words."

Too late; I've already typed it in. I crack up as the letters start turning.

"Ha! You can totally use curse words," I say triumphantly, showing him my phone.

"That's only because *bitch* has a regular meaning," John argues. "It would never use something like—I don't know—FUCKS."

"Wanna bet?" I ask, dangling my phone in front of him.

He holds his hand out. "Five bucks."

We shake on it. Two seconds later, he's digging in his wallet for a five-dollar bill, while I cackle childishly over my phone.

"I can't believe that worked," John says.

"I can't believe you doubted me."

"You're going to lose your streak, at this rate."

Oh, crap. He's right. Neither BITCH nor FUCKS got me any usable letters. (And wow, that's a sentence I don't think anyone's ever said before.)

"All right, all right," I say. "No more curse words." I think for a moment, drumming my fingers against my chin, then ask, "What's a five-letter word that means incompetent, condescending asshole?"

To my relief and intense annoyance, the Canada Day event is a total success. The weather is perfect, sunny but not sweltering, the food is delicious, and the music John's friend George is playing is perfect, sort of old-fashioned and folksy without feeling cheesy. I eat a hot dog and two (okay, four) cupcakes decorated in red-and-white icing and try not to sulk too much when I overhear the historical society ladies complimenting Shelley on the event.

While John chats with Kiara's husband, Jake, I head into the museum to say hi to Trey. The inside of the museum is dark and cool, and I blink for several moments in the doorway, waiting for my eyes to adjust to the light.

A few people are milling about, peering at the exhibits. Trey is working at his station, but he puts down his tools as soon as he sees me. The kids watching him exclaim in disappointment.

"Pee break," he says, making them giggle.

He beckons for me to follow him into the staff room and then turns to me with an uncharacteristically serious expression. "Kiara told me what happened," he says. "Why didn't you tell me?"

I shrug. "It's okay."

"No, it's not," he says sternly. "Shelley's way out of line. I have half a mind to talk to the historical society."

"Don't do that," I say hastily. "I don't want her to fire you too."

Trey scowls. "Like she could."

We're both silent a moment afterward, though. She definitely could. Shelley has all the power in this tiny little kingdom.

"Honestly, don't make a big deal about it," I say. "It's probably for the best anyway. I'm really busy working at the shop, and I've been looking into jobs at other museums . . . plus, I'm thinking about trying to turn my caregiving thing into a proper business."

I'm just making stuff up at random, to try to seem less pathetic, but as I hear myself say it, I think, huh.

*Should* I try to make it a proper business?

"What about the internship you applied for?" Trey asks. "And the degree in museum studies?"

I flush. "I never heard anything back. Things are so competitive these days . . . and it's not like I have a lot of experience."

"You worked here," Trey says.

I manage a small smile. "Yeah, for, like, a month." I peer over his shoulder. The kids waiting for him to come back look like they're starting to get antsy. "Listen, don't worry about me," I say, mustering a cheery tone. "I'm fine, and it's not like you're going to be rid of me. I'll still stop by and bug you once in a while."

"If you're sure," Trey says doubtfully. "But you just say the word and I'll go straight to the society. Or better yet, I'll go tell Shelley what I think of her right to her face."

"Thanks, Trey."

He heads back to his workstation, to the cheers and whoops of the waiting children. I do a loop of the museum, walking slowly, feeling very separate from the bright, happy atmosphere all around me.

I hear a woman asking how old the museum is, and I have to bite my tongue to keep from answering. I don't work here anymore. It isn't my place to butt in.

I know I'm being a little dramatic. Like I told Trey, I only worked here for a little while. And it wasn't exactly my dream job—it isn't in a big city, and the salary was exactly one hundred thousand dollars less than a hundred thousand dollars—but I really felt like I belonged here. Like I could make a difference.

I let out a strangled laugh, thinking of my Met internship application. I must have been delusional when I did that. I can't even make it as a volunteer in the tiniest museum in the tiniest town of the country's tiniest province. How on earth could I get an internship somewhere like the Met?

Floundering under a rising wave of misery, I make my way back outside and find John. He studies my face and then takes my hand.

"Time to go?" he asks.

I nod, blinking back stupid tears. "Time to go."

We walk back to his apartment in silence, hand in hand. The sound of the party grows quieter behind us, until all that's left is the chirp of birds and the distant murmur of the ocean. John suggests stopping for a pizza on the way home, and I force myself to smile and nod, though I'm not hungry at all.

He goes into the shop to order while I sit on the bench outside, watching a pigeon pick at someone's discarded crust. John emerges ten or fifteen minutes later with a pizza box in one hand.

"Cheer up," he says, taking my hand. "Things will turn around again soon."

I nod. "I guess."

He makes a reproachful noise and swings my hand back and forth. "They will. Who knows? Maybe you'll hear from a museum in Charlottetown this week."

"Maybe," I say doubtfully.

"You've been crazy busy lately, anyway," he says. "Maybe it'll be nice to have a break."

I glance up at him uncertainly. There it is again—that unpleasant, prickly feeling.

"I don't want a break. I want a job that I love."

"And you'll find one," he says. "It might not be tomorrow, but it'll come. You'll find something that you love."

"Like you and your job."

The words come out slightly caustic. I wait for him to call me on it. I want him to, even. But instead, he gives an easy shrug.

"Exactly."

I fall silent, my fingers slightly stiff under his. Even though his tone is casual, I can feel us teetering on the edge of a fight. It hovers between us, sharp and unpleasant.

*You don't really love your job,* I might say. *You're bored with windshield replacements and tire changes, and you have to squish all the race car work that you actually* want *to do in between the boring work that Fred approves of.*

*I'm happy where I am,* he might answer. *Don't get stuck-up again on me, now.*

A sharp pang of hurt. *I'm not stuck-up. I just want to do something I love.*

A cold, angry breath. *Well, then, maybe you shouldn't be dating a lowly mechanic.*

I shake my head jerkily and pull myself back from the words. There's no winning that fight, not for either of us. And why am I trying to pick a fight with him? What has he done all week, except be incredibly supportive of me, and kind, and understanding?

I sigh heavily. "Sorry. I'm in an awful mood."

His shoulders relax. "It's okay. You've had a rough week."

"It hasn't been the best."

He nudges me with our clasped hands. "What can I do to make it better?"

I manage a smile. "Nothing."

He lifts his eyebrows. "Are you sure? Because I'm not above slashing Shelley's tires. Or maybe we could ask Jim to get her car towed from the lot next week. He's the security guy, he has the authority."

I bite into a growing grin. "Don't you dare suggest it. He hates her so much, I think he'd probably do it."

"He hates her too?"

"He says he 'doesn't have much to do with her.' That's, like, Jim's version of calling someone the c-word."

John laughs. "That's amazing."

He nudges my side again, and this time I lean into him. "It'll be okay," I say more honestly. "I just need to sulk a bit more and then get over it."

"Well, you just let me know," he says, letting go of my hand to open the door to his apartment building. "If you want Shelley's tires slashed, I'm there. Or if you want to do some weird role-play with that old movie you love, Anne of whatever-it-was—"

"Anne of Green Gables!" I say. "Don't pretend you don't know what it's called. And we can't do *role-play* with Anne and Gilbert," I add indignantly. "They never had sex."

"Didn't you tell me they have children in the later books, though? I hate to break it to you, but that means they had sex."

"Blasphemy. They don't even kiss in the movie. It ends with him tucking a single strand of hair behind her ear, then they walk off together with a horse."

"We'll role-play that, then. You put your hair up, and I'll track down a horse."

I laugh, feeling the last vestiges of tension slip away from my frame. "Deal."

# CHAPTER 28

The next morning, my first Wordle guess is BRAVE. As in, I've decided I'm going to be brave today.

Before work, I head to the local hospital to visit Mrs. Finnamore. She was transferred back from Charlottetown to the local hospital to do a little more rehab prior to going home, and I've been too afraid to visit her until now. But like I say, today I've decided to be brave.

I buy a card and a vase of flowers from the hospital gift shop and ride up to the second floor with my heart in my throat, visions of Mrs. Finnamore groaning on the ambulance stretcher flashing before my eyes.

To my relief, when I walk into her room, I find her sitting up in a chair by the window, bossily lecturing the poor woman in the bed opposite hers.

"If you keep spoiling your grandson like that, he's going to grow up into an awful little— Emily!" Mrs. Finnamore interrupts herself, spotting me in the doorway.

"Hi, Mrs. Finnamore. Is it okay if I come in?"

"Of course, dear. Come in, have a seat." She gestures for me to sit on the end of her hospital bed. "This is my home care girl," she tells the other woman loudly. "You need to think about getting one of them yourself, Bertha. You're not getting any younger."

The woman, Bertha, waves Mrs. Finnamore away. "You worry about your own problems, let me worry about mine."

I stifle a smile at Mrs. Finnamore's affronted expression.

"How are you doing?" I ask, to distract her.

"Oh, I'm fine," she says dismissively. And actually, she does look pretty good. She's maybe a touch paler than before, but she's dressed in her own clothes rather than a hospital gown, and she has a crossword book on the little table in front of her.

"Does your hip hurt a lot?"

"Not at all," she says. "The nurses ask me a hundred times a day, and every time I tell them no. Even when it twinges a bit, I just take a bit of Tylenol. I'm not interested in messing around with street drugs."

"I don't think they use street drugs in hospitals."

She shakes her head. "Barberie told me—you know Barberie, from my old bridge club?—she told me her nephew stole all her pain pills after her knee surgery and sold them on the streets in Charlottetown. I'm not letting the doctors send me home with any of those, thank you very much. I'm on enough medicine as it is."

"Speaking of medicine," says a bright voice at the door. I turn and see a middle-aged nurse in scrubs bearing a cup of pills. "Time for your morning pills."

"Oh, lord," Mrs. Finnamore says. "Look at all these." She shows me the pills. "They've doubled my pills since I've been in here."

"I think that's about the same as before," I say doubtfully.

"Are you a family member?" her nurse asks me.

"This is the home care girl I told you about," Mrs. Finnamore says. "Emily."

The nurse looks at me with interest. "You work for VON?"

I recognize the name—those are the real home care nurses, the ones who can give needles and take blood and stuff. "Oh no," I say quickly. "I'm not a nurse. I just help out a few folks with laundry and groceries and things."

"Well, we certainly need more of that," the nurse says. "The wait lists for home care right now are appalling."

My heart flutters nervously in my chest. I swallow hard and say, "I actually do have time for a few more clients. You know, if there's ever a patient who needs a little help . . ."

"You should give your number to Jane, she's our care coordinator. I think she keeps a list of private places."

My heart thumps harder in triumph. "That would be great," I say, trying not to sound overly pleased. "Thanks!"

She smiles and leaves us to our visit. I sit with Mrs. Finnamore for another quarter hour before I tell her I have to head to work.

"Don't be taking on too many new folks while I'm in here," she says. "I'm going to need your help when I get home."

I hesitate. "Do you think Debra will still want me to? I mean, you might need professional nursing care while you're recovering."

"Oh, nonsense," she says. "The physiotherapist already said he's going to come to my house after I go home, and that's all I'll need for my hip. I don't want strangers traipsing in and out of my house."

"I think Debra was pretty upset about your fall," I say carefully.

"Debra's always upset about something," Mrs. Finnamore says. "That's my daughter," she explains to her roommate. "She lives out west. She used to be such a clever girl, but her father spoiled her rotten." She turns back to me. "You'll come visit me again tomorrow, then."

I smile. "Of course. And we can talk more about you getting proper home care."

Mrs. Finnamore pretends not to hear this. "Bye, now."

Chuckling, I head back to the nurse's station. The clerk tells me Jane is busy with a family meeting, but she takes my cell phone number and information and promises to pass them along. I feel a bit nervous thinking about my name going on some official hospital list of private caregivers, but then I remember Jim calling me his guardian angel, and I lift my chin up stubbornly.

I spend the rest of the day working at the shop, using my downtime to Google things like "how to start your own business" and "how much can you charge for caregiving services without being a greedy dick." At the end of my shift, I kiss John goodbye and head back to my house. After dinner, I put my cell phone on the kitchen table and stare at it for a few minutes. John offered to be here with me for this, but it feels like something I have to tackle alone.

I take a breath and dial Debra's number.

It rings five times, just enough that I start to secretly hope she won't pick up. Then—

"Hello?"

Oh, god, I forgot how mean her voice is.

"Hi." My voice squeaks. I clear my throat and try again. "I mean, hi, Debra. This is Emily."

"Emily. Hello." Her tone is forbidding.

"Hi," I say again. I steel myself and launch into the speech I've prepared. "I'm calling because Mrs. Finnamore told me she's being released from the hospital sometime in the next few weeks. She'd like me to come back to work for her."

Debra lets out a cold breath. "Oh, she would, would she?"

I grit my teeth. "Yes. She's nervous about getting around once she's home." This is a teensy lie—what she actually said was that if the doctors didn't let her go home soon, she was going to call the police on them—but I think she'd be fine with me saying it.

"And you're going to help with that, are you?" Debra says caustically.

I almost falter at her tone, but instead I lick my lips and say, "Yes."

"She shouldn't be going home at all. It's ridiculous the doctors are allowing it."

"She said they're really pleased with how she's done since her surgery."

"Oh, I'm sure *she* said that," Debra says.

I press two fingers to my temple and bite my tongue to stop from answering. I don't want to get drawn into a fight with her. "She'd like me to come back and do the same things I was doing for her before," I say instead, "but I'd also like to add a half-hour every other day, to be there in the house when she's showering. Not, like, be in the bathroom with her, I mean, but just to be nearby to make sure she doesn't slip, and to help her if she needs it."

"She needs a lot more than just that if she thinks she's going to stay at home much longer," Debra says. "She needs to get rid of that disgusting old tub, the rail is three feet high. No doubt that's what she fell over—"

She keeps ranting a little longer. I wait for her to run out of steam.

"I suppose you'll want more money now, will you?" she finishes nastily.

I almost say no, just to avoid a fight. Then I grit my teeth. "Mm. A half-hour every other day."

I can't see her face, but I imagine her pursing her lips unpleasantly. There's a long, cold silence, then she says, "I'll have to discuss it with my husband."

I let out a little breath of relief. I've won. I know I have.

"Of course," I say politely. "I can give you another call a bit closer to her discharge date."

"They'd better not discharge her next week," Debra says. "I've never heard of a woman her age going home after such a big surgery. I've told them they have to put her in a home, but she's got them all wrapped around her finger—"

She goes on in that vein for another minute or two, then huffs loudly and says, "I've got to go," like I'm the one holding her up. She hangs up, and I drop my forehead onto the kitchen table.

That woman is *exhausting*.

Still, I can tell that she's going to give in. Mrs. Finnamore told me that while Debra was here, one of the doctors asked Mrs. Finnamore if she'd ever thought about moving out west to live with her daughter.

"You should have seen the look on her face!" Mrs. Finnamore said, laughing. "Debra would rather eat chalk than let me move in with her. Not that I'd want to, mind you. She's got three of those terrible yappy dogs, always biting your ankles and getting fur all over the couch cushions." She shuddered. "I'd rather go to a home."

Anyway, if the wait lists for publicly funded home care are as long as that nurse said, Debra doesn't have a lot of other options besides me. Plus, Mrs. Finnamore would throw a fit if Debra tried to send a stranger into her house.

I sit back in my chair with a grin. I'm pretty proud of myself for how I handled that. It was a bit nerve-wracking, but I got through it.

I take a celebratory sip of my soda, grab my phone again, and call John to tell him how it went.

# CHAPTER 29

A few days later, I wake up to the sounds of birds chirping outside John's bedroom window and the quiet glug of the fish tank on the opposite side of the room. Fish 1 and Fish 2 are swimming lazily while Fish 3 hides in his (her?) favorite spot under the rocks.

"Is Fish 3 a boy or a girl?" I ask John, as he walks out of the bathroom.

"Which one is Fish 3 again?"

"The shimmery gray one."

"The *Geophagus*," John says.

"The geographer."

"*Geophagus*."

"Geology."

"I'm getting coffee now."

"Get me one too, please!" I call after him.

I crawl to the edge of the bed and stare at Fish 3. "Don't let him bully you," I whisper. "You're not a genealogist. You're a good little fish."

"Are you a bit insane?" John asks, reappearing with two cups of coffee.

"Little bit. But you love it."

He rolls his eyes. "Yeah, yeah."

The tips of his ears have gone slightly red. I hide a smile. I have this tiny, sneaky feeling that John and I are creeping toward saying "I love you" to each other. There's this way that he looks at me these days, with a fond sort of crinkling at the corners of his eyes that makes my heart beat funny. It's probably still a few weeks away, but we're definitely inching our way closer. Thinking about it makes me feel warm and slightly giddy, like I've drunk a bunch of coffee really quickly.

"Wordle?" I ask.

"Wordle," he agrees.

I curl up next to him and take a sip of coffee.

"First word?" he asks.

"LOVES," I say, because it's fun to nudge us a little closer. "As in, John *loves* how crazy Emily is." I type it in. "Crap. All wrong. I hope that's not a sign."

"A sign of what?"

"A sign that Wordle doesn't think we should be together!"

"We've talked about this," John says. "The Wordle answers do not hold any deep, secret meaning for your life."

"Um, what about the time the answer was BROKE and I *broke* my nail two seconds after I got it?"

"You broke your nail because you were spinning around on your chair like an idiot."

"Well, what about the time the word was PANTS, and I was *wearing* pants?"

"Okay," he says. "Quiet time now."

I chuckle, then turn back to my phone. LOVES was all wrong. I need to rule out some other letters and figure out what vowel is in the word.

BRAID, I type. If it's right, I'm totally wearing my hair in a braid today.

Shoot. Only the A is yellow.

I study the letters, hyper-focused, and type in a few more words. I get a few more letters right . . . a Y, a C, an H . . .

Aha! It's YACHT!

This is totally a sign that John and I are going to own a yacht someday. I'm going to tell him that once he's done, just to annoy him.

I swipe open my email while I wait for him to finish. A bank statement, a few emails from shops I bought stuff from a hundred years ago that I've been meaning to unsubscribe from . . .

I go totally still.

There's an email with the subject line "Your NYU Admissions Decision." Then below it, an email from the Metropolitan Museum of Art, with the subject line "Re: Internship Application."

Oh, god.

Oh god, oh god, oh god.

I put my phone down before I can accidentally see the little preview of the emails. I can't do this right now. I can't face the rejection. It would've been bad enough to just get one email, but *both*? Did NYU and the Met conspire on this or something?

"Did you get it yet?" John asks. "Is there a double letter?"

"Did I—what? Oh—yeah. I mean no. No double letter."

He looks at me. "You look weird."

"Thanks."

"No, I mean you've got a weird look on your face."

"Do I?" I say thinly.

His brow furrows. "Em."

Crap.

I have to tell him.

I take a nervous sip of coffee. "I just . . . got an email. Two emails."

He puts his phone down. "About?"

I lick my lips. "Well . . . you know how I've been trying to sort out what I want to do with my life? All that . . . dream job stuff?"

He nods slowly.

I swallow. "Well. I ended up applying to NYU a while ago, back before we were—you know, dating. And there's an internship program at the Metropolitan Museum of Art that I applied for too."

Oh, god. He looks so serious. "And?"

"And . . . I don't know. They've both just emailed with their answers."

"Did you get in?"

"I don't know. I didn't read them yet."

He stares at me. "Are you going to go, if you did?"

"I don't know," I say again. My voice sounds high and strange. "They're probably just rejections. There's no way my university grades are good enough for NYU, and the Met thing probably gets thousands of applications—"

"But if you get in," he repeats, "will you go?"

I attempt a thin smile. "Shouldn't I look at them first? If I didn't get them, it won't matter."

He looks at me for a long moment. "It matters to me."

Well, fuck.

I break his gaze and fiddle with the handle of my coffee cup. I want to say, "No, of course not!" I know that's what he wants me to say.

But . . . what if I got in? The Met internship is a long shot, but it's not entirely impossible to think that I might have gotten into NYU. And if I did . . . will I go?

"I . . . I think so," I say haltingly. "Yes."

A thick silence falls, then he lets out a short, disbelieving breath. "Seriously?"

"Well—yes," I say, defensiveness slipping into my tone. "It would be a huge opportunity—"

"A huge opportunity."

"Of course! You know I've always wanted to live in a city—to do something big—"

He puts his coffee mug down. "I thought you'd decided to stay here, actually."

"I—this is stupid," I stammer. "There's no point in arguing about it before I've even read the emails—"

"Are you serious? Of course there is."

"If I didn't get in—"

"What? Then you'll deign to stay here with me?" He lets out a humorless laugh. "This is an acceptable fallback option, is it?"

"That's not—that isn't what I said!" I push myself off the bed.

"Yes, it is," he snaps. "If you got in, you're going to go."

"Okay, well—why shouldn't I?" I demand, anger coming to my defense. "Don't you want me to be happy? Don't you want me to find a job I actually *love*? That I care about?"

He exhales impatiently. "Of course I do. But you can find that here. I know you, Emily. You like it here. You're happy here. You're just still convinced you're too good for it, or that there's some bigger, better life somewhere out there—"

"Well, there might be!" I say, gesturing to my phone.

"So you're going to throw away your whole life here just on the off chance you'll find something better?" He stands up and takes two angry steps away from me, dragging a hand over his face. "For fuck's *sake*. I know things have been a bit hard lately, with that lady breaking her hip and the museum stuff—"

"Yeah, they have been hard," I snap.

"—but I thought you'd decided you were going to make a go out of your caregiving business. Or was that just a second-rate fall-back plan too?"

"I—no. Not exactly." I throw my hands up in frustration. "Why are you making this so hard? It's not like this means we *have* to break up—we could do long distance, it'll only be for two or three years—"

He scoffs. "Only two or three years? You're telling me you're going to get a fancy museum degree and do a prestigious museum internship, and then after all that, you'll come back here to Waldon to live happily forever? Come *on*."

I hug my arms around myself, frustrated tears pricking at my eyes. He's right. Of course he's right. If I do this, my goal is to end up working full-time at a museum in a city like New York or London.

"This is my *dream*," I say tightly. "Can't you understand that? This is what I've wanted, for as long as I can remember."

"As long as you can remember?" he repeats acerbically.

"Oh, don't do that," I snap. "The museum bit is new, fine, but I know that it's what I want to do. I'm not like you, John. I can't be happy with *settling*."

"Oh, good," he says. "This again."

"Yes! *This* again. You aren't happy, John. Not as happy as you could be."

"Oh, what? Because I should have been a rich, stressed-out businessman like my father? Or a burned-out doctor like my mother? Grow up, Emily. Just because you think my job is beneath you—"

"I don't think it's beneath me!" I throw back. "But you don't like it as much as you pretend to. You say you know me, well, I know you too. You're bored with all the stuff Fred makes you do, but you don't have the guts to stand up to him, or leave the shop to start something up on your own, doing the things you want to do—"

John is shaking his head back and forth dismissively—I'm not sure he's even listening to me.

My hands curl into fists at my sides. "I know you think I'm a snob, that my dreams are idealistic and stupid, but you know what? I don't care. I *finally* have a job I can see myself doing forever, and to do it in New York City—to intern somewhere like the Met—" I throw my hands up incredulously. "Do you really expect me to turn all that down?"

He stares at me for one long, painful moment.

"I would have," he says. "Yeah."

My heart is beating loudly in my ears. My anger is fading, replaced by something ugly and painful. "Well . . . I can't. If I got in . . . I'm going to go. And if I didn't . . ." I shake my head, and two hot tears slip down my face. I give a rough shrug. "I guess you're saying we'll break up either way."

He stares at me incredulously, and for a moment I feel like we've been transported back in time, to when we didn't understand each other at all.

"Yeah," he says finally. "I guess I am."

A silence falls, so heavy and painful I can hardly stand it. The only sounds are my uneven breathing and the glug of the fish tank behind me. Ten minutes ago, we were laughing and making jokes. Now—now—

I wipe the tears from my face and pick up my phone. I open my inbox, and I don't have to look beyond the email previews to know. The answer is in the first three words of each email.

Dear Emily. Congratulations.

Thump-thump, goes my heart in my chest.

"Did you get in?" John asks.

I nod stiffly.

"Both of them?"

Another stiff nod.

"Well," he says. "Congratulations."

The word is a barb, hot and sharp in my heart.

"Thanks." My voice is tight, and an awful hot lump is swelling in my throat.

I look up at him, suddenly desperate for him to shake his head and relax a little, to tell me that it's no big deal, that we can talk about this properly. But instead, he stares at me like I'm a stranger and says, in a cool, distant voice, "I've got to get ready for work."

The lump in my throat gets ten times bigger. "Fine," I say thickly. "I guess I'll just . . . go, then."

"Yeah," he says. "I guess you should."

# CHAPTER 30

The rest of the week really sucks.

I wish I could find a better way to say it—maybe if I was the type of person who did crossword puzzles, I'd be more eloquent—but honestly, right now, I don't even have the energy to try. So, there it is. The rest of the weeks really *sucks*.

John and I haven't spoken a word since the breakup, and there isn't any time for us to sort things out, even if we wanted to. When I finally stopped crying and got around to reading the emails from NYU and the Met, it turns out I wasn't actually chosen for the internship initially. But one of the people they chose dropped out unexpectedly, and I was their next choice. Which means I have to be in New York City in a week.

A *week*.

I'm conscious, all the time, of how the days would have played out if I'd never started dating John. I would have been deliriously happy. Every phone call, every email, every decision would have been a thrill. Instead, every step that moves me closer to my new life is steeped in a thick layer of misery.

When I call Fred to tell him I'm quitting my receptionist job, he actually drives in from home just to berate me for leaving, pacing furiously around the shop and calling me a "typical flighty woman." I sit with my hands in my lap, trying not to cry, until he storms out with a final, furious "For fuck's sake. It's shit like this that makes me want to sell this damned shop."

I know John hears what he said, because he's in the break room when it happens, but he doesn't say anything to me afterward, not even when Dave makes a point of coming to my desk to thump me on the shoulder and say, "Ignore that old prick."

When I call the owners of my house to let them know I'm leaving, they drop another misery bomb. It turns out they've been thinking of selling the place, and now that I'm moving out, they're going to put it on the market. I stare at the phone a long while after they hang up, feeling heavy and cold all over. The last few weeks, when I was starting to sketch out my "stay in Waldon" plans, I had this secret dream that John and I would buy this house someday. Now, not only are John and I never going to live together, even if things go to hell in New York I won't ever be able to come back to my perfect little house.

Telling Mrs. Finnamore, Doris, and Jim the news is its own special species of awful. Well, not Doris, so much—"What are you looking for, girl? A hug goodbye?"—but Mrs. Finnamore and Jim seem genuinely upset to hear that I'm leaving. Mrs. Finnamore is still in the hospital, and when I tell her, she gets this awful crinkle in her forehead and gets uncharacteristically flustered, like she actually was counting on my help when she went home. Jim pats my knee and tells me he's proud of me, but he's quieter than usual the rest of the visit, and he stands on the porch with this strange, faraway look in his eyes as he watches me get in my car and drive away.

Rose and Trey, at least, are excited for me, and Kiara does a decent job pretending to be happy, but I can tell she's totally on John's side. And why shouldn't she be? He's her brother. I'm the jerk who doesn't think he's worth staying in Waldon for.

"No, I get it," she says hollowly, on our last morning coffee date. "It's like I said, right? Your happiest lives just aren't compatible."

I fiddle with my coffee cup. "It's not just that I'm going to New York. It's that he doesn't understand *why* I have to go. Or why I think that he's . . . "

"What?"

I clear my throat. "That he's settling."

A strange expression flits over her face, and for a split second, I'm sure she agrees with me. She's heard John complain about Fred. She's seen how much happier he is at the racetrack.

John wasn't lying when he said that he's happy. He is happy. But he could be happier. And that prickly feeling I've had in my gut . . . it's the resentment I have toward him for not trying harder.

Kiara is silent for a moment, swirling her coffee around without drinking it. "I think he really loved you," she says finally.

"I know," I say quietly. "I think I really loved him too. But love isn't a substitute for happiness."

Her lips turn up in a joyless smile. "Love isn't a substitute for happiness," she echoes.

From there I go to the bank, where I sign the paperwork for my new student loan. I've taken out a federal loan, which I'll use to pay for NYU as well as the payments on my existing provincial student loan. Because it's never a bad idea to use one loan to pay off another, right?

I did get a little discount on my dorm room, since I'm moving in at a weird time and agreed to be a dorm supervisor for the younger students, but it's all still going to cost an atrocious amount of money. I'll be lucky if I make it out on the other side with less than a hundred thousand in debt.

God, this had better be worth it.

The miserable days tick by, one after another. Even doing Wordle is depressing. All it does is remind me of John, and if I hit three hundred and sixty-five days, I'll do it alone in New York. Once, at the shop, John walked into the break room while I was doing Wordle, and just for a moment, I thought he wanted to say something. But then Dave ambled in and the moment was broken.

It's just as well. There's nothing good that can come of us talking. I've argued with him a thousand times in my head, and it always ends up the same way.

Before I know it, it's my last night in Waldon. I order a pizza (I've already spent about a thousand dollars this week on New York stuff, what's another twenty bucks that I don't have?) and eat it while I wander the empty rooms of my house. Even though all the furniture is still there—it belongs to the real owners, not me—the house looks barren and depressing without all my stuff, like my fridge magnets and stacks of books. All of those have been stuffed into five large boxes and a suitcase that my parents will pick up when they get back from New Zealand next week to store at their place. The two suitcases I'm taking with me on my flight to New York are already packed and set out by the front door.

I glance up as the doorbell rings. I'm not expecting anyone, unless the pizza guy's come back to tell me my credit card payment didn't go through.

I walk to the front door, swing it open, and there's John, looking as handsome as ever in a hoodie and jeans.

"Hey," I say uncertainly.

"Hey." He holds out a sweater, which I recognize as mine. "You left this at my place. I just found it in the dryer. Figured I'd get it back to you before you left."

"Oh." I take it from him. "Right. Thanks."

"No problem." There's a long beat of awkward silence. "'Kay, well. Night."

My heart twists painfully. "Night."

I wait for him to walk away, but he just keeps standing there, not quite looking at me. I open my mouth to say—something, I'm not quite sure what—but he beats me to it.

"I do have a dream job."

I blink. "What?"

He clears his throat. "A dream job. You know, like that weird list you have."

"It's not *weird*." Then, hesitantly, "So . . . what is it?"

He clears his throat again. "I want to own the shop. I know it's not that big or important, but . . . I don't know." He rocks on his heels. "You were right. Not about everything, I mean. I still think you're—well." He shakes his head. "I guess it doesn't matter anymore. But I have been bored with the shop. Fred's made enough to retire, so I don't think he cares how much money we make or about branching out at all. And there's a huge market for performance services, which is way more interesting. Plus I've always thought it would be cool to restore vintage race cars. I've got a buddy who does it in Ontario, and he's doing pretty well off it. And the shop could look cool if someone actually put some money into it, like a real vintage car shop."

I turn the idea over in my mind. I've seen enough of the You-Tube videos he watches to kind of understand what he has in mind. Camel-colored leather couches, chrome fixtures, maybe some old-fashioned posters of vintage cars . . .

"That would be cool," I say. "And you'd be great at it."

"Yeah, well." He shrugs. "Who knows? Maybe Fred will sell the shop to me, if I offer him a decent price. I think he's getting fed up with it. Dealing with flighty receptionists and everything." His eyes crinkle at the edges, the old John flashing through for a second.

My lips turn up. "You know what they say about women—hire them as receptionists for your auto shop, and a year or two later, they'll leave to do an internship at the Met."

"It's a stereotype for a reason," John says.

We smile at each other a little cautiously.

"You'd be great at running a race car shop," I say honestly.

"A performance shop," he corrects.

"Ooh, you should call it 'Race Cars 'R' Us.'"

He smiles. "See, this is why you should stick around and help. I never would've thought of such an exceptionally terrible name."

I open my mouth to respond, then close it again. Does he mean that?

I study his face. He's smiling like it's just a joke, but there's something underneath his expression, a seriousness that grows deeper as the silence stretches out.

"John . . ."

"You like it here, Em. I know you do. You could make a go of your caregiving business, and there's bound to be a job at a museum here, someday. I know it's not some big, fancy city, but . . . you could be happy here."

My throat grows a little tighter. I rub my arms against the chill of the evening air. "I know," I say quietly. "It's not that I wasn't happy here, it's just . . ."

"That you think you can be happier somewhere else."

I nod jerkily. "It's not that I *want* to leave . . . but I can't stay. It's too big." I look up at him, willing him to understand. "It's too big," I say again. "It's my life."

He stares at me for a long moment, his expression unreadable. Or rather, I *can* read it—the sharp flash of disappointment, the impulse to argue, the deep swell of regret—but I can't do anything to fix it.

I meant what I said. This opportunity is too big.

"Okay," he says finally. "I mean, it *isn't* okay." He lets out a funny, strangled laugh. "But . . . okay."

I blink quickly, fighting back sudden tears. I almost wish we could snap at each other again. This—this polite, quiet acceptance— is a hundred times more painful.

"I'm going to miss you," I say. "So much."

One corner of his mouth turns up. "Me too."

We stare at each other for another moment, then he clears his throat. "Okay, well. I'd better go."

I swipe a hand over my cheeks. "Right. Yeah."

"Good luck. I hope it's . . . yeah. Everything you want." He leans down to kiss me—my cheek, I think—but I shift to catch his lips with mine. It lasts just a second, not nearly enough.

"Night," he says, pulling away.

"Night," I echo. I rub my arms again. The evening air feels twice as cold now that he's stepped away.

He's halfway down the driveway when I hear myself speak again.

"Want to stay?"

He turns. "What?"

"Want to stay," I repeat. "I know we're—y'know. Broken up. But I just thought..." I trail off for a moment. "I don't know. Wouldn't you rather end things on a good note?"

He stares at me again, and for a minute, I think he's going to tell me no. But then he lets out a long, heavy breath, and the lines of his face relax a bit. "Yeah, all right."

I lick my lips, and nod a bit shakily. "Well... good." I try to summon up a brighter tone. "We can watch a movie or something. Plus, the people who own this place asked me to clear out all the cupboards for them, and I found a ninety-dollar bottle of wine that they've clearly forgotten about. I'd say it's our duty to drink it, don't you?"

With obvious effort, John puts on a smile.

"Yeah," he says quietly. "I guess so."

I PUT ON a movie—*Anne of Green Gables,* one last time—and we sip on wine and eat the rest of the pizza I ordered. It's a bit awkward at first. (Really awkward, if I'm being honest.) We're not together anymore—but we don't feel quite as broken up anymore either. For the first half of the movie, there's a stiffness in both of our shoulders, and when our hands brush reaching for a slice of pizza, we flinch apart like strangers.

But as Anne and Diana cry onscreen over the end of their friendship, something shifts in the air between us. *Farewell, my beloved friend,* Anne says. *Henceforth, we must be strangers living side by side.*

John exhales heavily and reaches his arm out to me, and I curl up in it without saying a word. I don't think about New York, or Waldon, or the fissure-like pain spreading through my heart. Tomorrow will come, whether I'm miserable about it or not. For now, I just want to breathe in the smoky scent of John's skin and sink into the warmth of his arms.

When Matthew dies at the end, I cry, but then John says, "Wait, who was that guy again?," which makes me laugh a little through my tears. He swipes the tears away with his thumb, and before I know it, we're kissing, as if nothing bad has ever happened between us. The real world is out there, threatening to swallow us up, but if anything, it only makes every moment with him sweeter, an undercurrent of pain that throws our time together into sharper focus.

His mouth moves over my fingertips, my wrists; his fingers dig into my thighs as I shift into his lap, letting my head fall back as his lips find my neck. The sound of his breathing is loud in my ears; the urgent heat in my veins is growing stronger. His hand shifts between us, two strong fingers slipping beneath layers of cloth to send widening rings of pleasure through my body. As we stumble to the bedroom, leaving a trail of clothes in the hall, I give myself over to the feel of his mouth and his hands, and I try not to think of it as a goodbye.

In the morning, I wake up five minutes before my alarm goes off. I'm not sure why. Maybe it's the half-bottle of wine I drank, or maybe it's some internal alarm warning me I only have five minutes left with John.

It's too dark to see his face, but I can hear the soft, deep sounds of his breath. I shift closer to him and feel him stir as I lay my head on his chest.

"'Larm go off?" he mumbles.

"Not yet," I whisper. "Five more minutes."

His warm arms wrap around me and I feel his breathing even out again. I must fall asleep again, too, because I'm woken up by my alarm blaring angrily. I turn it off as quickly as I can, but it's too late. The moment is broken.

It's time to go.

I slip out of bed and get ready for the day, pulling on comfortable clothes for the plane and braiding my hair into two French braids. At 5:15 a.m., I sit down on the edge of the bed and put my hand on John's shoulder.

"John," I whisper. "I've got to go."

He blinks blearily in the dim light and then drags himself out of bed to walk me to the door. He's still half asleep, but he wakes up as he helps me lug my suitcases to the car.

"Is that it?" he asks.

I know he's talking about the luggage, but the words still cut down to my bones.

"Yeah," I say quietly. "That's it."

We look at each other. Crickets chirp in the darkness. He moves first, wrapping his arms around me tightly. I press my face into his shoulder. I am not going to cry.

"Drive safe," he says.

I nod into his chest. "Will do."

We stay like that for another few seconds, then I lean up to kiss him.

*Our last kiss*, whispers a voice in the back of my mind. And yeah, that's no good. I'm definitely crying now.

I pull away first and say, in a strangled voice, "I hope things work out with the shop. You'd be really great at it."

"Thanks. You too. With the museum stuff, I mean."

"You don't think I could run a racing performance shop?"

He smiles thinly. "No," he says. "I guess not."

For a brief, painful second, I let myself imagine staying here. I know he's not really expecting me to stay and help him run an auto shop, but I think I can picture the future we could have together. Me, coming home from a day of caregiving work to laugh with him about whatever mean things Doris said, while he tells me about the new bit of equipment he's ordering, or asks my opinion on which billing system to buy. Going to dinners with Kiara and Jake and his parents, looking for houses together, embedding ourselves fully in our happy Waldon life.

I swallow hard. "Well—bye, then."

He lets out a heavy breath. "Bye."

We look at each other a moment, then there's nothing to do but turn away and get in my car. He stands barefoot in the driveway and watches as I back onto the road. I raise my hand in one last wave, then I put the car in drive and pull away. I watch my mirrors, wondering if he'll walk to the end of the driveway to watch me go, but if he does, it's too dark to see it. At the end of the street, I turn left at the stop sign, and that's it.

On to my next life.

# CHAPTER 31

The air in the city is hot and humid and smells like car exhaust and garbage. The streets are teeming with people, including a family of tourists who practically shove me and my suitcases off the sidewalk in their haste to get to Starbucks, and it's so loud I can hardly hear the scary guy with the angry political sign screaming obscenities at me. It's chaos—total chaos—and it's scary and intimidating and *brilliant*.

Don't get me wrong, I'm still totally torn up about leaving John. Part of me wishes he'd never come over last night, that I could have left when things were tense and angry. It would be easier to deal with than this strange, squicky feeling I have now, one that feels eerily close to uncertainty. But I can't give in to that. I need to focus, instead, on the immense, shiny buildings looming overhead, and the laughter of a group of girls my age passing by on the sidewalk, and the feel of the bright New York sun beating down on my skin.

As I wait for the lady at the NYU admissions office to get my dorm keys, I watch people walk by on the street. Even in the sweltering midsummer heat, everyone seems to be moving purposefully from place to place, striding along the hot pavement as though they don't have a second to waste. It couldn't be more different from Waldon, where some of the locals' favorite activities include sitting on a park bench and watching the ocean, sitting on a park bench and watching traffic go by, and sitting on a park bench watching absolutely nothing.

My dorm room is small but clean, and eerily similar to my old dorm at university. It's like I've gone back in time, like I've hit the reset button on my own life.

I don't want to unpack right now because I have a feeling if I stop moving my grief will catch up with me, so instead I just dump my suitcases in my room, change out of my grimy travel clothes, and head back out onto the streets. I'm not even going to look at a map, I'm just going to wander around and stare.

Every corner seems to hold something interesting to look at, whether it's a gorgeous building or a cute little park or a group of models decked out in head-to-toe Chanel. Some of it is kind of scary, like a group of guys that leer at me and a woman hissing nasty things at strangers, but as long as I keep walking, I can keep my nerves at bay. I'm like a shark. As long as I keep moving, I won't drown.

The shiny newness of the city keeps me going until late afternoon, but by the time I make it back to my dorm, I'm sweaty and sunburned and my feet are two solid blocks of pain. I sit down on my unmade bed with a thump. I briefly consider ordering a pizza for dinner, but that would be staying still, and staying still is death. Instead, I dig a summer dress and cardigan out of my suitcase and look up the fanciest restaurant within walking distance. My parents transferred two hundred dollars to my bank account as an early birthday present and ordered me to spend it all on a good meal.

I wind up at a restaurant called Frost, a small, ultramodern place with deep-blue lighting and white velvet booths tucked between faux ice sculptures. I hardly recognize a thing on the menu, so I pick something at random and order something called an Ice Melt cocktail to sip on while I wait. It's absolutely gorgeous, a very pale-blue liquid with a single ice cube in the shape of an iceberg in a fancy glass with a sugary rim. I take a sip—yikes, that's strong—and rest my chin on my hands, letting my eyes move over the restaurant. It's really early, barely six o'clock, so it's not that busy, but there are a group of young girls nearby dressed in cocktail dresses and an elderly woman with a heavy silver necklace sitting alone. Her hands tremble slightly as she takes a sip of her water, and I wonder if she has someone to help her at home. For a moment, I think about doing a little caregiving work here in New York.

Then I shake my head and take another sip of my drink. There's no way I want to mess around with US healthcare. If one of my clients fell and broke their hip here, their family would probably sue me for negligence. John's mother has a friend who works as an obstetrician somewhere in the States, and when she told me how much he pays in malpractice insurance, it literally made me sick to my stomach.

Plus, I'm not going to have time to do any caregiving. I'm going to be way too busy with classes, and my internship, and my duties as dorm supervisor. In fact, my life will be so exciting and full, I doubt I'll even have time to think about Waldon or John. The days will fly by, and before long I'll be like, John who?

I take another sip of my drink. While I'm just sitting here, waiting for my food, I may as well do today's Wordle.

FROST, I type in.

The R is green, the O is yellow.

My gaze wanders the restaurant again. At the table nearest me, the group of girls are giggling as they give the handsome waiter their order.

ORDER, I type.

Okay, now we're getting somewhere. The O is yellow, the R is green, the E is yellow, and the *second* R is yellow. That means it has to be—

ERROR, I type in.

Crap.

It's right.

I really hope that's not the universe's way of telling me I've made a mistake.

But it can't be a mistake. It just isn't possible. This is the start of my new, exciting life. In ten years, when I'm a curator at some fabulous museum in London and I'm married to some gorgeous British guy who's absolutely nothing like John, we'll be sitting in our white-marble kitchen one day and I'll tell him this story and say, "Can you believe I almost gave all of this up?" And he'll laugh and say, "Yeah, for some mechanic in Nowhereville." And then I'll say, "It wasn't *Nowhereville*, asshole, it was Waldon, PEI, and that mechanic was a million times better than you'll ever be—"

Wait.

No, that last bit's wrong.

I sigh heavily just as my food arrives.

"Everything okay?" the waiter asks. He's the same handsome waiter that the other table was giggling over, and his expression is warm and interested. Call it intuition, but I can just tell that if I say something witty right now, he'll banter back and maybe even wind up asking for my phone number.

"Mm-hmm," I say instead, lowering my eyes. The interest in his gaze falls away, and he retreats with a polite, impartial smile.

I stare down at my meal. It looks delicious—a glazed piece of fish and tiny little vegetables drizzled artfully with a pale-green sauce—but I've kind of lost my appetite. I make myself finish it all, but when the waiter comes to ask if I want dessert, I shake my head and ask for the bill.

It's still bright and hot outside, but I head back to my dorm room and set about unpacking. Maybe if I set up my new room, it'll start feeling like my new home. I leave my door open, just in case any other students are around, but three hours pass and no one walks by. The lady I got the keys from said the dorms are basically empty this time of year. Most of the students won't arrive for another month.

At ten o'clock, I give up and close my door. I sit at the little desk and stare out the window, which overlooks the street. People are still striding by purposefully, but the scene doesn't seem nearly as compelling as it did earlier. In fact, just for a second, the city seems loud and kind of exhausting.

I take out my phone and open my texts. My thumb briefly hovers over John's name, but I force myself not to click on it. Instead, I email my parents to tell them about the meal I had and wish them a safe flight home from New Zealand, and then answer Rose's cheerful text asking if I've arrived safely.

A few minutes later, my phone dings, but it isn't my mom or Rose.

[10:07] **Kiara:** Hope NYC is good so far.

[10:07] **Kiara:** We all miss you.

My eyes well up unexpectedly. I look up at the ceiling and blink quickly until the tears go away.

[10:08]: I miss you all too.

I hesitate, then type again.

[10:09]: This really sucks.

[10:10] **Kiara:** I know.

[10:10] **Kiara:** But you have to do what's best for you.

[10:10] **Kiara:** Sorry I was kind of weird the last time we met.

[10:11] **Kiara:** I'm just really going to miss you. ☹

[10:11]: It's okay.

[10:12]: I'm going to miss you too.

I send a heart emoji, then I put my phone down and press the heels of my hands into my eyes. The ache in my throat is so fierce I feel sick. But I'm not going to break down. I'm not going to spend my first night here crying. I'm not, I'm *not*.

I force myself to look out the window again. Look at those lights. Listen to the sound of this city.

I'm going to be happy here.

I am.

# CHAPTER 32

In the morning, I wake to the sound of an ambulance siren. It's 7:30 a.m., and sunlight is streaming in through my tiny window, warming the bare skin of my arms. There's a cold weight in my chest where my heart used to be, but I'm determined to ignore it. Not today, I tell it sternly. Today is the first day of my new internship. Today, I'm not going to be sad.

I dress in an outfit that I hope comes off as chic and professional—a knee-length skirt, ballet shoes, and a collared shirt. I almost put on the necklace John gave me, the one with the tiny sword that Kiara made, but after a moment I set it aside. I'm not going to keep holding on to the past. I'm going to move on properly, starting today.

I stride out into the sunlight and make my way to the nearest subway station. I get off at Seventy-Seventh Street and fall into step with the swelling crowd, many of them heading to the same place as me.

My feet slow as I reach the base of the steps, and my breath catches in my throat as I peer up at the towering pillars, the curving arches, the deep red banners hung on either side of the doors, emblazoned with two simple words.

The Met.

I float through the line in a bit of a daze, handing over my money when I get to the front. I guess I could tell them that I'm here for my first internship day, so I don't have to pay, but that doesn't start until one, and anyway, right now I just want to experience it like everyone else. I want to wander around aimlessly and breathe it all in.

I spend the morning walking around, twisting my neck up to look at the ceiling in the Great Hall and gazing in awe at the Temple of Dendur and the Charles Engelhard Court. I peer at ancient weapons and costumes and study intricate suits of armor. I eavesdrop on a couple having a (slightly pretentious) argument about whether or not you can create great art without experiencing trauma, and giggle at a rich woman who's snuck her tiny dog into the museum in a Prada bag. I watch a girl in her late teens stare at a painting for ten full minutes, her brown-eyed gaze soft and faraway.

*This.*

This is why I came here.

I love absolutely everything about this place. The smell of the air; the sound of my footsteps on the marble floors; the low, rolling murmur of the crowd. Working in a place like this, creating spaces where people can escape from the stress in their lives and get lost in the past for an hour or two . . .

It really is my dream job.

I find a bench in a quiet hall and sit down opposite a portrait of an elderly woman in a heavy gown. I take deep breaths in and out, trying to draw the feeling of this place inside of me. I can feel the muscles of my shoulders getting looser. I wonder if this is how people feel when they meditate. Not a single thought in their head, just a vague sense of contentedness.

I wonder how Mrs. Finnamore is doing.

The thought pops into my head out of nowhere. She's supposed to be getting out of the hospital today. I wonder if they've changed any of her medicines around. I wonder if she'll listen if they did.

I shake my head impatiently. Mrs. Finnamore isn't a part of my life now. There's no sense in worrying about her anymore.

I turn away from the painting of the elderly woman to face a marble statue of a naked woman carrying a vase.

Much better. She doesn't remind me of Mrs. Finnamore at all.

I space out for a little while, until a group of tourists pass by on a guided tour. I wonder absently if the Met does tours for New York nursing home residents. If they don't, maybe I could arrange some during my internship. Even someone as crotchety as Doris would be hard-pressed to complain about a place like this.

Actually, that's not true. She would definitely find things to complain about. The long lines, the abundance of "youths," the signs advertising free wi-fi for visitors ("So kids can look at their *phones* instead of the art," she would scoff. "What genius came up with that idea?").

I try to imagine how Jim or Mrs. Finnamore would react, but if I'm honest, I'm not sure they would like it either. Mrs. Finnamore would find the museum too cold and crowded, and I think it would all be too overwhelming for Jim. I think he liked working at the barrel museum because it gave him a reason to get out of his house and talk to people, not because of any deep-rooted interest in barrels or museums.

I hope he isn't missing me too much. Maybe I should call him tonight, just in case.

I shake my head again roughly. Seriously, what is wrong with me? I need to stop thinking about Waldon. I need to totally cut the cord, like I've done with John. Mrs. Finnamore and Jim aren't a part of my life anymore. They aren't a part of this dream.

I get to my feet again—staying still is the enemy—and wander determinedly until one o'clock, when I make my way back to the museum entrance and nervously ask a worker where the new interns go. He directs me to a room in the Egyptian Art wing and tells me to look for a woman named Benedita Ferreira.

A murmur of voices welcomes me into the room. There are a few tourists milling around, peering at the exhibits, but there's also a slightly awkward-looking group in the corner who must be my fellow interns. Most of them look younger than me, but to my relief there's a man and a woman who look about my age.

I smooth down my hair and approach them nervously. The man who looks about my age, a tall Asian guy with short dark hair, looks around as I approach.

"Here for the internship?" he guesses.

I nod. "Yeah."

He gives me a wide smile. "Us too."

He introduces himself as David, and the rest of the group offer me their names in rapid succession. There are so many of them that only a few of them stick in my mind, like Leah, the woman nearest my age, and Katarina, a short, dark-haired girl with glasses and a really friendly smile.

"Where are you from?" David asks me.

Before I can answer him, an older woman with an official-looking name tag strides toward the group.

"Welcome," she says, smiling at all of us. She has long dark hair, a stylish suit, and high heels that click along the marble. "Are you my new interns?"

"Yes, ma'am," Leah says, while the rest of us murmur in agreement.

"Wonderful. Do we have everyone yet?" She counts aloud. "Eighteen, nineteen—yes, that looks like all of you. Please, gather around."

We shuffle into a half-circle around her. One girl jostles for a spot in the center, making a big show of taking a notebook out of her bag to take notes. David, who's standing next to me, catches my eye and grins. I hide a smile. There's one in every group.

"I'm Benedita Ferreira," the woman introduces herself. "Program coordinator for internships, and curator specializing in early-twentieth-century art. How are you all doing today?"

"Nervous," I murmur under my breath, while the rest of the interns say, "Good."

Benedita tells us a bit about the internship program and then we do a round of introductions. I'm a bit anxious hearing all the things that everyone else has done. Half of them have interned or worked in museums before, and most of them are from the States, except for David, who moved to the US from China as a kid, and a girl named Gabriela, who's from Mexico. They all tilt their heads a bit when I say I was born in Nova Scotia.

"Is that a city?" the girl with the notebook asks.

"It's a province in Canada. But I was living in Prince Edward Island—that's another province—before I came here."

"Ooh, like in *Anne of Green Gables*," Katarina says.

I smile at her. "Yep."

Benedita leads us out of the Egyptian Art wing through a locked door, which opens on a long, plain hallway lined with doors. Some of the doors seem to be offices—I see a man talking on the phone at his desk, and a woman typing at a computer—while others kind of look like laboratories, with long white countertops and rows of glass cupboards. I feel a stir of excitement. This is so cool. Like going behind the scenes at Disney World or something.

We end up in a small classroom, where Benedita hands out shiny folders with our names on them. Inside, there are badges and brochures and a schedule of activities.

"As you can see in your schedules, you'll spend time in every wing of the museum, but I encourage you all to find a particular area that really interests you and dive into it as much as you can. You'll mostly be shadowing curators for the first few months, but down the road, there will be opportunities to get involved in research projects and acquisitions—perhaps even to help design installations."

A fizz of excitement runs through me as I read through all the different wings I'll get to see. Arms and Armor, Ancient Near Eastern Art, Drawings and Prints . . . they all sound amazing. I don't know how I'm going to pick just one to focus on.

*You wish you could do a lot of things.*

John's voice pops into my mind out of nowhere. I shake it away irritably. I'm not going to think about John right now. Or later, for that matter.

"For your first month, you only have one piece of homework," Benedita says. "And that's to come up with an idea for an exhibit. This is an exercise in creativity, so don't be limited by feasibility or budget. At the end of the month, you'll each present your exhibit idea to the group, for feedback and discussion."

An interested murmur passes through the room—several interns sit up a little, looking pleased, as though they already have great ideas. I feel a stab of nerves—all I can think of right now are exhibits of barrels. But I'm sure with a little bit of time, I can come up with something great.

Benedita pulls down a projector screen at the front of the room, and for the next hour, we watch a video on the history of the Met. Notebook Girl (whose real name, I think, is Lydia) scribbles furious notes, as do some of the others, but I just rest my chin in my hands and listen. Every word is like a balm on my soul. I've always wanted to be a part of something big and important, and watching the video, learning about all the amazing artwork and sculpture and pieces of history the museum's housed . . . it's every bit as wonderful as I always hoped.

Afterward, we do a few of those awkward icebreaker games to get to know one another, then Benedita releases us to enjoy the museum for the rest of the day.

"The names and office numbers of your first supervisors are written on your schedule," she says. "Who's starting with me—ah, Emily." I look up. "If you want to come with me for a second, I'll show you where my office is for tomorrow."

I edge around Notebook Girl, who's scowling at me a bit jealously, and follow Benedita to a room just a few doors down the hall. Her office is small and cozy, with hundreds of old books crammed into a bookshelf and a heavy desk covered in papers. There are a bunch of photos on the wall that must be of her family.

There's a wedding photo of her and her wife, and another picture of them with two kids.

"I hope it wasn't too hard to get here on time," Benedita says. "I know you didn't have much notice."

"Oh, no," I say. "It was totally fine." That's a tiny lie, but I mean it when I add, "I'm just happy to be here."

She smiles. "I'm sure you're going to love it. You worked at a museum before, didn't you?"

"Er—I was just a volunteer, actually. It was just a really tiny museum in PEI."

"There's nothing wrong with that. Small museums have their challenges, of course, but they also have their charms."

"Yes, ma'am. Ours was about barrel-making. We had a cooper who did demonstrations with old equipment."

She smiles. "Sounds wonderful. Now, if you'll excuse me, I've got to head out to attend to a few things. But I'll meet you here tomorrow at nine a.m."

"See you then."

I sneak one last glance around her office then return to the classroom, where most of the interns are still gathering their things.

"Some of us are going to explore a bit," David tells me, standing with a group that includes Leah and Katarina. "Want to join us?"

I smile, feeling a pleasant warmth settle over my shoulders. "Yeah," I tell him. "I'd love to."

# CHAPTER 33

The next few days rush by in a nerve-wracking blur, then it feels like I blink and two weeks have gone by. It's kind of strange how quickly I fall into a new rhythm: wake to the sound of sirens, eat a quick bowl of cereal in my room, rush to the subway to make it to the museum by nine.

I spend my days in the bowels of the Met, watching Benedita do her work. I'm so glad I've been paired with her first. She's so kind and knowledgeable, and she never makes me feel stupid for asking questions. Which is a good thing, because most of what she says is totally beyond me. Following her around is like a study in my own ignorance. I kind of thought curators just tracked down interesting things, came up with a clever way to display them, and then voilà! On to the next thing. The reality is much more complicated and sometimes—if I'm being perfectly honestly—a teensy bit dull.

Benedita spends a lot of her time doing research, for example, and although she tries to include me as much as she can, the fact of the matter is, a big part of research is just sitting quietly and reading. Those are the worst times, because whenever my brain isn't distracted, it immediately starts thinking about John and Waldon. Missing John isn't a surprise—I didn't expect my feelings to go away overnight—but I'm surprised by how much I miss Waldon itself. Sometimes I'll be walking along and suddenly remember something random, like the cute dog that used to trot out to see me every morning when I did my run, or the smell of the local library where I used to check out books.

It'll all fade the longer I'm here, I'm sure.

When I'm busy, it's easier, so I fill most of my days from dawn till dusk. I'm starting to get to know the other interns a little better, especially Katarina, Leah, and David. Katarina has lived in New York for a few years now, so she gives us a bunch of tips on free things to do in the city. In all my fantasies about living in big cities, I'd kind of glazed over how expensive they are. My dreams of going to art galleries and restaurants have been amended to reading books in Central Park, wandering the High Line, and eating ninety-nine-cent ramen for most of my meals. And while the energy in the city is just as amazing as I always imagined, it's also sort of—

Tiring. And loud.

But I try not to dwell on that. It's just different, that's all. I just need time to adjust.

I throw all my energy into my exhibit project, the one Benedita assigned us on our first day. Katarina and Leah and David all have great ideas for theirs—Leah wants to showcase this really eccentric local artist who makes art out of trash, Katarina is designing an exhibit of art by single moms, and David wants to do a display of children's toys from the 1300s to today. I spend night after night trying to come up with something equally clever, but I don't strike upon inspiration until one day in Central Park.

I'm jogging alone, trying not to think about this murder documentary I saw about a girl who was killed jogging in Central Park, when I spot a stooped, gray-haired woman sitting on a park bench, struggling to open a bottle of juice. She has a tiny, yappy dog with her whose leash is wrapped precariously around her wrist. My feet slow to a stop, sensing the impending disaster.

"Do you need help with that?" I ask, before I can stop myself.

She looks up at me, her eyes narrowing suspiciously. I've noticed that's everyone's first reaction in New York when a stranger talks to them.

I must look harmless enough, because her expression relaxes and she smiles at me. "Yes, thank you."

She hands me the dog's leash, and it throws itself eagerly at me while she uses both hands to twist off the bottle cap.

"He's so cute," I say, handing the leash back to her.

(This is a tiny lie—he's a scrawny, half-balding chihuahua with a horrendous pair of bright pink booties.)

The woman cackles. "You think so? Looks like a drowned rat, to me. He's my daughter's dog."

I stifle a laugh, then kneel to pat the poor little dog on his head. It's not his fault he looks like a rat. "Does your daughter live here?" I ask politely. The woman doesn't look like a local—for one thing, she's wearing an I ♥ NY T-shirt.

But she surprises me by shaking her head. "She lives in Jersey. She's just visiting me for the weekend. I've lived here for seventy-seven years," she adds. There's a distinct note of pride in her voice.

"Wow," I say. "And you—like it here?"

It's a stupid question, I realize as I say it. Of course she likes it here, why else would she have stayed so long (or be wearing that T-shirt)? But I'm curious to hear what exactly she likes about it. All the older people I knew in Waldon would despise living in New York City. They would find it too loud, too rushed, too crowded.

"Of course!" the woman says. "I was born here during the Blizzard of '47, and I haven't left since." She laughs, revealing very white, shiny dentures.

"Was that a big blizzard?"

"Big! It was huge. Nothing like these little flurries that people these days call a storm."

I grin. That sounds like something the older people in Waldon would say. No snowstorm is ever as big as the one happening in front of you. "That's really neat," I say. "Were your parents born here too?"

As it turns out, they were, and for the next half hour, the woman tells me about them—her mother, a seamstress, and her father, a painter. I ease myself onto the bench as she talks, feeling myself drawn into the slow rhythm of her speech. She talks like Jim does, dropping names of friends and family as if they're people I should already know. "And of course Aunt Mabel hated that," she says, and I nod conspiratorially, as if I knew Aunt Mabel too.

I ask her what she did for a living, and that's its own story—a clerk at a grocery store, a history teacher, a stay-at-home mom of six (six!). She's telling me about her youngest daughter, whom she hilariously refers to as the "least clever one," when all of a sudden she looks at her watch.

"Oh, would you look at that." She rises to her feet. "I've got to run. Pleasure chatting with you, dear."

She ambles off with her dog, and as I glance down at my phone, I realize with a jolt that a whole hour has gone by.

There's a strange ache in my chest as I rise to my feet. I try to make myself jog again, but my legs are slow and heavy. I walk the park instead, thinking and chewing on my lip.

I've missed talking to older people, I realize. I miss talking to people who grew up outside of my time. I miss that little spark of interest when I learn something about the past, like the time Jim told me about rumrunners during PEI's prohibition years, or when Mrs. Finnamore described the dress Queen Elizabeth II wore during her royal tour of the province. It's like time traveling, almost. Being transported back to a moment that happened before you existed.

I stop dead in my tracks as an idea hits me.

*That's* what I want to do for my exhibit. I want to give people that feeling.

The very next day, I bring it up to Benedita. I'm speaking quickly with excitement, leaning forward in my chair in her office. I know it's only an exercise in creativity, but I can't help but feel I've struck upon something really cool.

"Picture a dark, quiet room filled with little enclosed booths," I say. "And every booth has a video feed of an older person talking about their life growing up in the city."

"Like artists and historians, you mean?" Benedita asks.

"No, just average people," I say brightly. "Regular people telling regular stories. Like this woman I met yesterday in the park—she told me the funniest story about her family's milkman back in the fifties, and how he always got their order wrong on Thursdays." I hesitate, seeing Benedita's slightly bemused look. "It was funnier when she told it," I admit. "But that's the point, see? It's a glimpse into the past, told by people who actually lived in it."

Benedita smiles. "It's a lovely idea," she says. "Really creative."

I bite my lip. I can hear an unspoken *but*.

"I could do something else," I say, "if you don't think it's a good idea."

"Oh no," she says. "I told you, this is not about realism, it's about creativity!"

I nod, but I can't help wondering—why couldn't an exhibit like that be real?

"The Met focuses more on art and sculpture, that's all," Benedita says. "But it's certainly a clever idea. I would go to an exhibit like that."

I can't tell if she's just placating me. I muster a smile. "I'll keep thinking," I say. "I'm sure I can come up with something more . . . artsy."

"Let me know if I can help," she says kindly, then turns back to her computer, which is open to an article about an old painting.

I keep a bright, interested look on my face, but in truth, I'm a little disappointed. I thought it was a pretty cool idea. In fact, I had this secret daydream that when Benedita heard it, she would want to make it into a real exhibit. But that's pretty childish of me. The Met isn't a tiny barrel museum in Waldon where I can nail up a stack of barrels and call it an exhibit. It's one of the greatest collections of art in the world—and videos of old people telling funny stories about milkmen aren't art.

*Why not, though?* whispers a voice in my head.

I shake my head and push the thought away. But I'm distracted the rest of the day, and at lunchtime I find myself typing "private caregiving services New York City" into my phone. I close the tab before it can load, annoyed with myself. Yes, I miss talking with older people, but I've already decided I'm not going to try to do any caregiving here. I need to focus on my internship, my new friends, my new life.

I open a new tab and type in "young hot up-and-coming artists

NYC," and after filtering out the inevitable porn, I find a twenty-one-year-old artist in Queens who re-creates famous paintings out of candy. A *Mona Lisa* made of M&M'S, blue raspberry Twizzlers swirling in *The Starry Night*. In thirty minutes, I've done up my presentation for the end of the month. It's bright and quirky and young, the polar opposite of my first idea.

When I tell Leah, Katarina, and David about it at dinner, they smile and tell me they love it, and David suggests I call it "Candy Land," as a funny tie-in to his children's toy exhibit. I make myself laugh with them, but there's a hollow feeling in my chest.

Katarina tilts her head at me. "Everything okay, Emily?"

"Oh, yeah," I say quickly. "Just a bit tired. A bunch of sirens woke me up at, like, five a.m. today."

She grimaces. "Brutal. You'll get used to them after a while. I don't even hear them anymore."

"Yeah, but you're a city girl," Leah says. "Em and I are small town. Right, Em?"

"Small town!" Katarina laughs. "You grew up in Boston, Leah."

"Outside of Boston," Leah retorts. "My suburb was *tiny*, there were, like, barely two thousand kids at my high school."

"Two thousand is a lot, dummy," Katarina says.

David catches my eye and pulls an amused face. Katarina and Leah can bicker for hours about nothing. I try to smile back, but my mind is still caught on Leah's words.

*Em and I are small town.*

She says it like it's something innate and unchangeable, like someone's eye color or height. As if there's a small-town gene that makes you crave quiet mornings and wide-open spaces. My mouth twitches up a little at the thought. If there is a small-town gene,

John definitely has it. And Kiara, too, for all she liked to complain about Waldon.

As for me . . . I don't know. Maybe I am small town at heart. But that doesn't mean I have to stay that way. People can change their natures, if they want it enough.

I shake my head and refocus on Leah and Katarina's conversation, but the thought follows me home on the subway, echoing under the thrum of the rails and the noise of the crowd. In the relative quiet of my dorm room, the words get louder.

*People can change their natures, if they want it enough.*

I peer out of my window, watching all the people, staring at all the lights. This is what I came here for. The noise, the energy. I want this life.

Don't I?

# CHAPTER 34

On Friday, at the end of our third week, the intern schedule brings us all back to our classroom at the end of the day, where Benedita gives us some exciting news. We're all invited to come back to the museum tonight to attend a gala that one of the museum's major donors is hosting. A murmur of excitement spreads through the room. As Benedita passes our invitations around, I hear Lydia (or as I still sometimes call her in my head, Notebook Girl) whisper to her friend, "I am *so* wearing Prada."

Since I don't have any Prada (and probably couldn't even afford a Prada rip-off), I put on my nicest sundress and heels after dinner and head back to the museum at eight. The whole building is lit up from within, and there are a bunch of people in gowns and tuxes on the stairs. I feel like I've been dropped into a scene from *The Devil Wears Prada* (only I'm dressed like the girl was before her makeover).

Inside, it's loud and gorgeous and more than a little intimidating. I shake my head politely at a waiter who offers me champagne (can't he tell I'm not a proper guest?) and hurry to the corner, where I spy a group of my fellow interns. They all look as out-of-place as I feel, except Lydia, who's dressed in a seriously gorgeous gown and keeps flipping her hair and smiling at one of the guests nearby.

The interns' talk turns to everyone's school plans for fall, and I try to listen politely, but it's hard to hear much of what they're saying. The high ceiling and smooth marble floors make everything louder and yet more muffled at the same time. I smile and nod occasionally, shifting my weight surreptitiously as my feet start to ache in my heels.

After a while, my attention starts to wander. I gaze around the hall, taking in the general atmosphere. The Great Hall is staggeringly beautiful at night, with the dim light magnifying every intricate carving on the walls and ceiling, and all the guests look so fancy and glittery. It's exactly the type of event I always dreamed I'd attend—and yet I can't picture myself ever belonging with the people around me, no matter how hard I try.

I spot Benedita in the distance. She's walking across the room with her wife, whom I've learned is also a curator at the museum. They're both dressed in long gowns that I know probably aren't as expensive as the other guests', but that look just as lovely to me. They seem to be talking seriously about something, though they're interrupted every few steps by guests who want to talk to them.

I catch echoed snippets of their conversation as they come nearer.

"Ana can't do ballet the same night Molly does tae kwon do, unless we can find a place closer by— Evening Mrs. Bellmont! Yes, the collection is coming along wonderfully—of course, thanks again—"

"What if we let Ana take the subway by herself? She's fourteen now, I'd say she's— Oh, hi, Frederick, lovely to see you. How's your wife doing? She must be due any day now, right?"

"Lord, what an insufferable man. The last thing this world needs is more of his DNA— Well, hello, my lovely interns!"

The rest of the group swivels around at Benedita's greeting, and Lydia rushes forward to compliment her outfit. I hang back, smiling faintly. I may not be able to picture myself as one of the rich, fancy guests, but I *can* picture myself in Benedita's shoes. Working hard at a job I love, with a partner by my side who really understands me.

Two interns drop back near me to whisper to each other. "See that guy?" one of them says. "He works at the *New York Times.* I'm going to go introduce myself, wanna come?"

I jolt in alarm. The *New York Times.* Crap.

The day's been so busy, I forgot to do Wordle. I'm so close to hitting a year, I can't give up on it now.

I make noises about finding a bathroom and then hurry off to a quieter hall. I take out my phone and see I've missed a few texts.

[7:53] **Rose:** I heard a rumor today that Shelley might be moving to Charlottetown

[7:53] **Rose:** All the folks who worked with her at the store are thinking of pooling in to pay for her moving van ;-)

[7:53] **Rose:** Hope you're doing well!

[8:05] **Kiara:** Want to have a (virtual) coffee date this weekend?

[8:05] **Kiara:** I want to hear how things are going down there

[8:05] **Kiara:** Plus I have news

[8:06] **Kiara:** (And NO, I'm not pregnant)

[8:06] **Kiara:** (Thank god)

[8:06] **Kiara:** It's about John.

[8:07] **Kiara:** Hopefully it's not too weird to hear stuff about him, but I thought you'd want to know he bought the shop.

[8:07] **Kiara:** Or he's buying it, anyway

[8:07] **Kiara:** That douche Fred is totally gouging him, so John's buying him out slowly over the next couple months

[8:07] **Kiara:** Still, it's pretty cool!

[8:08] **Kiara:** Unless hearing things about him ISN'T cool and makes you feel sad

[8:08] **Kiara:** In which case please erase these messages from your brain

My heart twists strangely in my chest. John bought the *shop*? I look around the empty hallway. I feel—

I don't know how I feel. My fingertips are prickly, and there's the strangest feeling stirring inside me.

I can't *believe* John bought the shop.

My thumb hovers over my phone. The urge to text him is almost overwhelming. But what would I say? That I'm happy for him? That I'm proud of him for going after his dream? That I wish I could be there to see him do it?

I swipe an impatient hand over my cheek. I'm practically crying all of a sudden, which doesn't make sense. I've already put John and Waldon behind me. This news doesn't change anything.

Does it?

I flinch as a door bangs open down the hall. A pair of uniformed servers stride toward me carrying heavy bags of ice. They look at me curiously. I clear my throat and swipe open Wordle, just to have something to point my eyes at.

I try to think of a word to start with—some word that encapsulates the feeling of this gala, maybe—but for some reason I'm drawing a total blank.

*DREAM*, whispers a voice in the back of my mind. As in, John is going after his dream.

I shake my head roughly. I'm not going to use that. I'm happy for John, but his future has nothing to do with me.

OUIJA, I type instead, back to my old banker word.

After a few more guesses, I get the answer—STAND.

I stare at it for a second, feeling strangely flat inside. Each Wordle answer used to give me a little thrill. A sign that I was one day closer to my yearlong streak, maybe even a sign about some upcoming event in my life. Now all I see is a random, five-letter word.

I turn my eyes to the high, painted ceiling, but all I can see is John standing on my Waldon doorstep.

*I do have a dream job,* he said.

Footsteps echo again down the hall. The caterers are gone; David, Katarina, and Leah are headed toward me, all of them slightly flushed and smiling.

"There you are!" Katarina says brightly.

"Benedita said we could wander around the rest of the museum a bit while it's empty," Leah adds, "as long as we tell the security guards where we're going and don't try to steal any priceless art. Want to come with?"

"Oh—sure," I say automatically. "That sounds great."

"Just let me pee first," Katarina says, and pops into the ladies' room nearby.

"Way too much champagne," Leah adds, following her.

David smiles at me as the bathroom door swings shut behind them. He has a nice smile, I notice. Wide and straight, with a deep dimple on both cheeks.

"Are you having fun?" he asks.

I nod. "This place is gorgeous at night."

"Definitely." He glances at my phone. "Hey, is that Wordle?"

I look down. "Oh—yeah." I smile sheepishly. "Had to do it before midnight."

"Don't show me the answer," he says, putting one hand over his eyes. "I haven't done it yet. Don't want to cheat."

"Do you have a streak going?"

He nods. "Ninety-two days. You?"

"Almost a year."

He laughs, bright and easy. "That's awesome."

Katarina and Leah emerge from the bathroom, giggling and swaying slightly on their heels.

"C'mon," Leah says. "Let's go explore."

She and Katarina head off, arm in arm, and David takes a few steps after them. Then he turns back and smiles at me. "You coming?"

He holds a hand out to me, palm up.

As he stands there, smiling under the glittering lights, something happens to me—something I'm not sure I could explain if I live to be a hundred. I have this sudden—*vision*, I guess, of what my life will be like if I reach out and take his hand.

He and Leah and Katarina and I will grow closer and closer. We'll eat dinners together and laugh over coffee at lunch, we'll slowly start to share our hopes and troubles and fears. And then one night, way down the road, when the memories of John have faded away, David will smile at me and ask me to dinner, and I'll say yes, full of fizzy excitement and unbridled glee.

Flash forward another five or ten years, and we're both curators at some big museum. Maybe the Met, maybe somewhere else entirely. We're getting stopped by guests every few feet as we walk through an event, and chatting in between interruptions about our dog's flea medicine or a trip we've got planned. He says something funny and I laugh and smack his arm. Things aren't perfect—maybe we fight now and then, maybe some of our work is a bit of a grind—but at the end of the day, I'm happy. Really, truly happy.

I could have that. I can see it clear as day. And it would be a great life. A really, really great life.

But I could also have a different life. A life that smells like sea salt, where the hours move more slowly and my morning soundtrack is the whir of fishing boats. And maybe there is a museum somewhere in that life, or maybe there's not. Maybe my days are filled with fifties music and slow, easy voices and cranky old women who don't trust my flimsy modern car.

The details of that life might be different—maybe some of them are a little better, maybe some of them are a little worse—but the end result is the same.

I'm happy. Really, truly happy.

Jim's voice suddenly echoes in my ears. *There were thousands of things I wanted to do, I'm sure. But you can't do everything you want to do in life.*

I didn't understand, back then, what he meant. Now, standing here in the Met with David holding his hand out to me and Leah and Katarina smiling at me behind him, I think I do.

There are thousands of things I could do with my life. Millions of different winding paths I could take. And there might always be one that's brighter, or warmer, but at some point, I have to stop wandering around and choose *one*.

And this path . . . this brilliant, sparkly future life standing right in front of me . . .

This is not the one I'm going to choose.

"Emily?" David says. "Are you coming?"

I blink. David's hand has dropped back to his side, and all three of them are smiling at me, waiting.

After a moment, I smile back at them. There's a strange, perfect quiet inside my mind, like when a snowstorm finally comes to an end.

"Yeah," I say. "I'm coming."

My heels click on the marble as I head after them down the hall. I'm going to spend this amazing night with the three of them, exploring the Met without a single tourist in it. I'm going to drink champagne, and munch on hors d'oeuvres, and soak in every second of this incredible experience.

Then, in the morning, I'm going to dismantle this beautiful dream.

# CHAPTER 35

Three days later, I wheel my suitcases into my Airbnb in Waldon and collapse onto the couch in an exhausted, sweaty heap.

Oh, man.

Those three days were *long*.

Withdrawing from NYU was easier than I thought it would be. Two apologetic emails, one awkward phone call with an NYU admissions officer, and it was done.

Leaving the internship was far more painful. Benedita seemed truly disappointed in me, even though she said she understood, and I couldn't articulate my reasons for leaving well at all. After I left her office, my chest got all tight and panicky, and all I could think of was what people would say when they heard that I had quit.

"She chose some random *guy* over her internship," said Fallon's voice.

"They're not even planning to have *kids*," Martha added.

"Lollll," chimed in Divya.

But I gritted my teeth and told myself to smarten up. I'd made my decision, and I wasn't going to change it based on other people's opinions. And anyway, I wasn't just leaving for a guy. John was only part of my decision. An important part, yes, but still only a part.

Wrapping up the rest of the New York stuff was pretty easy.

My parents had already picked up my stuff from my old house in Waldon, so they brought it to the airport for me to pick up when I landed in Halifax, along with my car. I thought they might be disappointed that I'd left New York, but to my surprise, they both seemed kind of relieved. My mother even made a comment about how happy she thought I'd been in Waldon. And I haven't bothered telling Fallon or Martha or Divya, so I don't have to worry about them judging me.

Relocating back to Waldon was a bit trickier. My old house has already sold, according to the online real estate listing, and trying to find an affordable apartment in small-town Canada these days takes significantly longer than seventy-two hours. Until I have more time to look, I'm stuck in a tiny Airbnb that reviewers described as "cramped" and "inconvenient" and "yikes."

I look around, and it is indeed cramped and inconvenient and yikes. There are only two rooms—a tiny bathroom and an equally tiny bedroom/living room/kitchen/entranceway/laundry room—and the distinct smell of weed is wafting in from the apartment next door. But it's cheap enough that for now I don't care.

I crack open the bottle of red wine I bought on the way home (my only stop on the drive from the Halifax airport) and dial the number to the local pizza place. I order a large pizza, then take a swig of my wine and ask Johnny, the pizza delivery guy, if he can bring me whatever chocolate bars they have in the shop as well.

I can't afford pizza or wine or name-brand chocolate bars, not after losing my deposits for school and paying for the flight home, but tonight, I'm just not going to think about it. Because if I think about it—if I think about how I've got literally nothing right now, no job, no money, no permanent place to live, no boyfriend—I'll probably wind up curled into the fetal position on the floor, sobbing into my wine.

Instead, I've elected for positivity. Stupid, totally irrational positivity.

I will make a new job for myself. I will find a new place to live. I will get John back.

My pizza and chocolate arrive, and I curl up on the bed (slash couch) and unlock my phone. Somehow, through this whole mess, I still haven't lost my Wordle streak, and I definitely don't intend to lose it now.

MUSTY, I type. As in, the smell of my new apartment.

Hmm. The T and Y are both green.

TIRED. (Self-explanatory.)

Oh-ho! The D and T are yellow, and the I and R are green.

DIRTY, I type confidently, and watch as the letters all turn green.

I snort aloud. MUSTY, TIRED, and DIRTY. That sums up my current state quite nicely.

Well, never mind. I take out my laptop and open up a blank to-do list.

I've got a lot of work to do.

THE FIRST THING I do the next morning is head to John's apartment. And yes, I know, sorting out my job should be priority number one, not my love life, but I prefer to think that I'm prioritizing them *equally*. I'm just starting with John because his apartment is on the way to Jim's house. Obviously.

My heart is doing gymnastics in my chest as I punch in the front door code and walk up the steps to his apartment. I smooth down my hair and practice the speech I've come up with in my head. At first, I envisioned myself giving this long, passionate monologue about how leaving him to go to New York was the worst mistake I've ever made, but I discounted that almost immediately. First of all, it's not true. I'm glad I went, if only because it made me realize that what I really want is to be here, starting my caregiving business and (hopefully) being with John.

Second of all, John is not the kind of person who would appreciate getting a romantic speech. If anything, he'd listen to the whole thing, raise an eyebrow, and say, "Yeah, maybe it's a good thing we broke up."

So anyway, the *actual* speech I've come up with is just the blunt truth: I'm back from New York and I'm here for good, and I'd really like to get back together again, please.

Short, sweet, and to the point.

Oh, crap.

I'm at his door.

Swallowing hard, I knock loudly three times. I wait, fidgeting restlessly, then knock again. Still no answer. I check my phone. It's only 8:22 a.m. Maybe John went to work early, for some reason?

I sigh. I don't really want to try to reconcile at the shop, but it looks like I've got no choice.

I'm walking back down the stairs when I almost run straight into John's mother.

"Carla!" I exclaim. "I mean, Mrs. Smith." I'm not sure I'm still allowed to call her Carla, since John and I broke up.

But her eyes light up when she sees me. "Emily! What on earth are you doing here? Aren't you supposed to be in New York?"

"I'm looking for John," I say. "I'm . . . I've come back."

Carla tilts her head. "What about your internship, and school?"

I bite my lip. "I decided I wanted to be here more."

She studies me for a moment and then smiles. "That's wonderful. Come help me feed John's fish, will you?"

I blink at her, startled. I was kind of expecting more questions. But she's already turned away from me and is heading up the stairs.

"Er—is he not home?" I ask uncertainly, following her.

"He's in Toronto for his friend's wedding."

Oh, crap. I forgot about that. He would've left yesterday, if I'm remembering the dates right. "When does he get back?"

"Not till next week. Tuesday, I think." She unlocks the door to his apartment and we step inside. My heart swells up at the familiar sight, even though I feel a bit awkward being here without him knowing.

"He'll be glad to hear you're back," Carla says.

"Yeah, maybe," I say, flushing. "I mean . . . I'm not, like, expecting anything."

Carla opens the cupboards to find the fish food. "Why not?"

I chew on my lip. "I don't know. It's a lot to forgive, isn't it? I basically chose another life over him."

Carla chuckles. "I'm not sure that's true. Sometimes love and real life are incompatible, that's all. If Laurent decides to move to Antarctica tomorrow and spend the rest of his life as an ice fisherman, I'm sure as heck not moving there with him." She smiles at me. "People change, lives change. If you've decided that this is the life you want, then I'm sure you and John can work things out.

As long as your mind is made up, that is. It won't do either of you any good to get back together if you're going to change your mind again, or resent him for making you leave New York."

"I won't," I say. "Honestly, John is only part of the reason I came back." I lick my lips. "I really want to try to turn my caregiving work into a proper business. I think . . . I don't know. I think I could really make a go of it."

Carla smiles. "I do too." Then she tilts her head. "I thought you liked the museum work, though."

My heart twists in my chest. "I did," I admit. "A lot. But . . . you can't do everything you want to do, right? You have to choose one thing eventually." I lift my chin. "And I really love working with older people."

"That's great, then," Carla says. She sounds like she means it too.

"I'm going to go around begging all my old clients to take me back today," I say.

"Begging?" She chuckles. "Dear, you've only been gone what, a few weeks? Tell them you changed your mind and I'm sure they'll be thrilled to have you back. And if you want, I can ask around at the hospital to see if any of the staff know of someone who needs help in the community."

"Would you really?"

"Of course. I can think of five patients I discharged last month who desperately need some help at home. And a lot of them are retired out-of-province folks who bought homes here on a whim during the pandemic, so you *know* they can afford it."

"Carla . . . thank you." I try to inject all my gratitude into the words. Carla smiles at me, and I smile back, and for one crazy second, I think we're thinking the same thing. If John and I get back together . . . Carla might be my mother-in-law someday.

She turns away to measure out the fish food and sprinkles it over the water. We watch in silence as the fish eat. Fish 1, Fish 2, and Fish 3. Raspberry pudding, swordsmith, and geocentric.

Carla reaches out and squeezes my arm and I let out a long breath, feeling a bit of tension drain from my shoulders.

"Come," she says. "Let's go get a coffee."

# CHAPTER 36

If I had any doubts about returning to Waldon, they disappear as I pull into Jim's driveway. He's sitting in the big wicker chair on his front porch, and his whole face lights up when he sees me get out of my car. I'd be lying if I said I didn't tear up a bit when he calls my name.

We make a pot of tea and sit back out on his porch, watching his neighbor's horses graze and chatting a while. I tell him a little bit about New York and he fills me in on the latest Waldon gossip, but mostly we just sip our tea and breathe in the warm summer air.

"Will you be working at the auto shop again?" he asks me, as I pour more tea into his cup.

I grimace. "No, I definitely burned a bridge with my old boss. I'm going to try to turn my caregiving work into a proper business, actually. So if you have any friends who are looking," I add, with a teasing smile.

Jim chuckles. "All my friends are long gone, I'm afraid. That's the trouble with living as long as I have."

I study his face. "You're not too lonely, are you?"

"Ah." He waves a dismissive hand. "Don't you worry about me."

I make a worried noise, but I can tell he doesn't want me to press the issue. "Maybe when I get my caregiving website up and running, you can write me a review," I say instead. "I won't even be offended if you only want to give me four stars."

"You really think I'd only give you a four out of ten?"

I giggle. "I meant four out of *five*."

"Hmm." He smiles at me. "I think we can do a little better than that."

Impulsively, I reach over and squeeze his hand. His skin is dry and cool, but his grip is strong. "I missed you," I say.

He pats my hand, and a comfortable silence passes between us. I squeeze his hand once more before I let go.

"I suppose you've made up with John?" he asks.

I pull a face. "Not yet. He's in Toronto for the week. I haven't told him I'm back yet." I drum my fingers on the arms of my chair. "I could call him, I guess. But it sort of feels like something I should do in person."

Jim nods absently. "He's a nice boy."

We sit out on the porch for a while, watching the trees ripple gently in the breeze. The neighbor's horses flick their tails absently in the fields, and in the distance, someone is methodically chopping wood.

"It's good to be back," I murmur.

I'm not sure Jim hears me. He's looking out at the view, just like I am, with a faraway look in his eyes. I reach over and take his hand again, and smile as the time slips by between us.

THE NEXT THREE days, I spend every waking moment working.

And yes, okay, that's obviously an exaggeration. I do take breaks to eat, and do Wordle, and there's an hour when my brain is so frazzled that I binge-watch like fifty YouTube videos about puppies.

But most of the time, I'm working.

After my visit with Jim, I go see Mrs. Finnamore and Doris to ask if they want me to start up my services again. To my relief, they both accept without giving me any grief. I mean, Mrs. Finnamore is a bit annoyed that I've moved, because someone's already bought my old house and she's convinced they're going to be a "ruffian," and Doris makes a comment about how she knew I'd be back, because New York City is more of a place for "brainy girls" like her niece Florence, but I pretend I don't hear that.

After that, I spend an hour with a twenty-two-year-old guy named Kevin who lives in his parents' basement in Charlottetown.

Hang on, that sounds bad when I put it like that.

Let me rephrase.

After that, I spend an hour with a freelance graphic designer named Kevin, who I found on the web and who offered to make a logo for my caregiving business at half price if I wrote a five-star review for his graphic design business.

He's a bit of an intense guy—I make a polite comment about how fancy his computer looks, and he spends thirty minutes telling me how anyone who uses fewer than three monitors is a simpleton—but I actually really like the logo he designs. It's the outline of an old-fashioned-style house, the kind you see all over PEI with a gable roof and a brick chimney, with a tiny heart instead of a front doorknob. In a circle around the house, it says STAY-AT-HOME CAREGIVING, which is the business name I've decided on. I thought about putting my name in it somehow, but I think this is better. Because it's why a lot of older people get caregivers, and it's why I want to do this work. So I can help people stay in their homes a little longer.

Kevin also helps me design two flyers, and uses his printer to print out fifty copies of each. From there, I head to the university campus, where I wander around pinning my first flyer to every notice board I can find. This one isn't for caregiver services, obviously. It's for a part-time job providing in-home caregiving to the elderly. It's a bit of a long shot, looking for employees, but I figure if I'm going to do this, I may as well go big. And this way, I can expand the business outside of Waldon.

My plan is to be in charge of finding and vetting clients and coordinating schedules, as well as communicating with clients' families and dealing with any conflict or issues that arise. I'll take 10 percent of any employee profit for doing that part of the job. (I felt a bit squicky about that part, but then I reminded myself of how awful it always was to talk to Debra, and I decided that 10 percent is more than fair.)

It's a gorgeous summer day, and the campus is bright and bustling. I wander around for a little while, watching the students hurrying from class to class or lazing around on bright green lawns. I could have being doing that myself at NYU in a few weeks. Finding my way to my classes, nervously making friends, hunting out the perfect library nook to do all my late-night studying.

I feel a genuine pang of sadness at the loss of it, but then I look down at the flyers in my hand and the pain eases up a little bit. This is the life I've chosen. This is the path I've decided to take. It's not going to be perfect, or easy, but it feels as right as it did when I was standing under the glittering lights of the Met with David stretching his hand out toward me.

I take a deep breath and let it out again, then turn and head back to my car, humming a little as I go.

# CHAPTER 37

The next day, I make the rounds of Summerside, pinning flyers for clients on every grocery store, church, and community hall bulletin board I can find. The day after that, I paper the town of Waldon. I stop at the local hospital and put up flyers there—most of them are aimed at clients, but some for workers as well—then I make the rounds of the local shops. At the bakery, the cashier brightens when she sees the flyer and tells me that her great-aunt is desperate for some help.

"I'd do it myself," she says, "but she won't let me. I think it's easier for her to ask a stranger for help. She feels like she's a burden to us."

I smile and give her my cell phone number, and she promises to pass it along to her great-aunt. Then she gives me a free iced coffee and a chocolate chip cookie.

I walk back out into the sun and head to my car, sipping on my iced coffee as I drive to Jim's house. I don't think he's done any laundry since I left, and I want to tidy up his kitchen a bit as well.

When I pull into the driveway, there's another car there, a red Honda with a New Brunswick license plate. I peer at it in interest. Jim's son and daughter-in-law were supposed to arrive yesterday for a visit. They were taking him out for dinner last night at a restaurant in Summerside.

As I climb the creaky porch steps, the front door swings open, and a tall man in his seventies steps out. My first thought is that this can't possibly be Jim's son—he's old enough to be my grandfather himself. But then I remember that Jim is ninety-six, which means even his youngest son is in his midseventies.

"Hi, there," I say brightly. "I'm Emily."

"Ah—Emily, of course." Jim's son reaches out and shakes my hand warmly. I see why Rose called him a "total looker." Even though he's older, he has a really handsome smile and a swoop of wiry hair. "My father's told me about you. I'm Herman."

"Nice to meet you. Sorry to interrupt," I add. "I was going to do some laundry, but I can come back later if now's not a good time."

Herman's expression changes. "Ah. Well. I'm afraid that won't be necessary."

I blink. "No?"

His smile softens, and he gestures for me to sit down on Jim's wicker chair. I ease into it, feeling my heartbeat change.

"I'm afraid my father passed away last night," Herman says. "I just found him an hour ago. He must have passed during his sleep."

I stare at him, hearing nothing but the slow, steady thump of my heart in my ears.

"Passed away," I say numbly.

"I'm afraid so."

"I—" I turn my eyes to Jim's neighbor's fields, seeing nothing. "I'm so sorry—"

Herman shakes his head gently. "This was how he wanted to go. And he's missed my mother terribly." His eyes are sad, but his lips curve up softly. "It was his time."

I sink back into my chair, feeling—

I don't even know what I'm feeling.

"Is he still—here?" I croak.

Herman nods. "The coroners should be here any minute. Did you want to see him?"

I stare at him. *Do* I want to see him?

"Yes." I stand. "Yes, of course."

I walk through the house somewhat woodenly, feeling like I'm moving on autopilot. Herman doesn't follow me, which I'm distantly grateful for. I need to do this alone.

Oh, god. I can't do this alone.

I can't do this at *all*. I've never seen a dead person before. I'm not ready, I can't do it.

My feet come to a stop outside of Jim's bedroom door. It's slightly ajar. I can see the familiar mahogany dresser where I used to put his folded clothes.

A horrible grief is swelling up within me, stealing the air from my lungs and forcing a huge, hot lump into my throat. But my body moves without my permission—my hand pushes open the door, my numb feet carry me inside.

And then all the grief falls away in a whoosh as I see Jim lying there on the bed.

Ah.

There he is.

I don't know how to explain it, but looking at the relaxed lines of Jim's face and the strange, unearthly smoothness of his skin, I don't feel sad anymore. Or rather, I don't feel sad for him. I feel sad for myself, because I'm going to miss him so damn much.

But Herman was right.

It was his time.

I move closer to the bed and sit down on the edge of it. The old mattress creaks under my weight. The bedcovers are pulled up to his chest—he's wearing the soft flannel pajamas that he would never let me wash—and his hands are resting loosely at his sides. I slide my hand into his. His skin is cool and dry, his fingers loose and unmoving under mine.

Tears are slipping down my cheeks, but they aren't of grief, exactly. There's a sharp, almost painful sort of happiness in them.

"I'm really going to miss you," I whisper.

He doesn't answer me. Of course he doesn't. He's far beyond me now. His story has come to its end.

I look into his face and remember the low sound of his laugh, and the crinkle of his eyes when he smiled, and his knee tapping along to the Diamonds' song "Little Darlin'."

I hum a bit of the tune, smiling through my tears, and squeeze his hand one last time. I take a deep, shaky breath and turn to leave. As I do, my gaze lands on his bedside table. There's an old pair of glasses, a tattered paperback book, and a notebook folded back on itself. Jim's written two short lines in his wide, slightly wobbly hand.

*Emily is a great comfort to me. I highly recommend her services.*

I give a watery laugh and look back at him, tears streaming freely down my face. Then I lean down and kiss his soft, papery cheek.

"Bye, Jim."

# CHAPTER 38

The next morning, I wake with the sunrise. A loose spring in the Airbnb mattress is digging into my spine, which is probably what woke me, but I don't really mind. The whole apartment is suffused with a golden glow, and a warm breeze is sifting in through the window.

I dress in a T-shirt and shorts and head out into town. There's a small stack of flyers left in my bag, but I don't really have any intention of putting them up today. I just want to walk around for a while, thinking of Jim.

I'm half-expecting a wave of grief to hit me, but instead, I'm filled with the same strange peace I felt yesterday. Jim's son Herman and I sat out on the porch for a while yesterday, sharing memories of Jim until the coroners arrived. Afterward, I texted Rose and Trey, and the three of us met up for dinner. Rose cried for a little bit—she knew Jim even better than I did—but I could tell she wasn't really sad for *him*. She knew he was ready. He'd been ready since his wife died.

We spent the rest of the night telling stories about him, laughing and tearing up and lifting our glasses to his memory. There isn't going to be a funeral—Herman said Jim was very firm that he didn't want one—but in a way, remembering him with Herman and Rose and Trey felt like a truer way to honor him.

I wander toward the waterfront and wind up near the post office, which overlooks the water. I sink into a bench nearby and take deep breaths of ocean air. I know the weather doesn't really revolve around me and my life, but I swear the air feels a bit stiller today. Like the whole world is taking a minute to remember Jim.

Part of me wishes I could stay in this quiet, peaceful place forever, but the sun rises and the world wakes up like it always does. The lazy Waldon traffic picks up behind me, greedy seagulls swoop over my head looking for food, and a runner's dog wiggles out of his leash and leaps off the wharf to chase after a sea duck, sending about fifty of them springing into the air.

I smile and get to my feet, heading to the local bakery. As I approach, the door swings open and Kiara emerges, cappuccino in hand.

She stops dead in her tracks when she sees me, then gives a delighted shout that startles an old man walking by.

"No fucking way!" she says, making the same old man scowl at her. She crosses the sidewalk in two quick bounds and throws her arms around me, spilling cappuccino down my back. I hug her hard, beaming into her hair.

"I'm sorry I didn't text," I say, while she drags me to a little table outside the bakery. "I saw your mom a couple days ago, but I made her promise not to tell you. No offense, but—"

"I can't keep a secret," she interrupts. "Duh."

I smile. "I didn't want John to hear that I'm back secondhand."

"And are you back for good?"

"Back for good," I confirm.

She grins and leans back in her chair, pushing her sunglasses onto the top of her head. "John is going to freak."

I smile thinly. "In a good way, I hope."

"Of course! I've never seen him as bummed out as he has been since you left. I mean, it's *John*, so he's not, like, sobbing into a pint of ice cream or anything. But he's got this broody, pensive thing going on, it's been driving me nuts."

I make a noncommittal sound. I don't want to get my hopes up too much. "We'll see what happens when he gets back."

Kiara grins. "Either way, I'm glad you're back. Do you have time to grab a coffee? On me," she adds, seeing me hesitate.

I open my mouth to argue, then close it again and smile. "That would be really great."

We drink coffee and catch up until she has to head to work. As I take our empty cups back inside, the cashier waves me down.

"It's Emily, right?" she says brightly. "I told my great-aunt about you yesterday. I gave her your number, but she was wondering if you could give her a call sometime? She doesn't know how to use her phone that well, so she hoped you wouldn't mind calling her . . ."

A warm feeling spreads through me. "I don't mind at all!"

I put her great-aunt's number in my phone and promise I'll call her later.

"Thanks so much," the cashier says. "We worry about her so much. She's ninety-six and still living alone, if you can believe it."

I go a bit still. Ninety-six years old. Just like Jim. I wonder, for a moment, if I can take the pain of getting close to someone else, just to lose them. But then I shake my head. Of course I can. And anyway, what I feel about Jim isn't a bad pain. It's a happy pain, and I wouldn't give up a single moment with him to get rid of it.

"That's amazing," I tell the cashier. "I'll call her later today."

I head back out onto the sidewalk and wander in the direction of my apartment. Halfway there, I pass the barrel museum. My feet slow down automatically, and I turn to stare up at the beautiful building. I don't want to see Shelley, but I can hear the familiar clank of Trey's tools. And I've missed this place so much. It isn't the Met, but it's just as special in its own way.

I walk forward determinedly and swing open the door. The familiar smell of smoke and wood envelops me like a warm hug.

The girl at the front desk looks like she's in her early twenties, with long blonde hair dyed pink at the ends. She gives me a bright, welcoming smile. She must be the other university student Shelley hired. I wonder if they're related too.

Probably not. This girl looks way too friendly.

"Hi, there," she says. "Did you want to buy a ticket?"

"Uh—actually, I was just hoping to say hi to Trey. I used to volunteer here."

"Oh, cool! You can just go on back."

I thank her and head to the back, where Trey is doing a demonstration for an eager-looking family of tourists. He smiles when he sees me come in, but I can tell he's only a few minutes into his demonstration. I wave at him to indicate I'll walk around for a little while.

As I wander through the rooms, a bright, crisp voice catches my ear.

"Such a kind man," the voice says. There's a murmur of agreement.

I drift toward the voices curiously. In the eastern room, the one that houses tools from the 1890s, three older women I recognize from the Barrel Into Summer event are gathered around Shelley.

"I knew Jim since he was a teen. He used to work the ice-cream stand down on Lorway Beach," says one of the society women.

"I met him through his son," says another one. "Herman and I taught at the same school for a few years. He was the one who called me last night. He knew I'd want to know."

I edge closer, hidden from view by a convenient pile of barrels. I don't want Shelley to see me, but it's really nice hearing the women talk about Jim. I bet there are people all over Waldon who have stories of him, people who will hear that he's passed and spend a few minutes thinking of him. My lips turn up gently. I guess that's all any of us can hope for after we're gone.

"We just *loved* having him work here." Shelley's loud voice breaks into my reverie. "He was such a funny little man."

My head jerks back indignantly. *Excuse* me? A "funny little man"?

"We should put a plaque up," one of the society women says. "Something to commemorate his work here."

"Oh, of course," Shelley says. "It's going to be such a *wrench* working here without him."

The women titter sympathetically. Meanwhile, I'm so furious I can practically see the veins pulsing behind my eyes.

It's none of your business, I tell myself firmly. You don't work here anymore—it's not your place to stick your nose in—

"Jim was like a grandfather to me," Shelley says. "I wonder if we should give all the staff a few days of paid leave, to process the loss."

My temper splinters. Screw it. I'm *making* this my business.

"That's total crap!" I snap, emerging from behind the barrels. Shelley's face goes slack with surprise, while the society women blink at me, startled.

"Er—I'm sorry?" one of them says.

"That's total crap," I say again, my eyes on Shelley. "You didn't like Jim at all. You tried to fire him!"

Shelley's cheeks flush dark red.

"I'm sorry, who are you?" one of the society women asks, looking at me in faint alarm. She seems to be the leader of the group. Her white hair is short and tightly curled, and the shiny button on her dark-green jacket gleams in the dim light.

"A volunteer we had to dismiss," Shelley says quickly. "Mentally unstable," she adds in an undertone.

"I am not!" I say fiercely. "My name is Emily, ma'am," I add to the society woman. "I volunteered here earlier this summer, and I was Jim's caregiver for a while."

"Oh, *Emily!*" the woman says. Her suspicious frown melts away. "Of course." She holds out a hand to me. "I'm Elaine Mac-Quarrie. I think we met at one of the events. Jim told me all about you," she adds pleasantly. "He said you designed that fabulous new exhibit, the one children can take photos with."

I smile. "Yes, ma'am. And I organized the Barrel Into Summer event, and the Canada Day event. With Trey and Jim's help, I mean."

"She means she pitched in," Shelley says.

I glare at her. "I didn't *pitch in.* I organized everything. And you didn't even want me to do the events in the first place."

Shelley makes a dismissive noise and shoots the society women an incredulous look, as though she expects them to agree with her. But instead, all three women are frowning at her.

"Is that true?" asks Elaine.

Shelley lets out another scoff. "Of course not."

"No? Then who was the caterer for the Canada Day event?"

I demand. "What was the prize for the scavenger hunt? What brands of soda did we sell?" Shelley's mouth moves soundlessly for a moment, and she looks at the society women again, as though she expects them to jump in. "You can't tell me," I snap, "because you have no idea. You sit in your office all day scrolling through Facebook, letting this beautiful museum go to waste. You don't care about any of it! You just want to get paid to do nothing."

A muscle twitches furiously in Shelley's jaw, and her whole face has turned a red-purple color. I can sense how badly she wants to shout at me, but she also seems keenly aware that the society women are watching her.

"This is very inappropriate, Emily," she says instead, in an exaggeratedly patient, condescending voice. "We're all very grateful for your volunteer work, but what you don't seem to understand is that there's a little more to running a museum than picking *soda brands*. I'm terribly sorry for the disruption, ladies," she adds to the society women. She shakes her head regretfully. "All this, on the day after Jim's death—"

"You didn't give a *damn* about Jim," I say. "How dare you pretend like you cared about him? Don't you have any shame?"

"Ridiculous," Shelley says, shaking her head in that stupid way again. "Ridiculous."

"It is ridiculous," I say. "It's ridiculous that you're paid to scroll through Facebook in your office all day while volunteers do all the work. Trey is by far the best part of this place, and yet the minute you had the chance to give out proper salaries, you threw them at your daughter and her friend instead of him!" I let out a sharp laugh as I realize how terrible it actually is. I turn to the society women abruptly. "You should hire someone else as manager. This museum deserves someone who'll treat it with the care it deserves."

"Hear, hear," says a deep voice behind us. Trey is leaning against the doorway with his arms crossed, looking as though he's been standing there for quite a while. "And if it helps your decision-making process," he adds, smiling charmingly at the society ladies, "I plan to resign immediately if you don't."

I grin at him and turn back to the women, breathing quicker with triumph. Elaine and the others exchange uncertain glances. They don't seem to know quite what to make of the whole situation.

"This is insane," Shelley says, red with fury. "You two are slandering me. I could have you up on *charges*."

Trey rolls his eyes. "You do that."

A beat of awkward silence falls; the only sound is the heavy huff of Shelley's breath. The tourist family who were watching Trey earlier poke their heads into the room, then back out immediately when they see all of us standing there.

Smart family.

"Well," Elaine says finally. Then again, "Well." She glances at the other two society women. "I suppose we'll—take this back and discuss it."

"You can't be serious!" Shelley snaps.

She seems to realize right away that it's a mistake. She tries to backtrack hastily, adopting a calm, pleasant tone that doesn't match her reddened face. "What I mean is, of course we should all discuss it, obviously." She draws a circle with her hand to indicate herself and the society women. "If there are any problems at the museum, I'm perfectly happy to fix them. Not that I think we'll find anything worth fixing."

Elaine's eyebrows lift. Again, I can see Shelley realize she's made a mistake, but it's too late—the words are out. What Shelley meant, I'm sure, is that she wouldn't find any problems that *needed* fixing. But that's not what she said. And all the society women heard it.

"Hmm." Elaine frowns at her, and the tiniest flicker of distaste crosses her face, one that's mirrored on the faces of the other two. They aren't stupid, these women, and it's clear they care deeply about their society. Shelley's mediocre job performance over the past few years can't have escaped them.

Perhaps Shelley realizes it, because a fresh wave of mottled color perfuses her face. "This is ridiculous," she says again. "I have other job options, you know. I could make twice the money I make here managing the call center in Charlottetown. They already offered me the job," she adds pointedly. "And I was going to turn it down because of my dedication to this place, but if my work is no longer *appreciated*—"

"Perhaps that would be best," Elaine interrupts.

Shelley's face goes slack, like she's been slapped. "Excuse me?"

Elaine straightens her suit jacket. "Well, if you have another offer on the table, we'd hate to keep you from it," she says. "We certainly wouldn't expect you to turn down the chance to earn more money."

I exchange a wide-eyed glance with Trey. Elaine's voice is prim and polite, but there's a crispness to her words that warns arguing with her would be a very bad idea.

"I mean—" Shelley stammers. "If I'm not *appreciated*—"

"Certainly we appreciate you," Elaine says. "We're so grateful for your services all these years, aren't we, ladies?" The other women nod. "When does the call center want you to start?" she asks Shelley pleasantly.

"Well—I'm not sure there's a *date*—I'd have to email them—"

"And Emily." Elaine turns to me. "When might you be able to step in?"

I blink at her stupidly. "Step *in*?"

"This is the candidate you're putting forward, isn't it, Trey?" Elaine asks.

Trey grins. "Yes, ma'am. You know she did an internship at the Met, in New York?"

"How impressive," Elaine says.

"My daughter's been to that museum," one of the other society women adds, nodding knowledgeably.

Elaine turns to me again. "I assume you're interested in the job?"

"Well—I mean, yes—" I stammer.

"Wonderful." She claps her hands together. "I'd say this timing works out splendidly, don't you, ladies?"

"Perfect," says one of them.

"Quite convenient," says the other.

I swear their eyes are twinkling. I have a sneaky feeling I'm not the only one who's been holding a grudge against Shelley. But as much as the idea of running this place thrills me, my stomach twists as I think of my caregiving business.

"The thing is," I say guiltily, "I've already got a job. Or, well—it's only part-time right now, but I'm hoping it'll grow over time—"

"You can't be a part-time manager," Shelley says immediately, her eyes sharp with malice.

Elaine frowns. "We do need someone here full-time."

"What if she shared the job?" Trey chimes in.

The society women brighten. "You could do that, Trey?" Elaine says.

He pulls a face. "Oh, god, no. But Rose knows as much about this place as anyone. I'm sure she'd love to split the job with Emily."

My heart is beating faster in my chest. Working here as co-manager with Rose and building up my caregiving business at the same time . . . *Dream job,* shouts an urgent voice in my head. *Dream job.*

"Now hang on—" Shelley says furiously.

"I love that idea," Elaine interrupts. "Rose is such a pillar in the community. She'd have to interview for the job, of course—you both would," she adds, looking at me.

"Of course," I say eagerly.

"Well, then," Elaine says, while Shelley gapes at her furiously. "What an exciting day! Let's pop into your office, shall we?" she adds to Shelley. "We'll have to fill out some paperwork, I'm sure—"

She holds out a polite arm and guides Shelley from the room. Shelley barely has the chance to glare at me furiously before they're gone.

"We'll get your information from Trey, shall we?" one of the other society women says to me as she walks by.

"Er—yes, ma'am."

"Very good." Her eyes gleam mischievously. "Perhaps it'd be best if you made yourself scarce, while we're in the office."

I fight a giggle. "Yes, ma'am."

The second they're gone, I catch Trey's eye. We stare at each other for one long, incredulous moment—then we burst out laughing.

"Can you believe that?" I demand, between hiccups. "Did you see Shelley's face?"

"Rose is going to kill me for not taking a picture," Trey says.

"You really think she'll want to be comanager with me?" I ask.

He nods. "She's been getting bored at the grocery store. And she's always loved this old place. But I'll talk to her tonight and let you know for sure. Now get out of here before Shelley comes back out and strangles you."

I break into giggles again. "Her fingers are probably super strong from all that scrolling on Facebook."

"I'll call you later," Trey says, grinning.

I flee the room, still giggling, and wave goodbye to the blonde girl at the front desk, who looks amused, if slightly confused, by my laughter.

"Have a nice day," she calls after me.

"You too!" I call back.

She seems quite nice, really. I think I'll keep her on, even if Shelley hired her.

I can do that, now. Now that I'm going to be the *comanager.*

I let out a silly, giddy squeal and do a quick spin in the parking lot.

Holy hell. I just got myself a *job.*

# CHAPTER 39

On Monday, I meet with Elaine, Rose, and the rest of the historical society board to finalize the details. I start as manager (manager!) next week, since Shelley apparently decided that she couldn't get out of there soon enough. Rose will join me as co-manager at the end of the month, since she's required to give two weeks' notice at the grocery store. During the interview, it was like she and I were sharing the same brain, shooting off idea after idea for improving the museum and finishing each other's bright, eager sentences. The biggest thing we suggested was to expand the museum beyond barrels and make it a museum about Waldon itself. I even shyly suggested an exhibit like the one I thought of in New York, with videos of older citizens in Waldon talking about their lives growing up in town. The society women all loved it, even if they were a bit unsure about how to set up the technology. I assured them I could sort it out, and made a mental note to call my three-monitor friend Kevin as soon as I could.

For the back-of-house museum work, Elaine herself is going to train me. Apparently she's done most of the finance stuff the last few years, anyway, because of some errors Shelley made in the past. It couldn't be clearer that they're happy to be rid of her, though they were careful to speak of her in polite, even tones. I think they felt like firing her would be a disrespect to Josephine, the former owner. Plus, there probably weren't a whole lot of people sticking their hand up to ask for her job.

The pay isn't that great—in fact, when the salary is split between Rose and me, it's less than what I made at the auto shop—but I don't really care about that. Plus, I've got my caregiving business! I've already set up two meetings with potential new clients, as well as an interview with a nursing student looking for part-time work. It's going to be a lot of work, balancing the museum with building a business, but I know I can hack it. And the thought of working in the museum again fills me with warmth.

I grab an early celebratory dinner alone at the local fish and chips joint, then head out onto the sidewalk, singing happily under my breath. It's a little past five o'clock, and I tilt my head back as I walk along the waterfront, soaking in the warm evening sun. I really think things are going to be okay. Even if John doesn't want to get back together with me . . . I think things will still be okay.

I sit down on a bench outside the post office and take out my phone. Now is as good a time as any to tackle it: the three-hundred-and-sixty-fifth day of Wordle.

I stare at the screen for a long while, trying to think of a good word to start with. I want something that captures this day, this single moment in my life, but all of the words are way too long. Like hopeful. Or peaceful. Like the start of something new.

On paper, it still might seem insane, giving up a prestigious internship and an exciting life in New York, but in reality, it just feels—

"Right," I murmur quietly.

RIGHT, I type in.

It's all wrong—every single letter is gray—but I don't care. My lips curl up in a smile.

*Right.*

My phone dings in my hand. It's a text from John's mother.

> [5:27] **Carla:** Emily, I've just realized I told you the wrong dates for John's trip. He got back last night. Thought you might want to know!

> [5:27] **Carla:** Hope you are having a great day.

Just like that, the peaceful feeling vanishes, replaced by a fluttery anxiousness. John got back last *night*? That means he probably was at work today.

I glance at my phone. If I leave now, I might catch him at the shop.

Swallowing down an enormous swell of nerves, I stand and walk determinedly to my car. I give myself a stern pep talk as I drive. "Don't be a chicken, Emily. Don't be a wuss."

Still, I have to wipe my prickling palms against my legs as I drive, and my heart pounds frantically the whole way. As I head up the road toward the shop, the front door swings open and someone steps out.

My pulse rate doubles.

It's John.

Oh, man. I know it's only been a few weeks, but I forgot how handsome he is. (And how dirty his work coveralls always are.)

He heads to his car, pulling his keys from his pocket. I slow down and put my blinker on to turn into the parking lot, then have to wait for three of the world's slowest drivers to pass by. As I wait, the auto shop door swings open again, and a woman around my age hurries out, shoving her phone in her purse as she runs. She approaches John's car, says something to him with a smile, then walks around his car and gets into the passenger seat.

*What?*

I stare at them in icy horror until someone honks at me from behind. With numb hands, I force myself to pull into the parking lot. My heart is thudding loudly in my ears.

Who *is* that?

Could it be—

Has John moved on *already*?

Moving on autopilot, I pull into a parking spot. John and the girl in his car haven't noticed me. Dave's old van is parked beside me, partially blocking me from view. Sick to my stomach, I put my car into reverse.

I guess that's it, then.

No more John.

I reverse a few feet, then I slam on the brakes so hard they squeak a little.

Am I *insane*? There are a hundred different reasons John could be getting into a car with a girl. She could be a relative. She could be a friend. She could be a customer who needs a lift home. Am I really going to drive home and sob like a character in a rom-com without even *trying* to confirm what I'm seeing?

I throw my car in park and jump out without turning it off, running across the parking lot like a maniac to try to catch them. They're just pulling to the edge of the road, but John slows down as I approach. It'd be hard to miss seeing me, the girl waving her hands like a total idiot.

He stares at me incredulously for a moment (god, I missed that stare), then reverses back a few feet into the parking lot. He says something to the girl beside him and then gets out of the car. I fold over my knees, breathing a little heavily. That was a way longer run than it looked.

"Are you okay?" John asks.

"Oh, yeah," I wheeze. "Totally fine." With effort, I force myself to stand up. "How's it going?"

His eyebrows lift. "Good. This is Maya." He gestures toward the girl in the car, who's watching through the open window with an interested look on her face. "She's the new receptionist."

The new receptionist! I fight the urge to do a little dance, then sober just as quickly. John fell for the shop receptionist once already. I can't let it happen again.

"Nice to meet you," I say politely. Then, to John, "Can we talk for a second? Just—give us one second," I tell Maya as I beckon John away from the car.

"What's up?" he asks.

"What's *up*?" I repeat, slightly indignantly. "Aren't you shocked I'm here?"

"Er—no. My mom told me you were back. And Kiara. And Trey."

They *what*? Oh, I am seriously going to kill all of them.

That'll have to wait until later, though, because right now, I just want to know what's going on behind that handsome, inscrutable face. "And?" I say nervously. "What do you think?"

He shifts his weight a little. He looks sort of uncertain. "It's good," he says. "I mean, if you're happy about it."

"I am. They hired me as comanager at the barrel museum. I'm

going to share the job with Rose! And I'm starting up a caregiving business . . . and I got to see Jim before he died."

John's eyebrows lift. "Jim died?"

I nod. "A couple days ago."

"Shit, Em—I had no idea—"

"No, it's okay. I mean, I'm sad about it." My throat tightens a little. "I already miss him like crazy. But he was ready to go, you know?"

John nods. "Still, that really sucks. If I'd known, I would've— y'know, called you."

"Why didn't you? If you already knew I was here?"

He clears his throat. "Well . . . I don't know. I didn't want to, like, assume anything."

"*Assume* anything?" I shift uneasily. Is he saying he doesn't want to get back together? "We only broke up because I went to New York," I say feebly. "I sort of thought—now that I'm back—"

"That's not the only reason we broke up." John looks up at me again, and there's something sharp in his dark eyes. "I don't know if Kiara told you—I'm assuming she did, she can't keep a secret for shit—but I bought the shop."

"She told me."

"Yeah, well, that means I'm going to be here. In Waldon. For a very, very long time."

"I know!"

"Em . . ." He shakes his head. "You made it pretty clear you're looking for more than that. Just because New York didn't work out for you—"

"New York *did* work out for me," I interrupt. "The internship was great, and the city was incredible, and the people were really nice . . . There was nothing wrong with it. I just realized I wanted to be here more." I shake my head and look up at him, willing him to believe me. "I love Waldon. I love living here, and taking care of people like Mrs. Finnamore and Jim, and working at the barrel museum, and having early-morning coffee dates with Kiara and dinners at the pub with Rose and Trey. I want to be here. And I want to be with *you*."

My voice goes a bit wobbly at the end. John leans back to study my face, a little crease between his brows, like I'm a Wordle answer he's trying to figure out.

"You mean it?" he says finally.

I nod. "I mean it."

Just like that, the tension falls away from him. His handsome smile appears, a flash of lightning on his serious face. "Cool," he says easily.

"Cool," I repeat, a little thickly.

I don't know who moves first (okay, it's me), but all of a sudden we're kissing, as if nothing's happened since the day I left. My arms are around his neck, his hands are on my waist, and it's not like some dramatic movie kiss with rain pouring down or fireworks exploding overhead, but it feels even better than that. It feels easy. It feels *right*.

We break apart, and he uses his thumbs to wipe away the tears on my cheeks. I'm definitely going to have black grease marks on my face, but I don't care.

"I should get Maya home," he says. "Want to come over for dinner later?"

I smile so hard my cheeks hurt. "Yeah."

"I've bought a new place," he adds.

"In the three weeks I was gone?"

"Mm. I'll text you the address."

I chuckle. Classic John, treating a huge life decision like it's no big deal. It's kind of a shame, too. His old apartment was pretty cool. "Sounds good," I say, trying to mimic his casual tone. "See you later. Nice to meet you, Maya!" I add, waving to her as John climbs back into his car.

I wait until they've driven away before I throw my hands over my head and do the stupidest celebration dance of all time, complete with twirling and high-pitched squealing. I catch a glimpse of myself in my car window, and honestly, I look like the biggest loser.

I don't care, though.

I'm back together with *John*.

# CHAPTER 40

My excitement fades an hour later as I pull up in front of the address he texted me. His car is parked on the street, so I know I've got the right place, but . . .

Oh boy.

I don't mean to be judgmental, I swear, but when I tell you this place is a shack, I'm not being rude. It's a literal shack, a crumbling building the size of a garden shed. I've actually seen it before on my old running route. I always gave it a wide berth, just on the off chance it was haunted. It definitely looks like the type of place that would be haunted. The roof is collapsed, and almost all of the windows are missing.

I don't care how much I love John, I am *not* sleeping in that thing. As least not until I get an updated tetanus shot.

I get out of my car and approach John, who's leaning against his own car.

"So?" he asks, gesturing to the shack. "What do you think?"

I open my mouth to lie, but what's the point? Only a rabid raccoon would find this house appealing. "It looks like a good place to get murdered," I say honestly.

He snorts with laughter. "Maybe I *am* going to murder you," he says. "Maybe I'm actually pissed you went to New York, and I've tricked you into coming here."

"No, too creepy!" I protest.

He grins and pulls me toward him. "Sorry."

I let him hug me for a moment, enjoying the warm strength of his arms. "For real, though, is this actually where you live?"

"No," he says. "I just didn't want you to get lost. The streets around here are confusing. Hop in your car and follow me."

I roll my eyes. "The streets around here aren't *confusing*. I've run them, like, a hundred times. I own these streets!"

John laughs and gently pushes me toward my car. "Yeah, yeah."

I get into my car, shoot a quick reply to the text Kiara's sent me (YAY! Tell me everything at coffee tomorrow!!!!), and follow him down the street. He turns left, then right, then left again, then doubles back past the shack. I'm about to call him and tell him to stop being annoying when he finally puts his blinker on and turns into a driveway.

*My* driveway.

The driveway of my old house.

My hands are shaking a little as I pull in after him and climb out of my car. There's a hot lump in the back of my throat, and my eyes are prickling dangerously. The For Sale sign on the front lawn now says SOLD.

John holds his hands out to the house. "Voilà," he says. "That's French for 'look at this.'" He grins at me, then his smile falters when he sees my face. "Oh, shit. What's wrong? I thought you'd be excited."

"I *am*," I say in a tiny, tremulous voice. "I am excited. It's . . . it's . . ." I can't find the words. "Did you really buy it?"

"Mm. It's an awesome house. Needs some work done, but I can do most of it myself."

"But . . . *how*? Isn't this place really expensive? Plus with you buying the shop—"

John shrugs. "I've been saving up for a place for a while now, and my parents loaned me a bit." He looks up at the house. "Before you left, I heard you telling Dave that the people who owned this place were going to sell it, so I had my real estate buddy get in touch with them. I haven't actually moved in yet, though. Closing's not for a few weeks."

"You mean—" I go hot with mortification. "You got in touch with them *before* I went to New York?"

I can't believe it. I can't *believe* it. He must've thought I would change my mind. He must've thought I wasn't really going to leave.

He stares at me, bemused. "No. I did it the week after you left."

I stare back at him. "So . . . you knew I'd come back?"

That seems way out of character. And also sort of condescending. Did he really think I wouldn't stay in New York?

His mouth turns up in a fond, amused smile. "No, Em. I'm not a psychic. This is an awesome house. I bought it because I wanted to. But now that you're back, if you want to live in it with me . . ." He shrugs. "That's just a fringe benefit."

I study his face. "You mean it?"

He rolls his eyes. "*Yes.* I bought it because I wanted to buy it, so there's no reason to go into a big guilt spiral."

"No, I meant . . . you really want me to live here with you?"

"Oh! Yeah," he says. "If you want to."

I walk into his arms and hook my chin over his shoulder, staring up at the façade of my perfect little house.

"I want to," I say, as the first tears slip down my cheeks.

WE'RE IN BED at his apartment sometime later, curled up in the darkness and talking about the house—what colors I want to paint the walls, the outdoor fire pit John wants to build in the backyard—when I snatch a sudden breath.

John stares at me. "What is it?"

"Wordle," I say. "The last day."

"Oh, shit," John says. He sits up, reaching toward the nightstand to grab his phone.

I put a hand on his shoulder. "It's too late."

I can see the wall clock in the moonlight.

It's 12:32 a.m.

I missed the deadline. My streak is over.

John stares at me in horror. "Shit. *Shit*, Em—"

I shake my head. "Don't apologize."

"Er—I wasn't going to apologize," he says with a rueful grin. "I was just going to say that really sucks."

I laugh, surprised by the bright, easy sound of it.

I know I should probably feel devastated. I should be crying and swearing and kicking myself for forgetting. I was so, so close. Three hundred and sixty-four days. Three hundred and sixty-four words.

They're all floating around in my head, but the funny thing is, all I can think of is the last one I tried.

RIGHT.

I lie back down on the bed. "It doesn't matter."

"You sure?" John asks. "You were so excited to reach a year."

I smile and shift closer to him, letting my three-hundred-and-sixty-four-day streak go with a shrug of my shoulders.

"I'm sure," I say. "We can start again tomorrow."

# ACKNOWLEDGMENTS

First and foremost, I want to thank you, the reader. Whether you loved it, hated it, or something in between, thank you for giving this book some of your time.

Second, I want to thank the following people, without whom *A Five-Letter Word for Love* would not exist: my incomparable agent, Josh, and the impossibly swift-reading Anna; my wonderful editor, Tessa, and the amazing Avon team; the brilliant cover artist, Sam; my parents and sister, who filled my childhood with books; my in-laws, who let me take over their cottage every time I needed to write; my wonderful and unendingly supportive husband; and my equally wonderful but significantly less supportive dog, who feels that all the time I spend writing would be better devoted to giving her belly rubs.

Finally, to Rebecca, Julie, and Jen, to whom this book is dedicated. Thank you for your support all these years, and for believing even when I didn't. It means more than words can say.